ALSO BY MEG M. ROBINSON

<u>Chloe Chadwick Series</u>

Finding Salus

Waking Salus

Remembering Salus

Saving Salus

Megaverse Series

<u>Immortal Love Series</u>

Seeking Eternity

A Fury's Heart

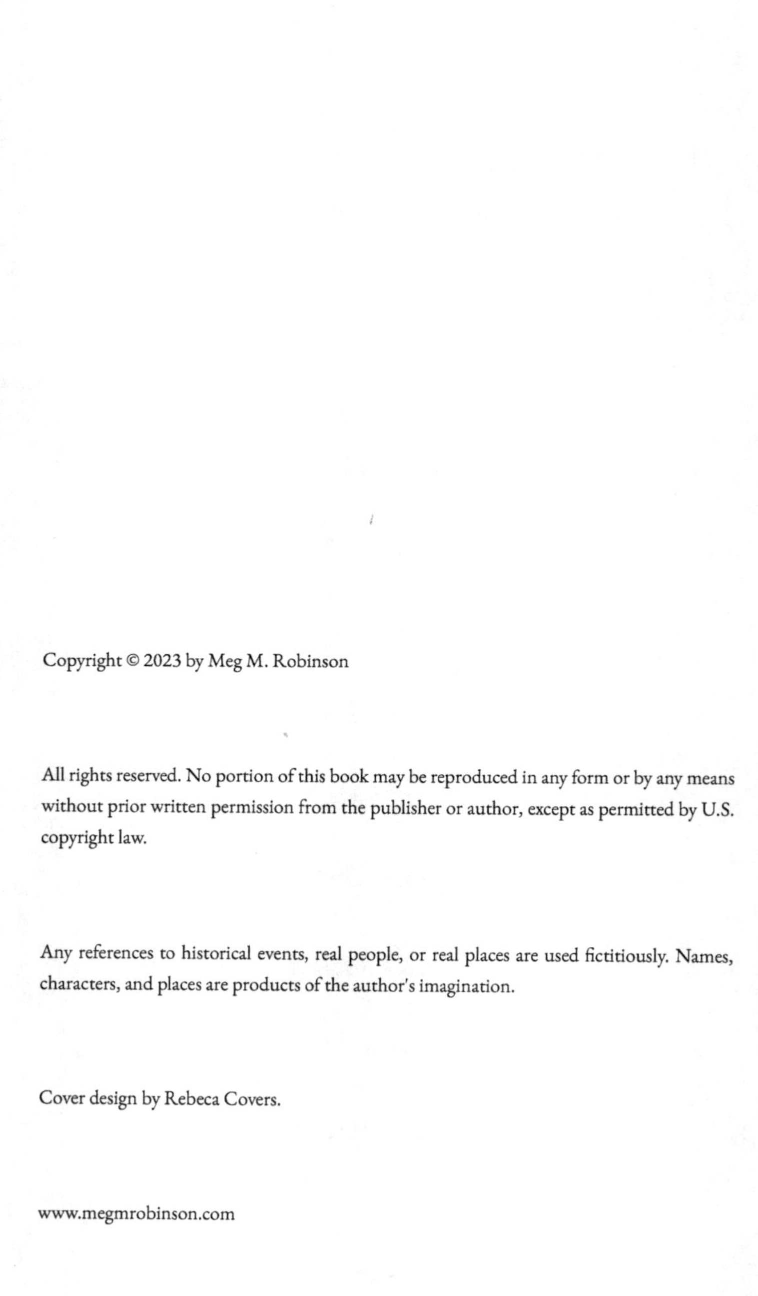

Cover design by Rebeca Covers.

www.megmrobinson.com

THE LAST LEMURIAN

IMMORTAL LOVE BOOK 3

MEG M. ROBINSON

ARCANE CROW PUBLISHING

DEDICATION

This one is for Andy, who is the best rubber duck I could ask for. He helps me more than he realizes.

PROLOGUE

A long, long time ago...

The stars had begun to fade in the sky as night gave way to dawn. Most in the already ancient city were sound asleep, leaving it hushed and still. Peaceful. The woman in the small house on the outer edge was no different. She lay on her side, breathing evenly as she slept and dreamed. Her auburn hair spread out around her, forming a dark halo.

A tall, hooded figure appeared silently in the room and walked to stand beside the bed. He looked down upon the woman, saw the serenity that was only guaranteed to be present when she slumbered, and sighed softly.

His task this night wasn't one he relished, but it was necessary. In only hours, everything would change, and unless he did this, she would likely never survive to see another quiet morning. As it was, too many would never enjoy another sunset.

A hand waved over her body and a bracelet made of a silvery-blue metal appeared on her wrist. It was a single, unbroken piece of metal, with writing as old as the figure who created it.

He brushed a lock of hair back from her face before pressing a gentle kiss to her cheek, letting his lips linger for a moment against her skin.

When he straightened, he held both hands out over the woman and spoke for the first time. His voice was hushed and somber. Even if she'd been awake, the words would have been indecipherable to her, but the anguish on the man's face would have been clear to any who had seen it.

The woman vanished and he let his hands drop. He'd done what he intended. She, at least, would be safe. Now he would have to see if his efforts made any difference. Shoulders slumped with a lack of hope, but he gave himself a minute—just one—before he turned to leave.

He got no further than the doorway before he was attacked.

CHAPTER 1

Present Day – Peru

He was going to kill TJ. Because of that mangy cat, Seth had been hiking around Peru for a week now, hunting for a lost...something. A temple—possibly—but gods only knew what the supposed structure really was. Or *where* it was. And while trying to find it, he'd been eaten alive by mosquitoes, had a banana spider meander into his camp—and onto his damn boot!—and had a fucking viper literally fall onto his head.

Even if this wasn't some wild goose chase, the trip certainly felt cursed.

He was going to give it one more day, just twenty-four hours, and if he didn't find what TJ had promised was an undiscovered ancient building, he was out of here.

No amount of riches was worth dying for. Not that Seth had all that much to live for—other than a job he loved—but he still preferred it to the alternative. Besides, he was too mean and too stubborn to die. And it would make his enemies—especially that asshole Aaron—entirely too happy, and he couldn't have that.

Yeah, TJ was definitely going to hear from him. The cat shifter had given him plenty of legitimate tips in the past—and had been well rewarded for them—but from time to time he 'overheard' things wrong, and passed that bad info on to Seth.

For now, Seth was going to continue heading west. He figured he could get to the top of the next peak before the end of the day, camp, then start back to civilization in the morning. While he liked hiking and exploring—enough to make it his profession—he also greatly appreciated modern conveniences. Like soft beds, hot meals, and, most of all, showers. He was in desperate need of the latter. Exploring the inhospitable areas of the world may have gotten him used to going without bathing for days at a time, but that didn't mean he enjoyed it.

He moved as quickly as was safely possible, something he only managed because he was used to punishing hikes and strenuous exercise. Even when he wasn't searching for lost ruins, he kept his six foot five frame in top shape. He was muscled, but had worked hard to make sure he didn't lose his agility. His quick body and quicker mind were his greatest assets. And on the trail, quickness—of mind or body—almost always won over pure strength. Especially when his strength could never hope to overcome that of some of the four-legged predators that roamed in the forests and jungles where he wandered.

Seth wasn't attractive in a traditional sense. His features were a little too rugged for a lot of women, and the stubble that he tended to sport did little to soften the edges of his face. Golden brown eyes could have been pretty in another face, on another person, but on him they tended to be distant and as cold as the metal they resembled. It didn't help that his body was just as rough as his face. His hands were far from soft and held a myriad of scars, as did the rest of him. The only place that had been spared such marks was, oddly, his face.

He'd let his black hair go a little long, so it was currently tied back at the nape of his neck, but a few strands stuck damply to his neck. It may only be in the sixties today, but he was pushing himself. He always pushed himself.

As he reached the top of a rise, he stopped and pulled out his canteen. The water wasn't anywhere close to cold, but it was clean and wet, which sufficed.

While he took his short break, he scanned the side of the mountain in front of him. There were no people there, not like there were just a few hours to the southeast. Machu Picchu was a big tourist draw, after all. And it was that very spot that had made him reluctant to follow up on this particular tip. Odds were good that everything that was here to be found had already been discovered, if only due to the proximity to that well-publicized site. But this wouldn't be the first time something had been located in a previously explored area.

The canteen stopped just before reaching his mouth, and his eyes narrowed.

Another asset of his was excellent eyesight. It wasn't as great as some of the people he knew, but it was damn good and better than a human's. And that keen sight had just spotted something...off...near the top of the next peak. He couldn't tell what it was, not from here, but he could tell that it didn't belong where it was. Which meant it was worth checking out.

The canteen was quickly put away so Seth could pull out his binoculars. He slowly scanned the area where he'd seen the oddness, but he couldn't pinpoint what had drawn his interest. All he saw were trees and rocks. Nevertheless, adrenaline raced through his veins now and he started moving again. Forgotten was the thought that this was a pointless trip, and his longings for civilized comforts disappeared. Replacing them was the rush of excitement he felt every time he found something time had hidden from the world. This was what he lived for. The money that came when he found hoards of long-buried treasure didn't hurt, but the thrill of discovery was the true goal. It was more addictive than any drug.

He barely noticed when he scraped his knuckles scrambling over a pile of loose rocks. Every fiber of his being was focused on reaching that dark gray whatever it was. So focused that he wasn't paying enough attention to his steps and put his foot down on an unstable stone. Cursing, he fell forward, landed face down, and slid a good ten feet until he managed to grab hold of a protruding root. His hands were scraped from the fall, and he was sure he'd have bruises later, but he barely noticed.

He only gave himself a minute to ensure nothing was broken or twisted before he got back on his feet. There was no point in dusting himself off, so he didn't bother. Getting clean was for the end of the hike, not the middle. Besides, he dressed for things like this. Standard hiking gear included sturdy cargo pants, hiking boots, and a light-weight, long-sleeved shirt.

Standard for him added a nine millimeter pistol and dangerously sharp combat knife. You never knew when you'd need them, especially when priceless treasures were involved.

Guns were largely considered taboo by the Arcane—the supernatural world. It was considered a form of cheating, but that wasn't something that Seth ever really worried about. He'd rather cheat than be dead, and not everyone he dealt with was supernatural, so the same rules didn't apply. And if it was good enough for demon hunters who had powers, it was good enough for him.

Besides, he didn't have the powers most of the Arcane did.

It took him almost an hour to traverse the gorge that separated him from his destination, then he started his ascent. When he was about three-quarters up, he slowed. Whatever he had seen was obstructed from view now, and he didn't want to pass it in his haste. Being patient was almost painful, but he was aware that rushing now could mean a lot more work for him in the long run.

It was a good hour and a half before he found what he was looking for. He'd passed the spot once, locating it only when he backtracked. But finally he stood in front of a flat, vertical area on the mountainside. It was smooth and untouched by vegetation, which was probably what had caught his eye. More, it was covered in carefully etched symbols, but looked natural otherwise. It almost looked freshly carved, which was unlikely, but he couldn't discount the possibility. It wasn't unheard of for people to present a hoax as real in order to profit from it. They'd been doing it for centuries.

Seth had done some checking before flying to Peru and knew there was nothing that had been discovered in this particular part of the region. Part of him wondered how no one had noticed it, then he rolled his eyes at himself. Humans were forever overlooking the obvious. It was a fact he knew well, and actually counted on. It wasn't really their fault, either. Quite a few temples and other sites were protected from human eyes by magic. Still, it astonished him on occasion.

He frowned as he studied the stone wall and the writing on it. He didn't see a seam or anything to indicate that this was a doorway.

Not so surprising, really. This could be a marker of some sort. *Or,* he thought, *it was just magical.* Stranger things had happened.

It was the writing that really bugged him, anyway. He'd picked up quite a few languages over the years, even if he wasn't fluent in all of them. Beyond that, he could at least identify several more. He didn't need to read cuneiform to know it when he saw it, after all. In his line of work it paid to recognize or read as many languages as possible. But this? This didn't look like any language he'd ever seen. The writing was in horizontal lines as most were, with the symbols a mix of swirls and straight lines that seemed incongruous with one another. They didn't really match with any of the alphabets he'd seen previously. A few characters were similar, but not all in the same language, so that was useless. Yet despite it not resembling any known language, it was somehow familiar. No, not familiar, he decided after a minute of study. It was more like something in him recognized it. Which didn't make sense, but that wasn't surprising either when it came to magic.

He slipped his pack off and pulled his camera out. This might not be something he wanted to share right away, or only share with the Arcane, but he wanted to record it regardless. If nothing else, it would allow him a chance to do research once he was home. After taking a couple dozen shots, making sure he included every symbol, he set the camera aside.

No matter how long he did this, or how unwise it could be in certain locations, he preferred a very hands on approach to things like this. It was more personal, and infinitely more exciting. Beyond that, there were some puzzles that could only be solved by handling them. Some required touch to activate, while others had clues that were so small they couldn't be seen, even by him, only felt.

Calloused hands brushed over the stone with a gentleness that would have surprised most people who knew him. Fingers traced the symbols as he tried to puzzle out their meaning. Guessing was pointless, since he had no frame of reference. If they were pictographs he might have a chance, but these looked more like letters.

Lips curved when he found himself wishing for something 'simple' like hieroglyphics.

With this closer inspection, he could see that the symbols didn't look carved after all. The edges were smooth and precise, which added to his magical theory. Such precise work was possible today, but there was no way this was a recent addition to the stone. It couldn't be, because that would mean this trip had been for nothing.

The combination of it being unknown and with magical origins had his heart beating faster. There was no telling what was inside—if anything—but it was sure to be something important. Potentially valuable, but he had enough money for his needs. More was always better, sure, but he'd be happier with solving a mystery. Or finding something that pointed him to a new one. *That* was why he did what he did.

Well, that and to keep magical objects and writings out of the hands of humans. The wrong text in their hands could be disastrous for the Arcane.

His fingers paused in their exploration when he heard a soft grinding sound. It grew louder and he stepped back several wary paces. To his delight, the stone split vertically down the middle, and the two halves of what he could now see was a door slowly swung inward.

With no obvious mechanism to cause it, he wasn't sure what he had done to have the doors opening, but he wasn't going to complain.

He quickly shoved his camera in his bag then found his headlamp before he slid the pack on. The weapons at his hips were checked to ensure they were secure before he switched the light on.

His heart pounded with eagerness as he stepped up to the doorway. Not inside, not just yet, but close enough to look beyond the door. No doubt this place was centuries old, perhaps more, but the construction was hardly primitive looking. The walls, ceiling, and floor were all smooth and level, and it looked like the hallway stayed uniform, rather than narrowing or widening slightly as some older structures did. It wasn't a large hallway, built only wide enough for a single person to pass at a time. He was surprised there weren't any carvings or pictures on the walls, as was the norm, but the lack only piqued his interest further. For a place like this not to have information could only mean that it was supposed to be kept secret.

Slowly, knowing that there could be any number of traps or dangerous creatures lurking about, he stepped into the hallway. Several dozen feet in, he heard the sound of stone grinding on stone again and turned back to see the doors closing after him. It made his heart quicken a little, but he wasn't really surprised. What was the point of a secret area within the mountain if the front door just stayed open to anyone who happened past? He only hoped he could open it again when he went to leave.

Sealed inside, Seth resumed walking, moving cautiously despite the urgency he felt. An urgency more acute than any he'd felt in the past. It wasn't a byproduct of being trapped, either, as it was hardly the first time he'd found himself stuck somewhere. He'd long since gotten over any claustrophobia.

The hallway curved to the left at almost a ninety-degree angle and he paused at the corner to peek around it. There was no obvious danger, but that worried him. Places like this weren't built without defenses of some sort, and it had been way too easy to get to this point. He waited and watched for a minute before stepping around the dubious safety of the wall and into the next section of the hallway.

He'd only taken two steps when he felt the stone beneath his foot depress lightly. He'd seen enough movies and been in enough tombs to know he'd just triggered some trap.

"Shit!"

That grinding sound was back, but this time it wasn't a door opening. No, it was the ceiling coming down, and he felt his heart skip a beat.

Worse, it was lowering a hell of a lot quicker than it did in the movies. Why wasn't everything as simple as it was on the big screen?

Despite the heavy pack he was carrying, he started running. Not back toward the door—he wasn't sure it would open anyway—but ahead, praying that there was some sort of safe spot. Logically, there had to be, or whoever had built this would have ended up flatter than a pancake.

Seth thought his prayers were answered when his light illuminated a doorway up ahead. It would be a race to see if he could make it before he got crushed by the tons of stone above him, but it was his only chance.

Pushing himself, he ran a little faster. The ceiling was only inches above his head when the floor dropped out from under him

He twisted and shot an arm out, barely managing to catch the edge of the floor with the tips of his fingers. The force of his body dropping made him wonder if his arm was going to be pulled from his shoulder, even as pain caused his breath to hiss out. Then he saw the wicked-looking metal spikes protruding from the bottom of the pit he'd almost fallen into. There were dozens of them in a space that was maybe three feet by eight. If he hadn't caught himself, there was no way he would have survived, even if they hadn't hit something vital. He'd have bled to death before he could have extricated himself from them.

Hastily he reached up with his other hand, giving his shoulder some relief, though it still screamed from the damage done to the joint.

The ceiling continued to descend, and he worried that it would keep going until it touched the floor, which would crush his fingers. If that happened, there was no way he was going to avoid being impaled. Sweat beaded on his forehead and ran down his cheeks as he watched the stone coming closer and closer. To his relief, the ceiling stopped with only a hair's breath between it and his hands. Though his fingers were starting to hurt, he held on, but he knew that he didn't have much longer before he lost his grip.

When the stone started to reverse, Seth wanted to shout with relief. He wasn't out of the woods yet, but it wasn't hopeless either. The moment there was enough room, he pulled himself up and laid on the floor, shaking his hands to try to relieve the ache. He didn't need to look at them to know that one hand was scraped raw. He could feel the blood dripping to the stone beneath him. But it didn't matter. He was alive, so they'd heal.

It seemed to take much longer for the ceiling to return to its default position than it had to lower. Once it had, he got to his feet and eyed the pit. Eight feet wasn't a hop, but it was doable, especially if he got a running start. To add to his chances, he tossed his pack across so he wouldn't be weighed down.

It was unlikely that there was another trigger for the ceiling, but he didn't risk moving back more than a dozen feet. He took a deep breath then ran as hard as he could, leaping at the last possible moment so he sailed over the pit to land beyond it. It wasn't the most graceful of landings, as he pitched forward and scraped his knee on the floor, but it did the job.

The doorway wasn't far, but not knowing what dangers lay beyond it, he took a minute to recover and get some water before venturing closer. Everything ached and his fingers had started throbbing, but he was too close to stop now. His innate curiosity wouldn't let him. He did pour some water over his raw fingers and pop a couple aspirin, but that was the most he allowed himself before he slid his pack on again. But to be on the safe side, he put his hand on the butt of his gun before he eased up to the wall beside the door and slowly glanced inside.

And found the last thing he expected to see.

CHAPTER 2

In the middle of the room was an altar about three feet high and seven feet long, made out of the same stone as the rest of the place. And lying on that altar was a woman. Not a statue, not a mummy, not even a skeleton, but a flesh and blood woman. She was covered from the mid-chest down by some sort of low metal dome, but he could see her face just fine.

And he liked what he saw. A lot.

Her features were delicate and perfectly formed, with high cheekbones and full, dark pink lips that were exquisitely shaped. At first, he thought her hair was black, but when the light from his headlamp shined on it more directly, he could see it was a deep auburn. It was long enough to be partially hidden by the covering over her, and was thick and wavy.

Drawn to her, he stepped into the room and torches he hadn't noticed before burst into flame. He hesitated for a moment before taking his headlamp off and tucking it in one of his pockets. If the torches went out, he didn't want to have to fumble to retrieve the lamp. And, light or no light, there wasn't any way he was leaving this place until he found out who this woman was and why she was here. He couldn't. If he had one major flaw, it was curiosity.

Maybe that was why he got along so well with TJ.

It was then he realized there was a breeze. It wasn't a strong one, but he couldn't figure out where it was coming from. The front door had sealed shut, and there was no exit from this room except the one he'd come through. As far as he could see, the walls were solid, without any sort of ventilation that wind could flow through. But when he got closer, he realized the wind was coming from her.

Was she an elemental? If she was a powerful one, that could account for the wind. Or maybe she was a goddess? That made more sense, because there was no way an elemental could still be alive after being sealed in what was essentially a tomb for so long. And she had to have been in here for centuries. A witch could have possibly cast a stasis spell, but witches had limits, and he doubted they extended this far.

That made him more hesitant, but he couldn't stop himself from moving closer. Unfortunately, when he was standing beside her, she only looked more beautiful, which reinforced his theory about her being a goddess. He'd never met one, but he'd also never heard of an ugly goddess.

The only question was, did he dare to wake her? *Could* he wake her? Sure, she was pulling a Sleeping Beauty, but while the thought of kissing her was appealing, the thought of kissing her while she slept, before she'd even laid eyes on him, felt...skeevy.

He'd save that for a last resort.

Instead, he laid a hand on her shoulder, intending to shake her gently, but the moment he touched her, he was hit by a gust of wind stronger than he'd ever felt before. It slammed him back against the wall, too quickly for him to do anything to protect himself. His head hit hard enough for him to see stars, an instant before his ass hit the floor almost as hard.

Dazed, he could only sit there, trying to focus past the pain and remain conscious. Then she opened her eyes.

Not quite steady after the blow, he got to his feet, a hand on his head. The movement alerted her that she wasn't alone, and her gaze sharpened as it turned to him. He was startled to see that her eyes were gray, the color of pale rain clouds, actually. Vivid hues like blue or green had seemed more likely to him with her coloring, but somehow the shade suited her, even if the look in her eyes was confused. No, it wasn't confused anymore. Angry. It left no doubt that she thought he was a threat and was preparing to defend herself.

His hands came up to show her that he wasn't armed. Well, to show her that he wasn't holding his weapons, anyway. "Whoa...not here to hurt you, lady," he assured her quickly.

Rather than looking relieved—or skeptical, which wouldn't have surprised him either—she looked confused again. He didn't get a chance to wonder what exactly was confusing her, because she answered that question a second later.

She spoke and he was struck by how beautiful her voice was. It made him wonder if she was part siren before he realized that the quickly rambled words made absolutely no sense to him. In fact, they didn't sound like any language he'd ever heard. They weren't even close. Yet, like the writing on the outside of the door, it was oddly familiar. For a moment, they wore the same baffled look.

Nonplussed, Seth did nothing more than look at her for a few minutes. It wasn't a hardship, really, but this was a first for him. He liked women, a lot. And though no one could accuse him of being the most suave man out there, he was never struck speechless. He was always able to come up with something to say, regardless of the situation. It might not always be the right thing to say, but that was hardly the point.

Luckily, since the problem was just a lack of knowledge of each other's language, he had a couple others he could try. Hopefully, she'd be familiar with at least one of the ones he knew. Otherwise, they were going to have to try to get by with charades.

He sucked at charades.

"Can you understand this language better?" he asked slowly in German. Her brow furrowed and he fought a sigh. German was a no. "What about this language? Can you understand me now?" he tried again, this time in an old form of Greek.

There was something on her face now. Not quite recognition, but more like it sounded more familiar, which was odd.

She pushed herself up to rest on her elbows and he tried not to stare. Drawing himself back to the task at hand, he realized she was probably older than she looked, not that it was easy to tell the ages of anyone in the Arcane. No way she was a human, though, given the structure they were in. Still, Mycenaean Greek was a weird language for anyone but historians and some of the older Greeks to know. With her reaction to it, he decided to stick to older languages. Thankfully, languages tended to get lost less easily in the supernatural community, given how long-lived the people were. He'd heard languages spoken in casual conversation that would make a human historian swoon with pleasure.

"Can you understand me now?" he asked, switching to Sumerian. It wasn't one of the languages he was fluent in, but hopefully he could find some way of communicating with her if needed.

Surprisingly, it was the one that made her eyes go bright with understanding. She nodded and responded in the same language, though much more smoothly and rapidly than he did. "I understand you, yes." And she sounded happy about that fact. There was more after that, but he couldn't understand it. Still, it was a start.

"Good. I do not want to hurt you," he was quick to assure her.

Her head tilted and she regarded him with a curious gaze. "I do not fear you," she told him as a slow, sultry smile curved her lips. "But I would like to know where I am," she added a moment later, the smile fading as she looked around.

"Ahh...Peru. In a..." He trailed off and gave her a helpless shrug. He didn't know what this structure was meant to be, or how to properly describe it.

She shook her head. "I do not know what Peru is. Is it a city?"

He started to ask if she'd been living under a rock, but that wasn't really too far off the mark. "It is a...kingdom...in South America."

Blank stare.

Frustrated, he asked, "Where are you from?" It might help him figure out how to explain their location.

"Lemuria."

Coming from her lips, the name was musical, and spoken with an odd accent that he found somehow appealing. Unfortunately, it was a name that he recognized, though it took him a moment.

Shaking his head, he told her, "No, Lemuria is not...true."

Well, she didn't like hearing *that*. Her eyes darkened abruptly, going from a pale, almost silver color to one that made him think of angry storm clouds. But pissed or not, she didn't get a chance to protest his blunt statement.

Two people suddenly teleported in, appearing near the doorway. One was a man about Seth's height, with short brown hair and olive skin, dressed in black slacks and a white button-down shirt. The other was a woman, several inches shorter, with blonde hair pulled into a ponytail. She was dressed similarly to the man, except her shirt was pearl gray.

Did they pop in from some office? Seth wondered before he saw that the man's hands weren't empty. He was holding a knife.

Fortunately, the witches—they had to be witches to teleport like that—looked almost as surprised to see him and the mystery woman as they were to see the witches.

"What—" was as far as Seth got before the blonde witch lifted a hand and pinned him to the wall with magic. Not for the first time, Seth cursed the fact that he had no powers. *That* was why he carried a gun.

Trusting that the woman had hold of Seth, the man focused on the woman who still lay on the altar, not having moved since company arrived.

"Who are you?" the man demanded, but since he asked the question in English, Seth tried to intervene.

"She can't—" Again, Seth's words were cut off by magic, though this time it was the feel of an invisible hand gripping his throat. Instinct had him trying to claw off the force restricting his airway, but since nothing was physically there, all he could do was struggle to draw in breath.

"Who are you?" the man demanded again, this time utilizing his magic as well. He wasn't as brutal as his companion was, but with a flick of his finger, a cut opened on the woman's cheek. Blood slipped down her cheek, dripping onto the altar.

The color of the woman's eyes flickered, much like storm clouds when lightning flashed behind them, and she pulled a hand from beneath the metal dome and brushed her fingers over her cheek. When they came away smeared with red, she glared at the man. And she was obviously done with dealing with strangers.

Her hand shoved toward the man, her palm facing him, fingers spread, and he was slammed back against the wall, hitting the stone much harder than Seth had.

She has *to be a goddess,* he thought, in awe of her power as he watched the effect that single motion had. If the witch had hit the wall wrong, it could have killed him. As it was, Seth was surprised he was still moving, though it was slight and sluggish.

Fortunately, the exchange distracted the other witch from Seth and he was dropped, landing lightly on his feet. He wasn't able to do anything more than suck in deep breaths for a moment. That, and watch as the women faced off against one another.

The witch made a grabbing motion, which had the mystery woman crying out and doubling over as much as the metal covering would allow.

Illogically, the thought of this goddess being harmed angered Seth. Once again thankful for his reflexes, he pulled his gun and fired. And he wasn't shooting to wound. Pissed off witches were too dangerous, and they'd already proven that they were aggressive and violent. Yes, it would be nice to question her and find out what was going on, but he couldn't chance it. Not when they had chosen to attack rather than listen. Not when she'd been willing to kill him without a word.

He'd had to fight to survive more than once. He'd killed before, even, but it was far from his favorite thing to do. Still, he didn't hesitate, and felt little remorse when the witch fell to the floor with a surprised look on her face and a hole through her chest.

A gasp came from the goddess and he glanced at her to see the tension the witch's magic had caused begin to ease. She said something to him, but he could only shake his head before lifting his shoulders in a shrug. Understanding that he didn't catch the words, she glanced at the other witch, who looked dazed, but still very much alive. Alive and gripping his knife.

"You made a huge mistake," he groaned, loosening his grip on the knife. For a moment, Seth thought he was giving up, or just too weak to hold on to it, then the witch's magic sent it flying toward the woman on the altar.

Seth knew he couldn't do anything to stop it. His reflexes were quick, but he was still recovering from being choked and had no magic of his own. Something tightened in his chest as he fired a second time, knowing it would be too late.

To his shock, he heard the knife hit stone and whipped his head around. The woman had a long cut from her chin to just below her ear, but she was alive.

Unwilling to just assume that the witches were dead, he made his way over to them, bending to check pulses. When he felt nothing beating beneath his fingers, he glanced to the woman. "You are not going to hit me again, are you?" It was a strain to keep speaking in the ancient language, to draw on his memories of it, but it was the only way to figure out who she was and what was going on.

She frowned. "Again? You helped protect me. Why would I hit you?"

He shook his head and almost smiled. "Not important. I am Seth."

"Tempest."

A fitting name for a woman who was radiating a breeze and had stormy eyes.

He didn't realize he was smiling until she gestured impatiently at him. "Instead of smiling like a fool, could you help me up?"

Feeling sheepish, he moved over to her. There didn't seem to be any latches or hinges that he could find that would let him move the metal dome, and it was too heavy for him to simply lift, especially with the injuries he'd taken in the last few hours. Instead, he moved behind her and gently grasped her under her arms and drew her back. And then he damn near dropped her.

Pulled out from under the covering, he could see more of her. Much more. The high-waisted gown she wore brushed the stone floor but had no sleeves, just two strips of cloth that crossed over her shoulders. But the fabric? Though it was a deep blue color, it was almost sheer. Almost. And it clung to her like a lover, showing him each and every beautiful curve. Not only that, but it was obviously the only thing she wore aside from a metal cuff-style bracelet. His eyes shot to the ceiling as he got her on her feet and stepped back. He couldn't resist a second look though, and nearly groaned.

He'd never thought of himself as an ass man before, but hers was absolutely fantastic.

To busy himself—or give himself the illusion that he was busy—he turned and set his pack on the end of the altar, sorting through it. "We need to leave," he told her as he pulled out a handkerchief and turned to gently clean the blood from her cheek. After a moment, she allowed it.

"Yes, that is a very good idea." Her gaze moved to the bodies and she scowled. "Did they follow you here?"

He frowned at her. "No. I think they wanted you. They…" He struggled to remember the words and settled with, "They did not see me."

"That makes no sense. There is no reason for anyone to mean me harm."

Unconvinced, Seth arched a brow.

"There isn't. I am not one of the priestesses and I am not the keeper of the relics," she insisted.

Keeper of the relics? That was interesting, but not relevant now. "Are you a goddess?" he asked, expecting her to admit she was, but she only gave him an odd look and shook her head. He didn't think he really believed her, but it would be pointless to argue. About that, anyway. "They did not see me. Only you," he reminded her. Him they'd just wanted out of the way. He was actually surprised they hadn't killed him outright.

He saw that she wanted to argue, but anything she could come up with would sound silly, and they both knew it.

"Perhaps you are right." There was a long pause before she sighed. "Regardless, will you take me from here?"

"Yes." He glanced down her body again and frowned. She was barefoot, and the gown wasn't something that should be worn while hiking through...anywhere, really. He had a spare change of clothes, but it wasn't ideal given the differences in size. Worse, there was nothing he could do for footwear, other than giving her a pair of his socks.

He dug the clothes out of his bag. "Here. Safer than your..." Again losing the word he wanted, he motioned to her gown. "Not a safe path," he explained. "These will protect your feet some," he added as he held up a pair of socks.

She looked down at her bare feet and wrinkled her nose cutely. "Thank you," she told him before giving him a pointed look until he turned around.

It took her only two minutes to rid herself of the gown and pull on his clothes. "I am dressed, but they do not fit well."

He turned and saw that she was having to hold the shorts up, since her frame was more narrow than his own. "Oh. Here." Another moment of rummaging in his pack netted him some rope. He quickly cut a length off it and passed it to her. "Belt."

Once it was secured, she grinned at him. "These feel odd, but comfortable."

Comfortable wasn't the word he would use. The tee-shirt was thin and loose, but not enough to hide the fact that she wasn't wearing a bra. But oddly, he liked seeing her in his clothes. Enough that he shoved that thought to the back of his mind.

"You good? It will be hard, but I will help you."

She nodded. "I'm ready."

Several minutes after they left, another woman teleported in. Dressed similarly to the witches, she looked equally as cold.

Stepping around the altar, she knelt beside the man, then the woman, confirming that they were, in fact, dead.

"Idiots," she murmured without a trace of grief. They weren't friends, just people she had worked with. For quite some time, sure, but there had never been any reason for them to get close. Nor had she wanted to.

Dismissing her fallen coworkers, she moved to the altar, running her fingertips along the dome, mildly curious about its construction. When she reached the head of the altar, she stopped and stared down at the stone. For the first time, she showed emotion, her lips curving into a smile.

A finger dabbed at a drop of blood and she lifted it, her smile growing as she studied the red smeared on her finger.

"Maybe you weren't completely incompetent after all," she said, summoning a vial. Using her magic, she lifted the blood from the altar and into the glass container, closing it tightly.

"Thanks for the help," she said in the direction of the bodies before she glanced at the doorway, then disappeared.

CHAPTER 3

When they left, Seth noted the spike pit was covered again, but he went first just to make sure that it wasn't going to drop again. Luckily, it didn't. It was like the defenses were turned off now that Tempest was awake. Even the front door was standing open.

Tempest was eager to leave the place and took a deep breath the moment they were outside. Her eyes closed and she smiled as she just basked in the afternoon sun, ignoring as the door closed tight behind them.

"It feels as though it has been ages since I last felt the wind, but it also feels like it was just yesterday," she murmured. "And it smells so *different* than it did before."

"You do not know how long you sleep?" Seth said as he watched her, making a note to brush up on his Sumerian as soon as possible. He was talking like a toddler.

"I am afraid not. What year is it?"

Sumerian numbers weren't his forte, and it took him a minute. "Two thousand nineteen. AD," he told her.

Her brow furrowed. "What do you mean AD?"

"Ahh..." Okay, she was *really* old if she didn't know what that meant. Something he really should have guessed judging by the fact that she spoke Sumerian but not an ancient form of Greek. "Our years go down to zero, then back up. Before zero is BC, after is AD."

Her head tilted. "Then your counting will be useless to me," she said, mildly distressed.

"Yes," he admitted. "Maybe you...tell me things about your time? Kings or...big weather? Could help," he suggested. *So would being able to communicate properly,* he thought, mildly annoyed by the language barrier. This really wasn't a language he was that comfortable with.

"That is not a bad idea," she said, giving him an approving look. She thought for a moment. "Since you do not believe my home is real, I will not tell you about it, though it leaves me little to go on," she admitted. "I did not pay much attention to the outside world. But last year—I mean the year before I went to sleep—there was a large eruption to the west. A very, very large eruption. I think it was the biggest eruption I'd ever heard of. Ash even made its way to Lemuria."

Unfortunately, the Sumerian word for eruption wasn't one he knew, and he shook his head. "I do not know that word."

She thought for a moment. "Mountain?" When he nodded, she went on. "It rained fire," she explained, and mimed something blowing up.

Understanding, Seth nodded. "That is good. Can you show me on a map?"

"I should be able to. At least an approximate location," Tempest agreed with a nod.

Unless she wasn't even from this dimension, but he was going to think positive. He had to. "Good. Before we sleep, I will show you a map." Which wasn't going to be for a few hours. If it was just him, he'd push on until it was fully dark, maybe even past that, but she didn't look like she was used to such strenuous exercise, especially without proper footwear.

As they walked, they started to teach each other their native languages by pointing out things they saw and giving their names. He was impressed by her. Very impressed. While he could admit he was good at picking up new languages, she seemed to soak up every word he taught her like a sponge. She kept her accent when speaking the English words, but it was charming and made it sound almost like she was singing instead of speaking. It was one of the prettiest accents he'd ever heard before, and he'd heard quite a few.

Her language, however, was a bit more of a challenge for him. Like the writing that had been on the stone, it sounded familiar, but it wasn't a forgotten language he could just remind himself of. He had to admit it was a pretty sounding language, though, and he was intrigued enough to want to learn more. He didn't believe for a moment that it was Lemurian, but new languages were always useful.

More than once they had to slow for Seth to help her cross some obstacle. There were a great many things that normal people never dealt with, and they weren't always easy, even for an experienced hiker. Loose rocks, foliage too dense to pass through, jagged boulders...Not to mention all the wildlife. But they didn't have much of a choice. And making sure that she didn't get hurt left him with little focus for actual conversation. Pointing out a tree and telling her 'tree' was easy. Thinking about something other than her safety was another.

His heart about stopped once, when he glanced back and saw a scorpion on her shoulder. Anytime he traveled somewhere new he took the time to research the natural dangers, so he recognized this as a

Yellow Scorpion, which could be fatal. Unless she really was a goddess, of course.

Tempest saw the horror on his face and froze, but before she could ask what was wrong, he closed the distance between them. She tensed an instant before he smacked the scorpion off her, then promptly stomped on it until he was absolutely sure it was dead.

After, she was almost as pale as he was. "Thank you, Seth," she told him.

Upset that she'd come so close to danger on his watch, he could only nod before continuing on.

Luckily, the next couple of hours were devoid of more encounters with wildlife—at least the dangerous sort, and they made camp.

At Seth's insistence, Tempest sat and watched as he got a fire going, then set up the tent. She seemed fascinated by the flimsy structure while he was annoyed by it. It was meant to be lightweight, which meant it was small. Unfortunately, he wasn't willing to sleep outside around here, which meant they were going to be getting very friendly come nightfall.

As he cooked their dinner—or rather, rehydrated and heated up their dinner—he found himself wanting answers to his questions about her.

"How did you come here?"

She sighed and lifted her shoulders in a helpless shrug. "I do not know. I went to sleep, and when I woke up, I was in there," she answered, brows furrowed with worry.

That wasn't an answer he'd been expecting. "Did anything happen before? Maybe a day or two before?"

He saw she actually thought about that before answering, which he appreciated.

"Yes...Vazi was acting...distant."

He cocked his head. "Who is Vazi?"

She gave him an incredulous look. "You do not know the name Vazi?"

The way she asked it implied that it was a name that everyone should know, so he searched his memory before shaking his head. "No."

That seemed to concern her, and she nodded slowly. "Much has changed," she murmured.

Since the subject seemed to upset her, he changed it. "What are you? You are air, but what kind?" For some reason, he didn't want to just come out and accuse her of being a goddess. Again.

"An elemental. And yes, I am of the air," she told him, smiling a little.

Now that was surprising and caused more questions. If she wasn't a goddess, then how had she not died after being sealed in a chamber for so long? If she didn't know about the numbering system for years, she had to have been in there for more than fifteen hundred years. Had a witch put her there? Except, if a spell could prolong life, then there would be a lot of very old witches walking around.

Then again, he did know of one, but she kept that a very closely held secret.

While he waited for the food to heat up he pulled out a map. It was deeply creased, and the edges were worn, but it still displayed the world, which was all he needed.

"Where was the fire mountain?" he asked, holding the map so they could both see it.

"This looks different from the maps I am used to," she told him, her brows knit in mild concern. "But there are familiar places." She touched a fingertip to a spot in the Pacific, drew it over the paper in a long oval. "This is where Lemuria is. I am not sure why it is not here. But the eruption was around here," she said, and placed her finger near the southern tip of Japan.

He noted the spot then nodded and folded the map. "Thank you."

They ate with only the most impersonal conversation, adding to the words they'd already taught one another. When she started to yawn, he rolled out the sleeping bag in the tent.

"Sleep. I will follow soon," he told her, holding the flap open and helping her to duck inside.

Before he banked the fire, he pulled out his phone. Normally, he wouldn't get any signal here, much less be able to go online, but he'd paid a witch to tweak his phone a little so he never had to worry about reception. It didn't matter how remote he was, or even if he was underground, he always had service.

For the next few minutes, he searched the internet, first identifying the volcano—Kikai Caldera—then finding out when it erupted. After a bit of hunting and some elimination, he found what was most likely the right eruption. Seeing it, he went cold.

The year of Kikai's largest eruption was more than six *thousand* years ago.

Astonished—and a little afraid—Seth sat back, wondering how it could be possible. She'd admitted to being an elemental, and elementals just didn't have the ability to survive for so long without food or water. If she had been a witch—or even a halfling with witch in her—he might have understood it, though again, he didn't see how a witch could have accomplished this. A god could have done it, but which one and why? Unfortunately, he knew relics and artifacts, not magic, not like this. But he knew someone who did.

When he discovered magical objects or texts in the tombs and temples he found, most of them all went to one place—the Athenaeum. It was a combination of library, museum, and hidden compound, and everyone who worked there was extremely knowledgeable. But the most intelligent person was the one who ran it all.

Grateful once again for his phone, he dialed a number that few outside of the Athenaeum knew.

"Hello, Seth."

Relieved he'd picked up, Seth leaned forward and ran his free hand through his hair. "Hey, Erasmus. You have a few?"

"Of course. Is everything okay?"

He let out a short, humorless laugh. "I wouldn't say that, no."

Erasmus's voice shifted from friendly to concerned. "What's wrong?"

"First, I need you to promise me that this doesn't go beyond you and me."

"Of course. You know I can be discreet when necessary."

Seth did know, which was why he'd called the man. Everyone in the Athenaeum was, and even most of the Arcane knew little about the Athenaeum other than rumors. Deciding not to beat around the bush, he asked, "Do you know if Lemuria was ever real?"

The silence that followed didn't give him hope. "I wish I could give you a definitive answer, but I honestly don't know. There isn't much written about it—not that we've found, in any case. Not even as much as Atlantis, and you know how little actual evidence we've found of that."

Seth groaned softly but hadn't actually expected a different answer. "If you had to guess, would you say it was real or myth?" he continued, hoping to get some idea of whether Tempest was crazy or not.

"To be honest, I've always secretly believed both Lemuria and Atlantis were real, but I can't say that I have any evidence to truly back that up. I am curious why you're asking this, though." There was a brief pause, then a thread of excitement entered his voice. "Have you found a reference to Lemuria?"

"That depends on what you consider a reference."

Erasmus made a low sound of mild annoyance. "It's not normally like you to be so vague, Seth. What's going on?"

"One of my sources led me to this place in Peru. He thought it could be a temple, but it turned out to be a doorway, a hallway, and a single room at the end of it."

"Peru?" Erasmus repeated with some surprise.

"Yeah. Anyway. The door had some writing I couldn't even identify, and in that room was a woman. Air elemental, and from what I can tell, she'd been in there since just after the Kikai eruption. An eruption that happened more than six *thousand* years ago."

"Really? That's extraordinary! Did you document the writing?"

"Of course. I'm going to see if she can translate it, or even just identify it. But I haven't gotten to the weird part yet."

"I wouldn't say any of that was truly weird, only unusual, but please, continue."

"As soon as I woke her up, two people showed up and attacked. And before you ask, they're dead and I'm okay."

"Good. I know you want to discover as much as you can, but you are just as valuable as anything you might discover."

Seth smiled faintly because he knew Erasmus meant it, and went on. "This woman—Tempest—told me she was from Lemuria, Erasmus. She seems pretty damn convinced of the fact. That's why I wanted to know if it was real."

Erasmus let out a deep sigh. "I really wish I could give you a better answer than it might be. At the moment, I'd be more concerned with the fact that you were attacked upon finding her. If two people showed up that quickly, then I'm surprised you haven't had more attackers show up."

"Same here," Seth admitted. "I don't even know why they showed up or wanted to attack us. Hell, I don't have any fucking clue how they found us. She woke up and they just teleported in, attacked me, demanded her name, then tried to attack her. It doesn't seem likely that both of us just came across the same place at the same time after it had been hidden for six thousand years."

"No, it can't be a coincidence," Erasmus agreed. "Lemuria or not, I think you should be very, very careful. Especially since I assume you're still with her?"

Seth glanced to the tent and nodded. "Yeah. I couldn't exactly just leave her there."

Erasmus let out a soft chuckle. "Of course you couldn't. I'm going to check the archives and see if I can find any reference that was missed, but until then, I do want you to promise me to be cautious. If you discover that these attacks are going to continue, get someplace safe until we can find out what's going on."

"That's the plan. And thanks, Erasmus. I owe you one."

This time it wasn't a light chuckle, but a full laugh. "After all the books and relics you've brought to the Athenaeum? No, you don't. But I won't object if you do end up finding out Lemuria is real and passing that information on."

Seth grinned. "I'll keep that in mind. Bye, Erasmus."

"Good bye, Seth."

He hung up, put out the fire, and crawled into the tent, making sure it was zipped fully behind him. Since she was already asleep, he took the time to study her with his new knowledge in mind.

Other than gods and demons, very few members of the Arcane lived longer than a millennium. Elementals weren't one of the few. The one witch he knew of was an extremely rare exception. Which meant he was lying beside one of the oldest beings on the planet. In fact, other than the gods, she might well be *the* oldest person on the planet. The thought was humbling and frightening. Especially since he could add at least a little time onto the 6,373 years since the eruption, given that she was an adult woman. But how was it possible?

It took him some time to get settled and ended up back to back with Tempest. It wasn't ideal, but it should work. If he was lucky, she wasn't the sort to move around in her sleep, but he was rarely that lucky.

The last thing he remembered thinking before he fell asleep was, *Damn. I'm going to have to pay TJ now.*

It wasn't a dark smoky room where the two men met, but a brightly lit private room in the back of a high-class club. At this time of night there were few others around, but those who were knew to avoid the area where the men sat.

"Did you feel it?" one asked, his tone demanding as he swirled expensive scotch in his glass, his stomach too tied up for him to dare sip at it.

"Of course I did. I don't understand how so many didn't," said the second, lips curved in a sneer. "Felt like a bomb blast, didn't it?"

"More like someone was taking a cheese grater to my insides," the first replied with a shudder. "Do you know who it was? *What* it was?"

The second man grimaced and shook his head reluctantly. "I don't." Though he had some ideas. "And since Regan and Thomas didn't make it back, they can't be any help."

The first man slumped in his chair. "And whoever it was will have moved by now."

"They have, yes," agreed the second. "Some blood was found, but it'll take time to do anything with it. We have to be careful, because whoever was there, they were powerful. And we have to find them. You know what he'll do to us if we don't," he warned.

Again, the first man shuddered, this time from fear. "I know. He's already contacted me." Urgency crept into his voice. "We need to send more in. Not just witches."

"Agreed. You'll arrange it? I'll try to stall for time."

"I think I like my job better than yours."

The second man sighed. "I don't blame you."

CHAPTER 4

When Seth woke the next morning, his body complained with every movement, especially his shoulder. Making a note to take some aspirin, he glanced to the side and realized Tempest was already up. He could hear her moving around outside and took just a couple of minutes before he joined her. He needed those minutes to try to process everything that had happened yesterday. Attacks weren't unheard of in his line of work, but the witches had felt more like assassins than people trying to steal treasure or glory. It was a slim distinction since both would leave you just as dead, but an important one to his mind.

Sighing, he shoved himself up and left the tent.

There was already a fire going, and she'd found the canteen, though the packaged food seemed to cause her some confusion. With a minimum of words—a mix of English and her native tongue—he prepared breakfast for her before slipping away for a few minutes of privacy.

Apparently, she'd been more hungry than he realized because she was done eating before he got back. Lips twitched as he sat down to eat his portion. After he'd finished and had cleaned up, he packed up camp. Rather than leaving immediately afterwards, he sat her down, his face solemn.

"What is wrong?" she asked, worried at his demeanor.

"I looked for the fire mountain."

Her worry vanished and she gave him a bright smile. "What did you find?" There was a brief pause, then her head cocked as she frowned. "How did you find it?"

Seth hesitated. He wasn't going to get into trying to explain smart phones with their language barrier, and the rest would be disturbing, at the very least. No doubt she'd forget all about the how once he let her know how long she'd slept in her stone tomb. "The fire mountain is the Kikai Caldera. I found one big fire like you saw."

There was such a long pause that she prompted, "And?"

"It was more than six thousand years ago, Tempest," he told her quietly.

It took a moment for that to sink in, and when it did, he was glad he'd had her sit down first. Her face seemed to lose her tan and her eyes widened as they flashed a darker gray. "You must have made a mistake," she whispered.

He shook his head. "No. I am sorry, but I do not think so. Nothing else will work. You were asleep for a long time."

She closed her eyes and swayed. Worried that she was about to faint, he quickly moved to sit beside her and wrapped an arm around her.

She sagged against him, but didn't open her eyes. "I cannot believe it has been so long," she murmured. "No wonder the world looks like it has changed so much." She looked up at him now. "Will I fit into it anymore?"

"Yes." Seth wasn't as certain as he sounded, but he wasn't about to do anything to upset her. She'd been through way too much already.

"You will have to learn new things, but you are smart. You will learn. Promise."

She gave him a wan smile. "Should we be going?" she asked, clearly not wanting to think about it too much at the moment.

"Yes." He offered his hands and helped her up. "It will be hours until we reach my...ahh...cart, but then we will not have to walk. We will find a town and get you clothes and shoes."

She nodded and took his hand. "That sounds good, yes. Thank you, Seth."

He smiled tightly and nodded. Hopefully it would only take them a couple hours to reach his SUV, but better not to get her hopes up. She wasn't wearing shoes, which slowed their progress, and there were always dangers when hiking. Always predators looking to find their next meal or protect their territory.

Their path got a little easier the further down the mountain they got, though they didn't make the progress he'd hoped. They were, however, able to teach more of their languages to each other. By the time an hour had passed, they were able to have brief, stilted conversations in English. It came in handy when they paused to rest and have a drink.

She was sitting on a fallen log when a butterfly fluttered into the clearing and delicately landed on her foot. Its fragile blue and black wings fanned lightly. Her face brightened and she was careful not to move and frighten it. "Seth? What is this called?" she asked in English.

Her delight at just watching the insect had him smiling. "A butterfly. It's safe," he assured her.

"Butterfly," she breathed, and she slowly lowered her hand to the delicate insect. Seth was surprised when it moved to rest on one of her fingers instead of flying away. "It is...good to look at?"

"Pretty, or beautiful when it is very pretty," he told her helpfully, but it was her face he watched, not the butterfly.

She smiled and nodded. "Beautiful. It is very beautiful," she agreed. It flew away then, but she didn't pout, just followed it with her eyes until it was out of sight. "I am happy," she told Seth as she gave him her attention again. "We should go?"

"We should," he agreed, taking one last drink before he put his canteen away and got to his feet. "It won't be long," he told her as they started walking again.

"This town...it is different?"

"Than you're used to?" he asked, and she nodded. "Very different. Don't be afraid. It's different, not bad." She still looked unconvinced, and he stopped walking and rested a hand lightly on her shoulder. "I'm not leaving you," he promised.

Tempest smiled faintly and covered his hand with her own. "Thank you."

He nodded and drew his hand back before continuing on.

A few minutes later, she spoke again. "I do not know why anyone would attack me."

He glanced back at her and frowned. "I don't know either. You've been sleeping for too long. No one knows you were there. Or they shouldn't know."

She started to respond, but then looked deeply troubled.

"What's wrong?"

"People do not know Vazi or Lemuria. They do not...remember...me either," she whispered in stilted English.

Something in his chest clenched when he saw a single tear slide down her cheek. Normally Seth wasn't much for patting backs and there theres, but he suddenly felt fiercely protective of this forgotten elemental. He found himself pulling her into a hug. She clung to him, her face pressed against his chest. "I know you," he said quietly. "Others will, too. It'll be okay."

Tempest trembled once before she gave a small nod and slowly drew back. "Thank you." She gave him a shaky smile. "I will be good. We can go."

He nodded, but they'd been in the same area for too long. Far too long. They'd barely taken a dozen steps before a blast of magic hit them both. It felt like jagged glass slamming into them and knocking them off their feet. Tempest was knocked into him and he wrapped his arms around her, just before her power flowed around them and cushioned their fall.

On the ground, holding Tempest protectively, Seth glanced in the direction the magic had come from and saw three people walking out of the trees.

Unlike the last two, these men weren't dressed in business wear, but wore black military-like clothing. Luckily, they weren't carrying guns, but the blast of magic proved they weren't human, which meant that their weapons were much more dangerous than any gun or knife, nor could they be taken away. Worse, it meant he and Tempest were outnumbered.

Seth sat up and moved in front of Tempest, his hand moving to rest near the butt of his gun. "What do you want?" He doubted they'd answer him, but it couldn't hurt to try.

The man on the left, a rough-looking man with a wide, square jaw and scar on his chin, looked at Seth for a moment then dismissed him to focus on Tempest. "Not you. Move away from the woman and we'll let you go unharmed."

Seth almost snorted. "Well now, I was always taught to protect a lady, and leaving her with three strange men in the wilds of Peru doesn't sound like protecting to me."

The black-clad man shrugged. "So be it." He flung a hand out and sent a fireball shooting toward Seth's chest.

Seth twisted around, grabbed Tempest, and jerked them to the side. The fire missed them by a fraction of an inch, shooting past them, but this time they didn't have her air as a buffer and he landed hard with her atop him. A rock jabbed him roughly in his lower back, making him wince, but it was the least of his concerns. He rolled with his arms around Tempest, putting her on her back, with his body protecting hers. His hand dropped, and he yanked his pistol from its holster while the witch prepared to throw another fireball, but it was a race he knew he wouldn't win.

The fire left the witch's hand and Seth tried to bring his gun up in time to at least get a shot off before he got hit, but the fireball never hit him.

Even pinned beneath his body, Tempest wasn't helpless. He knew she was a powerful elemental, but it had just been instinct to protect her. She got a hand out from under him and shoved it toward the witch, palm facing him. The fireball slowed abruptly, then was pushed back toward the witch. His eyes widened an instant before his own magic slammed into his chest and knocked him back several feet.

Seth took advantage of the shock of the other two witches, firing at the man on the right. His shot was rushed, so he didn't hit the heart, but it was close enough that he could shift his focus to the last remaining man. He fired again, aiming for the last witch's right shoulder. It hit, but this one was left-handed and didn't hesitate to bring that hand up, preparing to blast them.

Tempest's hand clenched into a tight fist then rose several inches, her air magic wrapping around the witch as tightly as a noose before it hoisted him into the air. Leaves swirled around him, like he was stuck in the center of a small but powerful tornado.

With his arms pinned, he couldn't fling magic at them, but Seth kept his gun pointed at the witch. Not all magic required hands, he knew. "Are you hurt?" he asked the woman beneath him.

"No. What do we do with him?" she asked, not sounding at all strained at the use of her magic. There was a thread of pain in her voice, but they were both banged up and a little bloody from the initial attack. And that was on top of the injuries both had sustained the day before.

"We question him." Slowly, he eased off of Tempest and moved to the fallen witches. He didn't want to assume they were dead and be surprised later, but the first witch was already gone, and the other breathed his last as Seth knelt beside him. Reassured, he walked back to Tempest, facing the hovering witch. "What do you want with her?"

The man's jaw clenched and he stared at Seth with hate-filled eyes.

Seth arched a brow. "You do realize you're helpless and your friends are dead, right? Talking is in your best interest. I just want to know why you and your buddies seem to want her dead."

Slowly, the man smiled, but it was filled with such malice that Seth's finger tightened fractionally on the trigger, almost firing.

"Yes, I want her dead. And she will be dead before we're done. It may not be me, but it will happen," he sneered before looking to Tempest. "Your time is up," he told her before he disappeared.

"Dammit!" Seth yelled, turning and kicking a rock hard enough that it ricocheted when it connected with a tree and almost hit him on the return journey. He shoved his gun in his holster and turned to Tempest, taking her hands and helping her to her feet. "We need to get out of here and get somewhere safe. I don't think they're going to stop coming."

Tempest looked calm until he saw her eyes, which had darkened far more than he'd seen before. Now they were a gray so dark it was nearing black. She was scared as well as pissed, and he couldn't blame her. "Where is safe?"

"I don't know, but we're going to find out. First thing, though, we have to get out of Peru. Come on." He gave her hand a squeeze, glanced at the bodies, then started walking at a quick pace. To her credit, she kept up, even with her feet only protected by socks and both of them hurting.

They were close to the SUV he'd rented, and it was parked only an hour from a town with an airstrip. If he was lucky, one of his contacts could get a plane there by the time they arrived. He hadn't known how long he'd be in Peru, so didn't have anything lined up, and, not for the first time, he wished he had the money for his own jet. Staying on the move was their best bet until they figured out why someone was after Tempest.

He pulled out his phone and breathed a sigh of relief a few minutes later. It had cost him a large chunk of change, but a plane would be waiting for them when they got to the airstrip.

"I know I promised you clothes when we got to a town, but I think that's going to have to wait," he said, glancing to Tempest.

She was getting winded, and a light sheen of sweat covered her forehead and throat, but she didn't lag behind. "I understand. It is good. Safe is more important."

He smiled a bit. "You're getting good with English," he told her, wanting to give her something else to think about.

The smile was returned, but it was faint and brief. "I have liked language forever."

"It shows."

That was the end of their conversation for a while. Tempest needed the air to keep up the hard pace, and Seth was keeping an eye out for threats both natural and mystical. He was shocked when they reached the vehicle without any further trouble.

Tempest frowned when she saw the SUV. "What is that?"

"It's a car. A cart that doesn't need a horse." He helped her into the passenger seat and showed her how to buckle up. The backpack was tossed in the back seat after he grabbed his canteen from it, then he slid into the driver's seat. When he started the engine, she jumped and stared in shock, and he couldn't help but smile. "It's just the engine. It's like a mechanical horse. It makes it move. It's all right. We'll be in town in an hour. If you want to nap on the way, feel free."

He handed the canteen to her, then put the SUV into gear and started down what could loosely be considered a road.

And hoped they made it to the airstrip.

CHAPTER 5

Seth was unsurprised when Tempest passed out despite the rough road they were going over. She'd been through a hell of a lot in the last day, and he was more than a little impressed with how well she'd handled it. If he'd woken up after six thousand years and been immediately attacked, he didn't think he'd be so calm.

He felt tempted to look at her quite a bit, but forced himself to pay attention to the road and their surroundings. If they were attacked again, she was, he had to admit, their best bet, so with her sleeping, they were both vulnerable. When they made it to the town without any other incidents, he was surprised, but wary.

Their speed slowed as he made his way to the airstrip, and he reached over to gently shake her awake. "Tempest? We're almost there."

She made a soft, adorable sound as her head turned toward him and she slowly opened her eyes. "Hmm?"

He smiled. "We're almost there. You need to wake up, I'm afraid."

Tempest caught a glimpse of the town they were driving through, which cleared the last of the fog from her mind. She sat up and looked at the buildings in wonder. "They look different. Very different."

Seth glanced at her. "Different bad?"

"No," she decided after a moment, "just different."

Considering that the last buildings she'd seen were thousands of years old, he had no doubt of that. Styles changed by the century, even the decade.

"You should be ready to move when we get to the plane."

"Plane?"

He'd almost forgotten that she'd only been speaking English for a day, and she didn't yet know the words for him to properly explain a lot of modern technology. "Like this cart, but it flies." Nothing wrong with simple. They could get into detail later. "Grab my back-pack. When we stop, we need to run to the plane. We could be attacked again."

She nodded and twisted around to grab the bag and cradled it in her lap, but the moment it was there, it was nearly forgotten. She was delighted by the unfamiliar sights and sounds that surrounded them.

Seth was going to thoroughly enjoy showing her all the things that the twenty-first century had to offer when he had a chance. The movies and museums, the people and architecture. He had a feeling she'd love every bit of it, good and bad.

They were only minutes from the airstrip when he realized they were being followed. It wasn't just paranoia, not after he'd taken several unnecessary turns which had led him in a circle. The SUV hanging back was perfectly nondescript, neither too new nor too old. It looked like dozens of others he'd passed once they'd reached civilization, but this was the only one glued to them.

"Damn. How'd they find us?" he muttered as he glanced in the rearview mirror and tried to figure out how they could ditch their tail.

Though he was quiet, Tempest heard and glanced to him. "What is wrong?"

"We're being followed." When she started to turn, he laid a hand on her knee and shook his head lightly. "Use the mirror," he suggested before he remembered this was all new to her. "It's the white box-like car a little back. It's been following every turn. What I don't get is how they keep finding us."

Tempest scowled at the side mirror and he knew her gaze was fixed on the other SUV. "I cannot say for sure," she murmured.

Neither could he. Sure, magical tracking was absolutely a thing, but these people didn't seem to actually know who Tempest was, so what about her were they using to repeatedly find them? Elementals, even powerful ones, weren't exactly rare. And people like him? He was barely more than human, so tracking him based on his magical signature was nearly impossible unless it was someone who knew him well, and these people were clearly out for Tempest, not him.

But the more important question at the moment was how they could get to safety. Starting a fight in the middle of a human population wasn't just frowned upon, it could be punishable by death, so he didn't want to risk it. Innocent until proven guilty was a nice sentiment, but it didn't always work that way.

"Okay. I don't have the knowledge—and we don't have the time—for me to try to lose them, so when we get to the plane, I'm going to park as close as I can to it. As soon as I stop, run. The moment we're on the plane, I'll tell the pilot to take off."

Tempest looked back to him, her face solemn, her eyes dark, and she nodded. "I understand."

"I don't know how things were back in your time, but now we hide from humans, so no using any visible powers unless you absolutely have to."

That was harder for her to take. Her jaw tightened slightly, but again, she gave him a nod.

He made the turn that would take him to the airstrip, relieved when it came into view without the SUV trying to run them off the road. He wasn't sure why. What did it matter if they died in a car accident or by a fireball? Both ways left them six feet under.

The plane was waiting, and to his relief, the door was already open and the stairs down. There were few other vehicles nearby, which could give them a little breathing room if it did come to a fight. He just had to hope that the people in the SUV were the only ones nearby.

He glanced at Tempest and saw her staring, baffled, at the plane. A chuckle slipped out before he could stop it. "That's the plane. It's safe, I promise." He wasn't sure how much of the English she actually understood, but she nodded regardless. "Remember, run when we stop."

"Yes," she told him, and fumbled with the seatbelt, looking proud when she got it undone.

Seth didn't slow down until they were near the plane, then made a quick U-turn to put the passenger side closest to the stairs. "Go," he told her as he undid his own belt and killed the engine. He split his attention between Tempest and the SUV as she hurried toward the steps. Leaping out after her, he raced for the plane, but didn't quite make it before something slammed into him from behind.

It wasn't a fireball this time, but a bolt of magic, sharper than any blade. It dug deep into his back and he stumbled forward, falling across the stairs. "Go!" he yelled to Tempest, his teeth clenched against the pain. Blood pulsed from the wound. He could feel it soaking his shirt and pants, stealing his strength with every beat of his heart. Fighting to get to his feet, he drew his gun and glanced over his shoulder. Five people climbed out of the vehicle; two men, three women, all looking cold. Merciless.

Before Seth could even raise his gun, one of the women lifted her hand and shot another blast of magic at him, but he was astonished when it crashed against nothing and the magic fizzled out. Glancing back at Tempest, he saw one of her hands outstretched toward the group.

Seth had known Tempest was powerful, that was why he believed her a goddess at first, but for her to be able to block a witch's magic with nothing more than air? It was hard for him to comprehend, but he wasn't going to waste his advantage. He scrambled up the stairs until he landed on the floor of the plane, smacking the button that would retract the stairs and close the door. "Get us in the air!" he yelled to the pilot as he aimed toward the witch and fired. A quick motion from the man beside her had the bullet veering off course and hitting the SUV. The woman on the other side of the witch started running toward them and shifted mid-motion, turning into a sleek black leopard.

They definitely weren't sweating Arcane laws, which chilled him. Either they were so psycho they didn't care...or they had someone extremely powerful backing them.

The plane started to taxi down the runway, quickly picking up speed. Seth didn't often have to make fast getaways, but he always ensured he had a pilot who could get him the hell out of Dodge if need be. This pilot was no different. In another minute, they'd be in the air. As long as the group down below didn't have an air elemental as powerful as Tempest, they might just get out of Peru alive.

Keeping his gun in hand, Seth managed to get to his feet and stumble to the nearest window. Tempest quickly took the window next to him. It was a good thing she did. The plane was starting to leave the runway, but the group outside wasn't giving up just yet. One of the men held his arms out, palms up, and slowly lifted his hands. Seth couldn't see what he was doing, but he could feel it. The plane jolted, hit from below by something large and solid. They bumped the runway before the plane lifted again, but the second hit was stronger and Seth feared they were going to crash the plane before it ever left the airstrip.

Tempest placed her hand against the glass, giving a harsh whisper in her native tongue. The leopard was blown back, landing hard on the concrete, quickly followed by another woman and one of the men, but the first witch and the man hitting the plane remained on their feet. They struggled against the wind, but it grew stronger, until even the vehicle he'd abandoned was tossed about like it was nothing more than a toy. It was enough to allow the plane to get off the ground.

"That's enough. We're safe," Seth told her as he slumped down into a seat. The back immediately pressed against his wound and he hissed out a breath. He shifted so he wasn't sitting directly on the injury, but now that attention had been drawn to the location, it throbbed painfully.

Tempest frowned and knelt in front of him. "You are hurt?"

Seth thought she looked so sweet sitting there, worried about him. Her eyes were slate colored with concern, and he fought to smile, but it came off as a grimace. "I'll be all right." He hoped so, anyway. He hated to think of Tempest alone in a world that was completely unfamiliar to her with no friends, only enemies who apparently wanted her dead.

But she didn't look convinced. "You are hurt," she said more firmly.

He opened his mouth to speak, but a figure appearing in the seat across the aisle from him stopped him. His gun was quickly lifted and pointed at the woman, which had Tempest twisting around and lifting her hands, preparing her own defense.

The stranger was tall and lean, almost to the point of being too slender, but it didn't detract from her beauty. Her hair was perfectly straight and as black as a moonless night. It fell past her hips, shrouding her in darkness. Her skin was a drastic contrast, no darker than the palest moonlight. Her lips were as dark as her hair, but curved in a warm smile, unconcerned about Seth's gun and Tempest's power. At first Seth thought she was monochromatic, since even her dress was black, with only a hint of silver in the hem and buttons, but she wasn't, not quiet. Her eyes were a pale blue, not gray like he thought, and ringed by a dark line of bluish-purple. All in all, she was a rather striking woman, and one who reeked of power.

"Who are you, and what are you doing here?" Seth demanded, fighting to stand, to move in front of Tempest. He couldn't seem to shed his protective instincts for her, even wounded.

The woman calmly crossed her legs and held her hands up in a gesture of surrender. "Calm down, Seth. I'm not here to hurt you." Her eyes shifted to Tempest. "Either of you. Quite the opposite, actually."

"You'll have to forgive me if I don't just take your word on that," he said dryly.

"I don't expect you to," the woman said, shaking her head. "You've had a rough couple of days, and paranoia will serve you well in the coming weeks. But I'll offer a bit of proof. A gift for each of you, if you'll allow it."

Seth arched a brow and exchanged a look with Tempest. Though she probably only understood a fraction of what was said, she nodded to Seth, deferring to his judgment in this. It was his world, he supposed, but he had no more idea of what was going on than she did. "Perhaps we will, but only once you tell us who you are. I barely have any magic myself, but I know you're pretty fucking powerful."

"As I should be," the woman said with a regal nod of her head. "A goddess without power is no goddess at all." She smiled again. "Though not all power is magical."

Suspiciously, he asked, "Which goddess are you?" Like all members of the Arcane, he knew that it was risky to trust deities of any pantheon. Most were apathetic toward mortals, and some viewed anyone less powerful than them as toys—and just as disposable.

"Hecate."

Seth dropped down in his seat, the hand holding his gun falling into his lap. "Well shit."

She laughed, and it sounded oddly like birds, but it wasn't unpleasant. "So you know of me."

"Of course I do. Goddess of witchcraft."

"Among other things. Will you allow me to give you my gifts?"

Tempest slowly moved to sit beside Seth and gave him a curious look. "It is good?"

"I...think so," he told her, but he was staring at Hecate and trying to recall everything he'd ever read or heard about her. "You're not known as a good goddess, but neither are you considered bad." And she wasn't one who was notorious for fucking with mortals.

"No, I'm more neutral, though most people don't see it that way." Hecate shrugged. "I'm the goddess of crossroads. The in between. So I am in between."

He was quiet for a long moment, then gave a slow nod. "All right. You can give us these gifts." Not that he could really stop her anyway. He could feel himself growing weaker by the moment as he lost more blood.

The cleaning bill for the jet would be insane.

She looked relieved—which confused him—then smiled. She leaned forward and rested her hand over Seth's. A tingling spread up his arm then down his back, where it centered in his still bleeding wound. No, not just there. Every injury he'd sustained in the past two days was tingling a bit. As soon as he noticed that, the pain receded, then disappeared altogether. "Better?"

He relaxed back with a sigh and nodded. "Much, yes. Thank you." In fact, he felt better than he had in years. His job was rough on the body and, though he occasionally saw a healer, it was rare.

"You're welcome." Hecate shifted her focus and smiled at Tempest. Her hand lifted from Seth's and reached for Tempest's face.

The elemental leaned back and gave Seth a questioning look.

"It's okay. It's good," he assured her with a nod, hoping Tempest's gift would be healing as well.

Tempest slowly nodded and straightened, allowing Hecate to rest her fingers lightly upon her temple. The contact made Tempest gasp and her eyes closed and fluttered, as though she were caught in some dream.

"What are you doing to her?" Seth asked, not afraid for Tempest, but still concerned. He could see the cuts on her face healing, but that wasn't all the goddess was doing.

"Shh," was Hecate's only response, her entire focus on Tempest. Only a minute later, Hecate released Tempest and relaxed in her chair.

Tempest's eyes opened wide and she stared at Hecate with something like awe. "What did you do to me?" she breathed, and Seth noted that her English was perfect, if still accented by her native tongue.

"Seth knows," Hecate said smugly, with a wave of her hand toward him.

"How did you know my name?" Seth asked. "Wait, never mind, doesn't matter." He turned to Tempest. "I think she just gave you the English language. You can understand everything I'm saying now, can't you?"

"I...can. This is very weird."

Seth chuckled. "I'll bet. You just had a language downloaded to your brain. Was that all you gave her, though?"

Hecate shrugged. "Mostly. I healed her as well, of course, and gave her a few tidbits to help her adapt to the twenty-first century."

"You're a little scary. But in a good way," he added quickly.

She laughed. "I don't consider it an insult either way, so rest easy."

Seth explained to Tempest, "Hecate is a goddess of witchcraft and the crossroads. Along with...what, the night, necromancy, and ghosts?"

"That's close enough, yes," Hecate said with a nod.

"There are still gods around?" Tempest asked, sounding excited.

Seth was confused by the reaction, but Hecate looked understanding. "Oh yes, we're still around, though not as prevalent as we used to be. My pantheon—the Greek pantheon—is still well known, of course, as are a few others. Quite a few have fallen in power as their worship waned, though they remain. There are even a few pantheons now that you likely wouldn't recognize, but with a few individual exceptions, all the old gods remain...except for one group."

Tempest's face fell. "The Lemurians," she whispered mournfully.

"Yes," Hecate said sympathetically.

"Wait, Lemuria's actually real?" Seth asked, shocked.

"Oh yes, or at least it was. And Tempest...I'm afraid you're the last living Lemurian of any sort," she said gently.

Tempest let out a soft sob. "I feared that when Seth didn't believe me about Lemuria. When he didn't know the name Vazi, but I hoped that they were just..." She shook her head and her hair fell around her face, shielding her tears from them.

Seth wrapped his arms around her and felt her body trembling as she cried over the loss of her entire people. "I'm so sorry, Tempest. So very sorry," he whispered against her hair.

Hecate remained quiet, letting Tempest take the time to adjust to the blow she'd just been dealt.

It took several minutes, but finally the tears stopped and Tempest turned her head to look at Hecate. "Are you absolutely sure?"

"I am. But that isn't why I'm here. Or not precisely."

"Yes, why are you helping us?" Seth asked, still holding Tempest.

"Because she is the last Lemurian, and there are those who want to ensure that there are *no* Lemurians alive."

"The people who have been attacking us," Tempest whispered.

"Yes," Hecate confirmed. "And they won't stop. So you can't stop either. Be unpredictable, stay mobile, until you find out how you can convince them to let Tempest live."

"Why is it so important to kill me?"

Hecate shook her head. "I can't tell you that," she said, looking pained. She clearly wanted to, which made him wonder if some sort of geas or compulsion had been laid upon her. It shouldn't be possible, not for her, not unless another god was responsible. "I shouldn't even be telling you this. I definitely shouldn't help you, but I'm going to add one more gift to those I've already given you." She held her hands out to them, palms up. When they placed their hands in hers, she gently squeezed them. Magic flowed from her hands into theirs, spreading over their bodies in a comforting wave. "It's what protection I can give you. And if you happen to see a crow, look on it kindly." She smiled at Seth. "Even you, though I know you're partial to falcons because of your father."

Tempest gave him a curious look. "Your father?"

"He's a falcon shifter," Seth explained. "My mother was human, so I can never shift, but I always admired the bird he could become." He looked back to Hecate. "Thank you. Even if this is all you can do for us, it means a lot. Even just healing us was more than enough."

"Yes, thank you," Tempest echoed. "I've been so afraid since I woke, but I'm a little less afraid now."

"You're both welcome. Now, plan well, think ahead. And I'll do what I can, when I can. Be safe, both of you," Hecate said before she smiled and disappeared.

This time, the two men met in the office in an expensive house, well away from prying eyes and sensitive ears.

"They still haven't done their job," one man said as he poured amber liquid from a crystal decanter into a heavy tumbler.

"No, and the situation has gotten worse," the other said grimly as he paced in front of the desk.

"How in the hell could it have gotten worse?"

"*He* showed up."

The first man downed the liquor in a single swallow. "Damn. What did he say?"

"He wants her dead at all costs. We're being offered a great deal if we can manage it..."

"And if we can't?"

The second man gave the first a dark look. "We'll be lucky if he only kills us."

"Shit." The first man started to pour another glass, then threw it at the wall instead, where it shattered. "Send everyone we have. I want her head on my desk by the end of this week."

"It's already done. And Marie claims to have her blood. She's working on a spell. If we can't find the woman, her spell should." He sighed. "I just hope it's enough."

CHAPTER 6

For several minutes, Seth and Tempest just sat there, reeling from all they'd been told. Seth spoke first.

"I'm sorry, Tempest. For not believing you about Lemuria, I mean."

She shook her head. "No need for apologies. It sounds as though we've been forgotten by everyone," she said quietly. "How could we not be, if we're all dead but for me, and there's no proof my homeland existed?"

"Still, I could have handled it a bit better. But...I really did think it was nothing more than myth."

Tempest cocked her head. "Lemuria is a myth? What is known about it?"

"Not much. It was a land in the ocean, though myths varied between the Indian and Pacific Oceans. And it sank, lost beneath the waves. That's it, really," Seth told her.

She sighed. "I don't know about it sinking, but it was more than just land, Seth. So much more."

"I'd love to hear about it sometime," he told her sincerely. "It's what I do. I look for lost places. Temples, cities, anything that has been forgotten to time."

"You rediscover places? So you're an explorer, then?"

"Mostly, yes," he confirmed with a nod. "Some call me a treasure hunter, and they're not entirely wrong, but a bulk of what I find goes to museums or to vaults held by the Arcane, depending on what it is. Non-magical objects go to museums, while anything that could reveal the existence of the supernatural goes to the Arcane."

She smiled faintly. "It sounds fascinating. Is that how you found me?"

He nodded. "I was told that there might be a temple in the area. I was looking for it when I came across your...resting place."

"I'm very glad you did, for my sake. But I'm sorry that it's caused you so much trouble."

"I'm not," he said simply. "And I'm going to do what I can to get us both out of trouble."

"How?"

"First, I'm going to get us some help. Hecate was a good start, but more is better," Seth told her as he pulled out a phone.

"What sort of help?"

He smiled. "My best friend. She's a halfling. A stone elemental and a witch. She's good with creating wards, and she's damn smart, too. We can rest up at her place, and maybe come up with a plan," he told her as he called Kara.

"I hope she's as smart as you," Tempest said with a nod.

"She is. Why don't you go rest up? There's a bed in the back, and a small bathroom. We'll be in the air for a while, and sleeping on the ground isn't very restful."

"I think I might." Tempest kissed his cheek then rose. "Thank you, Seth."

He watched her disappear into the back, distracted enough by the sight that he missed Kara's first, "Hello?"

"Sorry. It's me."

He could hear the smile in her voice. "Yeah, I know. You're programmed into my phone. What's up? You stuck in a caved in temple again?"

He grimaced. "One time and you never let me forget it," he muttered.

She laughed. "Of course not. It's too much fun. But I take it you don't need a rescue?"

"I do, sort of, but not that sort."

Her voice went serious. "What's going on?"

He sighed. "Long story short? I woke up the last Lemurian and now a shitload of people are trying to kill us. Hecate—as in the goddess—popped in and told us it's not going to stop until the Lemurian is dead, and I can't let that happen. We need a safe place for a few days, where we can't be found, while we figure out how in the hell to stop the never ending line of assassins."

Silence.

"Kara?"

"I'm here. I'm just not sure I heard you right."

"No, you did. I said Lemurian."

"Well, hot damn. I knew you were going to discover something big one of these days, I just didn't expect you to find out a legend was real."

"You think I did?"

She snorted softly. "Good point. I take it you're hoping my place will be that safe place?"

"You're the best I know at warding."

"You've got that right. Okay, come to my place. I'll reinforce the magic and do some research on Lemuria, though I'm not sure what I can find that you can't."

Seth felt a frisson of fear. "Be very, very careful in your research, Kara. They found us almost the moment Tempest woke up. You look in the wrong place or ask the wrong person, and they're going to be gunning for you, too."

Rather than take the warning, her voice perked up. "Tempest? So this Lemurian is a woman, huh? I'm betting she's pretty, too, isn't she?" she teased.

He rubbed his temple and sighed. "Not the point, Kara. Just be careful, okay? We only took off a few minutes ago, so it'll be a while before we get to you. Probably around eight hours to touch down, another hour to get to you."

"Fine," she pouted. "I'll make sure a car is waiting for you."

"Thanks, Kara. You're the best."

"Yeah, yeah. But when things calm down, I want some dish. There's gotta be more to this than you're telling me," she said before she hung up.

He put his phone in his pocket and glanced back to the bedroom. He had so many questions for Tempest. Questions about her life. Questions about Lemuria. Now that it had sunk in that Lemuria had been a real place, not just a story told to children, he was desperate to know more. Everything in him craved knowledge of lost lands and people. But now probably wasn't the best time. She needed time to process. In two days she'd lost more than six thousand years and her entire people, right down to her gods.

Seth stood and walked back to the door, listening for a moment. He heard the water running and decided to leave her be. A shower would be great, but he could wait until they reached Kara's home in Colorado. Tempest deserved it more.

Instead, he went to the cockpit and told the pilot about the change in destination. They hadn't been in the air long, so it wouldn't be too much of a course correction to get to Colorado. With that done, he sat in one of the reclining chairs and leaned it back. He wasn't quite ready for sleep yet, so he pulled out his phone. Researching magical things on the internet usually didn't yield much in the way of truth, but now and again a kernel of useful information could be found.

After half an hour of finding absolutely nothing useful on Lemuria, he gave up and considered. Hiding at Kara's wasn't a solution. It was, at best, a temporary fix, and it could be extremely temporary. No, he needed a way to get whoever was after Tempest off their backs. Except he'd never had assassins after him.

Then he recalled hearing the story of how one of his acquaintances had met his wife. Sometimes he disliked people, but right now he was thrilled for each and every contact he'd made.

Seth dialed and listened to the phone ring. Just as he expected to hear the voicemail message, the call connected.

A woman's laughter was the first thing he heard, then a man's amused voice. "Hello?"

"Wade, it's Seth. I'm not interrupting anything, am I?"

"If you'd been five minutes later, maybe," Wade admitted, and Seth could hear the grin in his voice. "But no, you're good. What's up?"

Seth blew out a breath. "Need some advice."

"Advice? I only went treasure hunting once, and I was pretty much just the muscle," Wade replied, mild surprise in his voice.

"Nah, not about treasure hunting," Seth said with a shake of his head. "I heard that you have experience being chased by assassins."

Like with Erasmus, Wade's voice went serious, though his held a hint of a growl. "You've got assassins on your tail? Who? Why?"

"Those are good questions. I wish I could answer them."

"Tell me."

Seth didn't know Wade well, had only actually met the guy once, but he was friends with several people who trusted the wolf implicitly. With only a brief hesitation, he gave Wade a brief run-down, including the bits involving Hecate and Lemuria. His focus, however, was on the people currently trying to kill Tempest.

When he was done, Wade said nothing for a full minute. "For three hundred years of my life, I knew the gods existed, but had never interacted with them or known of anyone who did. Now I've got what amounts to a sister who's friends with one, have one for a mother-in-law, and you've got Hecate secretly helping you. I said it when I met Sam, and I've gotta say it again...Did we just step into an alternate universe and no one told me?"

"No fucking idea," Seth muttered. "You have any ideas, though? I can shoot, sure, and I can throw a punch, but I just don't have the experience or knowledge to fight off trained Arcane assassins over and over again."

"Who the hell does?" Wade retorted. "Your idea about going to a warded location is a good one. So is keeping on the move, but I can tell you from experience that it doesn't always work. When Sam and

I were trying to stop Bellar, I can't tell you how many times we got ambushed while on the move."

"Shit." Seth ran his hand through his hair, grimacing as he felt the dirt clinging to the strands. He really did need a shower. "It was worth a shot. Besides, Hecate may help, and I've got someone looking into the Lemuria angle."

"I wish I could do more, but if you end up in my neck of the woods, let me know. Sam and I will help. And I don't know if there's anyone on the planet who can beat her in a one-on-one fight," Wade said proudly.

"I will. Thanks, man."

"No problem. I'll keep an ear out, too. If I hear anything, I'll let you know."

"Thanks," Seth said again. "Later."

He hung up and slumped in the seat. He hated feeling useless. At least if he was on a treasure hunt he could research, but this? It was a completely different sort of job, and he just didn't have the resources to work on it while in the air.

Exhausted from the last two days, he leaned the seat back and closed his eyes to try to get some sleep. He was reasonably confident that they'd be safe as long as they were in the air. But he knew nothing was ever certain.

After Tempest closed the door behind her, leaving her alone for the first time since she'd awoken, she nearly broke. She leaned against the door and closed her eyes, struggling to control her breathing, to calm herself.

It was too much to deal with. She was way past overwhelmed and she hadn't gotten a chance to really deal with any of it.

Just waking up had been disorienting. She'd fallen asleep, safe and sound in her own bed, and woken up on a stone slab, miles away from everything she'd known. And she had no idea how she'd gotten there. She suspected Vazi had something to do with it. Though he had been a god and she was just an elemental, they'd been friends for years, and they'd only gotten closer after her parents had died. Three days ago, for her, he'd been her best friend. But she couldn't figure out why he'd seal her in what some might call a tomb. If it was even him.

And if Seth hadn't found her, it might very well have become her tomb. She might have slept until the world ended and never have known a thing.

Seth...she had so much to be grateful to him for. Not only had he found her and saved her from a sleeping death, he'd protected her, even to the point of being badly injured himself. And he was still protecting her. He had no reason to. His life would certainly be easier if he just left her somewhere and moved on. If she were a good woman, she'd suggest he do just that, but she wasn't that selfless.

Besides, she liked him. He'd been good to her, and tried his best to make things easier on her. She felt an odd sort of connection with him, but that could simply be because he was the one who had woken her up. But the fact that he was extremely attractive didn't hurt either.

She pushed away from the door and explored the small room. When she found the bathroom, Hecate's gift let her know what it was all for and she nearly wept with relief. She had no clean clothes to put on, but she desperately needed to wash the last six millennia off her. She stripped off her borrowed clothes and turned on the shower, stepping gratefully beneath the hot water. She tipped her face up into the spray and sighed with relief.

If only it could wash away the revelations of the past hour as easily as it could the dirt. But instead she was stuck with the pain of knowing that everyone she'd known, every soul she'd grown up with, interacted with, was gone. She was alone in the world. A single Lemurian, cast adrift in a world that had forgotten her kind ever existed.

That fact confused her, though. How could the world have forgotten about Lemuria? Witches, elementals, and shapeshifters still roamed the world, though she didn't know in what numbers. And if they were here, where was the memory of her home? The two should never have been separated. Not unless someone had wiped the memory of Lemuria out along with the land itself.

It was a mystery she had a feeling she was going to have to solve before she could solve the problem of how to protect herself. And Seth. But that was a problem for a well-rested mind.

Twenty minutes later, she stepped out of the shower, clean, if not feeling better. She dried off, but didn't bother to put the dirty clothes back on, just crawled between the sheets. Within minutes, she was asleep.

CHAPTER 7

The plane was about to begin its descent when Seth knocked on the door to the bedroom. "Tempest? Are you awake?" It took a couple more knocks before he got a response.

"Minute," she called back, her voice slurred with sleep.

"Take your time. We're getting ready to land, but it'll take a few minutes. But once we're on the ground, we're going to have to move fast."

"Okay."

He was sitting and sending a text to Kara when she emerged ten minutes later, dressed in his shorts and tee-shirt. He glanced over and grimaced. "We need to get you some clothes. I'm so sorry we weren't able to back in Peru."

She shook her head. "It's okay. I'd rather be in dirty, ill-fitting clothes but alive, than in clean clothes and dead."

He gave her a half smile. "Wise words. We can't really stop on the way to Kara's either, but I think she's about your size. She's damn sure closer than I am, so at least you'll have clean, better-fitting clothes."

"I'll appreciate anything at this point," she told him as she sat down beside him.

He studied her face for a moment. "How are you feeling?" he asked, hitting send and setting his phone in his lap.

It took her a minute to answer. "I'm not really sure. More tired than I should be, I think, but that could simply be everything going on." She paused, then continued. "And a little numb, but I hurt. Here," she said, resting her hand lightly over her heart and rubbing gently.

He nodded, but did note that she looked exhausted despite sleeping most of the flight. "I'd be shocked if you didn't. Anyone would be hurting in your situation. And most people wouldn't be handling it nearly as well as you are."

"I don't know that I'm handling it at all," she admitted. "I don't think I can just yet. If I think about it too much, I'm afraid it'll just break me."

"If it does, just remember you're not alone. You've got me," he told her gently.

Her eyes went damp with tears and she nodded. "Thank you, Seth. Is there anything I can do to repay you?"

"There's no need for that, Tempest. Any decent person would be doing as I am now."

"Ahh, but that's the thing, isn't it? Not everyone is decent, are they? So please, if there's anything I can do, let me know."

"When things are calmer, when you can handle it, I'd like to know more about Lemuria. But only if you can handle it," he said after a minute.

"Actually, I think I need to talk about it now," Tempest told him.

He frowned. "You do?"

"I think it might be relevant to our current situation."

The plane touched down and he glanced toward the cockpit. "Then let's wait until we get in the car. I have a feeling this may take a bit."

"You're right. And I think I'd prefer to talk when it really is just you and me."

"I can get that." He grinned. "By the way, just because you speak English now doesn't mean you can't still speak Lemurian. I'd love to learn it."

She smiled. "It would be nice to have at least one person who I can speak it with."

"Excellent," he said, his grin widening. Despite their situation, he was thrilled at the thought of learning a language that hadn't been spoken in thousands of years. And maybe one of these days he might find the ruins of Lemuria, and then he'd be able to translate any of the words he found. Not that he was going to mention that to her. No reason to make her think of her homeland in ruins.

Minutes later, the plane had stopped and they were off it, with only the single bag Tempest had carried on board for him. It was a small airfield, one run by elementals and witches, so they didn't have any trouble getting out and to the car that Kara had sent for them.

Only after they were several minutes down the road did Seth broach the subject of Lemuria again. "You said that something about Lemuria might be relevant to our current situation?"

Tempest sighed and nodded slightly. "I believe so, yes," she said, her voice pained

"Take your time, Tempest. We've got a good forty minutes before we get to Kara's," he told her.

She nodded again and shifted in her seat to face him a bit better. "Before I slept, I thought how odd it was that there are witches and shapeshifters and such, but no memory of Lemuria."

He shook his head. "I don't understand."

"Which is the problem," she said with a faint smile. "Witches, shapeshifters, elementals, and sirens…They all owe their existence to Lemuria. It was their birthplace."

Seth nearly drove off the side of the road. "What?" he yelled.

Tempest flinched slightly and looked sad. "You heard me right. The Lemurian gods created the first magical species out there aside from gods and demons. You said your father was a shapeshifter, which means that one of his ancestors was born on Lemuria."

"Are you fucking kidding me? Are you saying I'm Lemurian, too?"

"I'm sorry, but no," she told him with a shake of her head. "We eventually learned that when one of the Lemurian gods' children was born on Lemuria, they were Lemurian themselves. But if they were born anywhere else, while magical, they were not Lemurian."

He frowned and shook his head. "I don't get it. What does geography have to do with it?"

She thought for a moment. "It's a number of things. Being Lemurian is magical, biological, and geographical all at once. Technically, I suppose you could say that any member of the four magical species are Lemurian by blood, but they aren't by magic or geography. When a Lemurian was born on Lemuria, it changed them. Maybe the magic of the land infused each person on their birth, I'm not sure. But they were more powerful than those born anywhere else."

"Now that explains a few things," he muttered.

"How so?"

He gave her a sheepish look. "I've met my fair share of elementals, even a few air elementals, but none that were anywhere near as powerful as you. I...may have thought you were a goddess at first, even when you said you were an elemental."

He expected that might make her feel proud, but instead she looked sad again. "So much has been lost..."

"Maybe that's the point," he said.

"I had the same idea. How could such an important fact be lost with the land unless someone worked to make sure it stayed beneath the water as well?"

"It would explain why someone's trying so hard to kill you," he told her grimly.

"It would, but it makes it less likely that we'll find a way to make them stop hunting me," she pointed out.

"We'll find a way, Tempest. I don't know how yet, but we will."

"I hope you're right," she murmured.

After a long pause, Seth glanced at her. "Ahh...there was something else...do you have any idea how you got to Peru? Or how you survived so long?"

"Ideas? Yes. Certainty?" She shook her head. "I have a feeling that it was Vazi, a Lemurian god I was friends with. I don't know why he would have put me in that place, though."

"Oh, yes, a god would have been able to manage it," he said with a nod. "I'm kind of glad he did. Otherwise, we never would have met."

She made a thoughtful noise. "Maybe, maybe not. If someone is trying to silence any word of Lemuria, then it's likely I would have been killed, but I might have survived."

"I have no doubt you would have, but you still would have been dead thousands of years before I was born," he pointed out. She frowned and he gave her a sharp look. "Why do I get the feeling you know something else I don't know?"

"How long do elementals and such live now?"

"How long...are you kidding me?"

She shook her head. "No. How long?"

"On average, most magical species live about a thousand years. There are some exceptions, but generally it's a thousand years, give or take. Gods and demons are immortal, of course, along with a couple of Arcane species who live equally as long."

Another sigh escaped her life. "I'd forgotten that," she murmured. "Lemurians are immortal. It was only once we left the island that we lost that immortality."

Seth's hands tightened on the steering wheel, his knuckles going white. When he spoke, his voice was tight. "Are you shitting me? We were immortal once? *You're* immortal?"

"Yes," she answered in a small voice.

Reeling, he just drove, not even able to look away from the road. "I don't think I can handle any more revelations, so if there's anything else, get it out now, Tempest. Please."

She shook her head. "Nothing I can think of, no," she said quietly. "I'm sorry, Seth. I really didn't think that part had been lost, too."

"It's not your fault, darlin'. It's just a lot. Twenty-four hours ago I didn't know Lemuria existed, and now all this?" He glanced at her briefly. "We'll need to tell Kara so she can help us, but I'd keep most of this to yourself for now. Maybe forever. It sounds like dangerous information to have."

"Yes, I suppose you're right about that," she agreed grimly.

He pried one of his hands off the wheel and took hers, giving it a gentle squeeze. "We'll get through this, Tempest. Somehow. So don't worry."

She gave him a faint smile and nodded.

He was quiet for a moment before he remembered the pictures he'd taken. "There is one thing that might help solve the mystery of how you got to Peru."

Her brows lifted. "What's that?"

"I don't know if you noticed, but the door to the place where I found you had carvings on it. Writing, but I couldn't decipher it. I was thinking that might be because it was Lemurian."

"If Vazi or one of the other gods was responsible, that would make sense. Did you write down what it said?" she asked, excitement creeping into her tone.

"I can do better than that. Grab my bag?" When she did, he directed her to the camera, then guided her into turning it on and pulling up the pictures. "I know it's small, and if you can't read it I'll put it on my computer later so it's bigger, but can you recognize that language?"

She moved the camera close to her face and studied the images silently for a minute. "Some of it, yes..." she murmured absently. "The part at the top, no. I don't even know what language it is, much less what it says. But this part?" she pointed to it but he couldn't make it out without taking his eyes off the road for too long. "That's my name. And this is Vazi's name."

"Can you tell what the rest of it says?" he asked, trying not to get his hopes up.

Squinting at the small screen, Tempest read and finally nodded. "Most of it. Some of it is too small, but it looks like it says that Vazi put me there to protect me, though it doesn't say from what. It also says that any who open the door should have the most honorable of intentions or would suffer a grave fate."

"Sounds like I was lucky, then," Seth said dryly. "I was just curious and wanting a big discovery, which wasn't exactly honorable. But neither did I want to steal or hurt anyone."

She lowered the camera and smiled at him. "I don't think curiosity is a bad thing, especially since you couldn't read the warning. Though *I* am curious why you went inside without being able to read it."

He shrugged. "I touched the door and it opened. I can't resist an open door."

She laughed softly and replaced the camera in the bag. "A dangerous impulse."

"Sometimes," he agreed.

They drove the rest of the way in silence. It wasn't until they pulled up at a stone house, situated halfway up one of the smaller peaks, that he spoke. "We're here."

"Are you sure it's safe here?" Tempest asked, making no move to leave the car.

Seth shut the car off and unbuckled before he looked to her. "No, I'm not," he said bluntly. "But it's our best bet for right now. I know Kara won't sell us out, and her home is warded. We shouldn't stay more than a day or two, but it's long enough for us to rest, eat, and get you some better clothes. Maybe even figure out what the fuck we're going to do."

She studied the house for a minute before she nodded and climbed out of the car. She felt a little self-conscious, and more than a little wary. Here she was wearing dirty, borrowed clothes that hung off of her, at the home of a stranger, when unknown people were trying to kill her. Likely, she wasn't going to feel like herself for quite a while. But she was going to trust in Seth. Trust that this friend of his was as loyal as he believed.

He was all she had right now, which was a little terrifying.

"Don't worry. Kara's pretty easy going, and she's going to like you. More importantly, I think you're going to like her. So just try to relax while we're here, okay?" Seth murmured as they started for the front door.

A wan smile curved her lips. "Relaxing isn't going to happen, but I'll do my best."

He nodded. "It's the best anyone can do." He rapped on the heavy wooden door.

From inside, they heard a cheerful voice call out, "It's open! Get your cute butt in here and bring that Lemurian with you!"

Tempest gave him a startled look and he smiled wryly. "She's got an interesting sense of humor. But she's harmless, I promise." He opened the door and led her inside.

The house wasn't at all what Tempest had expected, given Seth's description of Kara and the rough architecture of the exterior. She had expected stone colors and a spartan appearance, but she was complete-ly wrong. The living room was done in warm shades that mirrored those of a setting sun. There wasn't a lot of furniture, but what was there was plush and comfortable looking. Large windows let in plenty of moonlight, and during the day would bathe the room in golden sun. And while there weren't any stone colors, there were plenty of stones. Gemstones in a myriad of colors were scattered around the room. Some were tumbled and smooth, others sharp crystal points, while a few were carved into a variety of shapes.

Tempest liked it instantly.

Kara came out of the kitchen, dressed in a pair of denim shorts and a tee-shirt that had a picture of some big green man on it. And like her home, she wasn't what Tempest had expected. Her hair was brown and pulled up into a simple ponytail. Every inch of exposed skin was lightly tanned and flawless. In those regards, she didn't look like she was half stone elemental, but her eyes were the color of moldavite. Green, with tinges of yellow and brown, but on her they were striking.

She was only a bit shorter than Tempest's five foot six, but she had more muscle and curves, and they looked amazing on her. Tempest immediately felt a bit inferior to this woman, but Kara's smile was so open and welcoming that Tempest couldn't help but like her instantly.

"Seth! About time you got here," Kara said happily, hurrying over to them to give Seth a big hug. "And you must be Tempest. I'm so sorry to hear that people are after you," she said before giving Tempest a hug as well.

It startled the elemental, and she gave Seth a baffled look, but he just grinned and shrugged until Tempest returned the hug. "Ah...yes, I am. Thank you for giving us a safe place for a few days."

"Oh, no big," Kara said as she stepped back. "Seth and I go way back. I've bailed him out of a lot of trouble," she explained with an impish grin.

"Not that much," Seth said dryly. "But I won't argue anything else."

Kara laughed. "Because you'd be lying. Come on. I figured you guys could use some real food, so I've got some spaghetti ready. And you...look like you need some better clothes." She gave Seth an accusing look. "Did you dress her in *your* clothes? But forgot shoes?"

"It was all he had," Tempest said, instantly jumping to Seth's defense. "When I woke, I was only in my nightgown. It was hardly appropriate clothing for hiking through...what was the name of that land, Seth?"

"Peru, and she's right. This was the best I could do. I was hoping you'd have something she could wear. We didn't have time to stop, and it wouldn't have been safe in any case."

"Sure thing. You go grab some food, I'll find something for Tempest. Come on, girl. This'll be fun," Kara said, grinning and looping an arm through Tempest's.

Helplessly, Tempest was pulled along to Kara's bedroom. But only fifteen minutes later she had a couple pairs of jeans, a pair of shorts, and several shirts, along with some socks and a pair of sneakers that fit surprisingly well.

Kara showed Tempest to a bedroom and grinned. "You can sleep here until you guys leave. Feel free to go ahead and change before you join us. We'll be in the kitchen."

"Thank you, Kara. You've been very generous."

Kara laughed and shook her head. "It's just a few changes of clothes, and Seth's my best friend. This is the least I can do. Now hurry up and change. I want to hear the whole story," she said before closing the door and going to join Seth.

Tempest blew out a breath. She might be the one named for a storm, but Kara was a whirlwind.

Maybe they'd get along after all.

CHAPTER 8

When Tempest made her way into the kitchen, she found Seth and Kara sitting at a table eating. The food—spaghetti, Kara had called it—smelled different from anything she'd ever eaten before. Different, but amazing.

"What is that delicious aroma?" she asked, inhaling deeply as she moved to sit in front of the third plate.

Kara grinned. "Spaghetti. Or could be the garlic bread. I take it that you didn't have anything like it in Lemuria?"

Tempest shook her head. "No, but if it tastes anything like it smells, I'm sorry for that."

"Well, dig in. I don't make it as good as some, but it's good enough."

"Thank you, I will."

As she started to eat, Seth began telling Kara about how he'd found Tempest and woken her up. Tempest half-tuned it out, focusing on the new and interesting meal in front of her. Besides, she didn't need to hear most of it since she'd lived it. He even told Kara what Tempest had told him about some of the magical species originating on the sunken continent. There was surprise, certainly, almost to the level Seth had shown, but when he got to the part where Hecate had shown up and informed him that Lemuria was real, Kara shifted her focus to Tempest.

"Even knowing that Seth wouldn't lie, and with a goddess confirming it, I still have a hard time believing that Lemuria is real."

"I have a feeling that would be the general consensus if it was made known," Tempest said with a faint smile. "But we don't believe it's smart to let it get out. It's a shame, though. People should know where they came from."

"I don't disagree, but it's a good idea to keep it quiet."

"I just wish I knew what had happened. What caused Lemuria to sink, and why I was put into that place in Peru," Tempest murmured.

"That's part of what I wanted to talk to you about," Seth told Kara.

Surprised, Kara blinked at him. "Me? I don't know anything about Lemuria."

"No, I know you don't, but you know a lot of people," Seth answered. "Do you think any of them might know something?"

"Yes, anything we can learn would be useful. It might tell us why someone wants Lemuria, all of it—including me—buried," Tempest agreed with an eager nod.

Kara leaned back and picked up her glass of wine, swirling it lightly as she thought. After several minutes, she took a sip and nodded. "I might. I know a woman. She's a bit...mysterious and secretive, but she's been around for a while. Heard she's a historian. Could be she heard something when she was researching something else."

Seth frowned and cocked her head. "Who? I know a couple of people who like history, but I can't think of any who strike me as mysterious and really old."

"I'm not surprised. Like I said, she's secretive. I couldn't even tell you what she is. I know what I just told you and that her name is Aelia."

Tempest looked surprised. "Aelia? That's a Lemurian name."

Kara frowned. "Is it? I thought it was Latin or something."

Tempest shook her head. "Maybe it was adopted by the Latins, but I assure you, it's Lemurian. I knew a woman named Aelia. She was a siren."

Seth fought a smile. "Not Latins. Latin is a language. It was spoken by several people, including the Romans."

"Oh. Well, my point still stands."

"It doesn't matter, really," Kara said with a shrug. "Names are important, but don't necessarily mean anything when it comes to the origin of the person. And it's not like she could be Lemurian."

"No," Tempest agreed, deflating. "I suppose she isn't. Even Hecate said I was the last one."

"Do you know how to get in touch with her?" Seth asked.

"I can try. You guys eat. I'll give her a call," Kara said as she rose and retreated back to her bedroom.

They resumed eating, but after a minute Tempest glanced to Seth. "Are you two...together?" she asked, as casually as she could make it. They certainly seemed close enough to be in a relationship, but she hoped she was misreading the situation. Since the moment she'd opened her eyes and seen Seth, she'd been attracted, and not just to his body, though even clothed she could see he had a hard, admirable body.

Seth had just taken a bite when she asked her question and ended up choking. It took a slap on the back from Tempest and a minute of coughing before he could speak. "What?" He picked up his beer and drank to clear his throat. "Together? Kara and I?" A laugh burst out of him and he shook his head. "No, we're not together. Never have been. She's closer to a sister to me than a girlfriend or lover. I love her, I do, but we don't think of each other like that."

"Oh. You were just so close I had to wonder."

"No, it was a fair question," he assured her. When she went back to eating, he watched her surreptitiously and hid a smile. He'd wanted her even before she'd woken on that stone altar, but hadn't made a move on her, giving her time and space. But if her question was any indication, maybe he should stop giving her quite so much space.

"Well, I still can't tell you anything for certain," Kara began as she came back into the kitchen, "especially since I didn't want to say too much over the phone, but I've got us a meeting with Aelia."

"You did? When? Where?" Seth asked.

"Two days, near Denver."

"Two days?" Tempest asked, dismayed. "Why so long?"

"Couple reasons," Kara answered as she retook her seat. "First, she said she wasn't in the area, but I'm not sure I believe that. Still, she claimed she needed time to get here. Second, you two have been through hell. It gives you time to rest up and recover."

"Good point," Tempest allowed with a single nod.

"Hey, don't look so glum, girl," Kara said, nudging Tempest's foot with her own. "It won't be so bad. I mean, Seth isn't great company," she said with a wink to the man, "but I'm fantastic. And there's a lot of modern stuff you haven't even seen yet. Movies, music, not to mention the shopping. Which, okay, might be limited to online at the moment, but that's something else! The internet. Every piece of human information in one place, accessible to anyone who wants it."

Tempest's eyes went wide and she glanced to Seth. "Is she being serious?"

Seth grinned. "Except for thinking she's better company than I am, yeah, she is. She's pretty dull, though. She sends me jigsaw puzzles all the time, after all."

"Hey, there's a purpose to the puzzles," Kara protested. "You need to learn how to relax. They're relaxing."

He leaned toward Tempest, close enough for her to feel his breath against her ear when he stage whispered, "See? Dull." He felt her shiver lightly and fought not to let her see his satisfied smile.

Tempest cleared her throat and shook her head. "I don't see either of you as being dull. And gods know life hasn't been dull the past two days. A little dull might be nice."

"I'm glad to hear you say that. You can do puzzles with Seth," Kara said, giving Seth a smug smile.

Seth rolled his eyes. "I'm not going to be doing any puzzles tonight. I'm going to take a shower and enjoy sleeping in a bed. There's no telling when we'll get an actual bed for a while after we leave here."

Kara's smugness died and shifted into concern. "You really don't have any idea who's after you?"

"No," Tempest said quietly. "I don't know what happened to Lemuria, so I don't know who would want to keep it buried."

"And it's not a single group. Or I don't think it is. So far we've been attacked by witches, shapeshifters, and what was probably an elemental," Seth added. "For all I know, we had some of everything after us. Could be some sort of secret society, or they could just be hired assassins."

"There's not really any point in speculating until we have more information, so you two just rest while you can," Kara told them. "Relax tomorrow. Enjoy yourself. I'd say go shopping, but you two probably shouldn't leave my house. The yard is protected, too, but the house is the safest. No sense in putting yourself at risk before you have to."

Seth grimaced. "You're right, but that could be a problem. I'm wearing the only clothes I have with me."

"No problem. Just tell me your sizes and what you want and I'll go get it. No one's looking for me."

"That'll work. I'd give you my credit card..."

"But if they found out your name that could raise flags," Kara finished with a nod. "No problem. Just don't die and we'll call it square."

"Thanks." He got up and rinsed his plate before putting it in the dishwasher. "You need anything before I shower and sleep?" he asked Tempest.

She looked uncertain and glanced between Seth and Kara. "I slept fairly well on the plane, so I'm not quite ready for sleep. Is there something I might do to occupy myself while you two sleep? A book, perhaps?"

Kara grinned. "I've got something better than a book, though I've got those, too. You go wash off all that grime, Seth. I'll take care of your girl."

Seth's gaze shot to Tempest at the last two words, but she just smiled at him. "I'll be all right. Go. I know you'll feel better after you bathe."

He slowly nodded. "Okay. But behave, Kara."

"Never," she told him with a serious tone and impish smile.

Knowing that was the best he was going to get from her, Seth shook his head and retreated to the bathroom.

The moment he was gone, Kara nodded to Tempest's plate. "Eat what you like, then I'm going to show you where my books are, but after that? I'm going to teach you what a movie is. Both are good, but you've read books. You've never seen a movie."

Tempest nodded and took another few bites before she set her fork down. "It's delicious, but I couldn't eat another bite. Now, what's a movie?" she asked as she got to her feet. Hecate had filled her head with a great deal of knowledge, but it seemed to be activated only when she came in contact with various modern things. She hadn't known what a shower was until she saw it, so the same was probably true for everything else.

Kara laughed and stood, leading Tempest to the small but packed library. After letting Tempest look around for a few minutes, she introduced the Lemurian to the joy of movies, showing her how to operate the remotes before she went to bed herself.

Left alone, Tempest sat in the living room, but she didn't feel so lonely. Knowing that Kara and Seth were just in the other room, that she could go to them if she needed anything, loosened the tight knot that had formed in her chest the moment she realized how long she'd slept.

She'd taken a book from the library, one full of magic and adventure, but it rested in her lap, closed. The light from the movie that played on the screen flickered over her face and the music washed over her. Background noise, really, nothing more. The thought of a movie intrigued her, but she couldn't get her mind to shut down long enough to actually pay attention to it. Nor could she read.

Though Tempest knew it was probably due to the events of the last few days, she felt off. She was mentally tired, just as she'd told Seth when they'd been about to land, but it was more than that. Nothing she could pinpoint, but it continued to prod at the edges of her consciousness.

Her gaze slid to the door Seth was closed behind and her mind settled on one topic. She'd been upset earlier when she thought he was with Kara, which was silly, really. She hardly knew him. And he was certainly old enough to have been with multiple women. Yet, she couldn't deny how she felt. It wasn't love. No, she wasn't foolish enough to believe that. But she wanted him, even if this was no time to pursue a man. She'd stay alive first, then, perhaps, she could think of such things.

Tempest forced herself to look back to the TV. She set the book aside and drew her knees up loosely against her chest to get more comfortable. Her focus on the movie was scattered at best, but as she watched, as she half-heartedly listened to the people on screen, she began to drift off.

The dialogue influenced her dream, as did her thoughts before sleep.

Instead of the hero speaking to his lady love, in her mind she saw Seth speaking to her. Seducing her with words before ever touching her. But when he did touch her? Every cell within her body sang. Even when she turned into air itself and soared across the sky she didn't feel so free. So alive. And when he slid into her, her body fractured, exploded, then reformed, with every piece of her vibrating with pleasure.

It was that pleasure that shocked her awake, and she sat up abruptly, gasping, her body aching with need.

Tempest closed her eyes and fought to control her reaction to the dream. To press her desire down so it didn't distract her.

She fumbled with the remote until she found the right button to turn the TV off, then stood and walked to the hallway. Seth's door had her stopping and she stared at it for a long moment before she forced her feet to move again until she was safely tucked away in her room.

This time, sleep didn't come so easily to her.

CHAPTER 9

S eth slept long but not well. It wasn't really unusual for him.
After a hunt or dig, it always took him a few nights to relax and
sleep deeply, and this time, he hadn't gotten the chance to relax.

The hunt wasn't over yet.

But it wasn't his mind that woke him, nor was it the sunlight
beginning to stream in through the window. It was his phone. He
snatched it off the nightstand and squinted at the display. Number
blocked. He had no idea who would be calling him from a blocked
number, so frowned as he accepted the call.

"Yes?"

"You sound like hell," came the deep male voice from the other
end.

"Thanks," Seth said dryly as he rubbed a hand over his face.
"Who the fuck is this and why are you calling at," he pulled the
phone away from his ear to glance at the time, "six in the morning?"

"Damn. Now I'm hurt. You think you'd recognize the voice of
your rival. Though rival makes it sound like we're equals, and we
both know I'm the far superior archaeologist."

Seth bit back a groan. No, Aaron Fischer wasn't a rival. He was
a royal pain in Seth's ass. "You're my superior all right, but not in

archeology. Superior jackass, maybe. But none of that explains why you're calling me at all, much less this early."

"Early where you are, maybe, but the sun's up here, and it's a beautiful day."

"Aaron? Get to the point or I'm hanging up and going back to sleep."

Aaron tsked. "So impatient. I'm rethinking my choice to do you a favor."

Seth's brows shot up to his hairline. "A favor? Last time I saw you, you were causing a cave in that buried me in an underground temple. If my phone weren't enhanced, I'd have died in that fucking place."

"Eh, all's fair in love and money."

"Love and war," Seth corrected, his teeth clenched. "It's all's fair in love and war."

"Same difference. Besides, I didn't *want* to kill you, then. I just wanted to slow you down. You should really take it as a compliment."

Seth's head was starting to throb, but any interaction with Aaron had the same result. "How the hell is it a compliment?"

"I had faith you could manage to escape. But you're distracting me from my reason for calling."

"And what is that reason?"

"I was hired to kill a woman and a man matching your description," Aaron answered, all traces of mocking or laughter gone.

Seth went still. "What?"

"You heard me. They offered a hell of a paycheck, too, if I could manage it. A bonus if I did it in forty-eight hours and provided proof."

"And you're telling me this...why?" He slipped out of bed and started gathering his clothes. His phone probably couldn't be magically traced through Kara's wards, but there was no guarantee of that. And he'd been on the phone long enough that Aaron might have managed it.

"Because I'm not a fucking assassin, Seth," Aaron growled.

That made Seth pause. Aaron had a temper, and he'd growled at Seth before, but it had always sounded human before. This time, the tiger that Aaron could become was evident. "No," he said slowly. "I suppose you're not. But we're also not friends."

"Like I said, I didn't want to kill you before. I also don't want to see you dead now," Aaron answered. "I have a lot of fun scooping finds out from under you. If someone killed you to get to this woman, then I'd have to take the time to find a replacement." He paused a beat. "I don't imagine you'd be very easy to replace."

Seth sat down on the bed, thoroughly baffled. He and Aaron had never been friends before. They'd never even managed friendly. "If you don't want to see me dead, will you help me?" he asked skeptically.

Aaron snorted. "I don't know if I'd go that far, but I will tell you what I know, though it isn't much. They don't have your name. Either of your names, actually. Just a description of you and the woman. Who sounds hot, by the way. If you manage to stay alive, could you introduce us?"

"Fuck off," Seth snapped.

"Already taken? Well, we'll see. Gave your last known location as Peru, and I'd love to know what you were doing down there. Other than you flying away and the woman having impressive air magic, not much was really said."

"Why'd they contact you? I may not like you, but as you said, you're not an assassin."

"Hell if I know," Aaron admitted. "I know I'm well traveled, but there are probably plenty of actual assassins in Peru. Not to mention witches who can teleport. Maybe someone suspects your identity. Maybe they think if I'm the best archaeologist that I'm the best at everything. I don't know. They didn't tell me and I'm not a telepath."

"Shit." Seth ran a hand through his hair. "Who put the contract out?"

Aaron hesitated. "I don't know."

"A stranger called you up and asked you to kill someone?" he asked incredulously.

"Yep. Makes no fucking sense, but there you go. And they didn't give me a name, either. Probably would've been fake if they had."

"Probably," Seth agreed.

Aaron paused for a long moment before continuing, voice careful. "Don't freak out, but I didn't turn them down."

"What? I thought you said you didn't want me dead!" Seth yelled, surging to his feet. He heard the sound of a door slamming open, then footsteps, before his door opened and he saw Tempest standing there. She looked pale, with dark circles under her eyes. It made him wonder if she'd slept at all. A moment later, Kara joined her.

"Calm down. If they only offered the job to me, and I didn't turn them down, they might—and I emphasize might—wait before they hire someone else," Aaron explained.

"What is it? Is everything okay?" Tempest asked, brow tight with concern as she crossed to him.

Seth shook his head and gave her a signal to wait. "They might. I doubt it, but it might have bought us a little time." Though it burned, he added, "Thank you."

"You're welcome," Aaron said smugly. "You can be sure I'll remember this later. Especially since I'll call you if I learn anything else. Oh, and I suppose I'll send you my number. I want to know if you beat this. And try not to die before you introduce me to that woman with the sexy as hell voice, okay?" he said before he hung up.

Seth closed his eyes and took several slow breaths, trying to calm himself.

"Seth? What is it?" Kara asked, still standing in the doorway.

His eyes opened to find Tempest standing close to him. Very close. He could smell the subtle fragrance of her, like honeysuckle and storms. "Um...that was Aaron."

"Asshole Aaron?" Kara asked, surprised.

He nodded. "One and the same." He explained to Tempest, "We're sort of competitors. We both try to find old temples or tombs, but his methods are a lot less...Scrupulous."

Kara snorted. "That's putting it mildly. What'd he want?"

"To warn me." Kara looked skeptical, but Seth nodded and went on. "Seriously. He got offered money, a lot of it, to kill us."

"But he turned them down?" Tempest asked. "He wouldn't warn you otherwise, would he?"

"No, he didn't. Not directly. He bought us some time by not flat out refusing, but we should probably go sooner rather than later."

"I'll see if I can move the meet with Aelia up to later today, and I'll head out now to get those clothes," Kara agreed, nodding. "Even if they track you here, it'll take some time for them to get through the wards to actually locate you, so we've got time enough for that."

"Hopefully, yeah." Phone still in hand, he texted his sizes to Kara's phone. "Just be careful, okay? He said they only had our descriptions, but if they figure out who I am, it wouldn't be hard for them to find you."

Kara waved off his concern. "Yeah, yeah. You know I can take care of myself. You guys grab some breakfast and be ready to go when I get back. I'm sure I can be persuasive enough to get the meeting moved, even if we have to meet Aelia somewhere else."

"Thank you, Kara," Tempest said quietly. She still stood by Seth, staring up at him, her hands clenched into fists at her side. There was a little more color in her cheeks now, but not much. "And I'm sorry for all the trouble we're causing you."

"Pfft. It's fine. Life was getting pretty routine. And by routine, I mean boring. So you don't worry about a thing, girl." She flashed a grin, then left to run her errands, leaving Seth and Tempest alone in his bedroom.

"You okay?" he asked quietly, brushing her hair behind her ear.

"Not really," she admitted. "Your...competitor, did he know who wants me dead?"

"No, but I think he's going to try to figure it out. It pissed him off, being offered money to kill someone."

Her head tilted. "You said he was unscrupulous, though."

"I did, and he is, but I can't see him outright murdering anyone. He's a tiger, so he's lethal, sure, and I can see him defending himself without any trouble, or even hurting someone to get what he wants, but murder?" He shook his head. "No, it's not in him. Especially not murder for hire. So I'd put money on him doing his damnedest to track down the source of the offer."

"Will he help us aside from that?"

"I'm not sure," Seth admitted. "He might, if only to spite the money man, but I wouldn't count on it."

Tempest nodded and glanced downward, expression thoughtful. "After we meet Aelia, perhaps I should go on alone." She looked up at him and recoiled a step at the anger on his face.

"You're not going to deal with this yourself," he told her sternly, offended by the insinuation. "Do you really think I'm the sort of man who would let a woman deal with assassins by herself? Especially a woman who is completely unfamiliar with how the world works?"

"No, but—"

"But nothing. You're stuck with me. If, when this is all over and you're safe, you want to ditch me, you can, but not a second before."

She blinked rapidly, trying to keep her eyes from watering. On impulse, and partially to hide her face, she stepped forward and went up on her toes, throwing her arms around his neck in a tight hug. "Thank you," she whispered.

Stunned, it took Seth a moment before he could react. His arms came around her and pulled her a little more firmly against his body, almost lifting her off her toes. She was so tiny compared to him that it was the only way he could hug her without hunching over. Besides, it felt good to have her pressed against him. "You're welcome," he said in a rough voice.

Her face lifted and he felt a pang in his chest at the unshed tears in her eyes. It was nothing but impulse and instinct when he lowered his head and brushed his lips gently against hers. "Don't cry," he murmured before repeating the caress once more. She felt so good though, and when she returned the kiss, he couldn't help himself. He groaned and took her mouth. His tongue brushed against the seam of her lips until they parted, then pressed inside to stroke and tease.

Tempest trembled against him and tightened her arms around his neck, so he shifted his grip on her, sliding an arm beneath her ass to lift her up, easily supporting her slight weight. When her legs wrapped around his waist, he wanted to turn, lay her on the bed, and strip her borrowed clothes off her. Instead, he allowed himself another minute of tasting her before he pulled his head back.

Both of them were breathing hard, and Tempest could feel the proof of Seth's arousal against her. She didn't want him to stop, but she knew they needed to. Kara would be back all too soon. But she wanted him, badly.

She wiggled against him and he groaned with pleasure, then pain that he had to stop. "Tempest..."

"I know," she told him in a husky whisper. "We need to focus on the assassins. But soon...I'd like to continue this."

"Count on it." He stole one more kiss before her legs unwound and he let her slide slowly down his body. Her legs weren't quite steady when her feet touched the floor, and he held onto her until she was able to stand by herself. "You're not dealing with this yourself," he told her again.

She smiled. "No, I'm not." Slowly she stepped back and brushed a hand down his tee-shirt covered chest. "I should go get ready."

Seth nodded. "I'll be out in a few."

"Don't take too long," she said and gave a teasing look to the bulge in his pants.

While he fought the urge to adjust himself to make his erection less noticeable, she just laughed softly and left the bedroom, shutting the door quietly behind her.

That woman was going to be the death of him. But he couldn't help but smile.

After all, not all deaths were the permanent kind.

CHAPTER 10

Kara called on her way back and told them the meeting had successfully been moved up to noon, giving them plenty of time. Seth took advantage of that and showered once more before changing into the new clothes Kara had brought with her. Afterward, he felt better than he had since before he left for Peru.

With their few things packed up, they left the safety of a warded home and left for the meeting. If they were lucky, Aelia would be there early as well. It wasn't ideal, but they had few options at this point, and neither Seth nor Tempest were willing to be running for the rest of their life.

They piled into Kara's SUV, with Seth and Tempest in the back, and set off for Denver.

"Is Aelia going to be alone?" Seth asked.

"Doubtful. I know I sure as hell wouldn't be if I were in her position. A woman meeting with three strangers? Three magical strangers?" Kara shook her head. "Not smart."

"I thought you said you knew her," Tempest said as she absently rubbed at her temple. The headache had begun not long after she'd left Seth's room, and it had progressively gotten worse over the last few hours.

"Knowing is a bit of an exaggeration," Kara admitted. "We met...once. And you can barely call it meeting. She was at a friend's house, but so were a couple other people. We said hi, introduced ourselves, and that was mostly it." She glanced in the rear-view mirror at them. "She remembered me when I told her how we'd met, but it took her a minute."

Seth grimaced. "So we don't know if we can trust her."

She shrugged. "Do we know if we can trust anyone who isn't in this car? And it's not like you've got any better ideas. But I promise that if she tries to hurt either of you, I'll turn to stone and sit on her, okay?"

Tempest fought weakly against a smile while Seth shook his head. "I'm just glad I'm still armed."

An hour and a half later, they reached the meeting place, which turned out to be a closed down hunting lodge. Tempest's headache had gotten worse, and Seth had noticed something was wrong. The aspirin he'd given her hadn't helped, but she'd done her best to hide that fact. They needed to meet this woman, and it didn't matter if she was feeling ill. Ill was a lot better than dead.

"Well, this isn't ominous or anything," Seth muttered when Kara parked, checking his pistol before he got out of the car. "Stay behind me, Tempest."

She arched a brow, more for form than true offense. She was sure she looked almost as bad as she felt. "Just me?"

"Kara can turn into stone if she needs to. It takes a lot to harm stone."

Sick or not, Tempest just smiled and shook her head, but for now she remained behind him. He'd realize soon enough that she wasn't some vulnerable woman. She was Lemurian. And air was even harder to harm than stone.

Kara actually led the way to the door. "I don't see any other cars," she murmured as she checked the knob, finding it locked.

"Doesn't mean that we're the only ones here," Seth pointed out.

She gave him a bland look and said, "Duh," before she knocked.

They could hear movement on the other side of the door before a woman's soft voice asked, "Who is it?"

"It's Kara, and the two I mentioned before."

The locks were turned and the door opened. The woman standing on the other side surprised Seth. She wasn't at all what he had expected from Kara's description. To be fair, that description was basically 'weird historian', but Aelia didn't meet any of his expectations.

She was tiny, and he'd be shocked if she hit five feet. It wasn't to say she was childlike, because she wasn't, she was just dainty in every way. Her hair was a creamy sort of blonde color with darker gold highlights. Fair skin, almost as pale as her hair, wasn't flawless like he'd come to expect from most magical women, but had scars. Faint ones, but when he actually looked at her, he could see them. But it was hard to focus on those small, faded scars once he got a look at her eyes. They were violet. Not just an unusual shade of blue, they were actually purple. Very pretty, and something he hadn't seen before, on a magical person or not.

Seth started to speak, but he noticed that Aelia and Tempest were staring at each other, the former with surprise, the latter with something closer to shock. Tempest swayed and said something in her native tongue, but the only words he caught were 'how' and 'Lemurian'. Frowning, he looked back to Aelia as she responded in the same language. It wasn't as smooth as Tempest's had been, but halting, like she was rusty in the language or not quite as fluent.

Kara leaned closer to him and whispered, "What's going on? And what the hell language are they speaking?"

"Lemurian. And I'm not sure. I've only learned a few words," he murmured back.

"My apologies," Aelia said, taking a quick step back. "It's just been quite some time since I heard that language spoken. It caught me off guard."

"Apology accepted, but...what were the two of you saying?" Kara asked.

"Come inside, first. I don't imagine it's safe to talk about this out here," Aelia said, motioning for them to enter.

Once they were all inside, Kara put up a quick ward before they introduced themselves and sat down on the couch and chairs in the den. And Aelia and Tempest went back to staring rather than explaining.

"Do you two know each other?" Seth asked, studying Tempest with more than a little concern. He knew she was stressed, but he was starting to believe it was more than that. It could be a modern illness, as there was little chance her body had adapted to modern germs, but he doubted their luck was that good.

Aelia shook her head. "No, we've never met."

"But I have seen her before," Tempest corrected. "On Lemuria."

Seth took another look at Aelia, stunned by Tempest's words. "You're Lemurian?"

Aelia smiled faintly. "No, which is what she was asking me. I'm human, but I was on Lemuria, many, many years ago."

"What?" Kara asked, her voice rising an octave.

Tempest ignored Kara's shock and shook her head. "I don't understand. If you're human, and Lemuria's been gone so long that no one knows it existed, then how are you here? How were you there six thousand years ago when I was?"

Aelia drew in a slow breath. "I'm not going to answer all your questions, because the answers aren't relevant, and it's personal." They started to protest and she held a hand up. "Unless you all intend to tell me your deepest secrets, too?" she asked, brows raised in challenge. They all went quiet then and she nodded. "That's what I thought." She directed her focus to Tempest. "I'll admit, when I first got Kara's call, I thought it was a hoax or some sort of joke. No one's seen a Lemurian in thousands of years. I was prepared to give you the brush off and slip away."

"Then why did you agree to meet us?" Seth asked.

"On the off chance that it wasn't a joke," Aelia replied with a shrug. "There was no way I could just ignore you. I'd always wonder if I'd missed the opportunity to speak to a Lemurian again."

"So you'll help us? Since you know that Tempest is Lemurian?"

"I will. As much as I'm able, in any case."

"What happened to it?" Tempest asked quietly, clenching her hands together to hide the fact that they were starting to tremble. "What happened to my home? One night I went to sleep on Lemuria, and when I woke up, I was in another place, another time, and history had forgotten us. Or most of history. Except those who want me dead."

Aelia's face went grim. "I don't know everything, but I'll tell you what I can."

"Yes, please. Anything will help," Tempest said, desperate for answers.

"How much have you told them about Lemuria and its gods?"

Tempest shook her head. "Not much. Almost nothing, really," she admitted and gave Seth a guilty look.

Seth shook his head. "It's okay. There hasn't been a lot of time, and I know it's painful."

She gave him a grateful smile and nodded.

"Okay," Aelia said and drew in a slow breath. "The Lemurian gods were the first ones created or born, or so they said. They were also the most powerful. I don't know as much about them as I'd like, but I hadn't been on Lemuria long before..." She shook her head and went on. "Well, to put things simply, there was a war between the Lemurian gods."

"What?" Tempest asked, blindly reaching for Seth's hand. When he accepted the hold, she gripped it tightly.

Aelia slowly nodded. "I know, it sounds out of character, but it's true. They—the entire pantheon—were fighting in Lemuria. It was...devastating. All their powers were used on one another, but they struck the people, too, and the land. Tsunamis, earthquakes, volcanic eruptions..." She drew in a slow, unsteady breath. "They were killing their own people and destroying their own land. Some managed to escape Lemuria, those who could teleport or could swim such a long distance, but most..." She shook her head, her eyes haunted. "Most simply died as they tried to combat the magic killing them. In the end, it was the Lemurian gods themselves that caused Lemuria to sink beneath the waves. It was the most heart-wrenching thing I've ever seen," she whispered. "That beautiful, wonderful land being devoured by the sea. Its people terrified, confused, betrayed. I'll never get the sight out of my mind."

Tempest trembled beside Seth, silent tears streaming down her face. He carefully pulled his hand from hers and wrapped his arms around her.

"What happened to the gods?" Tempest whispered as she clung to Seth, but she didn't take her eyes off Aelia.

"I'm not sure. There were two theories back then. One was that they all killed each other. The other was that the other pantheons banded together to kill them. But I don't think either one's right," Aelia answered.

"Why not?" Kara asked. "What do you think happened? Because if they were fighting like that, and they're not around now..."

Aelia hesitated and Tempest said, in a whisper choked by grief, "Please." The pounding in her head had gotten worse, and was joined by an intense pressure centered behind her eyes. Knowing Lemuria had been forgotten was nothing compared to what Aelia was telling her now. The gods had loved their people and been loved in return. To hear that they'd *killed* their people sliced through her more painfully than anything she'd felt before.

"Like I said, they were the most powerful pantheon. It would have been extremely difficult to kill them, even if they were weakened by a civil war. Not only that, but to kill that many gods without destroying the world would have been...tricky. And if they were dead, then why hasn't the magic that stems from them died as well?" She shook her head. "No, I don't think they were killed at all. A few of them, maybe, but the whole pantheon? I believe they were put into some sort of prison or stasis."

"Like you were," Seth whispered to Tempest.

"But why would people want me dead because of a fight my gods had thousands of years ago?" Tempest asked, shaking her head. "It doesn't make sense."

"I don't know, unless they're worried that you being awake might wake your gods, too," Aelia said with a graceful shrug. "Because as far as I know, you truly are the last Lemuria who's alive and awake, including the gods."

Tempest closed her eyes and fought against tears. She didn't want to believe it, despite both Hecate and Aelia confirming it. She couldn't be the last one.

Seth rubbed a hand over her back, but it did little to comfort her. She wanted to go back a few days. Go back and wake up when Lemuria was still there, to when thousands of Lemurians roamed the Earth.

The pressure in her head intensified, blocking out her grief and causing her to cry out and double over. Her hands cradled her head and she heard a murmur of voices around her, but couldn't make out a single word. Her entire existence narrowed to the stabbing pain that began to radiate out and through her. Where it had just been a headache, it now spread down her limbs, until she hurt to the very tips of her fingers and toes. Her vision blurred, then went dark, though she thought her eyes were open. It felt like thumbs were digging into her eye sockets while a knife twisted in her head. Unbearable.

She didn't know what was wrong with her, couldn't think clearly enough to string a thought together, but she knew one thing with utter certainty.

She was dying.

CHAPTER II

When Tempest curled into a ball, Seth grabbed her before she could roll off the couch. That was bad enough, but then he saw blood and his heart stuttered with fear.

He'd heard of people bleeding from the eyes and ears, but he'd never seen it in person before. He hoped to never see it again, especially when he realized that blood was trickling out of her nose and mouth as well.

"What the hell?" Kara asked, lifting one of Tempest's hands and showing that her nail beds were also bloody. It seemed as though anywhere she could lose blood, she was.

"I don't know," Seth said as he tried to get Tempest's eyes to focus on him. "Tempest? Come on, darlin'. Don't do this. I'm not a healer." He knew the sudden desperation he felt made it into the words, but he didn't have the time to care.

She didn't seem to hear a word, just trembled in his arms until she let out a scream and the flow of blood rapidly increased.

"Did she get bit or stung by something in Peru?" Kara asked as she started searching for injuries.

"No," he said without hesitation. "And even if she had, Hecate healed us. I can't see her missing venom."

"Unless she didn't actually want to help you two," she said darkly.

"If she had wanted us dead, she could've killed us. We couldn't have stopped her." His eyes narrowed and shifted to Aelia, who was studying Tempest with sharp eyes.

Before he could say anything, Kara shook her head. "Couldn't be her. Tempest wasn't feeling good in the car, remember? Before we ever saw Aelia."

That was true, but it also meant he had absolutely nothing to go on. No reason for Tempest to be bleeding from every orifice, and no way to help her. Kara, despite being part witch, had no healing abilities. A fact they'd both regretted on several occasions.

Aelia moved closer, still looking intently at Tempest. "You said you were healed. Was she wounded then? Did she bleed?"

"What the fuck does that matter?" Kara asked with a frown, but Seth was willing to answer any questions if it would stop the bleeding. Tempest now looked like a victim in a horror movie, and all he could do was sit there. "Yes, she was. A couple of times. She was cut, on her face."

"Any chance someone could have gotten a hold of some of her blood? Even a few drops?" Aelia asked.

Seth thought back and wasn't sure how, but he wasn't going to rule anything out. Especially since it looked like Aelia had an idea. "And if they had?"

She blew out a breath, but didn't look happy. "Then it's a spell I recognize. A curse, actually."

Shit. Curses were never good, and while not all of them were lethal, many were. "Okay, great. So it's a curse. What is it doing to her, and how do we stop it?"

Aelia's expression didn't give him much hope, especially when Tempest let out another scream and bucked in his arms. He tightened his hold on her to keep her from hurting herself. "How do we stop it?" he snapped.

"I'm not sure we can, but I think I can...delay it."

He didn't know this woman. Had no idea if she could be trusted or how a human could possibly help with a curse. Yes, some humans learned magic—sorcery—and could do some types of magic, but was she really one of them? And could sorcery really counteract a curse?

A soft noise broke through the sounds of Tempest's suffering and the arguing that had begun between Kara and Aelia, and he glanced to the window. There, resting on the windowsill, was a crow. It did nothing but look at him, which made him wonder why it had caught his attention. Then he remembered Hecate's words.

He made a decision and hoped like hell it was the right one. "Do it," he said, voice cutting through the argument. After Tempest was safe he'd get more information.

Both women stopped and looked at him. Kara arched a brow but said nothing else. Aelia nodded and knelt on the floor beside him and Tempest. One hand came to rest on the side of Tempest's head, the other over her heart. She began to chant, which didn't surprise him, as sorcerers needed ritual of some sort to perform any kind of spell. It didn't sound like an actual language—or at least none he'd heard—but more like random syllables shoved together.

While she worked, Seth watched Tempest carefully. After a minute, the flow of blood seemed to slow. After two, it looked like it stopped entirely, but the exposed skin he could see still looked deathly pale. Nor had the trembling or soft sounds of pain ceased.

It wasn't until more than ten minutes had passed that Tempest's eyes cleared and met his. They were still a little glazed from pain and confusion, but she was coherent enough to frown at him. That quickly shifted to Aelia when she realized the woman was chanting. There was sweat beaded on Aelia's brow and her eyes were unfocused and unseeing. Clearly the spell was taking its toll on her.

"What's going on?" Tempest asked, her voice a hoarse croak.

"Shh." He shook his head, not wanting her to interrupt Aelia, not until he was sure that whatever the sorceress was doing was going to take. The last thing they needed was for a break in concentration to undo the progress Aelia had made.

By the time Aelia spoke her last word, there was a delicate tremor in her fingers as she drew her hands back. She looked at Tempest and gave her a feeble smile before her eyes rolled back in her head.

Kara cursed and dove for Aelia. While she couldn't prevent the woman's shoulder from smacking the floor, she did manage to prevent her head from receiving the same treatment. After a quick check of her pulse, she concluded the woman had simply passed out and relaxed a little.

Tempest made a noise and Seth reluctantly shifted her to sit beside him, though he kept an arm around her to keep her upright. "What's wrong with her? What happened? And why am I covered in blood?"

Kara and Seth exchanged a look, both equal parts baffled and relieved. Kara gently picked Aelia up and settled her in a chair before she answered. "You started bleeding and screaming. And I don't mean a little blood," she said, eyeing the clothes and skin that were now soaked in it.

Tempest followed Kara's gaze and swallowed hard. Blood by itself didn't truly bother her, but seeing herself covered in it, especially her own, was unsettling. "But I'm not bleeding now?"

"No, you're not," Seth confirmed. "Aelia said it was a curse. She wasn't sure how to reverse it, but she said she could delay it." His gaze flicked to the unconscious woman. "My guess is whatever spell she cast to do it, drained her."

"I had no idea she was a sorceress," Kara promised Seth.

He shook his head. "It's okay. If she wasn't..." He couldn't finish the thought, but found himself looking toward the window. The crow was gone, having done its job.

Tempest nodded slowly. "So I owe my life to her?"

"Seems like it," Kara agreed. "I don't think we can do anything until she wakes up, and depending on how strong she is—or how strong that spell was—she might not be up for a while. If, you know, you wanted to..." She waved a hand to indicate all of Tempest. "I'm sure she won't mind if you borrow her shower."

Tempest needed some help getting to her feet. She wasn't bleeding out anymore, but she was still weak from the blood loss and without Seth steadying her, she would have fallen. She wasn't sure how she was going to manage a shower, though she desperately wanted to be clean. If she had to sit on the floor of the shower, she'd do it, so long as she could get this blood off her.

"I'll go grab your clothes from the car," Kara offered. "And while you're showering, I'll strengthen the wards, to make sure we don't have any more surprises."

"If you want some help in the shower," Seth whispered against her ear, "I promise to be a complete gentleman."

She looked up at him and saw nothing but sincerity in his expression. Then again, only a vampire would be aroused by a woman coated in blood. And even that had never made sense to her. "Thank you. I don't know that I can stand up for that long," she admitted.

He nodded then bent enough to scoop her up into his arms. "Leave the clothes on the counter?" he said to Kara.

"I will. Just remember she's been—"

"I already promised to be a gentleman. What kind of guy do you think I am?" he grumbled as he went in search of a bathroom.

The third door he tried was a bathroom. He carried her inside, shut the door behind him, then set her on her feet where she could lean against the counter. "Give me just a minute to get the water going. Do you need help getting undressed?"

Tempest considered for a moment as he started the water. Her arms felt like they were weighed down. As much as she'd like to say she could handle it herself, she honestly wasn't sure she could. "I think I do," she told him on a sigh.

He nodded and stripped off his shirt, which drew her attention to the fact that his clothes were bloody as well. Considering she'd woken up in his lap, that wasn't surprising. What did surprise her was that he stopped undressing when he reached his boxers. To save her sensibilities, she supposed, though it wasn't necessary. He really was being a gentleman.

His hands were gentle as he pulled the wet fabric from her body, dropping each sodden piece in the sink until she was nude. There was only a brief hesitation as his gaze flicked over her, then he picked her up again and carried her to the shower. When he set her down under the hot water, she nearly moaned. Muscles she hadn't realized were tense began to ease under the heat, and she tilted her head back, letting the water rinse the blood from her hair.

He gave her a few minutes to bask in the soothing warmth before he turned her around. She wasn't sure whose bathing products were in here, but he picked up the shampoo and poured some into his hand before he started to work it into her hair. Her eyes closed as she savored the feel of his fingers massaging her scalp. She stopped thinking and just held onto his arms to steady herself as he methodically washed all the blood from her hair.

The sound of the door opening made his hands pause and his body go rigid.

"Clothes are on the counter. For both of you," Kara said before they heard the door close.

After finishing with her hair, he began to bathe the rest of her, and she had to give him credit for not taking advantage of the situation. He didn't linger like she knew some men would have, but simply ensured she was clean.

He shut the water off and stepped out, relieved to see Kara had found towels and set them beside the clothes. He hadn't thought that far ahead, but took one of the fluffy towels and began to dry Tempest just as thoroughly as he'd bathed her. In any other situation, he'd have lingered, but she was still weak. Yes, she'd indicated she wanted him, but now simply wasn't the time. Even if she had a body that—in normal circumstances—would have made him hard as stone.

"Are you feeling any better?" he asked when he'd finished drying her.

"A little, though I still feel shaky," she admitted.

"After we talk to Aelia, we'll grab some food. That should help." He hoped it would, in any case. Aelia had said she could only delay the curse. For all he knew, this was the best Tempest would feel until they broke it. But he seriously hoped not.

He helped her dress before pulling his own clothes on. "You need me to carry you again?"

She considered for a moment before she shook her head. "I might need some help, but I think I can manage."

"Okay, but if you do need more than just a little help, let me know?"

"I will." Holding his arm was enough, at least for the walk back to the den. The couch wasn't as bloody as she'd feared, but she still opted to sit in one of the other chairs. Kara was standing, but Aelia was awake and still in the chair Kara had moved her too.

"Are you okay?" Tempest asked Aelia.

"I'll be fine. I'm just a little tired. The spell wasn't a small one," Aelia admitted, and like Tempest, her voice was a little rough.

"If you'll point me toward the kitchen, I'll get you two some water," Kara offered. "Food, too."

"Thanks. I don't live here, but I do keep it stocked," Aelia said before directing Kara to the kitchen.

Seth perched on the arm of Tempest's chair, wanting to remain close in case something else happened. No one spoke as they waited for Kara, but he took the time to study both women.

They were impossibly old, though they both looked to be in their mid-twenties. And they both looked like they'd been through the wringer. Once again he wondered just what the fuck was going on. There were too many pieces, and none of them fit together. He knew there was more, a lot more, but he didn't know where to get the missing facts. If he was very, very lucky, Aelia had some. And he'd figured out where to get the rest.

Kara returned carrying a tray with four glasses of water and a plate piled high with sandwiches. She gave Aelia and Tempest each a glass and let them take a sandwich before she set the tray down where both she and Seth could reach it.

Both women devoured their sandwiches and drained their water, which relieved Seth. They needed it. He sipped at his water, but could only stomach a few bites of the sandwich, no matter how good it tasted.

"I'm sure you all want to know what's going on," Aelia said as she selected a second sandwich and took a bite.

"I'd like to know what happened to me, and how you fixed it," Tempest confirmed.

Aelia shook her head and gave Tempest an apologetic look. "I didn't. Fix it, I mean."

"I told her you said you had only delayed it," Seth added.

"I did, and I'm not sure for how long." She set the sandwich on her knee and sighed. "I've been alive for a long time, and I've seen a lot. I know I'm known as a historian," she said with a glance to Kara, "but my interest has always been in the Arcane. In magic. I've managed to befriend people from every part of the Arcane over the years, and I've seen all manner of magic. Including the curse that someone placed on you, Tempest. It's blood magic."

"Fuck," Seth muttered under his breath. Blood magic wasn't taboo. It was one of the few forms of magic anyone—including humans—could perform, but it could also be extremely nasty. Blood curses were different. They were also almost impossible to counter, and if caught, often punishable by death.

"How did you save me, then?" Tempest asked quietly.

"Like I said, I've seen all manner of magic. And while a lot of the Arcane looks down on sorcery, it can be powerful, too," Aelia said with a hint of a smile. "The spell I cast is only a temporary fix. It...for lack of a better way to say it, put the curse into stasis. It's still there, and it's unlikely you'll be able to use your magic at its usual potency, or have your normal stamina, unless it's removed altogether."

"And how do we remove it?" Seth asked. Aelia didn't answer immediately, which had dread curling in his belly. "There is a way to remove it...isn't there?"

"The one who cast it could remove it, though I don't imagine they'd be willing. I'm not even sure an extremely powerful witch could remove it. It's likely a god could, but there would be the issue of convincing one to help you." Her gaze slid to Seth. "You mentioned Hecate. Would she be willing to help?"

Seth shook his head without hesitation. "No."

"Why not?" Kara asked. "She helped you once. She healed you once. Why wouldn't she help with this?"

"Because if she would—or could—she already would have. She knows."

Tempest frowned up at him. "How do you know?"

"After Aelia offered to help you, when I was trying to decide to accept or not, I saw a crow in the window," he explained, inclining his head toward the window. "She told us to look out for crows, so it only stands to reason that she knows and was telling me to accept the help."

"Why wouldn't she help? Why help once, but not again?" Kara asked, throwing her hands up in disgust.

"I got the impression that she wasn't able to help as much as she'd like," Tempest murmured. "She couldn't even tell us much, though it sounded like she wanted to."

"It's gotta be politics," Kara muttered. "I hate politics."

"I actually thought it was more of a geas," Seth corrected with a shrug.

"Whatever. I still hate it," she said, folding her arms over her chest with a huff.

"There is one other potential option..." Aelia said hesitantly.

"What's that?" Tempest asked.

Aelia picked at the crust of her sandwich before she sighed and met Tempest's eyes.

"We could go to Lemuria."

CHAPTER 12

S ilence filled the room for a full minute, no one quite sure how to react to Aelia's suggestion. One made less than an hour after she'd told them Lemuria no longer existed.

"I'm sorry, I thought you just said go to Lemuria," Kara said, making a show of cleaning out her ear.

"Didn't you just say that Lemuria sank?" Seth added, looking to Tempest, who said nothing, just sat, staring at Aelia.

"I did," Aelia confirmed without breaking Tempest's gaze. "And it's a long shot, I won't deny that. It's also nothing I can confirm, but...I've heard that there's a small piece of Lemuria that still resides above the waves. However, it's also supposed to be shielded against everyone and everything but Lemurians, so I have no way of proving or disproving it."

Tempest went very, very still and was clearly fighting to keep her voice neutral. "How small?"

"I don't know. It could be as small as this room, or it could be miles across," Aelia answered. "I haven't heard anything about it in a few thousand years, and there's never been anything I've found written about it. It was just a rumor someone heard from someone else who heard it from a Lemurian."

"But it's possible that it's large enough to live on? I could go home?"

"It's possible, *if* it exists," Aelia stressed. "It might just be rumor or wishful thinking of some Lemurians who did escape that day. But, if it does exist, I think that you stepping foot on her soil could help you."

"Don't get me wrong," Kara began, "I'm all for Tempest being able to go home, but I don't see how that could help with a blood curse."

"We're stronger at home," Tempest whispered.

Aelia inclined her head. "Exactly. It was said that a strong Lemurian, when in Lemuria, could almost rival the gods. At least the gods from other pantheons. So my hope is that if we can find it, and we can get you there in time, that you might be able to fight it off."

"How likely is it that just being there would help her?" Seth asked, not wanting to think too much on the idea of finding Lemuria. He also didn't want to get Tempest's hopes up unnecessarily.

"I don't know," Aelia admitted, "but unless you have a god on speed dial, then this is the only option I know of."

Tempest looked up at Seth, hope shining in her eyes. "We have to find out. If it is shielded, then not only could it break the curse, but all these people who want to attack me won't be able to find me."

"But I might not be able to go," Seth pointed out. "I'm not Lemurian."

"I'm not sure that matters," Aelia interrupted. "I never heard that others couldn't step foot on it, just that no one but a Lemurian could find it. But again, it might all just be rumor," she reiterated.

"See? And maybe we can find something there to help us. Maybe we can find Vazi or one of the other gods," Tempest insisted, ignoring the warning.

Seth and Kara exchanged a look. It would give them a breather if it did exist like Aelia said, but that was a big if. And there was also no guarantee that they wouldn't find it only for Tempest to succumb to the curse. But how could he refuse Tempest a chance to return to her home, even if only for a little while?

"How big was Lemuria?" he said aloud.

"One moment," Aelia said, and she got to her feet and disappeared down the hallway, though she was still moving more slowly than before. When she returned, she held a messenger bag. "I brought along a few things on the off chance that Tempest was genuine," she explained as she sat down again. She pulled out a piece of paper, wrinkled and yellowed with age. She carefully unfolded it and set it on the coffee table next to the sandwiches.

It was a map. A very, very old map. The land masses didn't look quite right, and in the Pacific there was a new continent, long and thin, but it looked like it was only a little smaller than Australia.

Seth leaned forward, his attention grabbed. "How old is this?" he breathed, running his fingers just above the map, but was careful not to actually touch it.

"More than six thousand years old. It was made before Lemuria sank," Aelia answered.

"It's larger than I expected," he admitted. "I think I expected something more the size of England or Cuba or something."

"No, it was large. Which was good, because we had a lot of people. It meant we weren't crowded in." Tempest leaned forward and pointed to a spot on the northern half of the continent. "I lived here. It was mostly mountains and high hills, but I liked being up high. More wind," she said, a little smile curving her lips.

"Mountains," Seth murmured before he glanced at Kara. While she wasn't in the same business he was, she'd helped him with research on a number of occasions, was smart, and knew her geography and geology. "What do you think?"

Kara blew out a breath. "If we're going to look, the places that had higher elevation would be the most likely candidates to still be above water. Unless it was saved by magic, then it could be any damn where. But what the hell, I'm game. I haven't been on an adventure in...well, does pulling Seth out of a collapsed tomb count?"

"If you are going to do this, I'd like to go, too," Aelia said quietly. "Not only would I love to see Lemuria at least once more, but I may have to intervene again to make sure the curse doesn't take Tempest before we reach Lemuria."

Tempest stared at her for a long moment. "I'd like her to come, too. After me, she probably knows more about Lemuria than anyone else, and I'd like to stay alive long enough to see it."

"I'm down, but only if you two teach me how to insult people in Lemurian. Or curse," Kara said with a grin. "It'll drive some of the assholes I know crazy."

All three women looked at Seth and he shrugged. "Hell, I know when I'm outnumbered. Don't suppose you packed a bag, Kara?"

"Duh. Like I was going to let you fight off assassins by yourself?"

"Then give me a few and I'll arrange for a plane to...hell, Hawaii, probably. I can figure out a boat after that. You three just rest until I can make sure we've got a way off the ground. I don't want to leave the ward until we have to."

He stepped into the other room and made his calls. To his relief, it didn't take long, and he soon rejoined the others. "Good news. The plane's still at the airport and will be refueled when we get there. It'll take us to Hawaii, and I can arrange for the boat and equipment while we're in the air."

"Never thought I'd be happy for all your treasure hunting contacts," Kara said as she started up the SUV and put it in gear.

"Are you sure that a boat is the best idea?" Aelia asked. She was still pale and sounded tired, but still looked infinitely better than she had.

"Sure? No," Seth admitted. "It's a hell of a lot of area to cover. We'd see more from the air, but we can't just fly around aimlessly, and even if we did find it, there's no guarantee there'd be someplace to land. But if we get a big enough boat, we'd be able to stay out there for weeks, if not months, while we search." He twisted around so he could see Aelia and Tempest. "I'm not sure the hardest part is going to be finding Lemuria, though."

"What do you mean?" Tempest asked.

"I can handle a boat, sure, but I've only piloted smaller boats, and those in good weather. And sure, I can navigate fine on land, and can go to specific coordinates on the sea, but I'm not the best to handle searching thousands of miles of open ocean. We can find someone who can do all those things, yes, but finding someone we trust who can also handle the supernatural? More difficult."

"Oh. Yes, I see your point," Tempest said, biting her lower lip as she considered the problem. "The only people who know about Lemuria are us, right? None of your other friends know?"

"I've only told..." Seth paused as he recalled a few other calls he'd made. "I told two others," he admitted. "One is a bounty hunter—"

"Wade?" Kara asked.

He nodded. "Yeah. So he's good at tracking people, but not so much searching for a needle in a haystack the size of the Pacific. The other..." He had to tread carefully here. He trusted Kara implicitly, and somehow found himself trusting Tempest, but he didn't know enough about Aelia to give her the same trust. No matter what happened, the Athenaeum needed to be protected. "He's a scholar. I would feel comfortable saying he knows more about magic and the Arcane than anyone, except maybe the gods."

Aelia gave him a curious look and he had to wonder if she already knew about the Athenaeum. Its existence wasn't *that* much of a secret, but the location of it and people associated with it were.

"I'll call him when we're in the air," he continued, "and see if he's learned anything since I last talked to him. It's going to be a six-hour flight, so we've got time to make these calls."

"If someone else can drive, I can try to ward the car," Kara offered. "Warding something that's moving is harder than a stationary location, but since you said they kept popping up, I'm willing to try anything. Especially since you two are still recovering from that curse."

"It's a smart idea," Aelia said as she carefully folded the map and placed it in her messenger bag. "Let me grab a few things, then I'll be ready to go." She started to leave the room, then paused. "It sounds like you three were intending to go back to Kara's house when you left here. Is there anything you need?"

"Nope," Kara answered with a grin. "I got spare clothes for them, and toothbrushes and stuff, so we should be good. Unless they're picky," she added, giving a mock glare to both Seth and Tempest.

"You know I'm not," Seth said, though he appreciated her attempt to lighten the mood. It didn't really work, but he appreciated it.

Aelia's faint smile said she did, too. "Then I'll be quick."

She was true to her word, returning in under ten minutes with a duffel bag. He knew she was feeling better when she didn't look winded after packing it, though she was still pale.

They loaded up in the car, with Seth driving, Kara in the passenger seat, and their two ancients in the back seat. Before they went anywhere, Kara took a few minutes, getting the ward up around the vehicle.

"I'm not going to be all that chatty," she warned them. "So don't expect an answer from me unless it's an emergency."

"I honestly think I just want to nap until we get to the plane, so that's fine by me," Aelia said, and Tempest nodded her agreement.

When he was sure they were as safe as they were going to get, Seth put the car into gear and started the drive back to the plane they'd left only the day before.

The women in the back did pass out fairly quickly, and Kara was as quiet as she'd predicted, which left him alone with his thoughts. Not his favorite place to be at the moment.

He was absolutely out of his depth. No, puzzles weren't uncommon in his line of work. While not all traps in movies were truly feasible, people of the past—especially the Arcane—did love making it difficult to get to their hidden treasures. And then there was simply finding some of the locations. But none of that had prepared him for trying to figure out how to undo a blood curse, much less how to keep the last member of an ancient race alive when even the gods couldn't—or wouldn't—help her survive.

Finding Lemuria was a start, sure. It would give them breathing room, assuming they couldn't be tracked there. Oddly, he was okay with that assumption. If they could be tracked to the ancient land, then he had a feeling Lemuria would have been discovered sometime in the last six millennia.

Then again, he wasn't without contacts, and he was sure Aelia had plenty as well, given her longevity—and that was another puzzle he wanted to solve. Between them, they might know enough people to track down the source of these attacks. If they found the person responsible, then they could figure out how to eliminate that threat.

If they lasted long enough to start making those calls.

He glanced in the rearview mirror at Tempest and sighed silently. He'd known her less than a week, but he knew he was prepared to do anything to make sure she made it to Lemuria alive.

CHAPTER 13

When they parked at the airport, Seth nudged Kara out of her trance-like state before he woke the other women.

"We're here. Let's get on the plane and in the air. I want to keep moving."

Though sluggish, all three climbed out of the car and stretched out the kinks that sleeping in the car for an hour caused.

"Mr. Montgomery?"

He turned to see a stocky man wearing the uniform of the airport. "Yes?"

"Your plane's fueled and ready. You can leave as soon as you're all on board." The man glanced at the weariness on their faces and frowned. "You guys need anything before you board?"

Seth shook his head. "Just discretion, but thanks."

The man nodded. "Sure thing." He looked like he wanted to say something else, but just turned away to go back to work.

"Come on. That's our plane over there," Seth told them, pointing to the private jet. They grabbed the bags from the back of the car, then crossed the tarmac toward the plane.

Tempest quickened her steps until she walked beside him. He gave her a small smile. "You okay?" he murmured.

"I'm getting there. So much is happening so quickly. I just don't know how to handle everything," she answered.

"We'll get through this. Just try to focus on one thing at a time," he suggested.

She nodded, then brushed his hand with hers. When he didn't pull away, she smiled faintly and laced her fingers through his. "Thanks."

He said nothing, just gave her hand a squeeze.

Once they were on the plane and in the air, Seth ensured that the door to the cockpit was closed before they started got settled. He trusted the pilot...to a point. But he didn't know him well enough to fully trust him with their current situation.

"Since I'm now caught up in all this, I think I'd like to know the whole story," Aelia began as she tried to get comfortable in her seat. "Especially since you're worried about being tracked by somebody."

"Unfortunately, there's not really much more to the whole story," Seth said on a sigh as he dropped down onto the small sofa. It was next to Tempest, and sure, there were other chairs, but he wanted to be close to her. Especially if random bleeding was likely to occur again.

"He's not wrong," Tempest agreed. "Seth found me in a temple a few days ago. Almost immediately, we were attacked by two people. The next day, we were attacked by three more, then there was a van following us right to the plane out of Peru. And no, I don't know who. All I know is that people apparently want Lemuria to remain buried."

Aelia nodded as she processed that. "And where does Hecate come in?"

Now Seth smiled. "Right where you're sitting, actually."

She leapt to her feet and looked down at the chair as though expecting the goddess to be there. When Seth chuckled, she glared at him and sank back into her seat. "Explain?"

"She showed up on the plane right after we left Peru," Tempest answered before Seth could mess with Aelia again. "She healed us both and taught me English. She's the one who said that people don't want Lemuria resurfacing, but she couldn't tell us why."

"It sounds like a lot of bullshit to me," Kara muttered as she rose and poked around until she found the small galley. She grabbed some bottles of water, as well as a beer, and returned to the others. Seth was offered the beer, while she gave the waters to Aelia and Tempest, keeping one for herself. "You can have beer when you're not pale anymore," she told them before picking up her previous train of thought. "Not just why people would want all Lemurians dead, but the whole not telling us why crap. Okay, maybe there are gods who don't want it getting out that there was another pantheon stronger than them, but so what? Having one Lemurian alive isn't going to suddenly topple them off their thrones or anything."

Seth and Aelia both gave her incredulous looks, and the former said, "We're talking about the same gods, right? The ones who banned certain relics from existing and wiped out a whole group of people to ensure it? All because they wanted to make sure they were the most powerful things out there? And that's just one example I could give you."

Kara almost protested, then huffed out a breath and slumped in her chair. "Yeah, that's fair."

"Speaking of relics..."

Three sets of eyes fixed on Aelia with varying degrees of curiosity. "We weren't really," Seth said, "but what is it? Do you have one that can help us?"

"Possibly?" She drew her messenger bag into her lap and drew out something long and wrapped in cloth. The bag was set aside and she carefully unwound the wrapping, revealing a dagger.

It was beautiful. The hilt was some white metal. It reminded Seth of polished silver, but he doubted something that soft would have been used for a weapon unless it was symbolic. The pommel had an image of some four-legged creature, but not one he recognized. The guard was curved toward the blade with a design that looked vaguely Celtic, but was just a little off. The blade itself was what caught his eye. It had a double edge, but the metal wasn't like anything he'd seen before. He'd remember seeing metal that had a reddish hue like that.

"A knife?" Kara asked, her curiosity mild, but she wasn't immediately dismissing it.

"A dagger," Aelia corrected. "More specifically..." Her attention fixed on Tempest. "It's a Lemurian relic."

Tempest's eyes darkened even as her skin paled. Her attention shot down to the dagger as her voice dropped to a whisper. "That's from Lemuria?"

"It is," Aelia confirmed with a nod. "That's why I brought it. Though I had doubts about you being Lemurian, I'd decided that if you were legit and were a good person, I was going to give it to you. It belongs to a Lemurian, not a human. Not even me." She emphasized her words by lifting it slightly and offering it to Tempest.

Tempest reached across Seth, her fingers trembling lightly as she picked up the dagger and held it reverently. "This is from Lemuria."

She carefully cradled the blade against her chest and looked to Aelia. "Thank you. It's not the same as being able to see my homeland, but it helps."

But Aelia wasn't focusing on Tempest's words, she was looking at the bracelet on Tempest's wrist. It took Kara clearing her throat before Aelia snapped out of it. "Hmm? Oh, you're very welcome. Though it's yours by right, Tempest. You're the last Lemurian. All of Lemuria is yours."

"Pretty to think so, but there are plenty who would argue that," Tempest said with a wry twist of her lips.

Seth shook his head. "No, Aelia's right. And hopefully we'll find that part of Lemuria that she thinks still exists. Hell, if she doesn't, we'll figure out a way to go down and see if any of Lemuria still exists on the ocean floor. People pull stuff from ruins all the time. And most of them do it without magic."

"He's right," Kara agreed. "But since we're on the subject...how are we going to do this? Hire a human captain? Fuddle through the search ourselves? I don't really see a good idea here. No matter what we do there's the possibility of us getting lost or revealing Lemuria to someone we don't want to know."

They all went silent for a minute, processing the truth of Kara's words.

Tempest frowned as she lightly stroked her fingers over the cool metal of the dagger. She was so far out of her depth it wasn't even funny. Part of her wanted to stand on Lemuria so badly that she would ask anyone qualified to help, but she knew that would just put them in more danger. Although... "Once we're at sea, I can always fly up and get a view from above every so often. When I'm in air form, I can go extremely high," she offered.

"That's actually a really good idea," Seth said, slowly nodding. His concern was the curse. Would it prevent her from being able to do that? Aelia did say it sapped magic. He decided to save that for later. No reason to depress everyone. "Much better than flying over in a plane or helicopter. How often can you take that form?"

Tempest shrugged. "There's nothing that really prevents me from staying in that form constantly other than I like having a body." In fact, sometimes she'd felt like she never wanted to go corporeal ever again.

Kara's brows lifted. "Really? No elemental I know can hold their elemental form for longer than a few minutes, half an hour at the most."

"Lemurians are more potent than their non-Lemurian decedents," Aelia explained. "More powerful and longer lived."

"Oh. That's pretty damn cool. I'm a little jealous," Kara said, but she grinned to take any hard feelings out of her words.

Seth's phone rang and he frowned when he pulled it out. "It's a blocked number. Hopefully it's just Aaron again." If it wasn't, they'd deal with it. Though he wished Aaron had followed through and sent his number so he could know for sure.

"Who's Aaron?" Aelia asked, and Kara explained their history in a quiet voice as Seth answered the call.

"Hello?"

"You seem to be a very interesting person lately, Seth," Aaron drawled.

"What makes you say that?" Seth asked, leaning back in his seat and looking to Tempest.

"I keep having interesting conversations lately, and they're all about you and this mystery woman you're with."

"Oh?"

"Mmhmm. Got offered double to kill you and your woman, which I'll admit was tempting for half a second. It's an obscene amount of money. They were pretty pissed when I told them I wasn't an assassin."

Seth arched a brow. "You're calling me to tell me you turned down the job?"

"Nope. I did say conversations, and that was just one."

"You going to get to the point, then?"

Aaron chuckled. "So very impatient. This is why I'm the better archaeologist."

"Aaron," Seth said in a warning tone.

"Fine. The other was the more interesting conversation, anyway." He paused, then asked, tone amused, "Seen any crows lately?"

Seth went very still. "Crows?"

Tempest frowned and lowered the dagger to her lap. Even Aelia and Kara went quiet, sensing the tension the word had caused.

After putting the phone on speaker, Seth said, "What do you know about crows?"

"I was told that would get your attention," Aaron said smugly. "Had a nice chat with the crow lady. She said you'd understand if I refused to use her name."

"Yeah, I understand. What'd she tell you?" The fact that Hecate had apparently spoken to Aaron about him and Tempest was concerning, but she'd seemed genuine in her desire to help them. For that matter, he'd be happy if she were here now. Tempest looked like she wasn't quite back at a hundred percent, and he wasn't at his best either. And as soon as he got off the phone he'd have to remember to take something for the headache that had formed in the last hour.

"I'm on my way to Hawaii. Did you know that tigers love water?"

Seth cursed under his breath. "No, can't say I did. Do I want to know why you're telling me that?"

"I've got a boat waiting for me when I land. It's big enough for, oh, say, five people. More specifically, it's big enough for five people to stay out for a few months. And I'm well versed in navigating on the water."

"One second." Seth hit the mute button and ran his other hand through his hair. "What do you guys think? It solves the problem, but..."

"You don't know if you can trust Aaron," Kara finished.

"Who's the crow lady?" Aelia asked.

"Hecate," Seth answered.

"Well, it sounds like she trusts Aaron. If he can really help us find Lemuria, shouldn't we accept his help? I know Kara said you've had some problems with him, but if he already knows about Lemuria, wouldn't it be better to keep him close so you can keep an eye on him?"

"That's a fair point," Tempest agreed. "See if he knows what we're looking for. If he does, then trust Hecate. I can't believe she'd betray us at this point."

Kara nodded. "I agree with Tempest."

"So do I," Aelia added.

Seth nodded and took Aaron off mute. "Do you know why we need the boat?"

"You're really paranoid about this, aren't you?" Aaron asked, and he actually sounded serious rather than mocking. "Just how much trouble have you had so far?"

"We've been attacked three times in as many days." Four, actually, if he counted the curse.

"Damn. You've got good reason to be paranoid then. Okay, I probably don't know the whole deal, but I know it's about Lemuria."

Seth looked at all three of his companions and they all nodded. "Okay, Aaron. Where's the boat docked? We should land in about six hours."

"I'll text you the address. It's not too far from the airport if you're using the private one. I'll be landing in four hours myself."

"We are. Can you be ready to go the moment we all get on board?"

"Easily. Just text me anything special I need to get other than the typical supplies."

"I will." It rankled, but Seth added, "Thanks, Aaron."

"I'd say no problem, but it sounds like it's going to be a major problem. Just don't get me killed, Seth."

Aaron disconnected and Seth rubbed a hand over his face. "This has the potential to go very, very wrong."

"I don't think so," Tempest disagreed, "but we can only wait and see. Right now, we should all rest up. And didn't you say you wanted to call that scholar?"

"Yeah. Any information is welcome at this point."

"Well, I'm definitely going to sleep," Kara said as she stood. "I'm claiming the bed. If any of you want to join me, just be warned you might wake up being spooned. I probably won't grope you in your sleep, though."

"Spooning doesn't scare me and I'd love some sleep," Aelia said with a shrug as she followed Kara into the back.

Seth shook his head and smiled faintly as he dug out an aspirin and washed it down with his beer. His phone chimed, but when he looked up, Tempest caught his gaze before the phone did. More specifically, the way she was looking at him. She should be exhausted, but there was heat in her eyes that was difficult for him to ignore.

"You really shouldn't look at me like that right now," he murmured. "Not only are you still dealing with the aftereffects of the curse, there is now literally no privacy for us." Technically there was the bathroom, but he had no interest in their first time being rushed and in a cramped space. No, he wanted plenty of time to thoroughly get to know those curves.

"And that is the only reason I'm not kicking Kara and Aelia out of the bedroom," Tempest told him with a smile as she ran her hand down his arm. "But I am feeling better. So you should be warned...once we're on the boat and do have privacy..."

His lips curved into a smile that made her breath catch and warmth settle between her thighs. "I'm holding you to that, darlin'."

"Good." She leaned over and gave him a light, chaste kiss. "Make your calls. I'm going to get some rest, too."

"Stretch out on the couch," he suggested as he rose. She did, and he found her a pillow and blanket, making sure she was as comfortable as possible.

It was proof of how tired she was that she was out cold before he'd settled in another chair and grabbed his phone.

Aaron had texted the address as promised, along with his number. Seth sent back a reply and asked that Aaron grab some clothes for the women. That done, he took a sip of his beer and called Erasmus.

"Seth?"

"Yeah, it's me."

"I'm glad to hear you're alive and safe."

Seth gave a short laugh. "That is, once again, a matter of opinion."

"Tell me."

Like before, he gave Erasmus the full rundown, though he left out Aelia's name. He wasn't sure why, but he was sure that a human who had survived longer than most of the Arcane probably didn't want her name getting spread around.

"A blood curse? And this historian knew a spell to halt it? Extraordinary," Erasmus murmured. "I'd love to know that spell."

Seth almost smiled but kept them on topic. "Yeah. So...we're hoping to find Lemuria and break the curse. And if it is shielded or warded or whatever, it'll give us some time to figure things out."

"That isn't going to be easy. I've been searching, and the most I've found are vague references to its location and destruction."

"We've got a map and know where it was, but there's still one big problem. Lemuria was huge and there's no telling which part is still above water, and that's if any of it really is."

"Any chance of you sending a copy of that map this way?" Erasmus asked, trying to hide his excitement, but Seth knew him too well.

"It's not up to me. It's not my map, and Tempest may not want the maps getting out." He could sense Erasmus was about to argue, so quickly added, "However, I will let her know that I trust you and that it'll be safe. I just can't make any promises."

"That's absolutely fair. Now, other than trying to find anything on Lemuria, is there anything I can do to help?"

"If you can see if you can figure out who might want to keep all Lemurians dead and at the bottom of the ocean, that would be fantastic. Or a way to break blood curses."

"I'll do my best. Stay safe, boy. You may not want to join us, but I still consider you one of us."

That was high praise, he knew. Members were vetted thoroughly before they ever learned the location of the Athenaeum. Seth was actually one of the rare individuals who didn't work for the Athenaeum who knew the location.

"Thanks, Erasmus. Be careful, too. Don't go biting off more than you can chew."

The old man only chuckled and hung up.

Setting his phone aside, Seth reclined his chair and watched Tempest sleep. When he drifted off, his dreams were full of all that could go wrong.

The two men sat in the office. The one who sat behind the desk held a glass, empty but for a few drops of amber liquid. It was far from his first drink, and when he spoke, his words slurred.

The other sat opposite him, and though he too held a glass, it was untouched. He stared absently at the wall as he considered their problem. "Three teams have failed now."

"What about Marie?"

"No confirmation yet, though she said the curse was cast success-fully. But we have to kill this woman. Now."

"I know. All of the specialists I've called have either failed or refused the job."

"And that's a problem," came a third voice, deeper than the others and gravely.

"Shit," the man behind the desk exclaimed, dropping his empty glass.

The sober man looked more resigned and turned to face the stocky man.

The newcomer was dark in complexion, with hair even darker. It was windblown and deep brown, but not as dark as his eyes, which looked black in the shadows where he stood at the moment.

"We're going to send more teams," the sober man assured the newcomer. "I promise, we'll kill her, sir."

"You've had four days, Joseph," the newcomer said. "I had hope for you when you remembered my orders and acted so quickly, but you can't kill a single woman. Tell me why I should give you another chance when I'd prefer to gut you both and find more competent help."

"'Cause no one has connections like we do," the drunk man slurred. "We'll get her," he assured as he tried to sit up straight in his chair.

"Your connections haven't served either of us well so far, now have they?" came the cold reply.

"Every time she stops, we're able to zero in on her and send a team. It's only a matter of time before one of them succeeds," Joseph said. "It only takes one attack, done correctly, to end a person."

The newcomer strode across the office and around the desk, staring down at the man who was too drunk to realize the danger he was in. "So it does." His fist darted out and hit the man in the chest, breaking through the ribs until his fingers could close around the still-beating heart. He turned his head so he could look at Joseph. "Don't fail me." He yanked his hand free, pulling the heart with it, and tightened his fist, crushing the organ. "Or you'll end up like your friend," he promised darkly before he dropped the heart on the desk and disappeared.

Hand trembling, Joseph looked at his dead partner as he lifted the glass to his lips and drank deeply.

CHAPTER 14

Despite their exhaustion, none of them were able to sleep the entire flight. Seth was awake first, then Kara, Tempest, and finally Aelia. To Seth's amusement and chagrin, Kara pulled out a jigsaw puzzle. She really was shoving the things at him every time he turned around.

At her insistence, all four of them ended up huddled around the table, assembling the picture of the pyramids. Rather than relaxing Seth, his proximity to Tempest kept him on edge the entire flight. But to Kara's delight, they finished the puzzle only minutes before the plane landed in Hawaii.

The pain in Seth's head had died down to a dull throb, and he no longer felt quite so pessimistic about Aaron being involved, but his mind still wasn't calm. Tempest was the biggest cause of his turmoil now, a mixture of lust and fear for her safety. But then, he was worried for all of them.

Part of him was amused, though. Here he was, a man in his thirties, traveling with three beautiful women. True, he thought of one like a sister, and another was still mostly a stranger, but it remained a vaguely amusing situation.

The airport was similar to the one they'd left in Colorado, though this one was run by a mix of supernaturals. Since it was small, they went straight from the plane to the tarmac. Seth went first and frowned when he saw a black SUV sitting nearby, a uniformed man leaning against it.

The man straightened and approached Seth, which had Seth's hand moving to the butt of his gun. "Seth Montgomery?"

Suspicious, Seth nodded. "Yes?"

"I've been sent by my employer, Aaron Fischer, to drive you and your companions to the dock."

Seth relaxed a touch. Aaron did have money, a lot of it, and loved throwing it around. Still, it couldn't hurt to verify. "Okay. Give me a few." He stepped back on the plane to curious looks from the women.

"What's wrong?" Kara asked.

"There's a car and driver out there," he said as he pulled his phone out. "Says he's from Aaron. I just want to confirm that before we get in the car."

Tempest peered out the window and nodded. "Smart."

"Are you on the ground?" Aaron asked without a preamble.

"Yeah. Did you send a car? Black SUV, tinted windows, driven by a blond guy in a suit?" Seth asked.

"I did. He's been with me for decades, so you can trust him," Aaron answered. "At least enough to get from there to here. So just get in the car, okay?"

"Fair enough." Seth hung up and nodded. "He's legit. Let's go."

Twenty minutes later, they pulled up to the docks and Tempest was the first one out of the car.

They were so close to finding Lemuria, or what remained of it. She knew it could take months to find it, if it actually existed, but a few days ago she didn't believe she'd ever see it again, except in her dreams. Dreams that would be, she was sure, tainted with visions of Aelia's description of the events that had sunk the beautiful land. Instead of the largely idyllic setting she remembered, she expected to suffer through volcanic eruptions and earthquakes. So if they had to work with a man Seth didn't really trust, she'd do it. She'd do most anything to get back there, even if it wasn't a livable stretch of land.

And if Aelia was right, she didn't have any other choice. It was find her home or die.

"Is that the boat?" she asked when the others climbed out of the car to stand beside her.

"That's Aaron on the deck, so looks like it," Seth confirmed before he opened the back of the SUV to grab the bags.

"How can you even tell?" Aelia asked as she squinted at the boat. "It's at the far end of the dock."

"Though my mom was human, my dad's a falcon."

Kara leaned in close to Aelia and murmured, "He didn't get much in the way of powers, but he's got the eagle eye, so to speak."

Tempest heard the quiet words, but was focused on the boat. She hoped they weren't screwing up by putting their faith in Hecate. Still, when Seth rejoined her, she gave him a faint smile.

"You ready?" he asked.

"More than," she agreed with a nod. She glanced at Aelia and Kara, then started down the dock, Seth at her side. When he took her hand, she was surprised, but appreciated the support. She knew he was going against his instincts, so the fact that he was standing by her instead of abandoning her for safety meant everything. Even Vazi had never supported her like this, and he was a god who feared little.

"I guess he's not actually as bad as I made him out to be," Seth said quietly to her. "He and I just don't have the best relationship or track record."

Tempest laughed softly. "That's good, because you made him out to be pretty bad." She gave his hand a squeeze. "We'll get through this. And hopefully you'll make the biggest discovery of your career. The first archaeologist to see Lemuria."

"Assuming I see it before that jackass does," he muttered. "But yeah, that's a good point."

"Will you guys hurry up already? I thought time was of the essence?" Aaron called from where he stood on the deck, hands on his hips. He was a tall man, though he stood a few inches shorter than Seth, but his build was a touch more muscular. Attractive, too, Tempest mused, though she found Seth the more appealing of the two, despite the fact that their appearances were so similar. His black hair was a little longer than Seth's, and they both had tanned skin and weathered faces, but where Seth had golden eyes, Aaron's were the ice blue more commonly seen in tigers than people.

"Give me a break. I've been going pretty much for half a week straight," Seth yelled back, but he quickened his pace.

As the four tromped up the gangplank, Aaron looked appreciatively at Tempest, then Kara, before his head tilted and he frowned. "Aelia? What are you doing with this group?"

All progress stopped as three more sets of eyes fixed on Aelia.

"What? I'm a historian, he's an archaeologist. He's come to me for help before," Aelia said with a shrug. "Now, can we get on the boat, please? Before more assassins show up or I have to redo the spell?"

"Sure, but you could've mentioned this before," Seth said dryly as he continued onward.

Aaron surprised him by taking Aelia's hand and helping her on board, but the moment they were all on the boat he let go. He cast off, then nodded to the interior of the boat. "Let me get us out to sea, then I'll show you all to your cabins. If you want to talk, you're welcome to follow me," he told them as he led the way to the helm. Predictably, they all followed.

The engine was already running when they got there and Aaron expertly steered them away from the dock and out of the harbor, getting them into open water. He increased their speed so that the land behind them began shrinking into nothingness.

"So, from what I understand, you've been attacked three times, by a mix of supernaturals. You don't know who's sending them, but you do know it has something to do with Lemuria?" Aaron glanced at Tempest. "Possibly also you, because I've seen her before," he said with a nod to Kara.

"Yes. I'm Tempest. That's Kara." She glanced at Seth and he nodded, so Tempest told him about how she'd woken in Peru and everything they'd dealt with since then, leaving out little. If he was to help them, he needed to know what he was going up against.

"You really don't do anything half-assed, do you, Seth?" Aaron asked dryly.

Seth shrugged. "What would be the point of half-assing it? And it's kept us alive so far, so why change now?"

"Point. Okay, so do we have a starting point?" Aaron asked as he input coordinates to take them further out to sea while they spoke. "Or anything specific we're looking for?"

"We're looking for the piece of Lemuria that didn't sink," Tempest said quietly. When Seth stepped closer and slid an arm around her shoulders, she leaned into him gratefully. "According to Aelia, part of it is still above water—we hope—but warded against all but Lemurians."

Aaron arched a brow. "So how do you expect us to find it, then?" His eyes narrowed. "Unless you're Lemurian," he murmured as he studied Tempest more intently.

It wasn't something they could hide, not if they wanted him to actually help, but Seth didn't like it. "Don't think of trying to take advantage of that fact, Aaron," he warned, fingers itching to grab his gun.

"Wouldn't dream of it," Aaron purred. "I'd never put such a lovely lady at risk. But that means that you, my dear, are literally the only person on the planet who can find it?"

"If it truly exists?" Tempest nodded. "Yes."

Aaron sighed and walked over to a table and hit a button. A slit appeared in the middle of the table, then the two halves withdrew, exposing a map of the world. "Okay, so where are we looking?"

"That's where things get difficult," Aelia said as she stepped up beside Aaron. "It wasn't a small continent. It was somewhere around the size of the United States, but it was located here," she said, trailing her finger in an oval in the middle of the Pacific.

"Maps are different than they were back then, but that looks about right," Tempest verified.

Bridge of his nose pinched between two fingers, Aaron said in a pained voice, "No wonder it was suggested that I outfit the boat for several months." His hand dropped. "Lucky for you lot, I can handle setting up a search grid." He glanced between Kara and Tempest. "Do either of you have any powers that will help with searching?"

"Sorry. While I'm part witch, I'm not great at scrying or anything like that," Kara said, shaking her head.

"I'm an air elemental. I can search from the air whenever it will do the most good. I can go high and see far," Tempest answered.

"Good. That'll help. I'll set up regular intervals for you to go up and look. In between your trips, we should have someone on deck, keeping a look out. I'd be pissed if we missed it just because we didn't have someone on watch," Aaron said.

"We should do it in pairs," Seth added. "If we get attacked, I don't want anyone alone. These people aren't trying to capture anyone, they're shooting to kill."

Aaron gave a toothy grin. "I'd love to see the assassins try to attack me. I haven't had a good fight in ages."

"The last attack was a blood curse without a single person in sight," Seth cautioned.

"Was it really that bad?"

"Yes."

Aaron cursed under his breath and nodded. "Okay. We group up. Aelia, can you take the helm? Just make sure we don't crash into any boats while I show them to their cabins? The boat's been magically enhanced, but this close to shore I don't want to take chances."

"Of course," Aelia agreed, moving to the controls.

"I'll stay with her," Kara offered. "Just point out which cabin's mine and Seth can show me later," she said as she walked to stand by Aelia. "Can you show me how to drive this thing? No way we should let the boys have most of the control over where we're going. They never stop to ask for directions."

Seth's lips twitched and he shook his head as he fell into step behind Aaron. They went below deck, and he was unsurprised to see that the boat was very nice and very expensive. "How did you happen to get your hands on a boat like this so quickly?"

"Money talks, you know that," Aaron answered with a shrug. "But as it happens, this is actually my boat. I normally keep it in the Caribbean or on the East Coast, since there tends to be more to find there, but..." He paused and frowned. "I'm not exactly sure why I moved it here, to be honest." He glanced back at Seth and Tempest. "I had it moved a month ago, and you weren't awake then."

"Did anyone suggest you move it? Or make any hints?" Tempest asked curiously.

Aaron thought about it for a moment before he slowly shook his head. "My first reaction is to say no, but I had some dreams about hunting in the Pacific. It's possible someone planted those dreams in my head."

"It honestly wouldn't surprise me," Seth said. "A lot of weird things have been happening lately. I only found Tempest because I was told there was an undiscovered temple in Peru. Which is odd, because it wasn't a temple, and the tips I get are usually less vague than that." Though, saying it out loud, he had to wonder if wires had just gotten crossed somewhere. Tempest was awfully close to temple when said aloud. Ultimately, he didn't matter and shook it off. "But it came from a source I use a lot, so I didn't question it too much."

"What do you mean, about the tips?" Tempest asked.

"Usually when I go out, it's because someone came across a passage in a book or on a tablet or something, and it has a reference to some temple or whatever. So it's never really something undiscovered, just forgotten, hidden, or both," Seth explained.

Aaron nodded agreement. "That's how it is for me, too. Or I get tipped off that someone," he gave a pointed look to Seth, "is really interested in an area that supposedly has nothing in it. But you were literally just told undiscovered temple in Peru?"

"Well, it was a little more specific than just Peru, but yeah, basically," Seth confirmed.

"Who'd this tip come from?"

Seth frowned. "From someone who's given me dozens of tips in the past. Occasionally they don't pan out, but he's never screwed me over."

Aaron chuckled and inclined his head toward Tempest. "I don't think he screwed you over this time, but that doesn't mean he wasn't manipulated into getting you to Peru."

"That doesn't make any sense," Tempest said thoughtfully.

"It doesn't?" Aaron asked, one brow arched.

"It doesn't. Think about it. Just a minute after I woke up, someone tried to kill me, and they haven't stopped since. Someone wants all of Lemuria dead and buried. Maybe multiple someones. We have no proof that all these groups have been sent by the same person. So it leaves a couple of questions." Tempest held up a hand, counting off her points. "One, how did they know I was there? Two, how did they know I was Lemurian? Three, why do they want to hide the truth of Lemuria? And four, why are they willing to go against everyone else to do it?" She let her hand drop and shook her head. "It has to be someone powerful, too. It sounds like Hecate is fairly well-known and powerful, and even she wasn't able to help us directly. She couldn't even tell us what was going on, though I got the feeling that she wanted to."

Seth slumped against the wall of the corridor they stood in. "Shit. She's right. And so are you, Aaron. There's no way that I found her by accident. It'd be way too big a coincidence."

"Do you think it was Hecate who led you to her?" Aaron asked.

"I honestly don't know. If you'd asked me an hour ago, I would've said no without hesitation. But now?" Seth slowly shook his head. "I'm questioning pretty much everything now. Like how it is that my best friend just happened to know a historian who just happened to know all about Lemuria. It seems too easy."

Tempest snorted softly, and Seth was surprised that she made it sound almost ladylike. "Easy?"

"I don't mean the fights and assassins and curse," he assured her, a corner of his mouth twitching upward. "But the rest? We're all being led around by our noses, and I don't like it."

"Do either of you know any seers? Maybe they'd be able to tell us who's behind all this?"

"How would we know who to trust?" Aaron pointed out. "Even if we told them nothing, there's the chance they could learn quite a bit using their powers. I don't want to give us more enemies." He grinned. "I just want to be the one who rediscovers Lemuria. Maybe we'll find a nice temple or vault."

He was still speaking the last word when a sharp gust of wind had him pinned to the wall. Tempest got up in his face, her hair billowing about her head, her eyes nearly black with anger. He snarled at her but she wasn't cowed and simply spoke over him. "You will not ransack my home. I appreciate the fact that you're helping us, but this is *not* a treasure hunt, and my home is not your treasure chest. Are we clear?"

Aaron glanced to Seth, who had his hand on his gun, but didn't look at all ready to draw it. Looking back to Tempest, his eyes narrowed. "How powerful are you that he doesn't seem at all concerned right now?"

"You wouldn't really hurt her," Seth answered for her. "You want to find Lemuria too much for that. And even if you tried?" He smirked. "You wouldn't manage it."

"I'm a Lemurian, Aaron, even if I am cursed at the moment. You'll soon learn exactly what that means," Tempest said ominously as she stepped back and released the wind binding him. "But are we clear?"

"Yeah, we're clear." But he was giving her a considering look. "You know, I think I really do want to know what being Lemurian means," he said before he turned to show them to their cabins.

CHAPTER 15

Later that evening, after everyone had moved their things to their cabins and eaten, Seth rapped on the door to Tempest's cabin. It would be a while until they reached the nearest point where Lemuria used to be, so they were all hoping for a few quiet days. No one expected a bit of peace, but they needed it. Tempest most of all. He couldn't promise her that peace, but he could take her mind off it all for a little while. His mind, too, though he was finding himself more and more distracted by her.

The one kiss they'd shared was burned into his memory. Even with the danger surrounding them, he found himself thinking about her more than the assassins. What he needed was to get her out of his system. He wasn't quite the king of one night stands, but he traveled so much he never went for anything serious, and made sure the women he'd slept with in the past were aware of that. He wasn't an absolute asshole, after all. And while he didn't expect this to be a one night stand, he still wasn't looking for anything long-term. Oh, he was going to stick with her to get her to Lemuria and help keep her safe—even though she didn't really need his help—but this wasn't a good time for either of them to let emotions get in the way. Besides, they'd known each other for a week. He liked her, sure, but a week wasn't enough time to develop the feelings that would lead to serious.

Tempest opened the door, barefoot and wearing only a tee-shirt and shorts. When she saw Seth, she smiled and leaned lightly against the edge of the door. "Hi Seth. Everything okay?"

For a moment Seth just looked at her, the rational part of his brain warring with the part that needed, that ached. "It will be," he told her before he stepped forward. He cradled her face and lowered his mouth to hers. There was a moment of surprise, but then her lips softened beneath his and her arms lifted and circled his neck. The moment she sank into the kiss, he deepened it. He released her face and wrapped his arms around her, drawing her up close against him, until her toes barely brushed the floor.

Holding her like that, it was easy for him to step into her cabin and kick the door shut behind him. He turned them and pressed her back against the door before he took her mouth with a hunger he'd never felt before. While he wanted to strip the shorts off and slam into her, he did nothing but hold her and kiss her until she trembled helplessly against him. He groaned then broke the kiss, but only so he could press his lips against her throat, feeling the heavy thud of her pulse so close to the surface. "Tell me you want this," he said in a low voice against her skin, before he gently set his teeth against her neck, making her shiver and release a small gasp. "Not for forever, just for now."

"I do," Tempest breathed, tilting her head to bare her throat to him, the fingers of one hand sliding into his hair. "For as long as it lasts."

Seth moved one arm down beneath her ass, lifting her more tightly against him. Her long legs slid around his hips and he groaned as she pressed against his crotch, the pressure making him ache for her.

Fighting the urge to grind against her, he carried her over to the bed. It wasn't a large bed, but it would work. There wasn't going to be much space between them for the foreseeable future, anyway.

He set her on her feet to free his hands then slid the shorts down over her hips until they fell to the floor, leaving her nude from the waist down. His fingers brushed against her warm skin as his hands moved up and under her tee-shirt, her eyes dark with need as she watched him. Though he wanted to rush, he slowly drew the shirt up and off of her, giving him his first long look at her.

Her skin was the same lightly tanned color from head to toe, and every inch was soft and unmarked. Her full breasts and hips gave her an hourglass shape that he wanted to trace with his hands—or his tongue. Her dusky pink nipples had tightened in the cool air of the cabin and he reached out to cup her breast and stroke his thumb over one of the peaks, making her sigh and arch into his touch.

Voice rough, he said, "You're beautiful. I should take my time, show you just how beautiful you are, but I can't wait." He yanked his shirt off and tossed it aside before they dove at each other.

Tempest kissed him fiercely as her hands went to his jeans, eagerly unbuttoning them before she shoved them impatiently downward. While he kicked at the denim to get it off his legs, her hand wrapped around his cock, finding him hard as stone. His hips jerked and he let out a sharp groan of pleasure. "Not yet," he told her, grabbing her wrist carefully to pull her hand away from him before he lost it. "You can play later," he told her before he picked her up and half-set, half-dropped her on the bed. A heartbeat later, he followed her down, kneeling between her knees.

His fingers stroked between her thighs and he felt himself throb when he found her already slick with desire. For a moment he struggled against his instincts. He desperately wanted to be inside her, but he couldn't resist the urge to taste her, to make her go wild.

Nudging her legs further apart, he shifted down, settled between them, and pressed a kiss to her inner thigh. She watched as his lips moved closer and closer to where she wanted him, and her fingers stroked lazily through his hair. When he gave her a slow lick that ended at her clit, those fingers clenched and she let out a low moan.

"Don't tease me," she demanded in a breathless tone he loved.

"I'll save the teasing for another time," he promised with a wicked grin before he began to kiss her thoroughly. His tongue stroked and plunged into her before his lips shifted to wrap around her clit and suck, making her tug at his hair and clamp her thighs against his shoulders. When he slid two fingers into her, thrusting in time with the pull of his mouth, she cried out and threw her head back.

It wasn't enough. As desperately as he wanted her, he wanted to see her come for him first. He shifted his hand and sought that spot that would make her break apart under his mouth. And he was merciless, stroking it as he teased her clit, never taking his gaze off her face.

Though he always thought her beautiful, it was nothing compared to the way her face transformed when she finally shattered and arched against his mouth, her own opening in a silent cry.

"Now, Seth, now," she whispered when she was finally able to focus enough for words. Her fingers tightened and she tugged. All too willing to give in, he allowed her to draw him up her body until his hips were settled between her legs. At the first brush of his cock against her hot, wet flesh, his breath caught and it took everything he had not to plunge into her and just take her without any finesse.

Drawing his head down to hers, she kissed him without an ounce of restraint. Her nipples brushed against his chest as she shifted beneath him, drawing her legs up and wrapping them around his hips. When she tightened them, his control eroded to nothing.

With one smooth thrust, he sank deeply into her until he felt fused to her. He exhaled sharply at a pleasure more acute than any he'd felt before. Maybe it was simply the situation they were in, but no woman had ever felt so good around him. It was impossible for him to focus on anything but her and the way she felt around him, so figuring that out would have to wait.

There was no build up, no gradual increase in tempo, as neither of them had the patience for that. He lifted his head so he could stare down at her, could watch her face as he drove into her, joining them over and over. Her eyes seemed to flicker, going light and dark by turns as she moved under him, against him. She rose up greedily to meet his thrusts, her gaze fixed on him. It remained there even when her second climax hit her like the storm she was named after. She cried his name as her fingers splayed over his back, then curled, pressing her nails against the flexing muscles.

The feel of her squeezing him so intimately broke him. He'd been in a near constant state of arousal for days, and it was impossible for him not to bury himself inside her and let out a low, long growl of satisfaction as he joined her in the middle of the gale.

Seconds ticked by as they clung to one another, caught in a perfect moment they both knew would end all too soon. As Seth's body began to relax, he lowered his head, giving her a tender kiss. Not wanting to crush her, he slid his arms around her and rolled them onto their sides.

When the tremors caused by the intensity of her orgasm had ceased, she rubbed her cheek against his chest and sighed contently. "Is it later yet?" she murmured.

"Hmm?"

Tempest lifted her head so he could see the growing smile on her lips. A lesser man might be afraid of that evil, seductive smile. He just felt himself twitch with interest. "You said I could play later," she explained. In a quick move, and with more strength than her small form looked like it held, she pushed him onto his back and straddled him. As she grinned down at him, she asked, "So, is it later yet?"

He chuckled and slid his hands over her thighs, surprised to feel himself growing hard again already. "I suppose it is." But neither slept much for the rest of the night. They were too busy sating their appetites for each other.

Hours later, when Seth and Tempest lay asleep in each other's arms, sated and content, another couple dozed, wrapped around each other, caught in the state that exists between dreams and consciousness.

"They're getting close," the woman murmured. Though it was a comfortable temperature and she lay under a blanket, she shivered.

The man's arm tightened around her, pulling her in more fully against him. "Isn't that what you wanted, though, darling?"

She made a low sound in her throat before sighing. "It is, but if they fail..." She gave a distressed noise. "This is our one chance with them, and it's not even a good chance. Things will never be quite as I wish. But it would have been nice if fate had been accepted with grace rather than fought against."

"That, too, was fate," he murmured gently. "It couldn't be stopped, just as their actions today couldn't be stopped. And you've helped them quite a bit, my love. If you do anything else, it's you who is fighting against fate." A thought so laughable it made him smile, even in his half-conscious state. "Just be patient. Things will be as they are meant to. You, better than anyone, know that some things are simply inevitable."

She sighed and relaxed against him. "Too true. All right. I'll be patient, though I cannot promise I won't help where I can."

He chuckled and kissed the top of her head. "You wouldn't be you if you could make that promise."

She only smiled.

He was right. She did enjoy meddling.

Joseph had changed locations. He couldn't stand to remain so close to where his colleague—one of the few people he'd both trusted and liked—had been killed. He stood now on the balcony of one of the guest rooms, a phone to his ear.

"What do you mean you can't find her? How hard is it to find one woman? You're supposed to be the best tracker alive," he snarled to the man on the other end.

"Exactly that. We got a hint of them, but then their signature disappeared. I don't know if they have a teleporter or just some major wards, but they keep blipping on and off our radar. Last time we were able to get a read on them, they were at sea."

"That's unacceptable. I don't understand how in the hell they keep killing or evading us." Fear of failure, and what it would mean, had sweat beading on his forehead. He flung out a hand and telekinetically slammed a heavy concrete planter against the wall with enough force to shatter it. Dirt exploded over the balcony, but he didn't notice, even when it landed on his expensive black shoes. "Use all the men you have at your disposal. Do whatever it takes to find and kill her. No mercy. Don't just assume anything about them. We don't know what she is. Check the skies and the seas. Check underground. Search under every fucking rock if you have to, just find her. Am I clear?"

There was a long pause before he was answered. "Yes, sir."

"Good. Keep me updated. The moment you find her, let me know."

"Of course, sir."

Joseph disconnected and fought the urge to smash his phone. He was running out of time and he knew it. He had a few days at most before he ended up like his friend had. Actually, he could probably expect worse to happen to him. And given his lifespan, any torture for him could last for a very long time.

There was one more resource he could tap, but it was risky. His father wasn't too happy with him at the moment, though he knew his father wanted this woman dead as well. Not that he'd asked Joseph to do it, he'd only mentioned it in passing. Nor did he know Joseph had a long-standing contract to kill this woman. Well, not this woman specifically, but anyone or anything matching her magical signature. He'd tried over the years to figure out what that signature meant, but had come up absolutely empty. He just knew that if this woman didn't die, he was going to suffer.

He punched in a number, one he didn't dare save in his phone, and hit call.

The voice that answered was deep and booming, and though it was familiar, it made the hair on the back of his neck stand up. "Joseph."

"Hello, Father."

"I don't suppose you're calling me to tell me that the woman is dead, are you?"

Joseph cringed, but his voice was calm. "Not yet. My team is tracking them and has gotten some hits. But I've sent more teams out. I've got the best trackers I know searching for her."

Though there were only a few white, fluffy clouds in the sky, lightning flashed, striking a tree at the edge of the lawn. "Then why are you calling me?" his father asked, his voice dangerous, full of menace.

"Because I need help. I know you mentioned wanting this woman dead, and I've actually been contracted to kill her by a third party. I'm coming up empty, and if I don't kill her soon, I'm going to be worse than dead."

"So?"

Joseph clenched his jaw. He knew he was only one of many children his father had, but to hear so plainly how little he was cared for stung. "We want the same thing, Father. With your help, I know we can find and kill this woman."

Lightning struck again as the man laughed darkly. "I'm a god. Why would I team up with a demigod? I'll take care of this. Maybe it'll be soon enough to save your worthless hide. But if by some chance you manage it before I do, let me know. I might just reward you."

"Yes, Father," Joseph said stiffly, but his father had already hung up.

This time he couldn't control his temper, and his phone shattered on the stone of the balcony.

CHAPTER 16

Seth woke with Tempest curled up against him, his arm draped over her waist. A quick glance at his watch showed that they'd slept for almost nine hours. Not too surprising, really, given all they'd been through. His lips curved. And the fact that she'd kept him up for several hours before they finally fell asleep certainly helped add to their exhaustion.

He caught himself nuzzling at the back of her neck and froze. That was too close to getting serious, which left him torn. This was temporary, it had to be, and while he planned to enjoy it while it lasted, he didn't want to hurt either of them when it was time to end it. So rather than waking her up the way he wanted, Seth carefully drew himself away from Tempest. She made a tiny noise of protest and rolled over into the warm spot he'd just vacated, but stayed asleep.

Quickly, he pulled on his pants, grabbed his shirt, and slipped out of the cabin. But while Tempest slept on, he didn't get away clean. He'd barely closed the door behind him when he almost ran into Aaron.

"Shit," he half-whispered as he took a step back. "Make a little noise when you walk, Aaron," he said, annoyed.

Aaron merely smirked and folded his arms over his chest. "You sure you wanted noise? Looked to me like you were sneaking out."

"That's none of your business," Seth said as he turned to head back to his own cabin.

"I don't know, it might be," Aaron mused. "If you're sneaking out of her room, I'm guessing it's either over between you two, or going to be soon. Which means she's a free agent, doesn't it?"

Seth turned and shoved Aaron against the wall, holding him there with one hand gripping the man's neck. "Don't go near her. I just didn't want to wake her, that's all. So hands off, tiger," he snarled.

Aaron chuckled, completely unimpressed by the threat. "I had a feeling it was like that. Pity, though. She's hot. Of course, so are Kara and Aelia. Now let go of me, Seth, before I forget that we're, temporarily, on the same side."

It took a moment for Seth to shove down his sudden aggression and step back. "Just leave her alone," he said, stalking to his cabin and inside, barely managing not to slam the door.

Aaron grinned at Seth's back and shook his head as he wandered up the stairs. He had entirely too much fun picking on Seth, and it was going to be too easy for the foreseeable future. This trip was going to be enjoyable for so many reasons. He walked into the galley and found Kara and Aelia already there, working on fixing breakfast while they chatted.

"Ahh, there are the loveliest ladies in the world. How'd you sleep?" he asked as he moved to the coffee pot and poured a cup.

"Those lines might work with other women, Aaron, but I know your sort too well," Kara said dryly as she flipped strips of bacon in a skillet. But her stern countenance only lasted a few seconds before she grinned. "But I do like compliments, so keep 'em coming. And I slept like a baby. Taking shifts is weird, but the bed was surprisingly comfortable for a boat bed."

Aelia smiled and shook her head as she carefully cut out biscuits. "I slept very well, Aaron, thank you. You gave me a wonderful room, and were fantastic company last night." She paused as she transferred the biscuits to a baking sheet then slid them into the oven. "Can you get some plates and silverware out? Breakfast won't be too much longer."

"Ahh, a woman who appreciates me," Aaron said, moving over to Aelia to give her a loud, playful kiss on her cheek. "And I absolutely can, chérie," he drawled.

By the time food was being set on the table, Seth had joined them. "Okay, traveling with Aaron might have some perks," he decided after looking around the galley and food already prepared.

"Don't thank him," Kara said, jabbing the air in his direction with the tongs she was using to transfer the bacon to a plate. "Aelia and I cooked."

"Then screw him. You two are my heroes," Seth quickly corrected. "I'll take care of dinner tonight, so it's fair," he offered as he grabbed a cup of coffee for himself.

"Good. Now I don't have to kick your ass," she said with a grin. "Where's Tempest?"

"She was still sleeping a few minutes ago," he answered as he sat down. "It's been a rough week for her, so let's let her sleep as long as she needs."

"No, I'm awake," Tempest said as she stumbled into the room. Though she'd looked well enough when he'd left her, sometime in the last few minutes she'd grown pale. Even her eyes were so light a shade of gray that they were nearly white. It was a look he knew entirely too well.

"Tempest," he murmured as he jumped to his feet and crossed the room to slide an arm around her waist.

"I'm...no, I'm not okay," she admitted as she leaned heavily into him. "I woke up and felt all right, but then..."

More of her weight settled against his arm and he was close enough to see a drop of red leak from her right eye like a bloody tear.

"Shit. Aelia," Seth snapped without looking away from Tempest. He lifted her in his arms and moved to the chair he'd vacated, easing into it so he didn't jostle Tempest.

In the seconds between when he spotted the first drop to when he settled in the chair with her, more blood began to escape her body, dripping from her ears and nose.

"Holy shit. What's wrong with her?" Aaron asked, his eyes widening at the sudden deterioration.

"It's the curse," Aelia answered as she hurried around the table and dropped to her knees in front of Seth and Tempest. She pressed a hand to Tempest's cheek and over her heart and began chanting, just as she had the day before.

"Shit," Aaron breathed to Kara. "I didn't realize it was this bad."

Face grim, she shook her head. "It gets worse. I hoped Aelia's fix would've lasted longer," she said, keeping her voice quiet so as not to interrupt the sorceress. "This is why we need to find Lemuria so quick. Or one of the reasons."

"Should I ask what happens if we don't?"

Kara's gaze slid to Aaron, but the look in her eyes was all the answer he needed. The look...and the blood that was quickly starting to cover Tempest.

Aaron was an asshole. He knew that about himself and was okay with it, but he wasn't a complete bastard. Rather than standing here gawking at Tempest and Aelia, he nodded. "I'm going to check our position and see if I can get a bit more speed out of the engines. When...If they have anything that might pinpoint where I should head, let me know."

"I will."

It seemed to Seth that it took longer for Aelia to help Tempest than it had before, even though they'd gotten to her quicker. Which meant that this fix probably wouldn't even last as long as it had the first time.

This time, when Aelia finished, both women were unconscious, and once again, Kara caught Aelia before she could fall.

"I think we should let them sleep it off. Especially Aelia," Seth said as he reached for a napkin to gently wipe the blood from Tempest's face. It was going to take more than a napkin to get it all, but she wasn't awake this time to shower it off.

"Agreed. And as much as I hate it, when I'm in Aelia's room, I'm going to take the map of Lemuria."

Surprised, because Kara was the last person he could see going through someone's personal property, he paused in the act of standing. "Oh?"

"We're running out of time. Yeah, Aaron knowing the general location of Lemuria helps, but the map might help him more."

The map had indicated mountains, if not overall elevation, so he nodded with understanding. "Whatever we have to do." He rose, shifting Tempest to a more secure hold. "And when Aelia's feeling better, I'm going to see if she can teach me that spell."

Kara stood as well and Seth knew she was using her stone magic to make it easier for her to lift the smaller woman. "Never thought you'd turn sorcerer," she told him with a dim smile as they started toward the cabins.

"Honestly? I probably should have learned sooner. But if learning sorcery helps keep Tempest alive and Aelia conscious, then I'll do it without hesitation."

Since she was behind him, Kara didn't bother to hide her grin. Whether he knew it or not, Seth was definitely starting to fall for their Lemurian.

After making sure Tempest and Aelia were settled in their beds and the map was in Kara's hands, both Seth and Kara made their way to Aaron.

Hearing them approach, Aaron glanced back. "How are they doing?"

"Resting," Seth answered as he dropped into a chair. "If it's like yesterday, they won't sleep long, but I'd rather not disturb them unless we have to."

"Understandable. And I want to apologize."

Seth's brows winged upward. "For what?"

Aaron jerked a shoulder and looked back out at the water in front of them. "Underestimating how urgent this was. Thinking mostly about how I could be the one to find Lemuria."

"We've got something that might help with that," Kara said, carefully unfolding the map and setting it on the table. "Aelia managed to save this map of Lemuria when the continent went down."

Surprising neither of them, Aaron stalked to the table to devour the sight of the map. "Why didn't you give this to me yesterday?"

"It wasn't mine to give, but Tempest isn't exactly getting any better. And you can see it has mountains marked here and here," she said, running a finger over those locations. "We figured that they would be the areas most likely to still be above water."

"They would," he agreed in a distracted tone. "The problem is we don't know which range was higher. These are closer, but the southern range could be taller."

"And that's not even counting that whatever remains might be there not because of elevation, but because of magic," Seth pointed out.

"True. Still, if we focus first on this mountainous region, we might be able to save some time. Only issue is that it looks like this isn't exact so we can't really use it for precise coordinates," Aaron decided as he glanced up to Seth. "We'll still have to do some searching, but I do think this could help us." He shifted his focus to Kara and smiled. Not the toothy, playboy smile he normally gave to attractive women, but a genuine smile. "Thanks."

She shook her head. "Thank Aelia when she wakes up. She's the one who kept it safe for this long."

"I can and I will." He studied the map for a little longer before moving to his controls to adjust the course. Seth didn't feel the boat shift much, so they must have been at least somewhat on course previously. He hoped so, at least. They couldn't waste any time.

"Did you really tell me everything yesterday?" Aaron asked, his voice mild rather than accusing.

Seth nodded. "Except for a few of the details, yeah."

"It has only been a couple of days," Kara pointed out as she folded the map up so it wouldn't get damaged.

"I know, but I also know it's instinct to hold a few things back when you're around someone you don't trust, and we all know you don't trust me," Aaron replied with a shrug.

"No, I don't," Seth agreed with a shrug. There wasn't any reason to hide a truth they all knew. "But we also didn't really have a choice. It was you or hire someone who could just be luring us out to kill us. With you, at least, I don't believe you'd murder us."

"Gee, thanks for that rousing endorsement," Aaron said dryly. "I didn't ask just for shits and giggles, though. If people are targeting you, I'm now in the middle of it. I'd like to get through this alive, and I can't do that if I don't have all the facts."

It wasn't an unreasonable request, no matter how little Seth wanted to concede anything to Aaron. "I meant it when I said I told you everything but the details. The people trying to kill us didn't monologue or anything, they didn't hint about who they were working for, and I wouldn't intentionally leave anything out that could get us killed or keep us safe."

"That's all I wanted to know," Aaron said calmly, but Seth could see the tension in the tiger's shoulders. They'd never gotten along, so Seth had known things wouldn't be all puppies and rainbows, but with the situation as it was, he hoped they could avoid any actual violence.

But that might be asking for too much.

CHAPTER 17

Though neither Aelia nor Tempest slept as long as Seth had hoped, Tempest was up first. She found Seth on the deck and he was quick to hurry her back inside the galley.

"I feel fine," she protested as she was gently shoved into a chair.

"Darlin', you still look paler than a banshee, and you didn't get your breakfast this morning," he corrected as he grabbed her a bottle of water then started looking for something filling that he could make. Since he traveled so much, his culinary expertise began and ended with sandwiches, grilled cheese, and hamburgers. He just wasn't in a kitchen often enough to have time to learn how to make anything more than that. Since he wanted to get something in her belly sooner rather than later, he opted for the grilled cheese. Bread was easy to find, and he smiled when he saw that Aaron had smoked gouda. He probably intended it for something nicer than grilled cheese, but Seth didn't care.

"You do know how to make a woman feel beautiful," she said dryly as he started making her lunch.

"You are beautiful," he said matter-of-factly, "but that doesn't change the fact that you're currently cursed and it hit you again just a few hours ago."

She sighed and laid her head on her folded arms. "No, I suppose it doesn't. How's Aelia?"

"Still asleep." He was quiet for a minute as he buttered the bread and heated the pan. "When she's awake and feeling better, I'm going to see if it's a spell I can learn."

That seemed to surprise her. "You want to learn sorcery?"

"Sure. She might not always be on the spot and I don't want anything to happen to you. Besides, if I can learn one spell, maybe I can learn more." Which might help make up for his lack of powers and increase his life expectancy.

She said nothing and simply watched him until he placed a plate with two sandwiches in front of her. "Thank you," she murmured.

"You're welcome," he said before cleaning up.

Halfway through her first sandwich, Aelia walked in, looking just as tired. "How are you feeling, Tempest?" she asked, her voice weak, as she made her way to a chair and sat down.

"Better. Thank you for helping me again."

Aelia smiled faintly. "Of course."

Tempest nudged her plate until it sat between them. "Hungry?"

"I am. Thanks," Aelia said, picking up the second sandwich and biting into it.

Seth got another bottle of water for Aelia, then smiled at them both. "I'm going to check in with Aaron. He was updating our course. Last I heard, it was two days to the first set of coordinates, but I'm hoping it'll be sooner. Just no more passing out, okay?"

"I'll do my best," Tempest said and watched him leave the galley.

"Are you seriously feeling okay?" Aelia asked.

"I'm tired, but at least I'm not bleeding anymore." Though she was starting to run out of blood-free clothes.

"Definitely a plus. I'm just sorry it isn't lasting as long as I'd hoped it would."

"It's not your fault. Besides, without you, I would have been dead yesterday."

"Let's not think about that too much," Aelia said, shuddering a little. "I know I'd gotten used to the world without Lemurians, but now that I know that you're not all gone, I don't want to go through that loss again."

Tempest nodded slowly and sipped at her water. "I was actually wanting to talk to you about that," she admitted.

"About Lemuria sinking?"

"Not exactly. Just...Lemuria," she said quietly, her eyes darkening with grief. "No one else alive has ever been there. They don't have any idea what it looked like, what it felt like." She sighed. "What the people were like. I could explain in great detail, but it wouldn't be the same."

"No, it wouldn't. It wasn't quite like anyplace else on Earth, then, now, or anytime in between," Aelia agreed with a nod. "There are places that are very similar in some respects, and I've seen slices of it as I've traveled through the centuries. Lemuria wasn't my home, but seeing those pieces of it comforted me."

Tempest cocked her head. "You weren't born there? I know there were humans there, but it was rare."

"I know. But even then I was a scholar. Not a historian, not really." Aelia laughed a little and looked back outward, watching the sunlight glinting off the tiny waves. "That developed because I was seeing so much history. Living it. Back then, I was simply fascinated with magic."

Tempest frowned. "Even though you had no power of your own?"

"Even though. And I was very good at researching it. Ferreting out little details that others might miss. So I was allowed to visit Lemuria with a sponsor, a witch named Selana."

"Selana...I knew her. She took you to a party, didn't she? That's where I remember you from, isn't it?"

Aelia smiled sadly and nodded. "She did, yes. I was so excited to be mingling with so many magical people."

"What happened to her?" Tempest asked gently.

Shaking her head, Aelia glanced back to Tempest. "She didn't survive the sinking. Teleporting wasn't one of her abilities," she whispered.

"I'm so sorry, Aelia."

Aelia just shook her head again. "It wasn't your fault. It was quick, which I was thankful for."

Tempest turned to face Aelia more directly. "What happened to the others? I can't believe that they were all stuck on Lemuria and none escaped. There were people who could fly or survive underwater. People who were traveling or living outside of Lemuria." She was desperate to figure out how she had ended up the very last Lemurian.

Aelia pushed the plate away, her appetite gone, her expression, her movements suddenly weary. "They died. The ones who made it to other lands, they all died. One by one."

"But how? They should never have aged."

"And they didn't. But age isn't the only way death can come to an immortal. Some simply suffered tragic accidents over the years, taking too many injuries for them to heal. Others were killed. Some, I think, must have been murdered by the same person or people who are after you."

She hesitated, long enough that Tempest leaned closer to her and urged, "Tell me. Please. I need to know."

Aelia drew in a slow breath and nodded. "Some took their own lives, though that mostly happened right after the sinking...or after most of the survivors had died," she said quietly.

Tempest recoiled as the words hit her, shocked. "What? No. Why?"

When Aelia lifted her head and smiled, tears shone in her eyes. "For the same reason I tried myself," she whispered. "Life is lonely when you have no one else. When your home, your true home, has been destroyed, along with your people, your gods. Living even a day like that is hard, Tempest, much less a year, a hundred years, a thousand." She gave an annoyed swipe to the tears sliding down her cheeks. "It's hard watching everyone you care about die."

It took Tempest a moment before recognition crept over her face. "Oh...oh no," she whispered and reached out to Aelia. Her arms wrapped around the other woman and she held on a tight. "It was as hard on you as it was on the other Lemurians, wasn't it? You had to watch everyone die, just like they did. Except you..." She straightened and frowned in confusion. "You can't die, can you? That's how you're still alive after so long."

"No, I can't, and trust me, I should have, many times," Aelia whispered against Tempest's shoulder. "I've wanted to, on multiple occasions, but it's just...impossible."

Tempest slowly relaxed her hold and leaned back. "Do you know why?"

Aelia nodded slowly. "I do..."

It was clear she didn't want to get into it, so Tempest dropped it and switched the subject. "The knife you gave me. You said it was a relic, but you didn't say what kind and I didn't recognize it. What does it do?"

"I'm not exactly sure," Aelia admitted. "It's activated when it's used to stab someone, that much I know, but I haven't exactly gone around stabbing people to find out." She glanced down and touched fingers lightly to the bracelet on Tempest's arm. "You didn't need the knife to have a piece of Lemuria, though. Don't forget you have this."

Tempest looked at the bracelet and frowned. She ran a fingertip over it, studied it, and shook her head. "I don't know what this is. I'm not even sure where it came from. I know I wasn't wearing it when I went to bed in Lemuria, and I can honestly say I didn't notice it was there until you pointed it out just now. So it could have been there for six thousand years or six days."

Aelia's brows lifted. "You've been wearing it since I met you and you haven't seen it before now? That's...weird. But it's definitely Lemurian. I've never seen that metal outside of Lemuria. It's nalonium, isn't it?"

"It looks like it, yes," Tempest murmured. No other metal she'd ever seen had the same blue hue as nalonium. Nor did any other metal hold magic and amplify it like the Lemurian metal did.

One corner of Aelia's mouth tilted up. "I don't suppose you sense anything from it? Some kind of magic?"

"No, I can't." Tempest tried to pull it off, but it stayed precisely where it was. "It won't come off."

Aelia gently drew Tempest's arm toward her and looked more closely at the bracelet. There was no seam that she could see, and it fit snugly against Tempest's skin without being tight. "Does it hurt you? Or has anything weird happened since you woke up?" At the look Tempest gave her, she laughed. "Other than the obvious."

"No, it doesn't hurt. I can't even feel it unless I'm focusing on it," Tempest said, letting her arm drop. "But I'm concerned about what its purpose is and who put it there."

"Maybe the same person who put you in the mountainside in Peru?"

"We think Vazi did that, but I'm not not sure why he'd do something like the bracelet."

"It does sound out of character for him, based on what I know of him," Aelia admitted. "I'd try not to worry about it too much right now," she suggested. "You've got enough on your plate without adding this to it. But I would tell Seth."

One brow arched as Tempest said, "Just Seth?"

Aelia hesitated. "No, I suppose not. We're supposed to be a team. For one reason or another, we're all together, working toward the same goal, so if we can't trust one another, what chance do we have of succeeding?"

"Good point." Tempest nodded and got to her feet. "I'm going to go find Seth, I think. If you see Kara or Aaron before I do, will you let them know?"

"I will, yes," Aelia said, smiling.

"Thanks."

But as Tempest left the galley, Aelia's smile faded. She had spoken truth, but she wasn't sure how much she trusted anyone on this boat. Except, oddly, for Tempest.

And it only took one betrayal from one person to doom their mission.

Aaron was walking by in time to see Tempest disappear through the opposite door, and when a few minutes passed without Aelia following, he slipped in quietly.

Aelia had moved to a seat at the side of the room so she could stare out over the ocean as their boat skimmed along the surface. He couldn't see her face well, just her profile, but it struck him how sad she looked. Even the way she sat betrayed her sorrow.

And he wondered what caused it.

"Aelia?"

She jolted, even though his voice had been soft, gentle. "Aaron...you surprised me," she said as she turned to face him. "Did you need something?"

He scowled and shoved his hands into his pockets. "I saw Tempest leave, but you didn't join her. You okay?"

Aelia cocked her head, brows lifting in surprise at his question. "Why wouldn't I be?"

"Because you're sitting out here alone, staring sadly at the water," Aaron answered with a shrug. "Mind if I join you?"

She frowned but nodded and shifted her legs so there was room for him. "Oh, Tempest asked me to tell you if I saw you before she did...Have you noticed the bracelet she's wearing?"

"Sure. Odd looking metal, unique design that I assume is Lemurian. What about it?" he asked as he sat down, his knee brushing hers.

"She didn't have it on when she went to bed the last night she was in Lemuria," Aelia answered. "She didn't even realize she was wearing it until I specifically pointed it out just a bit ago."

"That's definitely unusual, but compared to her being in a magical stasis for six thousand years, it's minor," he pointed out.

"If we knew the purpose of the bracelet, yes, it would be," she agreed. "We're not actually worrying about it yet, but she thought the whole group should know."

"I appreciate the heads up." He shifted, adopting a relaxed pose. "So what'd the Lemurian say to make you go all sad? You're usually serious, but not really sad."

Aelia smiled faintly and tucked a strand of hair behind her ear. "Just remembering the past, that's all. She makes me remember it more than most."

Aaron cocked his head. "Why does the past make you sad?"

She couldn't help but laugh, though it was hardly an amused sound. "Isn't that what the past tends to do, Aaron? Especially once you've lived a few centuries? No one gets through life without some regrets, and the longer you live, the more regrets you can rack up."

"Mmm. True, I suppose. But why would Tempest make you remember more than most?"

"Ahh, that's right, you weren't there. She and I have met before. Using a very loose definition of met, anyway."

Aaron leaned back and gave her a skeptical look. "Didn't she just wake up after a few thousand years in a cave?" Aelia only nodded and he looked at her more closely. After a moment he leaned in, so his nose was nearly touching her cheek, and inhaled deeply.

She drew back and gave him a wary look. He wasn't bothering her or making her uncomfortable, but it was an odd action. Worse, it made her feel and she did her best to avoid that. "What are you doing?"

"Smelling you." He straightened and shook his head. "You're human. My nose may not be as keen as some, but I can smell that."

"I am."

"Did you reincarnate?"

"No. I was alive back then. In this body, even." Her brow furrowed as she fought to remember. "I think I was going by a different name, though, but it's hard to keep track of what name I used when." He started to speak but she held up a hand and shook her head. "I'm not going to get into it now, Aaron, for three reasons. First, it can't be replicated. Two, it doesn't matter. Three...not trying to be mean, but it's really no one's business but my own."

Aaron smiled slowly, showing off his slightly too sharp canines. "Oh honey, that's the wrong thing to say to me. First, I don't care if whatever it is can't be replicated. Second, everything matters, you just have to figure out the when and where. Lastly?" He leaned a little closer and dropped his voice to an intimate whisper. "Never dangle a secret in front of a cat. It's irresistible."

"Curiosity killed the cat," she said primly.

"Ah, but satisfaction brought it back. It might be very satisfying to learn your secrets." But instead of pressing, he only grinned as he got to his feet. "I need to check on our course, but we'll speak again soon." He was at the door when he glanced back. "You might want to consider one thing, though."

"What's that?" Aelia asked dryly.

"You're not so sad anymore, are you?" he asked with a wink before he started to leave.

She couldn't help it, a smile curved her lips and she shook her head. Because damn if he wasn't right.

CHAPTER 18

The rest of the day passed in relative quiet. There was some good natured bickering, which helped distract everyone from worrying about being attacked. Mostly, however, Aaron worked on ensuring the best course for searching as much area as possible. Each of the others spent time with him, learning about what he was doing and familiarizing themselves with the route.

There were zero certainties for any of them for the next little while, and they all knew it. Redundancy could save their lives.

Aelia was careful, however, to avoid being around Aaron without one of the others nearby. He was tenacious, and she didn't feel like being hounded about a secret she'd kept since Lemuria had disappeared beneath the ocean. It was made easier when Seth asked her about the spell she was using to counter the curse on Tempest.

She was hesitant, not because she didn't want to teach him, but because she'd spent thousands of years learning the sorcery she knew. Some of the Arcane thought of sorcery as simplistic, easy, and weak, but it was far from the truth. Yes, some spells were indeed no trouble to learn, but most involved a great deal more than simply reciting the right words. And while the spell to save Tempest appeared like it was nothing but chanting, it was more complicated than that.

Still, she'd seen the way Seth had been looking at Tempest and couldn't deny him. They spent several hours on deck, away from the others, as she painstakingly taught him the words in a language that hadn't been spoken in more than five thousand years and had never been written down. He had an excellent memory and by the time their bodies grew stiff from sitting in the same position for so long, he could recite seventy percent of the chant properly. He didn't have it memorized yet, but that would come.

Now she had to teach him the part that took the words from a recitation to a spell, but that would have to wait for tomorrow.

Seth was pleased that Aelia had agreed, though he told himself he wasn't avoiding Tempest. Gods knew he definitely didn't want the previous night to be their only time together, but he didn't know if she'd meant it when she said she was okay with it being casual, temporary. And given that the blood curse could affect her at any time, he wasn't going to risk upsetting her by asking. The time for serious conversations—if needed—could come after they'd found Lemuria and she was safe.

Seth and Aelia weren't the only ones seeking a distraction. Tempest was getting more and more anxious the closer they came to Lemuria. She wasn't anxious to see her home hidden beneath the waves if none of it existed on the surface. On the other hand, she didn't want to spend the rest of her exceptionally long life trapped on what might remain of it, with little to no company. That would be existing, not living.

"What would be the point?" she murmured, which had Kara stopping in mid-sentence. They were sitting in the room that doubled as

Aaron's office and library, with Kara using the computer, trying to introduce Tempest to TV shows.

"What would be the point in what?" Kara asked as she paused the show. Tempest hadn't been paying attention, so all she knew about it was that it involved someone who seemed to live in a big blue box.

Tempest sighed and shook her head as she used her air magic to levitate a glass paperweight into her hand, giving her something to fidget with. "Surviving. If I stay in the world where I can interact with people, I'll be hunted. If Lemuria exists, I can stay there, but for what? To spend eternity alone as the last Lemurian?"

"Hey, no. You can't think like that," Kara said sternly. She pushed her chair back so she could lean forward and lay a hand on Tempest's knee. "Listen to me. I don't care how hopeless you think things look right now, they're not. And I hate to criticize you, but you're not alone. You're on a boat with four other people. Okay, sure, so you only just met all of us, and we're not Lemurian, but that doesn't mean we don't give a damn about you. If you were alone, Seth would have ditched you back in Peru, I wouldn't have let him bring you to my house, Aelia wouldn't have come with us, and Aaron wouldn't currently be figuring out all the coordinates we're going to hit to find your home. So think about that, then think about how it might be insulting for you to say you're alone with all of us busting ass to help you out."

Shamed, Tempest slowly nodded. "I'm sorry, I didn't mean to insult you, and I know I'm not alone *now*, but you all have lives to go back to. You can't all just uproot yourselves and move to Lemuria."

"Maybe we can't," Kara said with a shrug, "but that doesn't mean we won't keep busting our asses to find out how to get your enemies off your back. And when we do, you can always have a summer home or whatever on Lemuria but still hang out with us. Hell, I'd love to have a neighbor I can stand and who knows what I am. And I know Seth wants to spend more time with you."

Tempest went quiet, mulling over what Seth had said the night before. "About Seth…"

Kara tried to hide a smile and failed. "What about him?" she asked innocently.

"Why is he single? I mean, he's a nice man, smart, talented, and extremely attractive. I'm shocked he isn't with anyone."

"Mmm. I could give you two answers, one easy, one hard, and both of them are true. I probably shouldn't tell you the hard one, but I've seen the way you look at him. Which answer do you want?"

Tempest didn't blush, even knowing that Kara was aware of her attraction to Seth. An attraction that went beyond the physical. "Both, please."

Kara nodded and went to the mini-bar, pouring herself a scotch and soda. A questioning look to Tempest had the woman nodding, and she poured a second. She passed over a glass and sat down before she spoke. "Easy answer? His job. I don't know how much he's told you about it, but it's a pretty complicated job, mostly because it has a magical and mundane side to it. To the humans, he's just an archaeologist, though I know some of them consider him nothing more than a treasure hunter. But whatever you call him, he's damn good at what he does. It's how he found you, actually. He was looking for another site to excavate. But it means he's traveling, a lot. He has a house, but I've been there and it's pretty much a place to research between digs and to store the artifacts he keeps.

"The hard answer..." She glanced to the door, made sure it was fully closed before she continued, though she lowered her voice. "Like I said, both answers are true, and his work does prevent him from forming any actual relationships, but I don't think it's the biggest reason. I think it might actually be an excuse. Has he told anything about his mom?"

Tempest shook her head. "I only know that she was human. And the only thing he's told me about his father is that he's a falcon shifter. He doesn't seem to really like talking about himself."

"It does take a while. We'd known each other for a year before he opened up to me, and I had to get him drunk to do it," Kara confessed. "But that also ties back into the hard answer."

"Which has something to do with his mother?"

"Yep. She died, giving birth to him, actually."

Tempest gasped softly, her eyes darkening with sympathy. "Oh no," she whispered.

"Yeah. That part fucks with him. He never knew her, but he saw how his dad mourned her. Still mourns her, actually. And he blames himself for her death, even though he's innocent. A child can't be blamed for that. I've tried to help him, but it's deeply ingrained. Decades of blaming himself aren't going to be easily forgotten, you know? So I think he avoids relationships with women because A, he's worried he'll hurt them since he, in his mind, hurt his mom just by being born. And B, he's afraid of ending up like his father."

"That's horrible." Tempest remembered her drink and took a deep drink. The taste of it surprised her enough that she glanced at the pale liquid, but it didn't distract her for more than a second. "It explains quite a few things, though." She slowly lifted her gaze to Kara's.

Whatever Kara saw in her eyes made her smile. "You're going to knock some sense into him, aren't you?"

"I think I'm going to try," Tempest decided. "I'm not saying I want him for forever—I don't know him well enough for that—but I like him, a lot. We may not be together, but we're..." She tried to think of a discreet way to say it, but opted to just speak plainly. "We're having sex, and I don't want him worrying the whole time. I also don't want him to be alone his whole life, either. I understand loss." She let out a humorless laugh. "I *really* understand loss. I lost my parents shortly before I was put to sleep, and now I'm dealing with the loss of my home and entire race. But I also know you can't dwell on it. If you're constantly wondering when you're going to suffer loss again, you'll never enjoy what you have."

"Tempest, I'm very tempted to kiss you right now," Kara said, beaming at her. "But I won't, because it'd be like kissing Seth by proxy, and eww."

Startled, Tempest repeated, "Eww?"

Kara wrinkled her nose. "Yeah, eww. I'm an only child, so Seth's the closest thing I've got a brother. I so don't want to kiss him. But I think you're going to do him some good, even if you two part ways after we find Lemuria. Which I don't think is going to happen, by the way."

"You don't?"

"Nope. At the very least, he'll stick with you until you're safe from whoever has a hate on for Lemurians."

Tempest smiled. "Yes, you're probably right about that. A man who would guide a strange woman who didn't speak his language to safety isn't going to just leave her alone to deal with people trying to kill her."

"Damn right. I wouldn't have a douche for a best friend, after all, and that would be a total douche move. And now that we've moved out of serious topics, you've got me curious. Seth said you and Aelia were speaking Lemurian back at the cabin, right?" When Tempest nodded, she grinned. "Can I hear it? I was a little too confused to actually enjoy it last time."

Tempest laughed and switched to her native tongue to say, "Seth is very lucky to have a friend like you. And if he doesn't realize it, he's a fool."

"I have no idea what you just said, but that was damn beautiful. Can you—"

Her words were cut off when the boat listed sharply to one side and felt like it actually came out of the water briefly, only to slam back down hard into the ocean. It jolted them enough their chairs tipped over and Kara's drink spilled all over her.

"What the hell was that?" Kara asked, surging to her feet.

"I don't know, but it can't be good," Tempest said as she raced out of the office and to the deck.

The others were already there. Aaron was in the wheelhouse, fighting to control the boat. Aelia was sprawled on the deck while Seth helped her to her feet, one hand holding tight to the railing.

"What's going on?" Kara shouted as she hurried toward them.

"Something hit the boat," Aelia said as she got to her feet. "Something big."

"A whale?" Kara asked as she peered over the edge.

Seth and Tempest looked into the water with her, and it was Seth who spoke. "I don't think so," he said grimly.

Circling beneath their boat wasn't a whale or anything the humans knew existed. If they'd spotted it, they likely would have just called it a sea monster, or perhaps a leviathan. It looked like an odd cross between a huge sea serpent and a shark, with a long, serpentine body covered in blue-gray scales. The way it coiled about in the water made it hard to tell exactly how big it was, but it was much longer than their boat. The head came closer to the surface, showing the snake-like features. Slit pupils almost disappeared into the sickly gray eyes, but the menace in them wasn't the real threat. The fangs as long as Tempest was tall were.

"What is that?" Tempest asked with growing horror.

Though she looked to Seth for an answer, Aelia was the one to provide it, her voice somber. "A cetus. A sea monster from ancient times, and a servant of the gods."

CHAPTER 19

"What is it?" Aaron asked as he ran out of the wheelhouse, his hands already shifted to show the lethal claws of his tiger form.

"A cetus," Aelia answered. "It's—"

"I know what it is." He looked to Tempest. "Who the hell did you piss off?"

"That's what we're all trying to figure out," Tempest answered bitterly. "Better question right now is...can we kill it?"

One of the thick coils of the cetus's body, as big around as a bus, slammed into the boat again. It hit hard enough that the boat rocked hard to one side. The railing Seth and the others held onto rose up in the air, while the other side of the boat dipped low enough it was almost submerged. Aaron managed to stay upright, but not everyone was so lucky. Kara grabbed hold of the railing and turned her hand to stone, making her grip almost unbreakable, though her body slid toward the water. Tempest may as well have been standing on dry land for all that she moved, but Seth had to grab hold of the railing with both hands to avoid falling. Aelia stumbled and fell, gravity pulling her toward the water. Aaron grabbed her before she could crash into the railing, but her momentum had them both hitting the deck hard.

When the boat righted itself, water splashed on deck, making it slick and harder to stay upright. Aaron rolled so that Aelia was beneath him, protected by his body until the boat settled. His body had shifted more toward his tiger, his five o'clock shadow more pronounced, his muscles thicker, his teeth sharper. He snarled as he lifted his head, pissed that this monster was threatening to destroy his boat, and them along with it. "That thing is dead," he snapped darkly.

"How do you kill something that freaking big?" Kara asked, manifesting a stone dagger. She threw it at the creature's eye, but it was just far enough under the water to protect it from any real damage. The water slowed the knife too much for that.

"Weaken it. Draw it to the surface and hit it with everything we got," Seth said, happy he'd decided not to leave all his weapons in his cabin. With some of their enemies being able to teleport, he simply couldn't just trust that being on the move and inside Kara's wards was enough.

"I've got spearguns. In the wheelhouse," Aaron told them as he climbed off Aelia and helped her to her feet.

"On it," Kara said. She released her hold on the railing and ran inside to get the weapons.

Seth drew his gun and fired several shots. It was hard to tell how many actually made contact with the creature, but at least one hit someplace sensitive because it thrashed its head beneath the water. The resulting waves rocked the boat about like it was a toy rather than a 142 foot yacht. "I'm annoying it more than anything," Seth yelled to the others. "And I'm almost out of ammo." The monster was definitely pissed off and smacked the side of its head hard against the boat, threatening to spill them all over the edge once more.

Aelia was still lying on the deck and called, "Do you have more?"

"In the duffel in my cabin."

"I'll get it." She scrambled unsteadily to her feet and hurried to the stairs below deck.

Aaron joined the others at the railing to glare down into the water at the cetus. "We need to get its head out of the water."

"I might be able to help, but I think if we make it angry enough, it might do it for us," Tempest offered.

He looked at her skeptically. "How?"

She glanced at him. "Does it matter?"

"Do it." He was so angry he was almost fully shifted to his half-tiger form. His shirt and pants were torn in places and straining at the seams in others. Black fur with even darker stripes covered his body and his head had a more feline shape to it than before.

Seth continued to shoot anytime the beast's head came close to the surface, but after just a few more shots, his magazine was empty. "I hope Aelia gets back soon," he said grimly, but Kara raced out of the wheelhouse holding two spearguns and a handful of spears.

"Here!" she called to Seth and tossed one of the guns to him. "You've got the best aim of all of us." The fantastic eyesight his father had given him made him an excellent marksman, and she knew it.

He caught it, relieved to see a spear was already loaded. Turning back to the water, he aimed and waited, not wanting to waste any of the precious spears. They'd need all of them to land in vulnerable spots if they hoped to kill the creature. Finally, the head grew closer to them again and he fired. The spear fared better than the bullets and sank into the creature's eye. It thrashed and screeched, loud enough that they could hear it as well as feel it, even with the huge mouth beneath the water. Unfortunately, in its thrashing, the cetus hit the boat again and sent Seth and Kara tumbling to the deck. The end of its tail surfaced—the first part of the monster to come out of the water—and smacked the boat, landing where Aelia had been laying not too long ago. It cracked several boards with the force of the blow before the tail snaked back into the water.

"Whatever you're going to do, do it!" Aaron snarled at Tempest as he clung to the railing.

"I am," she replied through gritted teeth. She'd assumed it was more reptile than fish, needing to surface for air, and had tried to pull the air from the water to suffocate it, but either she was wrong or it could hold great amounts of oxygen in its lungs. "It's not surfacing to breathe!"

Aaron gave her a sharp look when he clued into what she'd been trying to do. "Can you reverse that? Let me breathe underwater?"

"Yes, but it's too big to fight like that. It'd crush you!"

"Not if they keep shooting," he replied as he leapt over the railing and into the churning water below.

Tempest swore sharply in Lemurian but immediately shifted her magical focus. It would drain her too much to surround all of Aaron with a layer of breathable air, especially while he was tossed about by the cetus, so she only covered his face. Even then it was difficult to maintain it under these circumstances. But she watched as Aaron was pushed about like a rag doll through the water. As he moved, his claws slashed at any flesh he could make contact with, and soon the dark water was stained red.

"What the hell is he thinking?" Kara shouted as she got to her feet and gave Seth half the spears, then readied her own gun.

"Weaken it," Seth answered absently as he loaded a second spear. "Just be careful not to hit Aaron." He missed the incredulous look she gave him, and only fired again, sinking a second spear into the beast's eye. This time they were prepared for the jolt to the boat and managed to stay on their feet. Aelia wasn't so lucky. She'd just stepped out of the cabin and slammed into the door frame, her head smacking the wood with a dull crack. She nearly fell as the blow stunned her, but she managed to stay on her feet and keep hold of the ammunition she held.

Kara noticed and wavered for a moment before she rushed to the other woman's side. "You okay?" she asked, wrapping her free arm around Aelia.

"Yeah. Got the bullets," Aelia said, voice unsteady and weak.

"Shit." She couldn't put a gun in Aelia's hand. There was no telling how good she was with one, and with the head injury and Aaron in the water, it was too risky. "Sit." She didn't give Aelia a chance to argue, but gently pushed the woman to the deck before returning to the railing. When she looked back into the water, it was hard to see exactly what was going on. Seth and Aaron had been busy and it looked like there was more blood than water beneath the boat. She couldn't spot Aaron. For that matter, she could barely make out the thick length of the cetus.

Underwater, Aaron shifted fully, giving his tiger free rein. In this form, his claws were longer, sharper, his muscles stronger. He managed to grab hold of the cetus, digging the claws of one paw into flesh so he couldn't be easily dislodged. He tore into the creature, digging ferociously toward the spine. The cetus was large enough that destroying the spine might not completely stop it, but it would make it less of a threat.

Before he could reach the delicate spinal cord, he found himself pinned between two coils and the weight of them was crushing. He roared and tried to move out from beneath the heavy flesh, but couldn't manage to shift even an inch. He felt his bones threatening to shatter as they were ground against one another, and fought more viciously, tearing into the monster.

Just as one of his bones cracked, something he could almost hear, a light blazed through the water. It flickered and glowed like fire, but the source wasn't above him, it was in the middle of the tangle of flesh. It warmed the water around him and allowed him to see more than what was directly in front of him. But where had it come from?

The cetus moved sharply as it was burned by the magical flame, releasing its hold on Aaron. With a snarl of triumph, Aaron slashed deep, relieved when his claws hit bone. Anchoring himself with his back claws, he assaulted the spine, punching and clawing and tearing until the bone weakened enough to snap. He felt the shock wave as the cetus roared in agony and recoiled. He was thrown free but began to swim toward another loop of flesh.

Above the water, Seth frowned. "Do you see that?"

Aelia struggled to her feet and stumbled over to the edge, her eyes widening. "A fire? But how?"

"Who cares? Take advantage of it!" Kara yelled as she finally fired, sure she wasn't going to miss and hit Aaron. Her aim wasn't as true as Seth's, but she still hit the creature's face, which now held almost a dozen spears.

Beside her, Seth fired as rapidly as he could reload the speargun. When the creature turned toward them and roared, he smiled in grim satisfaction and fired a spear right down its throat. For the first time, the monster surfaced, its head rearing out of the water. The scream it gave was alien and loud enough to vibrate through them, making everyone on the boat cringe with pain. As they watched, the black tiger clawed his way up the length of the cetus, finally emerging from the water. One of his back legs didn't seem to be working too well, but to Seth's surprise, it didn't truly hinder him in his climbing. Seth and Kara continued to shoot at the thrashing head, most of the spears sinking into the thick skin. Freed from having to ensure Aaron didn't drown, Tempest joined in the fight, battering the creature with sharp gusts of wind, holding it elevated and vulnerable to the others.

Another shriek sounded, this one weaker than the last, and Seth felt a jolt of elation. The cetus was dying. If they could wound it just a little more, they'd be safe.

He had to shift his aim abruptly when Aaron climbed higher and began clawing at the sensitive flesh around the creature's eyes. Seth ran further down the boat so he could aim better, shooting another spear into the roof of the beast's mouth, just as Kara sank one in the throat, barely below Aaron's furred body.

The fire beneath the boat died as the cetus did, the light going out of both at the same moment.

Aelia was the first to see that the cetus was beginning to sink beneath the water and yelled at Aaron, "It's dead! Get away before it takes you under with it!" All it would take was one coil trapping the tiger beneath it to take him to the bottom of the ocean.

There was no reaction from Aaron at first as he continued attacking the monster. He was enraged and didn't seem to hear their yelling. Seth took a chance and fired a spear just to the left of Aaron, almost pinning one of his paws to the monster's body. With a snarl, Aaron looked back at Seth, who yelled, "Get off it! It's dead!"

Finally, Aaron leapt off the cetus, body twisting in the air so he dove toward the water. It was clear he wouldn't be able to make it past the sinking monster, but suddenly his downward progress was halted and he moved parallel to the water rather than toward it. Seth glanced at Tempest and saw one of her hands lifted and knew she was using her magic to guide Aaron to the boat.

When Aaron landed, he collapsed on the deck and shifted back to human. He lay there on his stomach, battered and naked, with the calf of one leg bent at a painful angle.

"Aaron!" Aelia ran to him, though with her head injury she didn't run straight, and she fell to her knees beside him. "Are you okay?" she asked, not wanting to touch him and make it worse.

Aaron groaned and rolled onto his side, leaving his injured leg as still as possible. "That fucking hurt." His eyes opened and fixed on the other three. "Any of you healers?"

Kara grimaced. "Sorry. I'm not that kind of witch. I can't heal anything bigger than a mild headache."

"I can't heal wounds," Aelia answered, swaying a little as she knelt there.

He sighed and moved fully onto his back, which had Aelia glancing over his body, then shooting her gaze back to his face. "Figured. Anyone know how to set a broken bone?"

"I do," Seth said as he watched the cetus sink further down into the water until it was out of sight, even to him. "But it's gonna hurt like hell unless you've got some pain killers on board."

Aaron let out a short, strained laugh. "'Course I do. Don't just have a first aid kit. Got everything short of an actual infirmary."

"Where is it? I'll get it," Kara offered.

"My cabin."

"Just hold tight," she said with a nod as she hurried inside to retrieve the medicine.

Tempest remained at the railing, staring down into the water as everyone else moved on. Seth noticed and asked, "What is it? Is there something else down there?"

She shook her head. "Not that I see. I was just making sure it was actually dead and not just faking it."

He frowned. "And is it? Dead, I mean?"

"Seems to be. It just sank and I don't see any movement."

Seth nodded and looked back to the tiger. "Good. I don't want to go through that again."

Aaron smiled tightly. "You and me both."

"I'll bet."

Tempest joined them and it really clicked in Seth's head that Aaron was naked, and not exactly an unappealing specimen. He yanked his shirt off, and though it was soaked, he still dropped it over Aaron's crotch. "Modesty, dude."

This time Aaron's laugh held real humor, though the pain still bled through. "What's the point of being modest when you look like I do? Let the ladies look if they wanna look," he retorted, though he left the shirt in place.

Seth rolled his eyes and crouched to look over the obviously broken leg. He could set it, yes, that wouldn't be a problem. However, even with a shifter's increased healing it would be a while before Aaron could actually walk on it, much less run. And if they could be found while moving across the ocean, they were bound to be attacked again. Tempest was fantastic in most fights, and Kara could certainly hold her own, but Seth would feel better if they had a tiger on their side, even if he still didn't full trust Aaron. Once they got him fixed up, Seth and Aaron were going to have to have a conversation.

A voice whispered in Seth's head, *"Ask for help..."*

He jolted and rocked back, falling on his ass.

"You okay?" Aelia asked him.

"Yeah...gimme a sec," he murmured. He took a moment then thought, *"Who is this?"*

"Ask for help..."

He frowned. It sounded like a woman's voice, but it was so quiet he couldn't place it. Still, there was only one woman he could think of who had helped him recently who might have the ability to speak into his mind. Then he saw it. Sitting on part of the rail that was undamaged, looking unruffled, was a single crow. The bird stared directly at Seth, which gave validity to his guess. He drew in a slow breath and closed his eyes. *"Hecate...please help us. We need all our people if we're to survive. We need the tiger whole."*

There was no answer, which disappointed him until he heard Tempest gasp. He opened his eyes and followed her gaze to his hands, which were emitting a faint glow. "Oh shit!"

"What the hell is that?" Aaron asked.

"Help, I hope," Seth said, shifting around so he could lay his hand on Aaron's leg, right where the break was.

Aaron hissed in a breath, but didn't move. "What are you—" He broke off when the glow brightened and seemed to sink down into his leg. Suddenly he went rigid and snarled, but his leg was moving beneath Seth's hand, the bones shifting back into their normal position. Only seconds later the glow faded, both from his leg and the hand Seth touched him with, though Seth's other hand still held a white halo to it.

"Aaron? You okay?" Aelia asked, touching his shoulder lightly.

Slowly moving his leg, Aaron nodded. "I think so. My leg feels better." He frowned at Seth. "How'd you do that? I thought you were powerless."

Seth clenched his jaw at the comment but nodded once, sharply. "I am, basically. That wasn't me. It was Hecate. I heard her, in my head."

"I don't think she's done helping either," Tempest said. When three sets of eyes turned to her, she smiled faintly and nodded to Seth's hand. "Both your hands were glowing. When you touched Aaron and healed him with one, the light went away. But Aaron isn't the only one hurt." She looked pointedly to Aelia and the blood dripping down the side of her face. When her head had connected with the door frame, she'd gotten a cut to go along with what could be a concussion.

"Oh, it's nothing. It's not going to kill me," Aelia protested.

"That doesn't mean it doesn't hurt or affect you," Aaron said as he pushed himself to a sitting position.

Kara came running out with the first aid kit in her hands, though she came to a slipping stop on the wet deck when she caught sight of Aaron and Seth. "What the hell?"

Seth gave her a sheepish smile. "Sorry. We didn't mean to send you on a wild goose chase. I'll explain the rest in a minute, okay?"

"You'd better," she warned him.

Seth got to his feet and moved around Aaron, careful not to touch anyone with his flashlight of a hand. "I can't promise this won't hurt, but it didn't last long with Aaron."

Aelia nodded and blindly took Aaron's hand, who squeezed hers reassuringly. "That's okay. And thank you."

Seth gave her a faint smile and laid his hand on her head where the blood was darkest beneath her blonde hair. Again the light seemed to sink down from his hand and into Aelia.

She made a small sound, more surprise than pain, before her eyes widened in surprise. "Oh! That feels better. A lot better." She smiled at Seth. "Thank you."

He shook his head as he returned the smile and got to his feet. "Don't thank me, either of you. Thank Hecate." He turned then and was met with an annoyed Kara, who stood with her hands on her hips, looking like she wanted to pound someone into the ground.

"You going to explain what just happened?" she asked and Seth had to fight off a smile.

"Come on. Let's let them get themselves cleaned up—and dressed," he added with a look to Aaron. "We'll make sure we get far away from this place and we'll tell you everything. Tempest, you're welcome to join us."

Tempest smiled and moved to Kara, linking her arm through the other woman's. "Love to. Come on, I, for one, want some distance," she said as she led Kara back inside.

Seth chuckled as he followed, tossing back to Aaron, "Seriously, get dressed. I don't want to see your bare ass again, Aaron. Once was more than enough."

"I make no promises," Aaron called after him.

CHAPTER 20

Everyone cleaned up and did what they could to repair the damaged boat before they gathered in the wheelhouse.

"So how sure are you that it was Hecate who helped you heal us?" Aaron asked once Seth was sitting.

"Pretty damn sure. I saw another crow, and that seems to be her sign that she's present, or at least paying attention. Why?"

"Because I'm wondering about that light or fire or whatever it was that injured the cetus. Do you think it could have been her, too?"

Seth considered for a moment before he slowly shrugged. "Anything is possible."

"It's not a power any of us have, and to the best of our knowledge, no other god or goddess is helping us, so who else could it be?" Tempest asked.

"Especially since she's the goddess of witchcraft," Aelia chimed in. "If anyone could cause a fire underwater, it would be her. I'm not even sure regular witches could do that. A fire elemental, maybe, but I kind of doubt it."

"Why are we even worrying about this?" Kara asked on a sigh. "Whoever it was wanted to help us. Even if it isn't Hecate, that just means we have someone else on our side. I, for one, would be delighted if someone else powerful wanted us to succeed."

"It just makes me uneasy, not knowing who was responsible," Aaron confessed with a shrug. "They might have helped us this time, but only so they can screw us later. For all we know, they *want* us to find Lemuria so they can follow us there and then kill us."

"Fair point," Seth agreed, though he hoped Aaron was wrong. They didn't need more enemies or more plots. Especially since Tempest could collapse again at any time. "Still, I think it's most likely it was Hecate. If she pops in again, we can ask. If she says it wasn't her, then we can worry about it. Otherwise, we're just stressing for nothing."

Aaron considered him for a moment, then slowly nodded. "True. Okay, then you four get out of here. I need to get us to the first set of coordinates, and I can't calculate if you're all buzzing in my ears."

"Don't forget you were the one who asked us to meet here," Kara pointed out as she rose to her feet and stretched.

"I didn't. But now I'm kicking you out," he told her, flashing her a grin. "Although if just one of you wants to stay—one of you ladies, anyway—then you're more than welcome. Or just kick Seth out. Either way works for me."

Seth rolled his eyes as he stood. "You're not as charming as you think you are."

"Yes, I am," Aaron said with absolute confidence as they filed out of the wheelhouse.

Hours later, when the sun had begun to sink beneath the horizon, Seth wandered back into the wheelhouse, relieved to see that only Aaron was there. He wanted to have a talk with the tiger, but also wanted to avoid any drama.

"You got a minute?"

Aaron glanced back and nodded. "Sure. We're still a few minutes out from the first set of coordinates, so mostly I'm just watching for any other sea monsters."

Seth grimaced and looked at Aaron's leg. "You feeling okay? Looks like you're standing all right."

"Yeah. Whatever you did seemed to do the trick. Your first time healing, right?"

"Right, though it wasn't really me."

"Handy, having a goddess wanting to help you. Any idea why she wants to help you?"

"No clue. Maybe she was fond of Lemuria back in the day. Whatever the reason, I'm not going to question it too much. And right now, I'm more curious about why you want to help us."

Aaron's lips twitched. "Suspicious of me, are you?"

"Considering we've been rivals since the day we met? Yeah, just a little," Seth drawled, his voice flat.

Aaron chuckled and shrugged. "Not my fault we end up going after the same things."

"Maybe not, but it is your fault when you try to kill me."

A low growl trickled out of Aaron's mouth. "Are you still on about that? Look, I knew you were friends with Kara. I knew you'd be able to get out. I just didn't want you following me. That headpiece was mine, fair and...okay, maybe not *fair*, but it was mine. Possession is nine-tenths, blah, blah, blah."

"Fine, whatever. But it doesn't explain why you're helping us now. You've never helped me before. Hell, I've never heard of you helping anyone but yourself. And I need to know what your motivation is so I know how close I need to stick to the women."

Aaron turned from the helm and got up in Seth's face before he could blink. "Let's get one thing clear, Seth," he said in a low voice. "I may be selfish and greedy, but I don't hurt children, and I don't hurt women unless they give me a damn good reason to. So far, none of the women below deck have given me a reason, and I don't see them ever doing anything horrible enough to be considered just cause. The worst they have to worry about from me is me hitting on them. Are we clear?"

Not the least bit intimidated, Seth nodded once, slowly. "We are, but you still didn't answer my question. Why are you doing this? Why spend the money to stock this boat? Why take time out of your schedule of plundering tombs and temples to go on what could be a wild goose chase?"

The tiger's mood changed abruptly when he stepped back and laughed. "I didn't think I was that complicated. Okay, it started off with two reasons. One, it's not every day you have a freaking goddess asking you to help someone. It's kind of a hard thing to turn down. I don't particularly want to be pissing off any of the gods, you know?"

That was a good point, so Seth nodded and said, "Fair."

"Of course it is. Second, Lemuria was mentioned. Now, it may not be as well known as Atlantis, but it'd still be the biggest archaeological find of the millennia if it does actually exist. You think I'm going to just sit back and bat around a ball of yarn after that gets dropped on me?"

Seth sighed. "Also a good point. Though you know that you can't actually report its existence, right?"

"Unfortunately, yes, though I didn't when I agreed to help. And while the first reason is still valid, there's are two bigger ones driving me now."

"Oh?"

"Mmhmm. Something attacked us. Something that was sent to kill us. You know me. I can be vindictive as hell, Seth. I'm not going to let that go. I'm also stubborn, and when someone tells me not to do something..."

Now Seth smirked. "You can't help but do it, even if it kills you."

"Oh yeah. Plus, I'm not going to let those three women down." Aaron turned serious again, though it wasn't the anger of earlier, just a knowledge of exactly what they were facing. "I can't say I know Aelia well, but I like her. And I've come to like Tempest and Kara, too. I'll be damned if I let whoever's orchestrating this whole thing just off her." He grinned broadly. "Even if it means working with your scrawny ass."

Seth rolled his eyes. "Yeah, yeah. Fine, we'll work together. But Aaron...don't screw this up. I'll trust you with their safety, but if you betray that, then no god in the world is going to stop me from killing you."

"Seth, if I thought any different, I wouldn't have the amount of respect for you that I do," Aaron said without a trace of humor. "You should go get Tempest. We're coming up on the first coordinates."

They all gathered on the deck of the boat, even Aaron. Seeing an elemental turn into their element was a rare sight for anyone who wasn't an elemental themselves, and they were all curious to know if she'd be able to see Lemuria yet. But with four sets of eyes watching her with anticipation, Tempest found herself uncharacteristically self-conscious.

"Don't get your hopes up," she warned them. "I might not be able to see anything yet. We're not really all that far from where we began."

"Maybe not, but none of us know exactly how far Lemuria was from Hawaii, or any other landmass, for that matter," Aaron pointed out. "The map was good, but it wasn't perfect."

Tempest nodded and turned her back to them. Becoming a breeze was as instinctual for her as breathing, but there was pressure now. Not only were they depending upon her to find Lemuria, but she could feel the curse trying to sap her power. She was a little concerned that it would trigger due to her doing this, but it couldn't be helped. They couldn't just sit on the boat and hope they ran across Lemuria. She just really hoped the curse left her alone while she was in her air form, especially since she didn't know how it would affect her.

Before she could question how safe or useful this would be, and get herself worked up any further, she transformed. To the others, she knew it looked like she had simply disappeared, but to her it still felt like she had form. No, she wasn't solid anymore, but she could move and interact with things. It was just different than when she was in her physical body. She turned and saw the almost awed looks on everyone's faces—with the exception of Aelia, who had no doubt seen it before. Sighing silently, she shot up into the air, faster than her other form could ever have tolerated, the boat growing smaller and smaller below her. After a minute, it was hardly a speck on the water. Any higher and she'd be getting dangerously far from the Earth. There wasn't any risk of her losing control of this form, and she didn't have all the same needs in this state, such as breathing, but elementals had died from rising too high. There came a point where even their magic couldn't hold the particles of air together.

Her eyes scanned the horizon as she turned in a slow circle. Though her eyesight likely wasn't as good as Seth's or some of the other shifters, she was still certain she'd be able to tell if there was something out of place. Unfortunately, all she saw, even from this height, were water and clouds. As best as she could tell, they weren't anywhere close to land.

Disappointed, she began to sink back down toward the boat. The odds of them finding what remained of Lemuria so quickly had been slim, but she had hoped. Oh, she had hoped. But their luck had been far from stellar, so this was simply no more than expected, really.

The others were speaking quietly when she reached them, so she didn't turn back into her solid form immediately.

"Do you think we're anywhere close to Lemuria?" Aaron asked Aelia.

"I honestly don't know," she answered with a shake of her head. "I hope so, but even if we were above where Lemuria used to be, that doesn't mean we're close to what remains of it. We could honestly be searching for months."

"I sure as hell hope we're not," Kara said grimly. "We've been lucky so far. The more attacks we have to deal with, the higher the chances at least one of us ends up dead."

"We'll find it," Seth said with enough confidence to make Tempest want to smile. "Even if there are gods fighting against us, which is likely considering the cetus, there's at least one on our side, and I have a feeling she'll do whatever she can to make sure we find it."

"I hope you're right," Aaron said, searching the skies for signs of Tempest.

While she was tempted to remain in her elemental form for a little longer, her luck had run out.

Though she didn't currently have a physical body and normally couldn't feel pain, a jolt of it ran through her, shocking her back to her human form.

The moment she stood on the deck, her knees buckled. It happened so abruptly and without the others realizing she was there, that she hit the deck before they could react.

She heard her name cried by several voices, felt someone gather her in their arms, but tuned it out to take stock of her body. As soon as she'd reformed, the pain had dissipated. Lifting a hand, fingers slightly trembling, to her cheek, she was surprised not to feel moisture there. Lifting her head, she gave Seth—because of course he was the one holding her—a curious look.

"What is it? Did you see something?" he asked, brushing her hair back from her face.

Slowly, in case it brought more pain, she shook her head. "No...I just saw the ocean."

"Then what's wrong?" Kara asked, and Tempest turned to see the halfling was only a foot away, watching her with a concerned look.

"I'm...not sure," she admitted as she settled more firmly against Seth, savoring the way he was holding her. Like she mattered. "I got back down here, but before I could change back, this...I don't know. It felt like someone was dragging a knife all over my body. It jolted me back to my physical form. But it doesn't hurt now," she explained, brow furrowing.

"Does anything else feel off?" Aelia asked. "I know I don't see any blood, but do you feel...normal?"

Tempest took another minute to focus inward and finally nodded. "I do."

"And how do your powers feel?"

Her chest chilled a little and she lifted a hand, intending to stir the air gently about them, but no one's hair so much as shifted, not even a strand. "Oh gods," she breathed when she realized she couldn't perform even the simplest of magic. "It's gone."

Aelia's lips firmed and she inhaled deeply. "If I had to guess...I'd say the curse tried to hit you, but without blood to affect, it did the only thing it could and drained your magic." At the look of horror that appeared on Tempest's face, she rushed to add, "Your powers should recharge with rest and food, but if you don't feel better in the morning, we'll see if we can fix that."

"Thank you." It was all she could say. Her mind wouldn't work. It just kept replaying three words—drained your magic. She wished her gods were here. She'd pray to each and every one of them to rid her of this feeling of...emptiness.

Aelia gave her a faint, understanding smile. "Of course."

Though he'd been quiet to this point, Aaron cleared his throat and took a step back. "I'll set the next coordinates."

Kara gave Tempest's hand a warm squeeze before she pushed to her feet. "I'll go with you," she said as she followed him.

Aelia glanced between Seth and Tempest before falling into step behind Kara. "Me too."

Neither Seth nor Tempest said anything until their footsteps had faded. "I feel like every time we move forward we get shoved back," she began quietly as she rested her head on his shoulder.

"I know. And I know you were hoping you'd see Lemuria when you went up there."

"I was."

"We're going to get there," he told her, tightening his hold on her. When she let out a shuddering breath and relaxed against him, he began to run a hand up and down her back. It wasn't his MO. It wasn't anywhere close. This was too close to forming a relationship, but he was too drawn to her not to comfort her. "You've been strong for so long, Tempest. Let go for a minute. We'll figure this out." He cocked his head and his lips curved. "You said that Lemurians were only Lemurians because they were born there, right? It wasn't just the blood that mattered?"

"Yes, that's right," Tempest murmured against his shoulder. "Why?"

"Two things just occurred to me. First, you said a bunch of types of supernaturals came from there. Like shifters, right?"

Not sure where he was going, she nodded cautiously. "Right."

"So they technically have Lemurian blood then, right? The only reason they're not Lemurian is because they were born elsewhere?"

Again, she nodded. "Right..."

"Well, doesn't that mean that, once we find Lemuria, if some of those supernaturals had children on Lemuria, that those children would be Lemurians?"

Seconds ticked past as those words began to sink in. The cold feeling she'd experienced at the lack of power was replaced by a blossoming warmth. "I think they would," she breathed. "Yes, I do think they'd be Lemurian. They might not have the culture, the history, but they could learn. They could create new history." Her lips curved in a smile that made his breath catch. "Thank you, Seth," she said before her lips were on his.

Her arms wound around him as she kissed him with joy as well as passion. Sure, it was currently a long shot, but it was still more than she'd had a few minutes before. And he'd given that to her. He'd given her hope that Lemuria wouldn't die with her.

Though Seth would have loved to keep kissing her, and his body was definitely on board with it, he drew back after only a minute. "That wasn't the only thing," he told her, unable to keep from kissing her lightly.

"What? Oh. What else?"

The dazed look in her eyes and huskiness of her voice made him grin. "It's related, actually. Lemurians have a connection to the land itself, right? That's why they have to be born on Lemuria?"

She drew back enough to see his face, her own filled with curiosity now. "Yes."

"How strong is this connection?"

"I'm not sure what you mean."

"Do you feel drawn to it? Or can you sense it or something?"

Her brows furrowed and she got a look of intense concentration on her face. After a moment, she closed her eyes and slowed her breathing. For a minute, neither spoke, but slowly her lips curved. "Yes," she whispered, her eyes opening. "It's faint, just like a humming in my blood, but I can." The smile dimmed. "But I can't tell where it is."

Seth shook his head. "That's okay. Just focus on that feeling. If it gets stronger…"

"We'll be getting closer," she finished, brightening again. "It won't really lead us to it, but maybe we can tell if we're getting closer."

"Exactly."

"Seth…That's brilliant. Thank you." Then, apparently deciding the conversation was done, she cupped the back of his head and drew him down for a kiss so intense he groaned. His arms tightened around her and he deepened the kiss, continuing until she trembled against him.

Seth didn't want to stop. He wanted to keep going until she was panting and sated, but he was acutely aware that they were still on the deck where anyone could see. He'd be surprised if Kara's nose wasn't glued to the window at this very moment, in fact. Still, he kissed her for a little longer before drawing back with a last brush of his lips over hers. "I should be brilliant more often," he murmured and made her laugh.

"Maybe you should. You're good at it. Let's eat. That flight made me…hungry," she said, but the look in her eyes and the way her hand slid down to give his butt a squeeze made it sound like she wasn't only hungry for food.

In the end, after they'd eaten dinner, they went back to his cabin and fed their other hunger.

CHAPTER 21

The next week passed slowly for the five of them. While there weren't any other attacks, the curse threatened to take Tempest out eight times. The first four times, Seth paid close attention while Aelia handled the counter-curse. The next three times, both Seth and Aelia worked to save Tempest, though he had to admit it felt weird doing magic, even if it wasn't the innate magic people like Kara and Tempest had. He was happy that he'd learned, though, when Tempest had begun bleeding while they were tucked away in her cabin. Aelia wasn't far away, but him being able to do the chant saved everyone some awkwardness.

But despite no one seeing any signs of those wishing Lemuria to disappear once more, they also didn't see any sign of Lemuria. Tempest was only able to transform and get a bird's-eye view twice, as the curse kept draining her. Not that it seemed to matter, not when she never saw anything more interesting than a pod of whales. While she took a brief bit of joy in the sight, it didn't quite counteract the feel of disappointment she felt every time she returned to the boat without any good news.

Still, the time wasn't completely wasted. She was able to learn more about the people who had become her allies. People who were quickly becoming her friends. Or, in Seth's case, becoming more.

Kara, she'd learned, was big on presenting a brash, even rude exterior, but she was actually a very loyal, caring person. And funny, though it was usually an odd sort of humor. Tempest liked it.

Aaron, despite Seth's misgivings, was actually a good guy, at least in her opinion. He was extremely flirty, yes, and loved to harass Seth, but it seemed more like a light, professional rivalry rather than anything malicious. Better, he was extremely smart, though his carefree attitude made it hard to see that without spending a great deal of time with him. He was also exceptionally driven. It didn't surprise her that he'd become so successful in his chosen career, even if Seth did deem some of his methods as 'shady'.

Aelia was the biggest mystery of them all, though she was outwardly the most friendly of their group. She smiled and joined in when the others hung out, but Tempest knew that she was hiding more than just how a human had lived for six thousand years. But that great age was a great asset to them. She was a historian, yes, but mostly because she'd *lived* it, not just read about it or studied it. She *was* history, so knew it more intimately than even the most devout researcher. But that history had made her sad, something she couldn't keep out of her eyes. Even when she was smiling, sorrow lived deep inside her.

And Seth…Tempest thought often about Seth. She'd agreed to his condition of their relationship being casual, temporary, but she was starting to want more. The more time she spent with him, the more she *liked* him. He wasn't perfect, no, but none of them were. He was a contradiction in a lot of ways, though. Ways that only made him more interesting. He was kind and generous, but not afraid of a fight or going against the odds. Largely powerless, he was still more than able to take care of himself in a world full of magic. And when they were in bed together, despite him claiming that it was just sex, he made her feel wanted, made her feel special. Never before had a man caused her to feel quite that way, and it made her heart yearn to see how much more she could get.

But it boiled down to Tempest liking them all. Even with the different personalities, they all shared one thing in common; they needed a break. Which is how they ended up sitting around a table playing poker one night. There had been gambling and games of chance and skill in Lemuria, yes, but they hadn't used cards, so the first half hour was spent teaching Tempest about the game. They used chips in place of money, which she appreciated given that she had no money, modern or otherwise. Aaron also made a cheat sheet for her, so she knew the rankings of cards and hands.

After a couple of hands were played open so she could get the hang of it, they started playing for real, though Tempest knew they were all going easy on her. While sweet in a way, she also found it a little annoying. She was smart and had her cheat sheet, after all. More, she'd spent a week in close quarters with these people. She'd learned enough about them to start spotting what Kara had called tells. A smile threatened to curve her lips upward, but she hid it. They could go easy on her, but she wasn't going to return the favor.

"If these chips aren't taking the place of money like they normally would, then what is their purpose?" she asked between hands as she held up a black chip with 100 printed on it.

Seth shrugged and shuffled the deck. "Nothing really. It's just a way of keeping the game as close to normal as possible."

Aaron grinned. "I guess whoever has the most when we're done can have bragging rights." He looked around at the others, a sly glint in his eyes. "Or we could make it more interesting."

Immediately suspicious, Kara asked, "Interesting how?"

Without hesitation, he answered, "We could play strip poker."

"No," was the answer from everyone but Tempest, who had no idea what exactly the game was. She had guesses, but couldn't know for sure.

"Party poopers," Aaron muttered. "Okay, then how about the winner could get a prize?"

"What sort of prize?" Aelia asked, just as wary of his intentions as Kara.

Aaron thought about that for a moment, but Tempest could tell he already had something in mind. "They could choose. Anything they want from us. A favor, basically."

"Nuh uh," Kara said instantly. "I'm not giving an unknown favor, especially not to you. You're too tricksy."

"Maybe if we agreed it can't be anything too out there? Nothing illegal or immoral?" Seth mused aloud.

Aaron threw his hands up in exasperation. "That takes all the fun out of it!" he complained.

Kara smirked. "That's the only way we're going to agree to those terms, kitty cat."

"I have to agree with them," Aelia said with a nod. "If it's too much, we can veto the favor, and the winner has to choose a new one."

"I agree with them, too," Tempest chimed in, smiling inwardly. She didn't know if she would win once they realized she was going to play as dirty as she could, but it could be interesting to get that favor.

Aaron pouted at them for a moment before his normal humor broke through and he grinned. "Fine, fine. I agree. Now deal the cards, Seth. We don't have all day."

Seth glared at him for a moment but began dealing. "Five-card draw, deuces wild."

Tempest picked up her cards and fought not to laugh after she had consulted her cheat sheet. She'd been dealt four bright red diamonds. If she could get lucky enough to draw one more, she'd have this.

They went around the table, making their bets while Tempest watched them closely from beneath her lashes. Aelia tugged lightly at her earlobe, which meant that she wasn't happy with her cards. Kara reached for her drink after a single glance, which she'd done every time she was excited about what she held. Aaron was harder to figure out, so Tempest had no idea what he held. Seth was almost as unreadable, despite the fact that she was sleeping with him. Still, she was fairly confident that she could win. She *wanted* to win. As a child she'd been competitive, and that hadn't changed when she'd grown older.

She called the bet and paid close attention to the others as the next round passed. To her delight she received the last diamond she was hoping for, but when Aaron laid down a full house, she blew out a breath in disappointment. The bet had managed one thing, however; she was now thoroughly distracted and invested in the outcome of this game.

Aaron occasionally left to check their heading. He'd had the autopilot magically altered so it was more reliable and useful than the mundane kind, but he wanted to be certain they were still on course. Something she could understand. But they played for almost two hours, and Tempest was surprised at how much she learned about her companions simply by how they played cards. It eased the sting of the hands she lost, usually to Aaron and Seth, but Aelia and Kara won their fair share as well.

By the time they called it quits, Aaron was winning by a margin of only five dollars. He grinned mischievously. "I think that means I win," he said, rubbing his hands together while he waggled his brows comically.

"Not so fast there, pussy cat," Kara drawled with an equally wicked smile on her lips. "I forgot that Tempest spotted me ten bucks half an hour ago," she said as she tossed a chip at Tempest's pile.

Tempest frowned lightly, sure she'd done no such thing, but she caught Kara's wink and caught on. "That's right," she agreed with a grin. "You were checking to make sure we were still on course."

Aaron eyed them skeptically, but one corner of his mouth twitched in amusement. "Is that so? Aelia, did you see it?"

Without hesitation, Aelia nodded. "Yep. Ten bucks. Guess that makes Tempest the winner, doesn't it?"

Seth was fighting against laughter as he nodded. "It does. We owe her a favor."

Tempest blinked at them. She'd only been trying to win. Ideas for what she'd ask for her favor hadn't even crossed her mind. "Um...do I have to decide now? I can't think of anything at the moment."

"Don't see why not. You've got time." Seth checked his watch and stood. "I think I'm going to head to bed, though."

She quickly stood as well. "That sounds like a great—" Words were cut off as a powerful jolt of magic surged through her body, simultaneously filling her with energy and leaving her feeling almost sated. Her eyes widened and she stumbled, arm flailing until her hand smacked against the wall. The rest of her body quickly followed, her knees barely supporting her. The sensation was overwhelming, and she struggled to contain it and not loose gusts of air on her friends.

All four of the others were out of their seats in seconds and at her side. They spoke over one another, concerned for her sudden and intense reaction to what they perceived as nothing. The only voice she could make out was Seth's as he scooped her into his arms and sank down to the floor, but she noticed Aelia's expression. Like Tempest, she was shocked, but she didn't show the confusion or concern the others did.

Seth stroked her hair back from her face. "Tempest? What is it, darlin'? What's wrong?" he asked, his deep voice gentle and worried.

"Lemuria," she breathed.

The others went quiet, each wearing an expression of bewilderment.

Kara frowned and knelt beside Tempest. "Lemuria? What do you mean?"

Tempest shook her head. "I'm...not sure," she admitted. "It felt—feels—like I'm home."

Aaron rushed out of the cabin and to the railing. Everyone else remained silent, their eyes fixed on him as he searched for signs of land. When he returned, he was frowning. "I don't see anything, Tempest. Not even a tiny island."

"Then what would cause her to feel like she was back on Lemuria other than Lemuria itself?" Kara asked as she stood and grabbed a bottle of water for Tempest, who was still cradled in Seth's lap.

"Nothing," Tempest said with a shake of her head. "I know things have changed, but Lemuria is—was—unique."

"She's right," Aelia agreed. "Even I felt it, and I don't have a speck of magic in my body. But I've been there. Which means we're probably *above* Lemuria right now." Her words struck them all hard, but none quite so severely as Tempest.

Tempest's eyes closed, tears wetting her lashes as she curled into Seth's chest. Above Lemuria. She'd known, intellectually, that her precious home was underwater, and she'd mourned, but it hadn't truly sunk in what that meant until now. This was as close as she was going to get to her homeland. Unless Aelia was right about part of it being saved.

A hand touched her cheek, and she instantly knew it wasn't Seth. His hands were larger, stronger, rougher. This hand was small, soft, and gentle. When she opened her eyes, it was to see Aelia crouching by her, sympathy and sorrow in her eyes.

"I know you want to be sad, to rant and rave about how Lemuria's gone," Aelia said in a quiet voice intended only for Tempest's ears, though Aaron's shifter hearing likely allowed him to eavesdrop, as did Seth's proximity. When the Lemurian nodded, Aelia smiled. "It's not gone. And I don't mean the island that may still remain."

Tempest frowned as she fought to understand what Aelia meant. It didn't take her long until she matched Aelia's smile with her own. "No, it's not, is it?" she asked, a touch of wonder entering her voice.

Aaron cocked his head. "How do you figure?"

"If it was gone, actually destroyed rather than just below the waves, then I wouldn't have felt a damn thing when we crossed over it," Tempest explained. "The land is still here, just inaccessible...for the moment. It's here and it recognizes me. Remembers me."

"The land is sentient?" Kara asked, surprised.

"No, but you have to remember that my magic comes from its magic."

"So it's like a parent recognizing a long-lost child?" Seth asked.

Tempest nodded happily. "That's a good analogy, actually." She looked to Aelia and grasped the other woman's hand firmly. "It's still here. Even if the island doesn't exist, Lemuria's still here."

Aaron scratched his jaw lightly, expression thoughtful. "If that's the case, it might not be completely inaccessible. Not making any promises, mind you, but we might be able to get down there. Depends on how deep it is. Hell, we might even get extra lucky and find an air pocket somewhere down there. But," he said, raising his voice to speak over the others, "let's not worry about that just yet, okay? Let's hunt for the island first. It's easier, and the only option that's really doable with the equipment we have on board now." He looked to Tempest. "You okay now?"

Tempest turned her focus inward, then nodded. She was better than okay. She felt more powerful than she had since she first woke up in her Peruvian tomb. Definitely more powerful than she'd been feeling with the curse sapping her strength. "I am. It didn't hurt me, just...startled me."

He grinned. "I'll bet. Why don't you go get some rest? Tomorrow we'll start seriously searching for your land, okay? Since we know we're in the right area now."

"I think I will." She got to her feet, accepting Seth's help since her legs were still unsteady. Aelia and Kara each got warm hugs before she turned to Aaron and kissed his cheek. "Thank you all, again," she told them with a smile. Though she headed for her cabin without any assistance, her hand did occasionally brace against the wall to keep her upright.

Seth watched her go until Kara rubbed his back soothingly.

"I know how you tend to think about relationships," she whispered to him, too quiet for Aelia and Aaron to hear, "but I'd seriously reconsider it this time." Before he could respond, she gave his shoulder a squeeze and joined the other two.

He blew out a slow breath before following Tempest below deck. But Kara's words stuck with him even as he slipped into Tempest's cabin. He was aware that she'd figured out years before why he kept his relationships with women so casual. He was equally aware that Tempest had already passed from casual into something more. Something he didn't really want to consider at the moment. All he'd wanted was sex and to keep her safe. When had it all gotten so muddled? He hadn't even known her for a month yet. Feelings, real feelings, couldn't form this quickly. Could they?

Tempest was slipping her shoes off when he closed the door behind him and she turned, her brows lifting. "Seth? I thought you were staying with the others."

"They can handle things," he answered with a shake of his head as he stalked across the small cabin toward her.

He wasn't sure what he was going to do or say when he reached her. He wasn't exactly sure what he wanted from her, either. All he knew was he needed her.

CHAPTER 22

Tempest watched him cross the cabin, keeping her expression neutral as she studied his face, the way he moved. She wasn't quite sure what sort of mood he was in. He moved like a predator and there was heat in his eyes, certainly, but there was something more, something she couldn't quite decipher. It went deeper than lust, that much she knew without a doubt. She also had a feeling he needed to get out of his head, no matter what was putting that intensity in his gaze. That was something she could help with. Something she *needed* to help with. Intensity wasn't a bad thing, but mingled in with the rest was something...darker. Sorrow? Fear? She wasn't sure, but neither were emotions she wanted him feeling.

Grinning at him, she let her eyes roam over his body, stopping when they reached the obvious bulge in his shorts. "Are you going to let me handle things tonight?" she asked teasingly as she lifted a hand and let her fingertips graze down the front of her body, drawing his focus. "You still haven't let me play, after all. You keep getting...impatient."

He paused and considered, then pulled his shirt off and let it drop to the floor. His shorts and boxers quickly followed, and she took a moment to savor the sight of him.

She'd seen a number of men—and gods—in various states of undress. None had ever drawn her attention or desire like he did. Apparently the hiking and treasure hunting kept him fit, because he was well-muscled and the only thing soft on him were his lips. She loved running her hands over his strong muscles, feeling how they leapt beneath her fingers. His skin, from his face down to his toes, was golden and, she knew, warm. He was scarred, and though she didn't know if they were from fights or accidents, she didn't care. Each scar was simply a part of him. Without them, he might not be the man he was. And one day, if he'd let her, she wanted to kiss each and every one of them.

Her gaze dipped and she bit her lip when she saw that he was already fully erect and, judging by the tense set of his shoulders, barely holding onto his control by a thread. She wanted to make him lose that control. To have it simply shatter as he'd made her shatter every time he'd taken her to bed.

He couldn't think, couldn't dwell, if he was lost in her.

Not wanting him to break before she had her fun, she kept her clothes on as she sank to her knees in front of him. Her name was said in a warning tone, but she ignored it. She was going to make him forget whatever was weighing on his mind and replace it with pleasure.

Her hands slid up his thighs, the muscles taut beneath her fingers. They moved to grip his hips as her mouth pressed lightly against his skin then moved up his thigh. When her breath brushed against his cock, she felt him stroke her hair back from her face. Her eyes lifted to meet his, and she held his gaze as her tongue lazily circled the head of his shaft.

His breath caught and his fingers sank into her hair. Though he tried to draw her closer, urging her to take him into her mouth, she resisted. He'd enjoy it, sure, but she wanted more than to give him a quick release to his emotions. Instead, her head tilted and she trailed her lips down his length, then let her tongue retrace their path.

He said her name again, but this time it was in a husky tone filled with need.

"Patience," she murmured, wrapping her hand around his cock before she gave him a slow stroke. "I'm playing."

This time, his voice was rougher, a hint darker. "Yeah, with fire."

She just smiled and took the head between her lips, sucking on him as though she intended to do nothing more for the next hour. When he groaned and bucked lightly against her mouth, the hand on his hip tightened but she didn't draw back. She couldn't. The way he reacted to her was arousing and just what she'd hoped for. Now she just had to drive him to the brink, to make the leash he had on his emotions snap. And she wasn't going to let him come until it did.

She let go of him for a minute without taking her mouth off him, sliding her shorts down, then carefully lifting one knee at a time until she could get rid of them completely. Now she did pull free of him, but only for a moment as she drew her shirt off, leaving her as bare as he was. His eyes darkened as he watched her, but she only reached for him again, her hands gripping his ass as she leaned in once more.

Her mouth slid down, taking as much of him as she was able, causing his fingers to flex in her hair. Gradually she increased the rhythm of her lips over him until she could hear his breath coming in ragged pants. But each time it felt like he was getting close to orgasm, she pulled back and spent a minute licking and kissing him while her hands roamed his body. Then her mouth would return to him to repeat the process all over again.

It had to be maddening for him, but it wasn't much better for her. Making him react like this made her feel powerful, and like no other woman on Earth could be so desirable. Which made it was hard for her to keep teasing him instead of laying back and begging that he put them both out of their misery, but the plan hadn't changed. She was going to drive the dark from his mind. But she had vastly underestimated the effect this would have on her. Knowing what she was doing to him had heat pooling between her thighs as her body ached with the need to be touched, to be taken.

But he didn't make her wait too long.

The third time her mouth left him, he let out a low growl and dropped to one knee in front of her. The hand in her hair released so he could wrap an arm around her. The other grabbed her knee and pulled, spilling her carefully onto her back right there on the floor.

The thrill of having pushed him to this made her smile and lift her head to kiss him. Immediately, he took control of the kiss, devouring her in a way that made her shiver beneath him. It was deliciously distracting, but not so much that she missed it when he positioned himself against her, making them both moan with anticipation.

Then, in one hard thrust, he was inside her completely and drinking down her shocked cry. He always felt so good, but tonight it was *more*. Her feet pressed against the floor so she could arch up and grind her hips against him. He rewarded the action by withdrawing, then slamming back into her.

As she moaned his name, Tempest's arms lifted to embrace him, but he stopped and grabbed both her wrists, lifting them above her head and pinning them to the floor with one hand. "You got to play," he told her with a light nip to her bottom lip, just hard enough to sting. "Now it's my turn."

She tested his grip lightly and found it firm, but she didn't truly want to escape, especially when he began moving again. It wasn't slow, it wasn't gentle, but she loved it. Not only had she driven him to this, but each stroke of him into her body sent ribbons of pleasure spiraling through her body, until she was rocking up to meet each one. When his mouth found hers again, she found herself just as wild and out of control as he was.

Though her plan had been to drive him crazy so his only thought was her, the knife had cut both ways. There was nothing but him and the feel of his body against her, inside her, and that brilliant moment of joy that was quickly approaching.

His mouth tore from hers, his head dropping to her shoulder as his thrusts lost the little finesse they'd had. The last proof of his loss of control was all that she needed to tumble into her climax. Her hips shoved up to meet his and her arms strained against his grip as she was assaulted by the rush of pleasure. The only sound she made was a gasp, her mind too muddled to form a word, even his name.

Seth only managed a few more thrusts before he buried himself in her and dropped over the edge himself.

It seemed an eternity before Tempest realized he was lying on top of her, his breathing ragged in her ear. He'd also forgotten he was holding her wrists. While it didn't hurt now, it soon would. She might tell him in a minute, because she didn't want to break the peace she hoped he'd found. Then, as the endorphins began to fade, she realized she was feeling more than just her wrists. While the carpet she was lying on was soft, being rubbed against it had left her skin feeling a little raw. It had absolutely been worth it, though. His body was relaxed above hers, while hers felt as loose as air.

"Seth," she sighed, hating to disturb him, even for something necessary.

"Hmm?" he sleepily murmured, his face still buried against her neck. He nuzzled the sensitive skin and sent shivers through her.

She shifted her arms slightly in his grip. "Wrists."

There was a pause before his fingers relaxed and stroked down her arm. "I didn't hurt you, did I?" he whispered before lightly kissing her throat.

The mere thought made her laugh softly. He'd been rough, sure, but no more than she'd wanted. She doubted he could ever hurt her, no matter how uncontrolled he was. "Gods, no. I feel amazing." A languid smile curved her lips. "Though breathing isn't easy."

"Oh." His arms slid beneath her before he rolled them over so she was atop him. The movement caused him to pull out of her, and she made a low sound of protest at the empty sensation it caused. To soothe her, his hand stroked up and down her back, though she couldn't truly get anymore relaxed without falling asleep. Something she was likely to do if she stayed there for a few more minutes. She moved slightly to get more comfortable before she sighed contently.

Just before she dozed off, his hand moved to her butt and squeezed lightly. "Don't think I'm done with you yet."

Laughing softly, she tilted her head back so she could see his face. "Oh?"

"Mmhmm. Just as soon as my body is working again, we're going to take a shower."

"Okay. And?"

He brushed a kiss over her lips. "And I'm going to show you how much fun shower sex is."

Tempest nuzzled at his neck to hide her smile. Whatever had been bothering him, it certainly wasn't bothering him now. "I look forward to it," she promised.

It did take a few more minutes before either of them were able to get off the floor, but once they did, he proved as good as his word, making her come three more times in the shower. And when they fell into bed, content and exhausted, he gathered her into his arms, unafraid of doing something that seemed to hold so much meaning. Feeling her heart beating against his chest, he drifted into sleep, no longer dreading what Kara's words had implied. Rather, he had come to accept the truth.

He was falling in love with the last Lemurian.

CHAPTER 23

Even though they hadn't found Lemuria, the overall mood on the boat was improved knowing they had, at least, reached where it used to be. Knowing that it and its magic still existed in some form. They were all still on the lookout for more trouble, also knowing that it was coming, just not when, but they all smiled a little easier, laughed a little more.

With the proximity to Lemuria, Tempest's magic was back—at least temporarily. They didn't think the curse was gone—they weren't that lucky—but she wasn't drained like she had been. She took to the skies almost hourly until the continued bleeding episodes sapped her strength too much to allow her to spend any extended time in her other form. But even though she managed a dozen trips, she saw nothing but seemingly endless water. Unlike before, this didn't discourage her, at least not as much. Lemuria had been large, yes, but now they had clear boundaries to operate within. They'd discovered fairly quickly that if the boat wasn't actually over Lemuria, she'd notice almost immediately, which helped keep them on course. It also helped Aaron and Seth update their information, albeit slowly, to make their maps of the ancient world some of the most accurate out there. A fact that pleased Seth to no end. He wasn't an artist so his map wasn't the prettiest, but he'd take accuracy over beauty any day.

At night, when it was too dark to see clearly, the boat slowed to ensure they didn't miss spotting the island, since none of them had any idea how large it might be. Those times were spent planning or simply just hanging out and enjoying the time with one another.

Yet when Seth and Tempest were alone at night, their lovemaking took on a frantic edge. Their time together could be ending soon, which destroyed them both, though neither would say as much to the other. Seth because he still fought against something as simple, yet monumental, as commitment, and Tempest because she was falling harder for the man who had rescued her from everlasting slumber. And she wanted him to be with her for her, not because he felt responsible for her.

Tonight they had taken each other with an intensity that surpassed even the night of the poker game and left them boneless and weak on the foot of Tempest's bed. Despite that, it wasn't rushed or frenzied. It was almost languid but for the need that drove them both.

They were still tangled together, still recovering, when the first crack of thunder boomed so close it vibrated the boat.

They jerked upright, a startled look on Tempest's face, a concerned one on Seth's. She recovered first and smiled. "I love storms."

It didn't surprise him, not with her name, but he shook his head as he gently extracted himself from her and yanked on his pants. "I don't think you'll love them out here. Storms can sink huge ships, much less boats like this one," he warned. "You should get dressed. Aaron will probably need help if the storm is bad, and from the sound of that thunder, it might just be."

She frowned but got up and started dressing when the boat rocked violently, knocking her off her feet so her shoulder hit the wall. She hissed in a breath at the sharp pain, but just leaned against the wall as she tugged her shirt on. "Are storms like this common out here?"

"I honestly don't know. I'm not much of a sailor," he admitted. "That's why we need to get to Aaron."

With that, Tempest paused to grab the dagger Aelia had given her—the only weapon she had but for her magic. Likely they wouldn't need it, not for a storm, but she'd rather be paranoid than dead. And since her magic was currently on the fritz due to the curse, it was all she had.

Seth barely got his shirt on before he grabbed her hand with one of his, throwing the door open with the other. She didn't protest as he half dragged her up to the wheelhouse, only to find that everyone else was already there. Through the windows, they could see that it was much darker than it should have been, especially with the moon being full overhead.

"Is it bad?" Seth asked.

Kara gave him a grim look. "There wasn't anything on the radar, Seth. The storm just appeared out of nowhere, and there's no way to avoid it."

"How can we not avoid it? Can't we just circle around it?"

Aaron shook his head but focused on steering the boat. "Look behind us."

Dread settled in Seth's gut as he turned to look and saw dark storm clouds behind them as well. He stepped out onto the deck, turned his face to the sky, and his heart clenched. They were surrounded by dark, angry looking clouds. There really was no way to avoid this storm.

There was also no way this storm was natural. Not that he should be surprised. They'd had to fight for every mile they'd gained since Tempest had first awoken.

Before he could duck back inside, it started to rain. Not a gentle fall that started off slow and light then gradually worsened, but one hard enough to sting his exposed skin. He cursed as he got under cover and made sure the door was firmly closed. "Please tell me you're a hell of a good sailor, Aaron."

The tiger's mouth was a tight line, and he was worried enough that his eyes had shifted. "I'm good, but I don't know if anyone is good enough to get through this except for a water elemental or storm witch," he said as lightning flashed, eerily illuminating everyone's face. The boat was bounced around on the waves, which were growing rapidly larger by the minute. It forced everyone to find something to hold on to or risk being tossed about like a rag doll. Even Aaron had to tighten his grip on the wheel.

"This storm isn't normal," Seth informed them grimly.

Aaron nodded sharply. "I know."

"Can the boat take it?" Aelia asked. Though she stayed close to Aaron's side, she was the calmest of all of them. It surprised Seth, given she was the least hardy of them all, despite her longevity.

"Depends on who's causing the storm," Aaron answered. "If it's a witch or elemental? Probably."

"And if it's a god?" Tempest asked quietly.

"Then we'd better hope we can make it to the life raft and they don't notice something so much smaller than this boat," he said bluntly as he fought to keep the vessel on top of the water. As it was, huge waves slammed over the railing and onto the deck while thunder rattled everything, down to their bones.

Seth thought for a moment, thinking worst case scenarios. "Okay. Aelia, stick close to Aaron. Tigers are naturally good swimmers, and he's the most likely of all of us to be okay if we go into the water." Tempest started to speak up, but he held up a hand and shook his head as he went on. "Just help him if needed to get to the life boat. Kara, you and me are with Tempest. You can't drown the air, so the three of us are going to grab some emergency supplies and get the life boat ready, just in case."

Aaron glanced at Seth, but nodded. "Life boat's outside. One of those rapid inflating deals. Make sure you grab some water, life preservers, and a first aid kit. I've got the sat phone."

"Will do. Kara, grab the kit, I'll get the water." Seth turned to Tempest and hesitated.

"I'll find the preservers and raft. I'll be the safest doing it." Before he could argue—and it was clear he was about to—she slipped outside. In the few seconds the door was open, wind and rain blasted into the wheelhouse, soaking them all with freezing water. Or all of them except for Tempest, who used a curtain of air to shield her better than even the best umbrella.

"Do the best you can, Aaron," Seth said, giving the tiger's shoulder a quick squeeze.

"I will, but hurry. I don't think she's going to last much longer." His voice dropped. "I think you're right—this storm is divine."

Seth nodded. "I know." He hurried away to get the water, knowing that dehydration would kill them quicker than hunger would. But it still wasn't his greatest concern. With this storm being caused by the gods, their chances of survival had dwindled beyond slim. He wished that Hecate could help, but she'd been afraid of being caught helping them from the beginning. And a storm like this? The two most likely culprits were Zeus and Poseidon. Neither of which was a god anyone—even another god—wanted to fuck with. Their brother Hades was probably the only one who would risk it within the Greek pantheon, but he had no reason to help them. And gods from other pantheons would need a better reason than five mortals in danger to interfere with other deities.

"This would be a good time for some Lemurian gods to wake up and help their last worshiper," he muttered to himself as he found the jugs of water. There wasn't going to be much room in the raft, so he only grabbed two. They'd have to ration, but hopefully they weren't far from the island and that would be plenty. It was their only chance if the boat did go down.

He'd just picked them up when he heard a voice in his head, which almost made him drop the jugs.

"Be careful what you ask for. It won't always turn out how you expect..."

His eyes went wide. "Hecate?" he whispered. When he got no response, he went cold. Who else would be listening to him? If it was Zeus or Poseidon, they wouldn't have whispered cryptic warnings. They would have attacked. It didn't help that the voice sounded neither male nor female, which didn't help narrow the list down any.

Trying to shrug it off, Seth carried the water back to the wheelhouse, slamming into the walls as he fought not to go down every time the boat got slapped with a wave or hit the bottom of one. When he got back, Kara was already there with the first aid kit, looking more freaked out than when she'd left. "You okay?" he asked, setting one of the jugs down near the door.

"Fine. I just don't like boats much. Stone sinks, after all," she told him, and he noticed she was looking a little green.

He forced a smile. "Let's not go shifting into your stone form right now."

"Already ahead of you."

Another wave hit the boat head on, and was followed immediately by lightning striking the nose. It must have hit something extremely flammable because flames began licking over the boat, despite the insane amounts of water splashing over it.

"Time to go," Aaron said. "Get the raft ready. When I yell, get it inflated and in the water. Aelia and I will be right behind you."

Seth hesitated. It felt like leaving them in here was akin to sentencing them to death. What if Aaron got knocked out and Aelia got trapped? They'd lose them both and, as he'd told Hecate, they needed every member of their small group.

Aaron noticed the delay and turned to look at Seth. "Go!" he snarled.

Seth nodded once and picked up the water. "Let's go. Stay close," he told Kara.

The moment they were outside, Kara grabbed hold of the waistband of his pants. It was the only way to keep them together as they navigated across the deck to the back of the boat where Tempest stood. She was faring the best of all of them, using her natural grace and air magic to stay fairly steady.

"I've got the raft, but I don't know how to inflate it," she yelled to them, using her magic to amplify her voice so it carried. "I couldn't find the preservers, though." She paused. "I grabbed the dagger. Before we left the cabin."

Seth thought the dagger would be useless if they didn't survive the storm, but didn't voice that aloud. He also didn't answer her until they were closer, knowing his voice would be lost in the wind. "We'll manage without the life preservers, but I know how to inflate the raft. We're going soon. The boat's on fire," he shouted as he passed the jugs to her, then got the raft close to the edge with the rip cord on the side nearest him.

She paled at the news, but nodded and took the water.

A loud crack sounded that Seth mistook for thunder at first, but a second crack carried over the thunder and he glanced toward the front of the boat. Boards were broken and splintered, like someone had tried to fold the boat in half but hadn't quite managed it. "Shit. We gotta go now. C'mon Aaron," he muttered as he watched for signs of the tiger and historian.

Seconds passed but felt like eons before he finally saw Aaron emerge, carrying Aelia over his shoulder in a fireman's carry.

"Go! Get it in the water!" Aaron yelled, running toward them.

Seth didn't pause, just yanked the rip cord and tossed the boat in the water, keeping hold of the line so it didn't go too far. It inflated rapidly and he yanked at Kara. "Get in! Tempest, can you help her?"

The elemental nodded and used the air to steady the raft and help direct Kara as she leapt over the side of the boat toward the raft. It was difficult with the storm raging around them, but Kara avoided landing in the water.

He reached for Tempest but she shook her head. "I'll go last. To keep the raft close and help get everyone on," she argued before she gave him a magical shove.

She was the only one who could guarantee getting into the raft by herself, so he nodded and jumped after Kara. Seth didn't like it, but it made sense. He landed half on top of Kara and quickly scrambled off so he could look at the boat. He couldn't see any of them and felt a rush of panic, a moment before a flailing Aelia came sailing over the edge like she'd just been tossed. Seth managed to catch her, but it was clumsy and it was likely she'd end up with a few bruises. With only Aaron and Tempest left, Seth urged the two women against the side, making room for the tiger. Aaron landed the cleanest of all of them before four sets of eyes looked back to the rapidly burning boat for Tempest.

"Tempest!" Seth yelled, fighting the urge to climb back onto the boat for her when she spoke from beside him.

"I'm here."

He turned and grabbed her in an embrace hard enough to make her ribs ache, relieved she was there, if not quite safe. "I couldn't see you."

"I transformed. It was easiest," she told him as she hugged him back. "I'm safe."

"None of us are safe yet," Aaron said grimly, watching as the waves carried them further from the boat. "Just make sure to hold on. This is going to be a long night."

CHAPTER 24

For hours, the storm tossed them about in the life raft. It was difficult to keep them all inside the raft, even with the strength Kara and Aaron had. And despite all five of them working together, they still failed to keep everyone safe throughout the night.

A large wave crashed down over them, shoving them all to one side of the raft. After, as they coughed up water, they realized that, despite their best efforts, Aelia was no longer with them.

Aaron jumped to his feet, only to be knocked on his ass as the raft was rocked about. "Aelia!" he roared as he searched the dark, choppy water for some sign of the petite woman. When no blonde hair bobbed to the surface, he dove in after her before anyone realized what he was doing.

"Aaron! Dammit!" Seth cursed as he stared at the spot Aaron had disappeared. His whole body itched to go in after him, but knew that the chances of finding either of them were slim. The water was too rough and even his eyes couldn't see more than a few inches below the surface. He'd only be creating a third victim. "Tempest, can you help?" he asked, and a glance toward her showed that she was pale, her eyes wide with shock.

"I can try," Tempest said, her soft voice almost lost in a loud crack of thunder. She leaned against Seth for balance and stretched her arms out. She sent her magic into the water, joining tiny bubbles of air together and using them to search the deadly ocean. Precious seconds passed without any sign of either Aaron or Aelia, until one of the larger bubbles brushed against something solid. Not wanting to get her hopes up, she gathered more bubbles and surrounded the form until it was fully encased in air, thirty feet below the surface. Carefully, she drew it upward until the bubble popped upon contact with the open air.

Kara's soft cry had Tempest's eyes flying open, just before she sagged with relief. It was Aaron, holding Aelia tight to his body. They were pushed beneath the water once more and she reached out again, pulling them into the raft. But her relief was short-lived. While Aaron looked fine other than being water-logged and so angry his eyes had shifted, Aelia lay limp across his lap, her eyes open but empty of life.

"She took in too much water. She's not breathing," Aaron snarled as he pushed the others back and repositioned her so he could start doing CPR.

Tempest, Kara, and Seth watched helplessly as Aaron fought to breathe life back into the tiny woman. Seth had known Aaron liked Aelia, but he was fighting like a madman to revive her. Seth could only pray that he was successful. Not just for Aelia's sake, but at this point, Seth had no clue how Aaron would react if Aelia didn't wake up.

"We can't lose her," Kara whispered. "I mean, we've only known her for a little while, but we can't lose her."

"I know," Seth agreed, wrapping an arm around her shoulders. It was as much to comfort as it was to ensure she didn't tumble out of the boat, too. She leaned into him, but her other hand was tightly gripping the rope around the raft.

"Aaron…" Tempest began after several minutes with no change, but Aaron just growled at her and continued doing what he could for Aelia.

Seth started to speak up when there was a small noise from Aelia, almost missed in the sounds of the storm. He stopped and watched her closely. Even Aaron paused. A moment later the sound came again, louder, then Aelia started to cough, vomiting up the water she'd inhaled. Aaron quickly turned her on her side, helping her clear her lungs, but he wasn't letting her go.

Tempest slumped with relief and turned to Seth, her arms wrapping around his waist. "Thank the gods," she whispered.

He slid an arm around her and nodded as he watched Aelia try to sit up. "I agree," he murmured. In a louder voice, he called, "Welcome back, Aelia," which earned him a weak smile from the woman.

Aaron gathered Aelia close, practically wrapping his body around hers, and ducked low in the raft. His gaze met Seth's, his blue eyes hard and filled with both fear and anger.

Seth glanced down to Tempest and understood completely. But at the moment, all they could do was try to ride out the storm.

It was another hour until the storm began to ease up. By that time, they were all soaked, exhausted, and sore from being battered around and fighting to stay on the raft. As the sea calmed, Aelia reached for a jug of water, taking several long swallows.

"There's something you should know," she said, not looking at any of them, her voice scratchy from all the water she'd inhaled.

"It can wait," Aaron argued, still holding her close. "You nearly died."

She shook her head, the motion slow and hesitant. "No, I didn't." Her gaze flicked up and met Aaron's. "I *did* die."

"I imagine it would feel like that..." Kara said after a moment of silence.

Aelia sighed and rested her head on Aaron's shoulder. "No, it isn't feeling like dying. It isn't coming to the brink and being resuscitated. I mean I was literally dead."

"Did someone on the other side send you back?" Seth asked. It wasn't something that happened often, but it did happen occasionally. One of the gods would take pity on a soul, or decide they were needed on Earth, and send them back to their bodies.

"No," Aelia said yet again. "I die and I revive It's happened...hundreds of times. Possibly thousands at this point. I stopped counting centuries ago. Drowning, murder, and countless other ways," she told them in a voice that was barely audible. "It's how I'm a human who's older than most of the Arcane. I literally can't stay dead."

Kara frowned and glanced at the others, but saw no more understanding on their faces than she felt. "I don't understand. How?"

The smile that touched Aelia's lips was bitter and feeble. "Doesn't matter, and I won't tell you. But given what we're up against, and given that I've come to trust you all, I decided you should know that I literally can't die."

Aaron's lips brushed against her hair, his expression pained. "While I'd love to know the how, I'm just grateful that we're not going to lose you like that."

Seth had a feeling Aaron had actually meant that *he* wasn't going to lose Aelia. It was a new side to the tiger, one that surprised him. Yet he doubted it would soften any of Aaron's rough edges. If anything, he was going to get more feral, despite Aelia's true immortality. Something that was beyond rare. Even gods could be killed. It could be that Aelia was literally the only being who couldn't die.

With the now gentle rocking of the boat and their exhaustion, sleep began to claim them, one by one. Yet they all slept fitfully, even as the skies cleared and the sun began to rise.

It was nearly noon when Seth began to stir. At first he was disoriented. Tempest lay against him, which had become normal, as had the rocking of the boat on the water, but it wasn't this bright in his cabin. It wasn't until he started to sit up and his bruised body protested that he recalled the previous night. Being tossed around, Aelia drowning, her confession. The memory made him sit up abruptly, which caused him to bite back a whimper of pain. But he had to see. He had to make sure everyone was all right.

A quick glance showed that all four of his companions were still in the raft, all of them still asleep. It didn't fully relieve his concerns, and it wasn't until he made sure all four were still breathing that he relaxed. The three women slept through his gentle touches to their pulse points, but Aaron awoke with a low snarl, his arms tightening around Aelia. Upon spotting Seth, he relaxed a little and looked around.

"Everyone okay?" he asked in a low, scratchy voice.

Seth nodded. "Everyone's alive. But they'll probably all feel like shit when they wake up," he replied quietly. After the night they'd had, he wanted the women to sleep as long as they could. At least until there was something to do. And since he still saw no sign of land, they had nothing but time.

Aaron moved testingly before he grimaced. "I see what you mean." He carefully extricated himself from Aelia and grabbed one of the jugs of water, pleased to see one, at least, hadn't been thrown free of the boat. Though he wanted nothing more than to chug the entire bottle, he took only a few sips before he passed it to Seth, who did the same. "How long have you been awake?"

"Only a few minutes," Seth answered as he closed the water and set it aside. "Just long enough to make sure everyone was alive and see that we're still in the middle of nowhere."

Aaron grimaced and reached for his pocket before cursing. "The sat phone's gone. Must have fallen out of my pocket when I jumped in after Aelia."

Seth echoed his curse. "Do you remember how far we were from any known land?"

The grim look on Aaron's face made Seth go cold. "If we were still on the boat? Three, maybe four days. In this thing?" He shook his head. "We have to hope we're close to the island. If we're not..."

The problem was, even if they were close to the island and found it, what then? They couldn't get back to the mainland, or even Hawaii. It was unlikely the raft could make it, and it was their only means of transportation.

"I hate to say it, but I think we need to wake Tempest up," Aaron said quietly.

Seth's first reaction was to argue, but he saw the logic in the tiger's words and nodded. "Let the other two sleep a little longer, though," he said as he carefully stretched out beside Tempest and shook her shoulder gently. "Tempest? Wake up, darlin'."

It took her a minute, but her eyes slowly opened. "Seth?" she asked, her voice raspy.

"Yeah, it's me. Don't move too fast. You're probably going to be sore," he warned her as he grabbed the water and helped her sit up and take a few swallows. Even after he moved the jug away, he kept a hand on her lower back, wanting the contact to reassure himself that she was okay.

"I am," she agreed as she sat up fully, her movements slow. Unlike Seth and Aaron, she woke more quickly and frowned as she looked around. "No sign of land?"

Seth shook his head. "Not yet. Does it still feel like we're over Lemuria?"

There was no hesitation before Tempest nodded. "We are."

"Tempest...I know you probably just want to rest," Aaron began, "but we're in a bad situation here..."

"You want me to go up and see if I can spot anything from above," she finished. When he nodded, she sighed. "We're that far from known land, then?"

"We are."

Except she wasn't positive she could transform. Being over Lemuria helped counteract the power-draining aspect of the curse, but it didn't eliminate it. And she had used her powers several times during the night to keep them all alive. Still, she had to try. "Okay. I'll be back as soon as I can."

Seth's arm fell away as her body disappeared, but she brushed an intangible hand over his cheek. She knew it felt like nothing more than a light breeze against his skin, but he smiled nonetheless. Keeping that image in mind, she shot upward. Her power could drain at any point so she didn't have any time to waste.

The raft and those within it grew smaller and smaller as she joined the clouds high above them. Only then did she stop and slowly turn, though that was really the wrong word for it. With no physical form, it was more just a shifting of her focus. But no matter which direction she looked, she couldn't see even the smallest hint of land. Part of her wanted to go searching and see if she could find the island, but it would be too easy to get lost and not be able to find Seth and the others. Reluctantly, she sank back down to the raft, though at a much slower pace than she'd ascended.

When she got closer, she saw that Kara was awake, but Aelia still slept on, with Aaron keeping close to her. Not that there was much room to really wander in the raft. Tempest had to be careful where she reformed, so she didn't land on someone. All eyes turned to her, each pair holding hope, though that emotion dimmed with a single look at her face.

"Nothing?" Kara asked.

Tempest shook her head. "No land, and nothing to indicate that we're close to it. No birds, no floating greenery, nothing."

Aaron cursed softly and stared out at the water, his eyes cold and hard, but Tempest could see his mind was working.

"How long can we survive with the water we have?" Kara asked, frowning at the jug.

"A few days," Seth answered grimly. "Five people and one jug of water just isn't going to last too long." And, as a general rule, a person could only survive for three days without water.

For several minutes, they said nothing, only worried about what was to come. Or what they feared wouldn't come.

It was then that Aelia woke. Unlike the others, she didn't wake groggy, but she did seem to be weaker than any of them. Seth idly wondered if it was because she was the only pure human, because of all the water she'd inhaled, or if it was because she'd died.

She started to sit up with a low moan, which is what alerted Aaron that she was awake. Instantly, he scooped her up and into his lap, helping her to lean against his chest. "You okay?" Aaron asked, brushing her hair away from her face.

"Hurts," she whispered.

"I know. We were thrown around a lot last night," he said, voice so gentle that Seth did a double take.

Aelia shook her head slowly. "Not that. Drowning always hurts."

Aaron's face went hard again, and Seth saw that the tiger went rigid, even though he continued to hold Aelia gently.

"Well," Tempest began, "it sounds to me like we just need to cover as much distance as we can in the next few days. Gives us a greater chance to find the island. I can help with that."

"What?" Kara asked, surprised.

"You can?" Seth added over her.

"As long as I have access to my magic, yes," Tempest confirmed.

"Do it," Aaron added only a moment later.

Aelia only smiled faintly. She was beyond being surprised at anything Lemurians could do. Of course, she was the only one of them, aside from Tempest herself, who had actually seen any in action aside from the elemental.

Tempest looked around before she frowned. "Anyone have an idea which way we should start?"

"That way," Aaron said, pointing. "We were headed southwest when the storm hit, so we may as well keep going that way."

She nodded and shifted around until she was seated on the northeast side of the raft. "You might want to hold on," she warned them before holding a hand over the side of the raft so it hovered above the water. A blast of air had the raft lurching forward, then speeding across the water. It wasn't as smooth a ride as it had been when they were in Aaron's boat, unfortunately. Now they bounced roughly along the waves, but they were moving almost as fast.

"How long can you keep that up?" Seth called to her.

Tempest shrugged a shoulder. "At this speed, and if the curse leaves me be? Not sure. I'll have to take breaks, but it's still better than just letting the current move us."

He scowled. "Don't overdo it, Tempest." He didn't want them to die, but the thought of her harming herself made something twist in his chest.

She shook her head. "I'll be fine."

She'd make sure of it, because she wasn't going to let any of them die. This time, she'd save those she cared about.

CHAPTER 25

Tempest ended up propelling them in twenty-minute bursts, taking thirty minutes to an hour between them. Every couple of hours she'd fly up in search of land, but by the time the sun had set, they'd found nothing.

They rationed the water, only taking a few sips each every hour or two, but with the sun baking down on them, it wasn't easy. Still, they tried to rest when possible. Aaron was propped against the edge of the raft while Aelia lay next to him, her head pillowed on his thigh. Kara was stretched out between Aelia and Seth, who had his arm around Tempest. The Lemurian had her head on Seth's shoulder, exhausted but not yet asleep. He was shocked she was still conscious, since she'd had another bleeding spell. With the dehydration, it had drained her more than the previous instances.

They stayed there as the sun began to lower toward the horizon, offering a break from its relentless heat.

"There's something you guys should know," Seth said into the silence an hour after dusk.

"About what?" Kara asked.

"Last night. When I was getting the water. I said something about how I wished the Lemurian gods were awake to help you, Tempest," he answered, looking down at her.

Tempest frowned and lifted her head. "Why would you want them awake?"

He shrugged. "You seem to think they're awesome, and you're the last Lemurian alive. It made sense to me that they'd want to help you if they could." His brow furrowed. "Were they not the helpful sort of gods?"

"Some were." She shook her head. "I don't know why it surprises me that you don't know about Lemurian gods, considering they're nothing more than a myth now."

"Very little knowledge of Lemuria survived, at least as far as I've found. And believe me, I've looked," Aelia offered. "The name, the general location, that it sank...that's about it. Everything else has been lost. Or deliberately hidden."

Tempest nodded and shifted her focus back to the others. "There were quite a few Lemurian gods. There were ten gods who...I won't say ruled over the others, but they did have more power than them. A lot of people sorted them into the ten major gods and everyone else, who were considered minor gods. But the real division wasn't in power level."

"What was the real division?" Aaron asked curiously.

"Light and dark," Aelia answered, and Tempest nodded her agreement.

"Wait, your gods were sorted by good and evil?" Kara asked, eyes wide with surprise.

"No," Tempest said, shaking her head firmly. "Light and dark aren't the same thing as good and evil. Is nighttime evil? Is daylight good? No, they just *are*. They're neutral."

Something on Tempest's face told Seth there was more to it, and he nudged her lightly with his shoulder. "What aren't you telling us?"

Tempest and Aelia exchanged a look. Aelia ended up shrugging, then giving her a nod, so Tempest sighed. "Like I said, they weren't inherently good and evil, but there was a strict balance between the gods. There were an even number of gods, and it was critical that it remain that way. Each light god had a counterpart in the dark, and they kept each other balanced. If one fell, then the balance was off and the remaining one *could* go evil. In fact, they were more likely to."

"What do you mean, counterpart? My mind's already come up with half a dozen things that could be considered a counterpart," Kara said. "Like couples, siblings, or something."

"No, it wasn't like that," Tempest answered. "Or it didn't have to be. Sometimes it was. But no, it was really as simple as the division. The counterpart was their opposite. For instance, Caron was the god of Darkness. His counterpart, Pyra, was the goddess of Flames."

"And *all* the gods had an opposite like that?" Seth asked.

Tempest nodded. "They did. The five major counterparts were Darkness and Flames, Death and Birth, Retribution and Justice, War and Healing, and Sky and Sea. But like I said, there were a lot of gods, so sometimes it was...I won't say simpler than that, but nothing as all-encompassing. Like there was a god of the sun and goddess of the moon."

Seth was beyond fascinated by this. "So if the god of the sun was killed, the goddess of the moon would go evil?"

"I actually had a theory about that," Aelia spoke up. She'd gotten stronger in the hours since she woke, and she sounded almost normal now. "I think that while it was important to have the opposite around, that it might be just as important that there be an equal number of light and dark gods."

Tempest thought about that for a moment before she slowly shook her head. "I don't know. I can't think of a time when one half of a pair died that the other didn't go evil."

"True, but did you ever see an instance where a dark god died, and a light god who wasn't his counterpart died?" Aelia challenged.

"Well...no," Tempest admitted. "It's not like Lemurian gods died often or easily."

"No, they didn't. They were extremely powerful. And it's not a theory I'll ever be able to prove or disprove, I just wanted to share it with people who knew about the Lemurian gods." Her head tilted and Aelia looked to Seth. "But we've gotten off the topic, haven't we? I don't think you just wanted to tell us you wished for the Lemurians to help us."

"Oh. No, that wasn't it," Seth confirmed. "It's what happened after that was...disconcerting." He paused, but no one interrupted, so he continued. "I heard a voice in my head. It didn't sound like a man or woman. Just...androgynous. It said..." He closed his eyes and tried to remember the exact wording. "Be careful what you ask for. It won't always turn out how you expect."

Aaron frowned. "That sounds ominous."

"That's what I thought, too. It's why I wanted you guys to know about it," Seth agreed. "But like I said, I have no idea who it was. I haven't heard anything since."

"I just wonder if it was a friend trying to warn us, or an enemy threatening us," Kara murmured. "The way our luck's gone, it's more likely to be an enemy. I don't think for one second that the storm was just a coincidence."

"No, it wasn't," Aaron growled. "I'd been watching the satellite imaging as well as the sky, and there's no way that storm just appeared like it did. Yeah, storms can come up quickly, but not that quick."

"It hasn't all been bad, though," Tempest argued. "We only made it this far because of one particular friend helping us along the way," she pointed out, reluctant to mention Hecate's name. Odds were they weren't being watched at the moment, because if they were, they'd probably have been attacked again, but she didn't want to risk it.

"True, not to mention that we started off as two and we're five now," Seth agreed. "But friend or foe, I'm more wondering what they meant by it. Be careful what I ask for? Are they saying that Lemurian gods are alive? Or that they're against us?"

"I don't know, but I also don't think that it's what we should be worrying about," Aaron said. "Right now, our biggest problem is finding land. If we can't do that, then none of the rest matters. Aelia and Tempest might be okay, but the rest of us?" He shook his head. "We can die, and we can't travel large distances easily." It made it a little better for him, knowing that Aelia would get out of this no matter what, but he really, really didn't want to die. Not before giving a big fuck you to whoever was targeting them and seeing Lemuria with his own eyes.

Those words from Aaron bothered Seth. It wasn't that Aaron wasn't a realist, because he could recognize danger as well as any man, but Aaron preferred to flirt and charm and make jokes. He'd been far too serious, which only drove home just how severe their situation was.

"Aaron's right, but I refuse to believe that we've gotten to this point only to die in the middle of the Pacific," Seth decided aloud. "Yes, things have sucked. Yes, we've almost died…a couple of times. But we haven't, not yet, and our enemies have. So we're going to find Lemuria, then our enemies, and kick some ass. Got me?" he asked, looking to one face, waiting until they nodded before he moved onto the other. "Good. Now, let's get some sleep. Tempest is exhausted after using her powers all day and dealing with the curse, and Aelia is recovering from dying. Not to mention the rest of us haven't eaten since yesterday. Tomorrow we'll get back to it."

"That's a good idea," Aaron agreed, shifting down until his head was pillowed on the side of the raft.

"Yeah, I know I could use some sleep, too," Kara said as she got as comfortable as possible in the crowded raft.

Tempest kissed Seth's cheek and whispered against his ear, "Thank you. I think we all needed that."

Seth smiled faintly and kissed the top of her head. "You're welcome. Now get some sleep."

She nodded and rested her head on his shoulder. In under a minute, she'd fallen asleep.

Tempest walked along the pale stone road of the town nearest to her home. She wore typical clothing for Lemurians in the northern part

of the continent; a sleeveless gown that reached her feet, made of a light, breathable fabric. Hers was a blue so pale it was almost white, with the hem decorated in silver and dark blue threads, the former gleaming in the midday sun. Her hair hung around her shoulders in loose waves, partially held back from her face with a silver comb. She wore no jewelry except for a single bracelet, but there was a dagger hanging from a belt at her side.

She smiled as she passed the various homes, stalls, and shops, listening to the sounds of people, young and old, going about their daily lives. Children laughed and played while the adults haggled for wares or talked with friends. Unlike most towns of that time, there was magic. Items levitated from person to person at one stall, while in a store, the proprietor cleaned the floors with water controlled by his powers. Magic was as commonplace here as breathing was in any other part of the world. It wasn't even uncommon to see their gods visiting a market or the theater.

Lemuria was unique in the world.

Tempest exchanged a coin at a stall for a piece of purplish fruit that only grew on her homeland and tasted like a mix between an apple and mango. She bit into it, savoring the sweet taste of it before she realized something was off. The fruit no longer tasted quite so delicious as she stopped chewing and looked around, trying to figure out what was wrong. At first glance, there was nothing. The people looked like they always did, and neither the buildings nor the landscape looked off, either. It was a perfect summer day.

Then storm clouds darkened the sky until it appeared closer to dusk than noon. Yet none of the people reacted. Tempest lifted her head and frowned at the heavens, sending a tendril of her own magic upward, but it stopped only inches from her body. It was then she remembered the storm. The temple she'd awoken in. The bracelet that mysteriously appeared on her wrist. The dagger Aelia had given her.

Seth.

"This is a dream," she whispered in horror, using the language of her birth, rather than the one implanted in her mind by Hecate.

"Yes, it is," came a woman's soothing voice from behind her, using the same language flawlessly.

Tempest whirled around then shifted back a few steps, immediately on guard. The woman in front of her was a goddess, there was no doubt about that, but she wasn't one that Tempest recognized. She was taller than Tempest by several inches, with a curvaceous figure that said mother more than siren, though she was absolutely stunning. Her hair was blonde and curled down to her hips. Tempest couldn't figure out what color the woman's eyes were, because one moment they looked blue, but the next they were brown, then green.

This goddess radiated power. It wasn't as blatant as some gods she'd known—it was quieter than that—but there was an aura that made Tempest feel almost ill. Something was coming.

"Who are you? And why are you in my dreams?" Tempest asked, knowing that, even in her dream, it was unlikely she could beat a goddess.

The goddess smiled sadly and shook her head. "I'm afraid I can't answer your first question. Doing so would cause more harm than good, and I don't want to cause you any harm. You've been through quite enough as it is."

"Why would you care what I've been through?" Tempest asked. After the last few weeks she'd had, she distrusted essentially all deities.

Even Hecate. She had no idea what the goddess's true intentions were. She would accept the help, certainly, but the only people she currently trusted were her four companions.

"To explain that, I'd have to tell you who I am, and as I stated, it would do you no good. Beyond that, it would take quite a bit of time to explain to your satisfaction. So I'll answer your second question instead. At least as much as I'm able." The goddess sighed and looked around at the Lemurians who still moved around them, actors continuing their lines, with no idea their play was being interrupted and ignored. But when she spoke, she didn't mention them. "You are going to find what you seek. It's fate that you do, and few can truly alter fate. But what you find isn't going to be exactly what you expect."

Tempest shook her head even as she thought of the reply Seth had received. "What is it you think I seek?"

The goddess looked back to her and smiled sadly. "Home."

Tempest frowned. "You came into my dream to tell me I'll find Lemuria?"

"No," the goddess answered with a shake of her head. "I came to tell you that there are some things even the gods cannot prevent. You will soon need to trust in yourself." She stepped closer and something had Tempest standing her ground, even when the goddess laid her fingertips lightly against Tempest's cheek. "Even more importantly, you will need to trust in those you've taken into your heart. A time will come when you'll have to make a decision between logic and trust. If you choose logic, then everything you've suffered through will be for naught. And I'm sorry, Tempest, but the decision will not be an easy one."

A jolt of fear raced down Tempest's spine. "How will I know if it's the right decision?" she whispered.

The goddess gave her another sad smile and shook her head as she drew her hand back. Before Tempest could say anything else, the powerful woman faded from view.

Tempest looked around in the darkness of the approaching storm and went cold. The people who had been so abundant just seconds ago had disappeared as completely as the woman, leaving Tempest all alone in Lemuria.

CHAPTER 26

"Tempest? Wake up, darlin'."

Someone was shaking Tempest's shoulder and she jolted back to consciousness. She sat up so quickly she almost rammed her forehead into Seth's face. Only his quick reflexes saved him from a broken nose.

He watched her face as she looked around, her eyes wide, her breathing rapid and shallow. "Tempest? What's wrong?" he asked, his hand going automatically to where his gun usually rested against his hip. Unfortunately, it was still on the boat, which by this point was probably at the bottom of the Pacific.

She went still and looked at the anxious faces of Aelia, Kara, and Aaron, then shook her head. "Nothing...just a dream." Her eyes closed and she took a few deep breaths. It had to be a dream, but something about it had felt so real. She could still taste the fruit on her tongue. No other dream had ever been so vivid and clear. Nothing she could do about it now, so she asked, "You were trying to wake me?"

"Yeah. Look."

Tempest opened her eyes and followed the direction he was pointing. At first she didn't see anything of note, but then she frowned and crawled over him as she stared into the distance. "Is that..."

"Land? Apparently," Aaron said with a nod. "Hawk-boy—"

"Falcon," Seth corrected from between clenched teeth.

Aaron smirked and continued, "Spotted it about ten minutes ago, but none of us could make anything out until just before he woke you up."

"Is it Lemuria?" Kara asked, her gaze fixed on Tempest rather than the sliver of land barely visible over the horizon.

Tempest shook her head and started to tell them she didn't know, but stopped. "It...I think it is." She turned back toward them, hope blossoming in her chest. "I have the same feeling I've had since we first crossed over Lemuria. It can't be anything else."

"It does make sense," Aelia agreed. "There's nothing else it could be. The only other option that's even remotely feasible is that another island moved here, which could happen with the gods, but that would be extremely unlikely."

Seth rubbed Tempest's back in slow circles. "It has to be. It's still a good ways out, but if you feel up to it, we can probably be there in an hour or so." His voice dropped to a whisper meant only for her ears. "I know how badly you want to go home."

The last word brought the memory of her dream to the forefront of Tempest's mind and she frowned. Stepping foot on Lemuria, even just a piece of it, should bring her joy, but instead she felt a sense of dread. The dream was playing with her emotions, and she wasn't even sure it had been an actual goddess in her dream and not just some piece of her subconscious.

"Tempest?"

Seth's concerned voice broke her out of her thoughts and she nodded. "Yes, I can help." She moved to the other side of the raft. "Hold on," she warned the others before she used her magic to push the raft forward. For a while, the tiny piece of land didn't seem to get any closer, which only served to prove just how far away it really was. Luckily, the others weren't quiet, which kept her from slipping back into her thoughts.

"I wish we had any real idea of where we were," Kara said as she watched the piece of land, which was what all five of them were doing.

"Does it really matter?" Aaron replied with a shrug. "At this point, land—any land—is the same as life."

"It might. If we knew where we were, and knew where exactly Lemuria was, then Tempest might know what part of Lemuria we were heading toward," Kara explained.

"Even if we knew, it wouldn't stop us from heading toward it," Aelia pointed out. "We haven't seen any other land since we left Hawaii, and we're basically out of water. We *need* to get to land."

Aaron made a thoughtful noise and nodded. "True. Hopefully, wherever the land was, it'll be someplace that has something edible and fresh water."

"I'd settle for fresh water," Seth said dryly. "We can survive longer without food, and we are heading toward an island, which means we're surrounded by lots of fish-filled water."

"Lemuria was a very fertile place. Lots of fruit-bearing plants grew all over the island. Other edible plants, too. I'm sure wherever it is, we'll be fine," Tempest murmured.

Aaron, Aelia, and Kara started talking about what Lemuria had been like, but Tempest tuned them out. Seth settled down next to her and rested a hand on her knee. "You okay? You've been a little...distant...since you woke up," he said quietly.

Tempest smiled faintly. "I'm fine."

"You sure? Because after everything, I expected you to be excited to be this close to Lemuria. Hell, I figured you'd be thrilled to be so close to getting rid of the curse. But you almost seem like you'd prefer we didn't get there."

"No, I want to get there, I'm just worried," she admitted. "It's not like anything has gone according to plan. We've been attacked at every turn. I'm honestly surprised we've gone a day without any sort of problem."

"I was wondering about that myself," he agreed. "Which just means we have to be on our guard. But if we're tense every second of every day, we'll go nuts. And this should be a thrilling time for you. You're almost home. When you first found out what happened to Lemuria, did you ever think that would happen?"

Reluctantly, she shook her head. "No."

"But here we are, just miles from it," Seth said, motioning to the slowly growing piece of land. "If we get attacked again, we'll handle it." He smiled, though his heart wasn't really in it. "We're not exactly a bunch of humans, remember? I mean, look at us. We've got the guy who can shift into a lethal tiger, the woman who can turn into stone, the woman who can't die—at least not for long—and the immortal woman who turns into literal air."

Tempest's head cocked and she glanced away from the island long enough to frown at him. "We've also got a man who can see exceptionally well and has amazing aim. Not to mention never gives up, maybe not even when he should."

His lips twitched. "I guess so. But see? That just means we've got this. So relax a little and think about what you want to do when we get to Lemuria." He tapped a finger on her knee. "You know, unless we're a lot closer to it than I think we are—which is doubt-ful—then what remains of Lemuria isn't just a tiny little piece of nothing. It's miles across, which means it's probably someplace you could actually live."

Aside from the fact that she'd be the only one there, which didn't sound as appealing as it might have if she hadn't made the friends she had. Or fallen for the man who'd found her. But she didn't want to make him feel bad for bringing that thought to mind and only smiled and nodded. "I'll try to focus on that. And see if I can get us moving a little faster."

Seth smiled and kissed her cheek. "Sounds good."

Unfortunately, Tempest had to take several breaks on their way to the island. The constant use of power drained her of course, but the curse also had to hit once more. They gave her the last of the water and let her rest for half an hour before she insisted she was okay.

"You sure?" Aelia asked, her brow furrowed with concern. "It won't hurt anything if we arrive a little later. We're not on any sort of schedule. We'd be fine if we didn't get there until tomorrow."

"I know, but I want to get off this raft. I'm tired of being on the water," Tempest insisted, which was true. She'd never been on a boat before this trip, and while her body had mostly adjusted to the constant rocking, her mind wanted to be on solid land. Worse, the feeling of dread had only increased, and she wouldn't be able to relax until after they'd gotten to Lemuria without any problems.

"If you're sure," Seth said after a moment, but he stayed close to her when she resumed using her magic.

They were close enough now to make out vegetation on the island, which was, as Seth had suspected, a good size. And whatever piece of Lemuria this was, it was still fertile. Unfortunately, from this distance it didn't look familiar, which didn't really surprise her. It had been thousands of years. Any piece of land would change a great deal in that amount of time.

"There's something that's been bothering me," Aaron said as they watched the island gradually growing closer.

"What's that?" Kara asked from where she'd stretched out on the floor of the raft, her head on Aelia's calves, her feet propped up on the side of the raft.

"Aelia said that this piece of Lemuria was hidden from anyone who wasn't Lemurian, which is why no one else has ever found it, right?"

Aelia frowned as his point hit her. "I did, yes. But we all saw it before Tempest even woke up."

Aaron nodded. "Exactly my point. So how did we see it? We're not Lemurian. And yes, I know, we've all got to have Lemurian blood aside from you," he told Aelia, "but we're not Lemurian."

No one answered for a minute.

"Could it be as simple as we were with a Lemurian?" Seth asked, but without any real conviction.

"Maybe, since I don't think that whatever magic has been hiding it would just coincidentally wear off just as we were looking for it," Aelia mused. "But do remember that everything I heard was just rumor. It could be that any Arcane could spot it."

"I doubt that," Aaron disagreed. "We can't be the first Arcane to come this way."

"True. Could it be that we're touching a Lemurian?" Kara asked. "With the raft this small, everyone's touching everyone else."

"That's a fair point," Aaron allowed with a nod. "That or we're in the influence of her magic."

"I don't think worrying about it is going to change anything at the moment," Tempest said, though the question bothered her, too. "And we're not going to confirm anything right now. Besides, we'll be there soon enough."

It was almost an hour later when the raft made it to the shallows around the island.

The island was beautiful. Lush green covered the majority of the land, though it was dotted with vibrant colors that marked flowers and fruit. Along with the green there were slashes of gray where stone rose up above the trees in what were once tall mountains, but now were more like oversized hills. It was a perfect tropical paradise, one to rival even the best tourist destinations.

To everyone's shock, Tempest stopped the raft and stared at the island. The current kept them moving slowly toward shore, but that alone would take another half hour to push them onto the sand.

Seth looked at her and frowned when he noticed tears were in her eyes. "Tempest?"

"I know this place," Tempest whispered.

"What?" He looked back to the island, staring at it with a sharper curiosity. "Where was it?"

"We're on the northern side of Lemuria. There," she said, gesturing, "was a town. Not one of the bigger ones, but it suited us."

"Us?" Kara asked.

Tempest nodded. "Us. I had a house a little bit away from the town." Her lips curved in a trembling smile. "I liked being in the mountains, remember? We got a lot of wind, which always felt comfortable. It made it feel homey." She took a slow, unsteady breath. "I wonder if it's still there."

"It depends," Aaron answered. "If it was made of wood? Probably not. If it was made of stone or something similar?" He turned back to her and smiled. "Then yes, it could still be there, though it's probably full of plants and wildlife."

Her eyes closed and she felt like everything inside her was coiling up, just waiting to explode, along with her sanity. It wound tighter and tighter, her heart beating faster and faster, everything building to a devastating peak. For a minute, it felt like her heart was going to burst and her head implode. It was honestly as bad as when the curse hit. She started to hyperventilate as she struggled to try to calm herself. And then arms wrapped around her and gathered her close.

"It's okay, darlin'. Just breathe," Seth whispered against her hair. "Take as much time as you need, but it'll be okay."

Tempest turned into him and held him tightly as she focused on doing as he said, just breathing. A minute passed without her breaking. Then another minute, and she could breathe a little easier. Another, and the tension started to leave her body. Only then did she remember that it wasn't just her and Seth on the raft. They had an audience. She groaned softly, pressed her face against Seth's shoulder, and peeked at the others. To her relief, they were looking at the island rather than her, giving her what privacy they could.

"You okay now?" Seth asked quietly.

She nodded. "Yes, thank you." She drew back and wiped tears from her cheeks, tears she hadn't even realized she'd shed. "I don't know that I really believed it still existed until I recognized this place."

"Understandable." He gently stroked a thumb across her cheek. "You ready to get to shore, or do you need a few minutes?"

She loved that he gave her the option and smiled. "I'll be okay. And I'm sure everyone's as hungry as I am."

"You got that right," Kara said with such an exaggerated air of desperation that Tempest had to laugh.

"Fine, fine. I'll get us ashore, but someone else is doing any fishing. I'll just point out edible plants and fresh water," Tempest assured Kara as she got them moving again. "There's a pond and creek not too far from the town, so we'll be okay."

"What I wouldn't give for all my equipment," Aaron said with a sigh. "Mapping Lemuria would be amazing…"

Seth bit back a retort and just watched the approaching beach.

The raft sped through the turquoise water until it finally slid up onto the pure white beach.

"This is even more beautiful than I remembered," Aelia breathed.

"Even Hawaii wasn't this gorgeous," Kara agreed, trying to look at everything at once. "Tempest, you might have a neighbor. Just as soon as we break that curse on you."

Seth couldn't think of anything profound enough to say. He'd visited a lot of ancient sites, many of them absolutely stunning, but this outshone them all. Instead, he gave Tempest one last squeeze.

"You should be the first one to step foot on Lemuria. No one else deserves it more than the last Lemurian."

Choked with emotion, she could only nod. She wasn't quite steady as she got to her feet, so Seth reached up to support her. But even with all the build up to this moment, she had to take several deep breaths before she stretched her leg over the edge of the raft and set her bare foot on the warm sands of Lemuria.

CHAPTER 27

Tempest let out a soft cry as her body jerked. She fell to all fours in the damp sand, panting softly.

"Tempest!" Seth started to leap out of the raft after her, but she shook her head and lifted one trembling hand, signaling for him to wait.

"It's fine. I'm okay." Her eyes closed and she lowered her forehead to the sand. "I'm okay," she repeated, more quietly.

"Girl, that doesn't look like okay," Kara said, but she sounded worried, too.

Tempest shook her head before she slowly sat back on her heels and smiled at them. "No, I'm really okay. It didn't hurt me. Just...surprised me. It's safe to get out."

"What surprised you?" Seth asked as he climbed out and crouched next to her, his hand resting on the small of her back.

"Was it the jolt of power from being home? From stepping foot on Lemuria?" Aelia asked as she reached out and trailed her fingers through the pale sand.

"Partially," Tempest said, still a little breathless. "But it's also the curse. You're a smart woman, Aelia," she said with a laugh as she leaned into Seth. "I couldn't actively feel it before, not unless it was trying to drain me dry, physically and magically. But I can feel that it's gone, now."

"Not just smart, knowledgeable," Aaron corrected as he got out of the raft, then reached in to effortlessly lift Aelia out and set her on the sand beside him.

"Yes, well, being around for as long as I have, you're bound to pick up things here and there," Aelia mumbled, a little embarrassed by the praise, but obviously pleased as well. "I'm just glad I was right."

"Anyone else glad she's on our team?" Kara asked as she joined them on the sand and stretched.

"Definitely," Aaron said in a low purr, so only Aelia heard.

Seth helped Tempest get to her feet, and though she still wasn't steady, she looked better than she had in the raft. "You okay now?"

"I am. We should get some water and find some food." Tempest looked around, spotting half-recognizable signs of the town she'd once spent so much time in. All the buildings were covered in plants, just as she'd been warned, and only her knowledge of the place allowed her to see them. Covered in as much growth as it was, it was unlikely she'd even recognize her own house at first. "I wonder..."

"Hmm? You wonder what?" Seth asked. He was looking around, too, but unlike her, he was looking for potential threats.

"It's just...if this part of Lemuria remained, isn't it possible that some Lemurians didn't...that they could still be here? Like I said, there's food, there's fresh water, so there's no reason they couldn't have survived..." she said wistfully.

While Seth supposed there was a possibility some survived the initial sinking, it was unlikely anyone was left. The source of fresh water could have been tainted, they could have had difficulty getting enough food to eat...or they could have grown insane with solitude and took their own lives. That was if they'd even survived the attack by the gods. The chances of finding anything alive here beyond some animals were astronomical in his opinion. But he couldn't be the one to erase the look of hope on her face, so just said, "It's possible. Let's see what we find, okay?"

"Okay." Tempest looked to the others. "You ready?"

"For food? Hell yeah. Lead on!" Kara said with a grin, while Aelia only nodded and Aaron gestured for her to go first.

There were trees just off the beach, tall and lush, but just beyond them were large, square shapes, hidden almost entirely beneath vines and behind bushes and flowers. It was obvious there were man-made structures under all the green, but seeing them as buildings was difficult despite Seth's archaeological experience. Even the road under their feet was hard to recognize as such, the stones cracked and most covered in moss and other plant life. It looked alien, despite its beauty. The silence only added to the oddness, though they could see signs of animals and insects. Occasionally they'd hear a bird let out a trill, but the locals—if there were any—were suspiciously quiet.

Tempest led them toward the vine-covered structures, her steps slow despite the hunger of her companions. A moment this important simply couldn't be rushed, and she couldn't have forced her feet to move any quicker if she'd wanted to. It was hard for her to believe that she was actually here, back in Lemuria. It was harder to see what had been a thriving town full of people so empty and overrun by plants. The warring emotions tightened her chest, but she refused to let even a single tear fall. Crying wouldn't change anything, and their situation was far from ideal. They didn't have the luxury of giving into emotions, no matter how understandable it might be.

"So you lived in this town?" Kara asked as they passed a building and she peeked inside the open window. Inside, it looked like it had been a house because she saw what looked like a bedroom. The bedding that had once covered the bed was gone, and the bed was more a vague shape than a piece of furniture, but now a blanket of green had replaced it. It was sad, but at the same time, Kara wished she had a camera. It looked oddly peaceful and beautiful.

"Not in the town, no, but not too far from here." Tempest pointed to a blob of green on a nearby hill. "My house was there. Probably still is, it's just hard to see it from here."

"We can go there, you know," Aelia said gently. "We've got time." Her lips twitched as Kara's stomach growled. "After we eat, anyway."

A smile touched Tempest's lips. "This way. There's an orchard near the spring where we got our water. Or there used to be," she said, leading them through the village of trees and vines.

Minutes later, as they left the buildings behind, they could hear the soft tinkling of water. Ahead, a slender stream wound its way through the vegetation, the water more clear than most of them had ever seen before. On the other side of the stream they could see trees laden with colorful fruits. At one point it had been a carefully planted orchard, but now it was a jumble of trees.

Tempest frowned lightly at the differences, but moved to the stream and knelt beside the water. She dipped a hand into the stream and lifted it to her lips, sipping cautiously. She couldn't help but smile. "It tastes just like I remembered it," she said, glancing over her shoulder at the others. She took another, larger drink before she stood. "Drink up. I'm going to grab some fruit."

Aaron, Aelia, and Kara didn't hesitate to move to the stream and start drinking their fill. Seth, however, enjoyed only a single handful of water before he moved to Tempest's side. "I'll join you. I'm curious about the fruit you have here, and there's no way one person could carry enough fruit to satisfy those appetites," he said, inclining his head toward the trio.

"I could float it to them, but you're right. This makes more sense," Tempest agreed with a smile.

They started toward the nearest tree, one with almost black bark that reached high but had drooping limbs heavy with a pinkish-white fruit. Before they could reach it, a figure appeared in front of them.

He was shorter than Seth by half a foot, but since he stood six foot five, that was hardly short. The man had a stocky build that reminded Seth of a bodybuilder, but his features were rather ordinary in comparison. His hair was short and brown, streaked with lighter shades, while his eyes were dark, probably a deep brown. But what struck Seth the most was the look of loathing on the man's face as he looked at Tempest.

Automatically, Seth moved to stand in front of Tempest, who simply stood there, shocked.

"Jalvas?" she asked, her voice uncertain despite the recognition.

"You know him?" Seth asked in surprise.

"Of course she knows me," Jalvas said, and though he didn't yell, his voice echoed. "I'm one of her gods. She'd *better* know who I am. Even if she has caused me no small amount of hassle."

Footsteps sounded behind them, but Seth didn't dare take his eyes off Jalvas. Lemurian god or not, something told him not to trust this man. Because of that, he only felt the other three take up positions behind him and Tempest.

"Yes, he is one of my gods. He's the god of mountains." She shook her head and focused on Jalvas again. "But I was told all the gods were dead or sleeping," Tempest said, starting to smile with happiness. "How did you survive? How are you here?" This was more than she could have hoped for when she learned that part of Lemuria might have survived. If one of the gods had as well, then maybe there were others. Maybe she wasn't alone. Could this be what the goddess in her dream had meant? She didn't expect this, after all. But if that was true, what was the decision she had to make? Who was she meant to trust? Jalvas? It made sense, but so did trusting her companions.

The god only scowled harder and gave her a killing look. "The more important question is, how did *you* survive? I was told the last of your kind died more than four thousand years ago."

Tempest shook her head, confused by his attitude. "I don't know. I wish I did."

"How could you not know?" he demanded.

"I went to sleep one night, here, just like any other night, and the next I was waking up far away, only to find out thousands of years had passed," she explained. "I had to be told by others what happened to Lemuria," she added with a motion toward her companions.

He narrowed his eyes at her, clearly uncertain if he believed her story, but then he saw the bracelet and made a noise that reminded Seth of stones grinding together. "Where did you get that?"

Tempest lifted her wrist and looked to the bracelet. "I don't know," she said again. "When I woke up, it was on my wrist. Or at least I think it was. I didn't even notice it was there until it was pointed out. Do you know what it is?" He only kept staring at the bracelet, so she let her arm drop. "What happened, Jalvas? Are we truly the only two Lemurians alive? Did none of the other gods survive the sinking?" His glare and attitude had the smile fading from her lips. What should have been a joyful reunion felt dangerous, and she didn't understand why.

Jalvas let out a humorless laugh. "What happened? You screwed up my plans, that's what happened. You and one of the other gods, it looks like."

Tempest took a step back, her body bumping lightly into Seth's. The menace in Jalvas's tone was chilling. "What do you mean?"

"You really think anyone short of another god could have saved you for so long? Or given you that bracelet?" He shook his head. "And now that you're awake, it means the other pantheons are hunting for Lemurians again, even if they couldn't properly follow the fucking beacon that bracelet's emitting." His fists clenched. "You couldn't just die, could you? No, you had to evade the teams that went after you in Peru and get everybody freaked out. I picked the wrong people to trust with what should have been a simple task," he said with a sneer of disgust. "And do you know what happens if they keep hunting for Lemurians, Tempest? Do you?" he roared, his voice sounding more like an avalanche than a man now.

Being yelled at with such fury by one of her gods, one of the beings she'd worshiped, had her shrinking back. She was powerful, yes, but the Lemurian gods had far surpassed even the strongest of their worshipers. It was instinct as much as intelligence that had her unwilling to anger such a being.

"No, of course you don't," he said in a disgusted tone. "But I'll tell you. They find *me*. And if they find me, they'll put me to sleep like the rest of the useless pantheon. If they don't just kill me! After all these centuries, I'm sure they've found a way of doing it. That's what you've done!"

Tempest shook her head repeatedly. "No, I didn't do it. I didn't do any of this! I only wanted to live!"

"So do I!" he exploded. Before any of them could draw breath, he attacked. Rocks, larger than a man, tore themselves free from the earth, shredding vines and trees as they flew toward the group.

Seth jumped in front of Tempest, who was too shocked by the attack to react at first. The boulder hit him mid-body and sent him flying back into a tree. The rock had broken quite a few bones inside his body and likely damaged most of his organs, so he could only watch in horror as his friends were attacked just as callously.

Kara turned herself to stone, which helped her absorb some of the worst of the impact, but even her formidable form literally cracked under the strength of a god's magic. She staggered and dropped to one knee, but didn't go down completely. Aaron grabbed Aelia and twisted, taking the brunt of the impact of another rock on his back, which sent both him and the woman flying. When they landed, neither moved. Neither made a sound. Seth couldn't see even a hint of life. Aelia, he knew, would revive shortly, but that didn't matter if everyone else was dead and she ended up facing a pissed off god by herself. And for all he knew, a god could kill her and make her stay dead.

Tempest was somehow untouched by the rocks, but had gone stark white with panic and grief. She stumbled back as Jalvas approached her, and when he got within feet of her, Seth saw her start to fade into her elemental form. Before she could fully transition, Jalvas's hand shot out and wrapped around her throat. He jerked her face close to his, her body completely solid once more. "I don't think so," he snarled cruelly. "It's your life or mine, little elemental, and gods do not bow to those who should worship them."

She clawed at the hand around her throat as she struggled to draw in a single good breath. Even that movement stopped when Jalvas flung his hand toward Kara and the limp figures of Aaron and Aelia. Her mouth moved as she tried to scream when the earth rumbled, then split apart in jagged lines. Kara was swallowed first, plummeting into the deep chasm the god of mountains had created, her scream one that would torment both Tempest and Seth for the last few minutes of their lives.

Aaron and Aelia were taken only seconds later, the earth simply pulling apart beneath them so their lifeless bodies could be disposed of, ensuring that neither troubled the god again.

Tears streaming down her cheeks, Tempest looked up to the merciless face of Jalvas and managed to croak out, "Why?"

"With you dead, I can live. And since that bracelet of yours prevents me from killing you with my powers, it just means I get to do it the old-fashioned way," he said with a sadistic smile. "Good bye, Tempest." His voice dropped as he whispered harshly in her ear, "Long live the last Lemurian." As soon as the last word was spoken, his hand tightened and twisted, snapping her neck.

Watching the earth take his friends had been hard enough, but seeing Tempest killed by someone she'd been so happy to see broke Seth. Not caring that his body was all but destroyed and he was dying, he screamed, "No!" and used the tree behind him to help him get to his feet. He only managed it for a second before he collapsed again, his shattered legs unable to support his weight. Giving up wasn't an option and again he grabbed the tree and pulled himself upward.

Jalvas dropped Tempest's body like she was nothing but an inconvenient insect and looked to Seth with a hatred that was only surpassed by what he'd shown Tempest. "And you...you brought her here. You're as much to blame as she is." He smirked and kicked Tempest in the side, hard enough that her body rolled closer to Seth. "There's no way off this island, and I can think of no better punishment for you than to die in pain, alone with the body of the woman you cared so much for." He stomped his foot on the ground, which sent a tremor through the earth, an aftershock to the quake that had taken his companions. It wasn't intense, but it was strong enough to undo Seth's progress and make him crumble to the ground. "In your next life, remember not to fuck with the gods," he said coldly before he disappeared.

His whole world was gone and every piece of him hurt more than he thought possible, but Seth slowly crawled to Tempest and gathered her in his lap. "Hecate! Hades! Osiris!" he yelled, his voice thick with anguish, his cheeks damp with tears. "Someone...please...don't let her be dead," he whispered as he placed a gentle kiss to her cooling lips. "Don't let her be dead..."

The air stirred around him and power hit him hard before it immediately dimmed to a point where it was difficult to ignore, but not so painful.

"They cannot help you," came a deep, smooth male voice. "But I can."

CHAPTER 28

Seth looked up, his arms tightening around Tempest.

The man standing in front of him was clearly a god. At first Seth thought it might be Zeus, since he matched the depictions of the head of the Greek pantheon with his sturdy frame, gray beard, and immense power, but immediately dismissed it. Zeus wasn't prone to acts of altruism, and Seth had his suspicions that Zeus was one of those who had wanted Tempest dead. Nor was Zeus likely to look at someone with so much sympathy.

"Why? And who are you?" Seth asked suspiciously.

The man shook his head sadly and crouched in front of Seth. "I'm afraid I cannot tell you that. By all rights, I shouldn't be here. I shouldn't interfere, but neither could I stand and just allow this to happen." He gave a tiny smile. "Someone I care about would have been very upset if I had." A strong hand motioned to Tempest. "Besides, the world needs her. Not just her either. It needs you and the rest of your friends. You're all more important than you realize."

Seth shook his head. "I'm just a halfling treasure hunter."

"While technically accurate, you're much more than that," the man corrected. "But are you really going to argue with me when I've told you I can help?"

Seth swallowed down all the reasons why he should tell the man to fuck off and shook his head. "No, but I do want to know how. And what the catch is." Though if it meant bringing Tempest back, he'd pay any price. If it brought Aelia, Kara, and Aaron back, too? He'd find it impossible to say no.

"The catch is a simple one. You'll owe me a favor in the future." The man's lips twitched and he arched a brow, and Seth knew he was waiting for a protest.

"If you can do what you say, then done," Seth said without hesitation. Favors to the gods rarely turned out well for the mortals who owed them, but it had to be worth it.

"Well, perhaps I should clarify. I can't bring her back to life, or retrieve your friends from the bowels of the earth," the man explained. "What I *can* do," he said, cutting off Seth's angry words before they can form, "is give you a chance to ensure they never die. Of course, if you fail, you owe me nothing."

Seth frowned. "I don't understand. What do you mean, chance to ensure they never die?" Everything hurt so much, and his mind was still reeling over the events of the last few minutes, that it took him a moment for a thought to sluggishly occur to him. "Are you talking about sending me back in time?"

The man nodded once, solemnly. "I am. I will send you back to the moment before you first stepped foot on Lemuria. You'll have all of your memories, which means you'll have a fighting chance, but I cannot interfere anymore than that."

That was a great boon, and no easy feat. There were only a handful of gods who were said to be able to affect time like that, and Seth had always doubted the accuracy of those claims. But that wasn't the biggest concern. "Even if we go back and I warn the others...Jalvas was too powerful. We don't have any way of killing him before he kills us. He's a god."

Now the man smiled, bright enough that his eyes actually shone with humor. "Ahh, that's where you're wrong." He sat down in front of Seth, moving with more agility than could be expected of a man who looked as old as he did. "Fate is a funny thing, Seth. Sometimes kind, sometimes cruel, but it has an odd way of giving you exactly what you need. The trick is recognizing the boon when you see it."

Seth's brow furrowed and he shook his head. "I don't understand. What did it give us?" The man—who Seth was starting to think of as Father Time—motioned to Tempest's waist. It took Seth a few seconds before he noticed the dagger, the same one Aelia had given her. The one Aelia had said was Lemurian. "Tempest's knife?"

"Indeed. Don't you agree that it's kind of odd how it traveled the world for more than six thousand years, only to find its way into the hands of the only person on earth who deserved to own it?"

"And it can kill Jalvas?" Seth pressed. It was all well and good that fate wanted Tempest to have the knife, but that didn't mean it was capable of what Seth wasn't.

"It can," Father Time confirmed with a nod. "But you have to be careful what you tell them, Seth. Every word you say differently this time has the potential to alter things in a way you don't want. Tell them too much, and Jalvas might not waste time like he did this go around. I'd suggest not telling them anything, to be honest," he said as he got to his feet. "But do we have a deal?"

Seth hesitated. It was another chance and he had to take it, but there was still so much that could go wrong. "When you send me back..."

"It'll be like none of this ever happened, except in your memories," Father Time said, anticipating Seth's question. But then, maybe they'd gone through this before, and Seth had asked the same question then. It made as much sense as anything else.

Seth steeled himself, then nodded. "Then yes, we have a deal."

"Excellent. Good luck, Seth. Don't fail me. More importantly, don't fail her," he said, nodding to Tempest. "I'll see you when it's time to call in my favor." He straightened, then clapped his hands together, the sound reminding Seth of a sonic boom. But just as soon as the thought occurred to him, everything went black.

Seth heard the sound of Tempest letting out a soft cry when he came back to himself. For a second he struggled with vertigo as he tried to get his bearings.

Tempest was on all fours in the sand, panting, while the rest of them were in the raft. All alive, all unhurt.

"Oh thank the gods," he whispered, eyes closing.

"Well, that's a shitty thing to say when a woman's in need," Aaron snapped.

"No, that's not—Tempest, you okay?" Seth asked, though he knew what was going on this time. He climbed out of the raft and helped her to her feet, so relieved to see her alive. Before he could stop himself, he was pulling her into his arms and kissing her like it was the last time—which, if he screwed up, it might well be. He didn't care that there was an audience. When he'd seen her killed in front of him, he realized just how much she'd come to mean to him. He wasn't going to let another day, another *hour*, go by without showing her.

Tempest's eyes widened with surprise for only a second before her arms wrapped around his neck and she returned the kiss. It was only when the others started laughing and teasing them good-naturedly that she drew back and smiled at him. "What was that for?"

"You cried out. I just wanted to make sure you felt okay," Seth murmured. It bothered him not to tell them everything that had happened, but for some reason, he trusted the god. Not to mention if he tried to explain, they'd probably think he was going crazy. And he wasn't entirely sure he wasn't. "Everything good?"

"Yeah, it's fine. I'm okay."

"Girl, other than Seth kissing you, that doesn't look like okay," Kara said, tone lightly amused.

Seth was struck by the strange sense of déjà vu, except he truly *had* lived all this before. He let their conversation float around him while he tried to figure out how he was going to play this.

"We should get some water and find some food," Tempest said, looking around, still in Seth's arms.

"We should," he agreed. "But before we do...could I see your dagger?"

She looked back to him with surprise. "My dagger?"

"It's Lemurian, right? And we're actually on Lemuria now. I'm just curious if that affects it at all," he told her, which wasn't entirely untrue. He *was* curious. Was it that only a Lemurian weapon could kill a Lemurian god? Or was it some magical property the knife had? Aelia had called it a relic, which implied powers of some sort.

Tempest cocked her head and studied his face. She looked thoughtful for a moment before she nodded slowly and glanced down at the dagger she'd been holding onto since they'd made it to the life raft. "Of course. Are you feeling okay? You're acting a little odd."

"I'm fine," he told her before giving her a light kiss. "It's just my first newly discovered land." Lying didn't sit well with him—especially not lying to her—but he had no choice. Luckily, she accepted his explanation and handed him the blade before leading them through the town.

Seth only half-paid attention to the chatter from the other four. He'd heard it already—literally—and he was more concerned with studying the dagger in his hands. It looked impressive, yes, and he'd never seen metal tinged red like this was, but it didn't *feel* like some important relic. That didn't necessarily mean anything, though. Some extremely powerful relics hid what they were as part of their powers. By the time they reached the stream, he realized he wasn't likely to figure out the importance of the dagger by study, at least not in the next few minutes. Most likely, the powers wouldn't be revealed until it was used as it had been intended to. Not without a skilled witch examining it.

His heart began to pound as Tempest knelt by the water and pronounced it safe, but his gaze wasn't on her or the others, it was fixed on the spot where Jalvas would appear. When Tempest started toward the fruit trees, he fell into step beside her, taking her hand with his free hand and giving it a squeeze.

"Do you trust me?" he murmured, his heart pounding so hard it sounded like it was in his ears.

Tempest glanced up at him, her brow furrowed in confusion, but she nodded. "Of course I do."

Seth smiled faintly. "Then follow my lead, okay? Please? I'd never do anything to hurt you."

Slowly, she gave a second nod. He could see her unease written on her face, and only loved her more when she said simply, "Okay."

He released her hand and hurried away from her, to stand beside the tree Jalvas had appeared in front of the first time. Tempest gave him an odd look, but he just shook his head and lifted a finger to his lips. The three still by the stream had noticed his odd behavior, too, and were frowning in his direction, but when he called for silence, Aaron murmured something to the others and stood. Having fought beside him, Seth recognized his posture as one that showed he was ready for trouble.

Good. If he failed, he wanted the tiger on alert. If nothing else, he'd give them some time so Jalvas didn't just kill them all. Again.

The god appeared in the same spot as before. Though Seth couldn't see his face, he was sure the Lemurian was busy glaring at Tempest again. Luckily, Jalvas surprised the others so much they looked at him rather than at Seth, which meant he had a chance to catch the god off guard.

Seth heard Tempest begin the same conversation with Jalvas from before and began to creep forward. He may not be the stealthy hunter Aaron was—no one could match a feline in that department—but there weren't any dead leaves or twigs to give away his approach. His hand tightened on the handle of the knife as he closed the distance between him and Jalvas. For a moment, it looked as though he might actually reach the god and be able to kill him without any difficulty.

But of course it couldn't be that easy.

With his focus fixed on the god, he noticed as soon as Jalvas tensed—something he hadn't done the first time. For several seconds, which seemed to last an eternity, neither moved, then they both acted in unison.

Jalvas spun around and shoved his hands toward the ground, palms parallel to the earth. The ground started to shake just as Seth lunged toward the god, which ended up being both blessing and bane. While it knocked Seth off his feet, it also had him falling toward Jalvas rather than away from him. Unfortunately, while he crashed into the god, the knife only skimmed along Jalvas's side, doing a bare minimum of damage. But the fact that the blade drew blood gave him hope. Not just any blade could draw blood from a god of any pantheon.

"Who the hell do you think you are?" Jalvas snarled as he sent another blast of power through the earth, making Aelia and Kara stumble. Aaron and Tempest used their natural grace and powers to remain on their feet, but they weren't able to help him or the others. The most Aaron was able to do was crouch protectively over Aelia and watch as Kara turned herself to stone.

Seth didn't waste breath trying to answer, just brought the knife up sharply. Jalvas grabbed his wrist before the tip of the blade could penetrate his skin and scowled until he got a look at the knife. Though he could be imagining it, Seth thought he saw a flicker of fear in the Lemurian's eyes. Good.

"Where did you get that?" he demanded, his free hand lifting to Seth's throat.

Though Seth felt his air supply abruptly cut off, he still didn't try to answer, putting all his strength into trying to lift the knife. He only had this one chance to kill Jalvas and prevent them all from dying. If he failed now, he wasn't sure he'd get another chance to try to fix things. Yet each moment that passed sapped what little strength he still had, his arm trembling with the effort of trying to kill this god. His gaze flicked over Jalvas's shoulder and met with Tempest's. Her eyes were wide with shock, her powers causing wind to swirl around her, pulling at her hair and clothes.

Seth tried to put his apologies and feelings for her into his eyes before he broke the connection and turned his entire focus back to Jalvas. He was stunned when his arm started moving upward again, and it took him a moment to realize it felt like his arm was being pushed. There was nothing there, but a glance at Tempest showed that she had a hand outstretched, and it clicked. She was using her powers to help him. Even without knowing *why* he was attacking her god, perhaps the last of her gods here on Earth, she was helping him.

The moment Seth had asked her if she trusted him, her mind had flashed back to the dream, to the warning she'd been given. At the time, she'd thought maybe just giving him the Lemurian relic had been the choice. But when she saw her lover attack one of her gods, she'd realized it had only been part of it. The sight of the two of them locked in battle, both trying to kill the other, made her realize this was the choice. Did she choose logic, which said attacking one of her gods was not only suicide, it was also bordering on evil? The gods had loved and protected the Lemurians like no other pantheon she knew of. And as Jalvas might well be the last Lemurian god alive and awake, killing him was simply wrong.

Or did she choose trust, which told her that Seth would never do something so callous without a damn good reason? He wasn't a murderer, and he knew how much it meant to her that she wasn't alone.

It took her a moment, but when she saw Seth's face turning colors at the lack of oxygen, she chose trust. She had no idea why Seth would be attacking Jalvas, was horrified at the thought of killing one of the gods she'd known and worshiped her entire life, but she *knew* Seth. She knew that, for some reason, he *had* to do this.

Between the two of them, they fought against Jalvas's strength and the knife moved closer and closer to the god's chest.

"No! You can't kill me! I'm a god! I'm *your* god!" Jalvas roared when the tip of the blade pierced his flesh.

"My gods are dead," Tempest said flatly, though tears flowed down her cheeks, showing just what this act of faith was costing her. She was helping to kill the last of her gods, even though it meant she would truly be the last Lemurian.

With a final surge of strength, Seth shoved the dagger into Jalvas, angling it upward so it punctured his heart. Then the world seemed to stop as several things happened at once.

Jalvas's hand loosened around Seth's throat and the god threw his head back, roaring in pain and defeat.

The knife that connected them pulsed and turned red hot, no longer solid metal, but lava that flowed between Seth's hand and Jalvas's heart.

Seth let out a scream of agony as a pale, orange-red glow flowed up his arm from the weapon and enveloped his body. He trembled, unable to release the knife or pull it free of Jalvas's body, despite the pain that was beyond anything he'd ever felt, ever imagined. At the height of the pain, he thought he was going to die, because no one could suffer like this and still live.

Dimly he heard Tempest scream his name, a word echoed by Kara. He felt hands reach for him, trying to pull him away from Jalvas, but they disappeared almost as soon as they touched him.

Aaron cursed behind him. "He's too hot. I can't get a hold of him!" he shouted to the others.

"Seth, just let go," Tempest cried as she ran toward him, but she heeded Aaron's warning and didn't touch either Seth or Jalvas.

Seth tried to speak, but the pain was too much. He couldn't unclench his jaw long enough to get out even a single word.

Then suddenly, it was over. Jalvas and Seth collapsed to the ground. The glow around Seth disappeared, and the knife returned to its former appearance as it slid free of Jalvas's body.

Aaron grabbed Seth and pulled him away from Jalvas, though it wasn't necessary as the god's eyes were dull and lifeless, his body still in death.

"Seth!" Tempest dropped to her knees beside him, running her fingers lightly over his face and throat, the latter of which had already started to bruise. "What was that?"

"Don't know," Seth said, his voice more a croak from the damage Jalvas's hand had caused.

Aelia and Kara joined the others so he was circled, and he closed his eyes, so relieved he wanted to cry. It had worked. Even if Jalvas had done irreparable damage to his throat, it was worth it. They were alive, all of them. That was what mattered.

"Are you okay? Don't tell me you're going to let some puny...was he seriously a Lemurian god?" Kara asked.

"He was," Tempest said quietly, still stroking Seth's skin soothingly.

"Shit. Well, he was a puny god, so suck it up," Kara finished, though her eyes were damp with worry.

"I'm going to get him some water," Aelia said, jumping up and running to the stream. She managed to find a piece of bark she could pry off a nearby tree and filled it before bringing it carefully back. Aaron helped Seth sit up enough to sip at the water.

"So why'd you attack a god, Seth? You're not normally the sort to start shit like that," Aaron said, though Seth thought he sounded half-impressed.

An angry man's voice came from behind the group. "I'd like to know that myself."

CHAPTER 29

Five sets of eyes shot to the newcomer. Unlike Jalvas, he was impressive, both in appearance and power. He stood nearly as tall as Seth, and with a similarly athletic build. But where Seth was dark, this man was light, with bright blue eyes almost the exact color of a clear summer sky and blond hair that brushed his shoulders. And he looked supremely pissed, right up until he spotted Tempest. The angry facade faltered, replaced by one of confusion, then happiness.

"Tempest?"

"This isn't another god you're going to attack, is it?" Aaron whispered to Seth, who could only shrug.

Tempest wasn't so uncertain. The concerned expression on her face was replaced with one of joy as she leapt to her feet and rushed to the man, throwing her arms around him in a hug, one that was immediately returned. "Vazi! I thought you were dead!"

"And I hoped that you were alive. I'm so sorry I wasn't able to release you. Did you sleep for long?" Vazi asked, forgetting about his initial question.

"I've only been awake for a few weeks," she admitted as she drew back.

"And how long has it been?" he asked, apprehension sliding across his features.

Hesitantly, she answered, "More than six thousand years." She frowned. "How is it you're speaking English and not Lemurian?"

He shrugged. "I'm a god," he said as if it answered everything, and no one there questioned it.

Tempest nodded slowly as she tried to process everything that had happened in the last few minutes. "Then you are the one who put me in that...chamber?" She couldn't quite bring herself to call it a tomb, even though it could have easily become just that.

Vazi nodded slowly. "I was. I knew that Lemuria was going to fall, and I wanted to ensure you remained safe."

The conversation between them had Seth's gut twisting. Clearly, these two had a history, and Tempest had mentioned the name Vazi on several occasions. The way they were acting now, he had to wonder if they'd been an item before Lemuria's fall, but he couldn't bring himself to ask.

"Vazi? The god of the sky?" Aelia asked instead as she rose to her feet, though she remained next to Aaron.

The question drew Vazi's attention back to the others and some of his anger returned. "Yes. And would one of you care to explain why Jalvas, the god of mountains, lies there dead?" He looked down to Tempest. "And why you apparently permitted this?"

Tempest stepped back, retreating until she could sink down to the grass beside Seth, but it was obvious she wasn't afraid of Vazi. "A lot has changed since you put me to sleep, Vazi. Lemuria sank. This island seems to be all that's left of it. Since I woke, I've been hunted, attacked, and had a blood curse placed on me. As to Jalvas..." Her gaze dropped to the god's still form and she faltered. She reached for Seth's hand and Vazi's eyes narrowed as he caught the action.

"I killed Jalvas because if I hadn't he would have killed us," Seth managed to say, and he was surprised to find that speech hurt less than it had a minute ago.

His companions were vocal about expressing their shock.

"What?"

"How do you know?"

"I knew he looked like a bastard!"

"Are you sure?"

Vazi only crossed his arms over his chest. "Explain. To all of us, it sounds like."

Seth sat up slowly, and only then realized he was still holding the knife. He had to all but pry his fingers off the handle so he could drop it in his lap. His hand was burned, but oddly, it didn't hurt. It also seemed like it was healing. Flexing it testingly, he frowned, but there were more important things at the moment.

"The first time—" He broke off when questions were fired at him and he held up a hand until they subsided. "The first time when Jalvas showed up, he asked her how she survived, yelled at her for ruining his plans. Said that as long as they were looking for a Lemurian, he wouldn't be safe. That they'd find him and he wouldn't escape. He sent the assassins after you, Tempest," he said quietly, only to watch her face fall.

He reached for her, but she shook her head and scooted a few inches away from him. "I'm fine. Continue, please."

It hurt not to comfort her. It hurt more that she moved away, but he nodded. "When he got done yelling, he attacked us. I was thrown against a tree and broke nearly every bone in my body," he admitted. "Then he grabbed Tempest around the throat and made the ground split open." He sent an apologetic look to Aelia, Aaron, and Kara. "You three fell into the chasm, just before he...before he killed Tempest."

"What do you mean, the first time?" Vazi asked, and that was a voice Seth wasn't willing to ignore.

"Exactly that. After he'd killed Tempest, he left me to die. He...thought it was crueler than killing me outright." And he'd been right. Luckily, things hadn't worked out the way Jalvas wanted. "Then someone else showed up. Another god. And no, I don't know who. He wouldn't tell me his name. He looked older, but really muscular. Like a weird mix between Hephaestus and Zeus. I just thought of him as Father Time."

"Why Father Time?" Aelia asked with a frown.

"Because he told me that he'd send me back in time to just before Tempest first stepped onto Lemuria, in exchange for a future favor.," Seth explained.

"That's when you started acting oddly," Tempest whispered.

He nodded. "And I'm sorry I didn't explain," he said as he tried to catch her eyes. She refused to look at him and he fought back the regret that pooled in his belly. "Father Time told me that it was best if I didn't tell you guys anything. Said things would play out differently if I did. But he did tell me that your knife would help us. It couldn't have turned out any worse than it already had, so I agreed. You know the rest of it."

"Not quite," Aaron disagreed with a shake of his head. "All that makes sense, yes, though I'm very curious who this god was. There are only a handful who are really linked with time. But what did that knife do to you? And how did it kill a *god*?"

"It's a Lemurian dagger," Aelia explained. "I found it ages ago and gave it to Tempest when we met, once I was sure she was actually Lemurian. But as far as I can tell, it just healed me faster when I used it, but I never killed anyone with it."

"May I?" Vazi asked as he stepped closer and held out his hand, but despite the apparent politeness of his words, it was clearly a demand.

Seth wanted to know more anyway, so he gingerly picked the knife up and offered it to Vazi, handle first.

The blade was clean even though it should be bloody, and it lay dormant in Vazi's hands as he looked it over. "What happened when you stabbed Jalvas?" he asked, looking up to Seth.

Seth's mouth opened, but all he could really recall was the blinding pain.

Seeing Seth's inability to answer, Kara spoke up. "The knife looked like it turned red hot, both Seth and Jalvas screamed, then Seth glowed a weird orange color."

"Did it look like lava?"

Kara nodded. "I mean, kinda, yeah."

"Then that explains quite a bit, including why I'm here," Vazi said as he gave the knife back to Seth. "That knife is called Lemuria's Fire."

Tempest's head jerked up and she frowned at him. "Are you sure?"

Vazi's gaze softened, and he nodded. "I am."

"What's Lemuria's Fire?" Aaron asked, his archaeologist coming to the surface.

"A knife forged in the heart of the one volcano on Lemuria." Vazi looked to the west. "It may or may not still exist," he murmured thoughtfully before he shook his head. "But that doesn't matter." He looked back to Seth. "It can only do one thing, but it's extremely powerful. It transfers power from a person killed by it to the one wielding the knife."

Seth blinked and, once that sank in, shook his head. "That's...not possible."

Vazi shot him a dangerous look and a strong breeze began to flow around him, teasing the grass and their hair. "Are you really going to argue with me?"

"No, I just mean...If that's true, then I took in his god powers. And I don't feel like a god. Shouldn't I feel different? Shouldn't I have powers?" Seth protested.

"And how do you know what being a god feels like?" Vazi asked with a smirk, arching a brow. "And have you tried using any powers?" Without waiting for Seth to answer, he continued. "I thought not. But you *are* a god. Specifically the new Lemurian god of mountains. A god of light."

"Light? You're telling me that murdering jackass was a light god?" Kara asked in disbelief.

"Remember what we were saying about balance?" Aelia interjected quietly, staring at the look of anger on Vazi's face. "If he was the only Lemurian god alive and awake, then there wasn't any balance."

"Oh. Yeah, I guess that makes sense," Kara mumbled.

"You said the knife explained why you were here," Aaron said. "What did you mean?"

"Like your friend said, balance. A new god of light was born, so a dark god was revived to be a balance," Vazi said with a shrug. "As to why it was me specifically and not Jalvas's counterpart...The only thing I can think of is that my powers are connected to Tempest, since I was the one who made her slumber, and it's my magic she wears on her wrist. Which meant mine was the only power still around to grab hold of."

Tempest sharply lifted her wrist to stare at the bracelet. "What is this thing, anyway? I didn't even notice it until it was pointed out."

Vazi sighed and ran a hand through his hair. "It was meant to protect you. It made it so that you wouldn't die of starvation or dehydration while you slept, and it ensured that no god could use their powers on you."

"But one did," she protested. "Not long after I woke, a Greek goddess used her magic to heal me and teach me English."

He inclined his head to her. "I misspoke. It meant no god could use their powers on you to harm."

"Oh."

"Jalvas mentioned that," Seth murmured.

"What?" Tempest asked in surprise.

"Right before he..." No, he wasn't going to go there. "He said something about how the bracelet kept him from using his powers to kill you." Seth looked accusingly at Vazi. "It didn't stop him from snapping her neck, though."

Regret shone on Vazi's face, and he crouched by Tempest. "And I am so sorry for that, *agapila*. I had hoped that I'd make it through alive, that I could retrieve you after just a few weeks. I never once dreamt that you would be trapped, asleep, for so long."

Tempest drew in a shaky breath and shook her head. "Don't apologize." She looked to Seth, then back to Vazi. "If you hadn't put me in that chamber, I'd likely be dead." She hesitated, then added in a quiet voice, "Like the rest of our people."

Vazi flinched back, horror showing on his face. "Dead? All of them?"

"Unfortunately, Tempest is the last Lemurian alive, as far as anyone can tell," Aelia said gently. "Most died when Lemuria sank, and the rest died over the next few centuries. And you—and now Seth—are the last Lemurian gods alive and awake."

Vazi shot her a look of disbelief. "Are you sure?" he demanded.

She nodded. "I am. I was here, just before it sank. I'm one of the few alive who know the truth of Lemuria, other than the gods."

His eyes hardened. "Yes, the gods would remember. And they have much to answer for," he said darkly.

"Vazi," Tempest said quietly. "Don't. Not now. Please."

"Unfortunately, he does have a point," Seth reluctantly said. "Jalvas hired assassins. It sounded like he went through some sort of company or group of people. So there are still people hunting for you."

"Doesn't matter," Aaron said, a little too casually.

"What?" Seth snarled, only to jump when his voice came out as an echoing boom, just as Jalvas's had. It was going to take some time to adjust to his new status.

Aaron arched a brow, his lips twitching upward. "And that is part of why it doesn't matter. She's not exactly an easy target, you know. And she's got not one, but *two* Lemurian gods who would go through a hell of a lot to keep her safe. Not to mention she's got friends, including a tiger shifter, stone witch, and an immortal who knows more than just about any person on the planet. *And* she can take refuge on an island that even the gods can't find. I think Tempest will be fine until you guys come up with a more permanent solution."

Everyone went quiet as they processed the truth of his words, and he smiled smugly. "The way I see it, the only thing we have to figure out is how to make some of these homes habitable. I'm overdue for a vacation, you know. Even if I doubt there's any wi-fi way out here. But that's what satellite uplinks are for."

"You know...I haven't had a vacation in a while," Kara mused a moment later. "And I've been in my house for a little too long. People are going to start noticing that I haven't aged."

"I don't remember the last time I had a vacation. And it'd be nice not having to hide the whole undying thing," Aelia agreed with a nod.

Astonished, Tempest looked at each of them and asked, "You would stay here with me?"

"Of course. That's what friends do," Kara said with a grin. "And this is pretty much a tropical paradise. Seems big enough that we can all have space so we don't feel crowded, but still can drop in and hang out whenever we want."

Aaron and Aelia could only nod their agreement of Kara's words, though the former added, "I mean, after my vacation I will need to go back to work, but I could do worse for a home base."

Tempest looked to Vazi. "And you? Are you going to go hunting the other pantheons?"

Vazi looked mutinous for a minute before he sighed. "I suppose not. At least not right away. It sounds like much has changed that I need to learn about. I don't know what this wi-fi is, for example."

Aaron glanced between Vazi and Seth, then got to his feet. "Oh, have I got a lot to show you. Come with me and I'll tell you the joys of technology, my friend. I'm Aaron, by the way."

Vazi frowned down at Tempest, but she gave him a pleading look and he nodded. "Very well. And who are you two lovely ladies?" he asked to Aelia and Kara, who stood and followed after Aaron and Vazi, introducing themselves.

Alone, Tempest looked apprehensively to Seth. "And you? I know you didn't want any of this. You found me by accident, and it's caused you no small amount of trouble."

Seth brushed the backs of his fingers across her cheek and shook his head. "I don't think I found you by accident. Father Time had a few interesting things to say about fate, and I have to agree. I think I was meant to find you. I think all this was meant to happen." His hand slid into her hair and he drew her closer until he could brush his lips against hers. "I only regret one thing in all this, and it's that I had to see you die." The image of it flashed in his mind, and he wrapped his arms around her. Pulling her into his lap, he buried his face against her throat and reveled in the feel of her, alive and warm against him. "That's not something I ever want to see again, Tempest. No matter how bad it hurt when I killed Jalvas, it doesn't even come close to how it felt to see you die."

Tempest stroked Seth's hair, overwhelmed by the emotions his words caused. "Seth...I'm alive. I'm not going anywhere. I'm right here."

He lifted his head before he slowly shook it. "You don't understand, Tempest. You were literally dead. And I..." He closed his eyes and expected to have to build up his courage, but found the next words came surprisingly easy. "I never told you I love you."

When his eyes opened, he found hers were full of tears and his heart stopped. "Tempest?"

"Say it again," she whispered.

A wave of relief hit him and he smiled, giving her another kiss. "I love you. I didn't mean to, but it happened. I love you. And if you tell me that Vazi's an ex-boyfriend and you're going to run off with him, I'm going to have to see if this dagger works as well the second time."

Tempest laughed and shook her head, hugging him tightly. "No, no. I mean, there was this one time, but my parents had just died. We're just friends. Good friends, but it's not like that. I love him, but like I love Aelia or Kara. It's not him I'm in love with. It's you."

"Oh good. I wasn't really in the mood to fight another god today. Twice was enough," Seth told her, grinning.

"Really? Fighting one god twice is all you'll fight for me?" she teased.

"Everyone's got to have a line," he told her, and before she could retort, he covered her lips with his own. They kissed deeply, savoring the fact that they were both alive, and would be for a very long time.

Someone clearing their throat had them reluctantly drawing apart, and they looked over to see a grinning Aaron.

"What do you want, Aaron?" Seth grumbled.

"We just wanted Tempest to point out which house was hers before we go picking out crash pads. So stop making out with your girl and come join the victory celebration."

Tempest hid her face against Seth's shoulder and giggled. "We probably should join them."

"Fine, but we're continuing this tonight," Seth said on a sigh, setting her on her feet before he stood.

"I'm counting on it," Tempest said, before they joined the others, walking hand in hand.

It was time to shed the weight of what might have been, and embrace the new life she'd found.

"Why are you calling me now?"

"I know you said that you would take care of the woman. I was just curious about the status of that," Joseph told his father, struggling to keep his voice steady. His father abhorred any signs of weakness and was quick to take advantage of them.

"Why? So you could offer to help again and bungle it? Again?" his father asked snidely.

"I've only done my best, Father," Joseph said, rubbing his temple. "I sent the best trackers and the best assassins after her."

"And they failed, didn't they? But I didn't. Her body's either been eaten by some sea creature or will be washing ashore somewhere any day now," came the smug reply.

Joseph froze. "She's dead?" He almost couldn't believe it. For that matter, he wasn't sure he did. His father was arrogant to a fault and wasn't one to admit to his failures. "That's wonderful," he said anyway. "Will you tell me what was so important about her? Now that she's no longer an issue?"

"There's no reason for you to know. Just know that she was the last of a dangerous race, a race that's now extinct. The status quo has been restored."

"I'm so happy to hear that, Father. Congratulations."

"I don't need your congratulations," his father sneered. "Now, don't call me again unless it's something important."

"Of course, Father. I'll—" He broke off as his father ended the call and forced himself to set the phone on his desk.

No, he didn't believe this woman was dead. And he wouldn't believe it until he saw the proof of her demise for himself. So rather than call his men off the search, he'd continue to pay them for what could be a waste of money.

Except now he didn't want her dead. He smiled slowly. No, he wanted her alive and in his custody. If she was important enough that his father would get involved, then he had no doubt she could give him just what he needed.

A way to strike back at the man who had never acted like a father to his son.

CHAPTER 30

Though the others had mentioned claiming homes, their first order of business was finding food. They'd gotten distracted before eating a single bite, and they were still all suffering from hunger and dehydration. Fortunately, the fruit trees were as healthy as they'd ever been, and thanks to Vazi and Tempest, they were able to find several vegetables to round out the meal.

By the time they had sated their bellies, they were all too eager to claim a house and get some actual rest. Sleeping on the raft had been far from satisfying, and they knew it would take time to get a bed fit enough to sleep in. Though Seth was pretty sure they were all—except for Vazi—so exhausted that they could sleep on stone and not notice.

Vazi promised he was okay and would help them get situated, but Seth had a feeling he wanted to stick close to Tempest. That made him itchy, but he mostly let it pass. Tempest had already explained their relationship and told him that she loved him, not Vazi, so he wasn't going to argue about someone else keeping her safe, especially not another god.

God. That was going to take some getting used to. He was a freaking *god*. It still didn't feel real that he'd gone from being a powerless halfling to a full-fledge deity.

His dad was going to flip.

But that was a problem for tomorrow. He might be immortal now—or so he assumed—but he wanted eight hours of sleep before he tried to figure out what he could do now.

Tempest's house was, in fact, still standing. However, it, like all other stone structures they'd found, was covered in plants and showed signs of animal occupation. While he found himself curious about what sort of animals made Lemuria home, that too was an issue for tomorrow.

After his first glance, he watched Tempest, watching her reaction to the state of her beloved home. She didn't fall apart. Not even after all she'd gone through. Her eyes were sad and damp, but that was the only obvious reaction to the mess that was her house.

He slid his arm around her waist and pulled her into him. It was then he could feel the slight trembling. Pressing a kiss to her hair, he murmured, "We'll fix it, darlin'. I promise."

"I know," she whispered. "Thank you."

He smiled and nodded before turning to the others. "I don't think any of us want to clear out a bunch of houses right now. Why don't we just do this one for now, and you guys can pick out your new homes later? Looks like this one's big enough."

Tempest smiled at his suggestion and leaned into him.

"Sounds good to me," Aaron said with a nod. "Since we've already died once today, I think we can be a little lazy."

"Not funny," Aelia muttered and jabbed him lightly in the ribs.

"What's funny is that you don't think so," Kara said thoughtfully. "Don't you ever use dying as an excuse to be lazy?"

"What do you mean by that?" Vazi asked, giving Aelia a considering look.

"Not now, Vazi," Tempest interjected. She could see how uncomfortable Aelia was, and Vazi could be relentless when he wanted to know something. While she was still curious about Aelia's longevity, they had time to work it out.

He didn't want to let it go, but at a look from her, he did. It helped that they all got to work.

Though Seth, Aaron, and Aelia went with manual labor to clean the place out, the other three all used their powers. Tempest swept the place with air, and Kara used her meager plant magic to encourage vines to grow elsewhere. And though Vazi was known as a god of the sky, he was, after all, a god, and his powers weren't that limited. Though he didn't just snap his fingers and instantly make it perfect, he was able to restore the furniture to its previous state. A good thing, as the mattress and cushions had deteriorated in the millennia since Tempest had last seen them.

By the time they were done, the house was livable. She couldn't say it was just as it had been the last time she'd seen it, but it was close. It nearly brought her to tears. She refused to let them spill, though. After all they'd been through—including dying, apparently!—she wasn't going to let a little thing like a homecoming make her cry.

"You want to get some rest?" Seth asked quietly as he walked up to her and rubbed a hand over her back.

"I do. I know there's still a lot that needs done—like you figuring out your godhood—and we need to make a plan on how to find the people after me, but my brain is just...fuzzy," she admitted.

"That's understandable," he said with a nod. "I think everyone feels that way. Even Vazi. He might have just woken up, but I figure it's kind of how you felt when you first woke up."

She tipped her head back to smile up at him. "Probably."

"Then you go on back. I'll get these guys settled and join you."

She leaned up to kiss him lightly. "Thank you."

"Anytime."

He watched her leave, then turned back to the others. "You guys all know where you're sleeping?"

Kara answered simply, by pointing at the pallet Vazi had conjured.

Aelia nodded. "I do," she said, sinking down onto the sofa. When Aaron dropped down onto it beside her, Seth arched a brow, but said nothing when Aelia gave him a sidelong look. Since she didn't protest, he wasn't going to say anything.

Vazi studied them—or maybe just Aelia—for a moment before he turned back to Seth. "Apparently, I've slept entirely too long already. I'm going to see just how much of my home remains, and in what condition."

Seth was actually relieved to hear that. It wasn't something that had been at the forefront of his mind, not with Jalvas and Vazi popping up, but it was important. He was just happy that they'd found the chunk they did. A livable chunk. It could be that there were other islands remaining somewhere, and Vazi could likely find them quicker than anyone else.

"Hopefully..." Vazi continued after a moment, but he trailed off before finishing the thought. Seth got where he was going, though. If they were lucky, there were other Lemurians somewhere out there.

"Good luck," he told the god.

"Thank you." Vazi glanced at the bedroom, then disappeared.

Seth turned back to the other three. "Sleep well," he said before he joined Tempest in the bedroom and shut the door behind him.

He had half expected to find her already asleep, but she was stretched out on the bed, beneath the blankets Vazi had conjured, staring up at the ceiling. "I'd ask if you're okay, but it seems like a stupid question," he told her as he stripped off his shirt and took his boots off. No way was he getting into a clean bed while wearing dirty clothes.

"Not stupid," she disagreed, her eyes flicking over to him. "I can't say I'm bad, though. Overwhelmed, but not bad." A smile began to form on her face. "Lemuria exists, after all. And not all my gods are gone." She laughed. "There's even a new one!"

"Yeah," he said, drawing the word out as he rubbed a hand over the back of his neck. "Let's save that for tomorrow, okay?"

"I'm okay with that," she agreed. "In fact, I'd love nothing more than to not talk until we've both gotten some sleep." Since her statement was accompanied by a slow look over his body, he didn't think she wanted sleep right away.

His lips twitched as he undid the button of his pants. "Oh yeah? And what'd you have in mind?"

"Well...you told me I died today. I think it'd be nice if you proved to me that I'm alive," she told him as she drew back the blankets to reveal that she wasn't wearing a thing beneath them.

He hooked his thumbs in the waistband of his pants, drawing them and his boxers down, showing his rapidly hardening cock. "I think that can definitely be arranged."

As he approached the bed, she moved to her knees, lifting her chin and offering her mouth to him. His fingers speared into her hair as he kissed her fiercely, trying to replace the sight of her lying dead with this. This sight, this memory. But he kept it brief before drawing back just enough to look into her stormy eyes. "You're going to have to be quiet," he murmured, letting his hands slide down over her shoulders to her breasts, pinching her nipples lightly, but it was enough to draw a soft gasp from her. He pressed kisses along her jaw until he reached her ear to whisper, "Think you can manage that?"

"I don't know," she admitted as she tilted her head to accommodate the lips that now roamed down her throat.

"Try." One hand slid down her belly until his fingers found the damp flesh between her thighs. Automatically, she parted her legs for him and was instantly rewarded. She had to bite her lip to stifle the moan when one digit eased into her and the heel of his hand rubbed against her clit.

"More," she breathed as she rocked against the lazily thrusting finger.

"You're going to have to be patient, but don't worry. I won't keep you waiting too long," he promised. He bent his head to capture one nipple between his lips, at the same time a second finger was added to the first.

Tempest gasped and her hips jerked. Her hands found his shoulders and gripped firmly, needing the support as he began to suck and tease in earnest.

Seth felt a gentle breeze begin to swirl around them and would have smiled if his mouth wasn't otherwise occupied. It was something that only happened when she was exceptionally aroused—or emotional—and he loved the small sign that she wasn't in full control of herself.

At least he wasn't the only one who lost it when they were together.

He kept up the sweet torment, switching to her other breast to pay it the same attention. When the rocking of her hips became frantic, he lifted his head and found her mouth once more. His fingers curled to stroke against the extra-sensitive spot within her, then captured her cry when she splintered and spasmed around his fingers.

Despite the orgasm, Tempest was not done with him yet, her body far from sated. "More," she half-moaned, half-demanded against his lips. Her arms wrapped around him and she twisted, using her powers to add strength when she pushed him onto the bed. Though he landed on his back, she was well aware that he'd allowed it. He might not know his powers yet, but few were as strong as the god of mountains.

His smile was hot and a little smug as he watched her straddle his hips. Roughened hands stroked over her thighs before he shifted to rub his cock against her. "Impatient, are you?" he teased in a voice that had gone rough with lust. She loved it.

"Definitely," she agreed as she reached down to press the head of him against her folds, then lowered herself to take him deep inside her. This time when she moaned, his own mingled with hers. His hands tightened on her thighs as he ground up against her.

Leaning down to kiss him caused sweet friction to slice through them, and her breath caught. "This time," she breathed a moment later, "you're going to have to be patient."

He shook his head and moved one hand to her hip, the other to where they were joined, his thumb stroking over her clit. "I make no promises."

"Good." Straightening, she stroked her hands over his chest, shook her hair behind her shoulders, then began to ride him. Though she intended to go slow, to draw it out, the feel of him sliding in and out of her was just too good. It had always been wonderful between them, but there was something more this time. Maybe it was all they'd been through, or their earlier confessions. It could even be that this was their first time together on Lemuria or with him as a god. Whatever the reason, it didn't matter. Nothing had ever felt like this, affected her like this. Every cell in her body sang with pleasure and need, and every touch he gave her made her feel supremely loved.

Before she realized it, her languid movements were rapid and nearly frenzied. The rise and fall of her hips helped brush his thumb over her, only adding fuel to her desire. When she felt her climax begin to build, she panted his name, unable to look away from his face.

Something about his name on her lips made him snap. He couldn't lay there and just accept what she was giving him any longer. With one hand, he pushed himself upright and his other arm banded around her lower back. Holding her firmly, he helped her to lift, then slam back onto him. The pace and strength of the thrusts shot her over the edge and changed the light swirling of air into something rougher and more chaotic. Her cry was lost in the wind as she clung to him, body trembling.

Seth drew her down onto him only once more before his muscles went rigid and he poured himself into her.

Her forehead fell against his shoulder and she struggled to calm her breathing and her magic. With his arms still around her, he slowly leaned back until he was horizontal and she was draped over him, his breathing just as ragged.

"So…do you feel alive, now?" he asked a minute later, the humor weak in his voice, but present. His arms loosened so he could run a hand along her back, making her shiver and sigh in contentment.

She smiled and brushed her lips across the pulse that still thudded heavily in his throat. "Mmhmm. I feel wonderful. Suddenly tired, of course, but wonderful."

He kissed her brow. "Good. Make sure you stay that way." He reached out and grabbed the blanket, pulling it over them. It felt like his ass was sticking out, but it was a comfortable enough temperature for him not to worry too much.

"We've got a lot to do tomorrow," she said after a long pause, her voice growing thick with sleep.

"That's for tomorrow. For now, just sleep."

Tempest nodded and let her cheek rest on his chest, her body relaxing further as unconsciousness began to claim her. Just before she drifted off, she mumbled, "Love you."

Exhausted or not, he grinned at the almost absently spoken words. "I love you, too," he replied quietly.

Though Seth had expected his sleep would be filled with nightmares of Tempest's unseeing eyes or worries about the future, he found himself dreaming of a tropical island full of magical people. And a magnificent woman standing by his side.

CHAPTER 31

Though Seth thought they would all sleep late, he was shocked by exactly how long they slept since it was well after noon when then woke. Especially if he was, as Vazi insisted, now a god. Shouldn't gods need less sleep than mortals?

Vazi certainly didn't seem to have slept nearly as long as they did—if he slept at all. When they made their way out of Tempest's home, they saw he'd found or conjured a table, six chairs, and several clay jugs. The latter he'd filled with water and a juice that tasted remarkably similar to orange juice, but a little sweeter. He also had a large platter covered in fruit he'd gathered.

They were mostly silent while they filled their bellies, but the mood was tense. They'd slept, which meant they now had to discuss the issues weighing on them all.

"What'd you find out?" Aelia asked Vazi when she'd settled back in her chair.

Vazi smiled thinly when five pairs of eyes fixed on him, and settled his ankle on his knee as he linked his fingers over his stomach.

"What does she mean? What'd you do?" Tempest asked, having missed the conversation the evening before.

"I went to see how much of our home remained...and if anyone else was hiding somewhere on the remnants," Vazi explained, his voice gentle.

She leaned forward slightly, her eyes widening. "What'd you find? Are there others?"

He shook his head slowly. "I didn't find a single sign of another person. There are quite a few animals, but no people," he answered quietly. "I found a surprising amount of land considering what Aelia told us, but it's empty."

Seth reached for her and Tempest had to fight the urge to go immaterial. It wouldn't lessen her emotions, but it would keep them from seeing her tears. Instead, she let him wrap her in his arms and pressed her face against his shoulder as she fought to get herself under control. Vazi's findings weren't a surprise, but it did eliminate the last of her hope that her people still lived.

Except...they did. Vazi was an old Lemurian. Seth was also Lemurian now. And while it was unlikely that the rest of the land could be raised from the bottom of the sea, there was the possibility that Lemurians could inhabit the world again. Kara's children. Aaron's children.

Her own.

That calmed her racing heart, and she was able to lift her face and draw in a deep breath.

"You okay?" Seth murmured, rubbing her back.

"I am," she told him, and meant it. "You said you found a surprising amount of land. How much, if you had to guess?"

Vazi hesitated. "Before I answer that, I should tell you that I did discover something...interesting."

Aelia shifted in her chair and glanced to Tempest, then away. Tempest noticed, but filed it away for later. "Interesting how?" she asked instead.

"There seem to be some islands, smaller ones, that exist where Lemuria used to be, but...they aren't Lemuria."

Tempest shook her head. "I don't think I understand."

He blew out a breath and shrugged. "I don't know how it happened, but there is land where—back in our time—Lemurian land existed. But none of our magic lies in that land. People are there, too. Humans, mostly, but not entirely. Perhaps some of the other gods placed the land there, or it rose naturally over time...I just don't know."

Though she considered that for a moment, it didn't matter right now. It wouldn't matter unless somehow there was a way to raise the entirety of Lemuria. "This land is Lemurian, though. Even if this island is all that still remains, it's something. Is it big enough for us to start over? To have actual lives here?"

Vazi smiled and nodded. "If we're comparing it to what we once had, it's almost nothing. But for us? For the family you're building? Yes. It's large enough for several good-sized villages, a number of farms, and plenty of land for the animals to continue to thrive."

She returned his smile and her hand found Seth's and squeezed. "Good. That's all we need. We still have a *home*."

"We do."

"We need to make sure you keep that home," Aaron said as he grabbed another round fruit, one that was a pale shade of blue. He broke it open and took a bite of the tender flesh. "We need to figure out how we're going to, well, figure out who's after you, and how to stop them."

"I agree. Which is why I'd like you to tell me what happened from the moment you woke, Tempest. The troubles you had, how you found Lemuria, everything."

"Seth?" she asked, given that the story really began with him finding her.

He nodded and began detailing everything for the god. The attacks, Hecate's visit on the plane, recruiting the others to help, and the struggles they'd had in the Pacific. The others chimed in to add details or give their points of view, but they gave Vazi their entire journey from Peru to where they currently sat.

Vazi nodded now and again, and looked intrigued when they talked about Hecate and the dream Tempest had experienced. It was the former he focused on first. "You said she was a Greek goddess? Of magic?"

"And other things, yes," Seth verified.

Again, Vazi nodded, his expression thoughtful. When he said nothing for several minutes, Kara broke the silence. "I know we need to plan, but we also need to figure out what's here and pick out where we're going to live. Any reason why we can't multitask?"

"I'm all for multitasking," Aaron said as he rose and polished off his fruit.

"I'd definitely like to look around. I haven't gotten to see much," Tempest added with a smile.

They all got to their feet and Tempest ended up in the lead, with Seth on one side of her, Vazi on the other. There weren't any other structures in the immediate vicinity of Tempest's house, so they made their way down to the village. By unspoken agreement, they stayed together. None of them truly believed the assassins could find them here, not when Lemuria had been hidden for so long, but there was always safety in numbers.

"You don't think any of them would mind us just...taking over their homes, do you?" Aelia asked in a hushed voice.

Vazi smiled at her and shook his head. "No, they wouldn't mind at all." He arched a brow. "Didn't you say you'd been to Lemuria before?"

"I did," she confirmed, "but it's been a lot longer for me than it has for you, and I didn't get to spend as much time interacting with your people as I would have liked. And while I know there aren't bodies in any of these homes or anything, it just feels a little...odd."

"It does, but he's right," Tempest reassured her. "I like to think they'd be happy that we're rebuilding, even if it's on a small scale."

Aelia seemed to accept their words and offered no further protests as they explored the village.

Kara was the first to find a house that suited her, though that was a vast understatement. Despite the natural decor covering in it, it took her only a single pass through the eight-room house to fall in love with it. "This one's mine!" she cried as she stepped out the front door and did a little dance. It was silly, with lots of arm waving and booty-shaking, and helped clear some of the somber mood. "It has an amazing bathroom with a freaking *pool* for a tub. And it has a library! With books! I can't believe they survived, but they did. Not that I'll be able to read any of them—yet—but there are so many books in there!" The hip wiggle turned into a full on spin before she turned back to face them. "Can we start working on it now?" she asked, pressing her palms together and giving them all hopeful looks.

"Oh gods," Seth groaned. "She's doing the eyes. I hate it when she does the eyes."

Tempest laughed and walked to the witch, linking her arm through Kara's to head back inside. "Of course we can!"

While they worked, they talked. About the homes to an extent, but mostly going over what they knew and how they could learn more. To Seth, it seemed like they were primarily just thinking out loud, but that wasn't necessarily a bad thing. A lot of problems could be worked out that way, so he didn't hesitate to join in.

"You know, when we were talking to Hecate on the plane, it seemed as though she *couldn't* tell us more, not that she didn't want to," he said as he swept millennia of dirt out of the kitchen.

"What, like a curse or something?" Kara asked.

"I was thinking a geas, but yeah." He paused and looked over to Vazi. "If she is, it makes me wonder how trustworthy she is. I mean, she did help us, and I'm not entirely sure we'd be here if she hadn't, but what did she leave out?"

"I knew her—a little—before the battle," Vazi said as he worked on restoring the furniture. "I can't say we were the best of friends, but what I knew of her was that she tended to be the mediator." His lips twitched. "That isn't to say she was a pushover, she could be fierce if necessary, but I don't see her betraying you like that if she had any choice."

Seth looked at Tempest and arched a brow questioningly at her. She responded with a little frown. "What are you thinking?" she asked.

"I'm wondering if it's possible to summon a Greek goddess to an island hidden from the world."

With that statement, Vazi again found himself the subject of scrutiny. He chuckled and sat down in one of the chairs he'd finished fixing. "In general, deities are able to go almost anywhere, so long as they have a worshiper to call out to them or aren't blocked from a place. Others can summon gods with the correct spells as well."

"Great, but can she get here?" Aaron muttered irritably. While he was at home digging in the dirt for artifacts, this kind of manual labor wasn't something he normally bothered with and it was annoying him. That, in turn, amused the hell out of Seth, who understood exactly why his former rival was so snippy.

Vazi rolled his eyes at the angry tiger, but nodded. "Of course." His gaze lifted upward. "Hecate. Join us." The words weren't any louder than the ones before it, but it seemed to Seth that they carried farther.

A handful of seconds passed before Hecate appeared in the middle of the room. She glanced around, then beamed when she saw who she was surrounded by. "You survived," she said on a happy sigh. "I was a little concerned when the storm blocked my ability to see you."

"It blocked our ability to see much, too," Aaron grumbled, but he didn't hesitate to drop what he was doing and move closer to the others. Right next to Aelia, in fact, who elbowed him lightly. "Sorry," he murmured to her.

Hecate only smiled. "Thank you, though, for agreeing to help them."

"Yeah, well, when a goddess asks for help, it's not smart to say no."

"Still." Her smile shifted to Aelia, though there was more curiosity in it, before her focus moved to Vazi. "I had hoped that they'd make it here safety, but I have to say, I didn't expect to see you here, Vazi. I'd be very curious to hear how they not only made it here, but managed to wake you."

"Perhaps I'll tell you. If they don't beat me to it," Vazi said with a grin.

"I think we can let you tell that one," Tempest teased. "After all, we've been the ones telling stories...over and over again. I think I need a break."

"I know I do," Seth agreed as he leaned the broom against the wall and joined Tempest, draping an arm around her shoulders. "Thank you for the help, Hecate."

The goddess's eyes sharpened as she finally focused on him. "I definitely didn't see this coming," she murmured as she stepped closer to him, moving right into his personal space. She lifted a hand and moved it along the line of his face, never touching him. "I definitely would like that story, Vazi. Sooner rather than later," she told him absently.

"How about we trade stories?" he suggested, drawing her attention away from the now-uncomfortable Seth.

Hecate took a step back and looked to Vazi, her expression apologetic. "I'm afraid I won't be much help to you."

Vazi nodded understandingly. "Seth told me he believed you might be under a geas. A powerful one, if it prevented a goddess of magic from breaking it."

Unable to confirm or deny, she only gave him a weak smile.

"Would you permit me to try?"

"If you think you could manage it, I would welcome the chance to be able to speak freely. There—" Her voice cut off then, and she scowled, proving to Seth the geas had forced its will upon her again. "Yes, please," she said through gritted teeth.

Vazi walked over to her and placed one hand over her heart, the other on her shoulder, and closed his eyes.

Before Vazi's divine house repairs, Seth had never felt magic before, not like so many of the Arcane did, but this was different. Stronger, more intense. It made his bones hum and he found himself drawn closer to the two deities. He wasn't sure why as he still didn't know what powers he had, or how to use them, but he couldn't stop himself from moving to Vazi's side as he worked.

Hecate let out a low groan as the magic seeped into her, her beautiful features contorting into an expression of intense pain. Seth looked at Vazi's face and found it stony with concentration. Apparently, the geas was stronger than even the Lemurian had realized.

Unsure of what he was doing, Seth lifted his hands, resting his fingers lightly against Hecate's temples. The moment his fingers touched her skin, he felt Vazi's power moving through her, felt the unyielding wall that was the geas. Then he felt his own power—power he hadn't truly believed he had—join with Vazi's in attacking the geas.

The geas fought back and Hecate screamed as the three powers warred within her body. Then, as though their magic had found the weak spot in the spell, it splintered.

Hecate dropped the instant she was free of the magic. Before Seth could drop his arms to reach for her, Vazi had done so, catching her on a cushion of air. They eased her into a chair, but by that point, she was already recovering.

"Thank you," she told them, voice still a little weak.

"You're very welcome," Vazi said as he took a step back to give her some space.

Seth, on the other hand, drifted back to Tempest's side, frowning as he tried to figure out exactly how he'd participated in breaking a geas the Greek goddess of magic and witchcraft hadn't been able to counter.

As though he could read minds, Vazi looked at him and smiled faintly. "Later," he promised.

Seth nodded as Tempest leaned into him. She was a steadying presence, and he didn't hesitate to slide his arms around her.

Aelia, Aaron, and Kara spoke quietly, everyone wanting to give Hecate a chance to recover. Still, it was only a few minutes before Hecate looked to Vazi, then Tempest, and smiled.

"Why don't you get comfortable, and I'll tell you what happened to Lemuria."

CHAPTER 32

With every person in the room wanting to know the truth of Lemuria's destruction, they quickly got settled on chairs or on the floor—or against the wall, in Vazi's case.

"I'm going to start at the very beginning, because I know most of you haven't heard any of this," Hecate began as she shifted to get comfortable. "The Lemurian gods were, as a whole and on average, more powerful than any other pantheon. And, as you know, there are several gods—I won't name names—who are jealous and power-hungry. There were some who began to sow discord among the Lemurians, encouraging them to fight. They may have even been the cause of a few deaths, in hopes that they would throw the balance off enough to spark a war."

"And they succeeded," Tempest said softly.

Hecate nodded and focused on Vazi. "They did," she agreed, voice equally as quiet.

"I had wondered why so many normally level-headed or neutral gods began to grow...argumentative," Vazi admitted. "I'm ashamed to say not even I was innocent."

"I can't say it was entirely your fault, but neither can I absolve you of whatever guilt you may be feeling."

"I don't know that I'm worthy of absolution," Vazi murmured, more to himself than Hecate.

She must have agreed because she went on. "They incited the Lemurians to fight amongst themselves until, one day, a huge battle broke out. I don't know what the final straw was, but I also don't know that any gods stayed neutral."

Vazi's head dropped and his shoulders hunched. "No, none of us stayed neutral." He let out a sharp, mocking laugh. "A few days ago, I would have said there was only one of us who remained sane, but it seems he was a great deal more involved than I realized."

"Jalvas?" Tempest asked, pressing more firmly against Seth's side.

"Jalvas?" Hecate repeated. "Why would you mention him?"

Vazi shook his head. "Later," he promised. "The point is, we all fought, and all because Scuris and Machelis decided to have it out in the middle of the capital."

"The gods of War and Healing," Tempest whispered absently to Seth, but her attention was fixed on Hecate.

"That would do it," Hecate said sadly. "Regardless, it was something that was planned for. When you were all dead or weakened from the battle…multiple gods, from multiple pantheons banded together." She gave him a sad smile. "They weren't able to kill you. I'm not entirely sure why since I didn't participate, but I'm sure they tried. Instead, they locked you—all of you—in an eternal sleep in another realm."

Seth was pissed. Tempest had slept for six thousand years, her people wiped out, all because some gods were jealous that they weren't the most powerful things out there? It made no sense. There was always someone more powerful. Always.

Tempest closed her eyes and leaned more fully against him, but there wasn't much he could do to comfort her except hold her, which he did. He glanced at Kara and the others, finding looks of shock and anger on their faces. But when he turned to Vazi, he was reminded that Vazi was considered a dark god. He was getting pissed, and everyone in the house could feel it. The air literally vibrated with it, making the room uncomfortable. And instead of the sharp breezes Seth had felt before from both Vazi and Tempest, what felt more like small shock waves radiated from the enraged deity.

"Vazi." The air god ignored him, so Seth yelled, "Vazi!" This time his voice came out in a boom that almost startled him, but it got the man's attention.

"What?" he snarled.

"Tone it down," he snapped. "I get it. You're pissed and have every right to be, but you're going to destroy the house and hurt someone if you don't calm the fuck down."

Vazi's gaze shifted around the room. Only Hecate seemed unaffected by the magic itself, but even she looked nervous. With great effort, Vazi drew his power back into him and the air calmed as he did. "I apologize," he ground out, still angry, but in control now.

"We get it," Kara said with a shake of her head. "I'm not even Lemurian and I'm pissed."

"Anyone would be," Aaron added. "Hell, I'm more than happy to claw the shit out of some assholes for you. Except for, you know, the part where they're gods and I'm a shifter."

"Later." More level now, Vazi asked, "Hecate, did you know Jalvas was still awake?"

"Ah. That explains your reaction." She shook her head. "I didn't know it was him, no. I could sense something Lemurian was still around, but when I felt Tempest wake, I thought she was what I'd been sensing."

"You felt me wake?" Tempest asked, surprised.

"Oh yes," Hecate agreed with a nod. "I wasn't alone, either. It's why you were attacked so quickly. I imagine there were multiple deities who were—let's say—tuned to the frequency of Lemurian magic. It may have been thousands of years since one was last awake and alive, but it's not something you forget the feel of."

"That explains the instant attack, but are they going to continue?" Seth asked.

Hecate sighed and began to fiddle with one of the many rings on her fingers. "I would say almost certainly. There were too many gods who rejoiced when Lemuria was essentially killed. Some, I imagine, have moved on or grown, but there are at least a few who would do anything to ensure it remains dead."

"Who?" Vazi demanded. "Who is responsible for Lemuria's fall? Who has been targeting Tempest?"

Hecate didn't answer right away, but glanced at Tempest uncertainly.

"I'd like to know," she told Hecate. "We can't plan on how to stop them, how to stay safe, if we don't know who's after us."

The goddess sighed and again played with her rings. "I can't say I know everyone who was involved back then. They weren't exactly making a list. If their plan had failed, they wouldn't have wanted their part in things to be known. I know Zeus was one, as was Ares. He loves war, of course, and will do most anything his father tells him to.

I would feel comfortable saying Apophis, as well as several of the war and battle deities."

"And who is still gunning for Tempest?" Seth asked, though it concerned him that the Egyptian god of Chaos could be involved.

"That's harder. Ares is mostly loyal to Zeus, but his attention span is minuscule. I would say Apophis has probably moved on as well, if only because Lemuria returning would cause chaos."

Kara shook her head. "We need to figure out for certain," she said, brow furrowed as she looked to Seth and Tempest in concern.

"I promise that I'm working on it," Hecate assured her. "I have to be extremely careful, though. Zeus is absolutely involved, and he's always been a paranoid god. If he gets wind that I'm helping, if he even *thinks* I'm involved, then he'll kill me." Aaron started to speak, but she went on without pausing. "That said, I'm not without my own powers, and for all that Zeus pretends like he's the most powerful god around, he's not all-knowing or all-powerful. I'll find something." She smiled a touch. "And, like me, there are gods who mourned Lemuria's loss. I'm fairly certain I know who at least some of them are, and I'm going to reach out—discreetly—and try to enlist their help."

"Who?" Seth and Aaron asked at the same time.

To their surprise, she laughed. "Would you believe Zeus's mother? A few others, but she's the one I intend to go to first."

"I believe it," Aelia said, smiling genuinely. "After all, Rhea went against her husband to save her children. She doesn't ignore the bad in people. Never has."

"Exactly," Hecate said, inclining her head to Aelia. "So I'll do what I can and provide information whenever I learn something." She turned back to Vazi. "I'm afraid I need to ask you something. It's not normally something I'd consider, but under these circumstances..."

Understanding, Vazi nodded. "I know. Though even if these were normal circumstances, you would be welcome. It's not the same thing as asking admittance to Thelaria. Lemuria was our home, yes. Protected and beloved, but it's not quite the same thing. And, as you said, these circumstances require some flexibility."

"Thelaria?" Seth asked.

"It's like Olympus, but for the Lemurian gods," Aelia explained.

"A simple answer, but yes," Vazi agreed before he offered his hands to Hecate. She took them, tilting her head in question. "I permit you the ability to see and visit Lemuria as you wish, so long as you never use this gift to bring an enemy of me or my people to our lands."

Again, Seth felt that tingle of power as Hecate nodded solemnly. "I understand and accept. Thank you."

"That is most definitely mutual," he said as he turned and walked to where Kara, Aelia, and Aaron sat. He offered Kara and Aaron his hands first and repeated the process. There was a pause, then he took Aelia's hands. It took him a moment to speak, and Seth saw Aaron scowl at the Lemurian. "Aelia, I permit you the ability to see and visit Lemuria as you wish."

He stopped there and had Seth and Tempest exchanging a look, while Aaron let a little growl trickle from between his lips.

Vazi looked at the tiger, then released Aelia's hands and stepped back.

Hecate cleared her throat and stood. "Then I'll be back if and when I learn something. Hopefully it'll be sooner rather than later." She smiled at Seth. "And still keep an eye out for crows. And if you need me, call out to me. I can't promise to appear in person, of course, but I'll do what I can. Not that you need as much help as you did getting here."

"I wouldn't go that far," he said dryly.

"Before you go," Vazi interrupted, "we did promise a trade of stories. If you'll join me outside, I can fulfill my part of the bargain and we can let Kara continue to boss people around."

"Hey!" Kara said indignantly, but then she grinned and shrugged. "Okay, you're not wrong. Now shoo. I want to get my house ready."

Hecate and Vazi left the house, the former smiling, the latter chuckling. After watching them go, Seth grinned. "Speaking of bossing people around...Not too many people would boss those two around."

She shrugged and went back to getting the house in order. "Vazi likes me—I think—and he knows he needs people he can trust until Lemuria is safe. Which means I'm safe, at least for now."

"Ballsy," Aaron decided, "but I like it."

"Still not falling for your crap!" Kara called to him in a singsong voice.

"I can see why she's your best friend," Tempest whispered to Seth, who smiled and kissed her temple.

"She keeps me from getting too far in my head," he explained.

"Good."

For twenty minutes they worked, with Kara now singing—mostly on key—and dancing around happily. Then Vazi returned without Hecate. Before he could get distracted by anything else, Seth walked over to him.

Vazi's head tilted. "Is everything okay?"

"It will be. I was hoping we could talk about the powers I apparently have now."

"Of course." He considered Seth for a moment, then looked over to Tempest and sighed. "Considering we may be fighting other gods, we need you to be as strong as possible."

Though the insinuation that Seth was currently weak stung, he also couldn't truly argue against it. Having powers was different from knowing how to use them. That went for any weapon, mundane or magical. Anyone could fire a gun, but it took practice and skill to hit what was aimed at. While he might hope that using his new god powers would be instinctive, he doubted it would be that easy. Nothing had been easy since he'd reached Peru.

"Agreed. I'm not going to risk Tempest. Or the others, but I'll go against Zeus if I have to, if it means keeping her safe."

Vazi's eyes seemed to glow as he watched Seth. Tiny gusts of air came off the god—the other god—and Seth arched a brow. "Do you have a problem with that?" he asked.

"No, I don't," Vazi admitted easily. "Tempest and I are close, I'm sure you know that, but we're friends. I don't love her the way you do, but I still want her to be safe."

"Good."

Vazi smiled. "I hope you all don't mind if I steal Seth away for a bit," he called to Tempest.

"Not so long as you return him in the condition he's in now," she retorted.

"I can only promise to do my best." Vazi turned to leave, paused, then looked over his shoulder. "I would ignore any loud noises you're going to hear for the next little while. And some of them may be...rather loud."

"That's not ominous," Kara decided, giving Vazi a wary look.

"We're going to play with his new powers, and he's the god of mountains. Do you really think we're going to be quiet?" he replied.

"I hate it that he has a point," she muttered, but sighed. "Fine, just try not to give me a heart attack, okay?"

"That's entirely up to Seth," was Vazi's answer as he left the house, a sighing Seth following after.

CHAPTER 33

The moment they were outside, Vazi laid a hand on Seth's shoulder and he felt a jerk in his gut as his entire body dematerialized and was yanked sharply. He reformed only a few seconds later, but it was a jarring experience that left him a little unsteady.

He looked around and saw that they were on the top of a cliff, looking down over a lush green forest. "Where are we, and why are we here?" he asked when his stomach settled enough that he could stop worrying about vomiting.

Amused by his reaction, Vazi said, "We're still on Lemuria, just a few miles away from where they are. Not only is it safer for them, you should find it easier to practice here, on the source of your power."

"You could have warned me you were going to do...whatever the hell that was," Seth pointed out. It had felt like teleporting, but not any kind he'd ever experienced before.

"I could have," Vazi agreed. "This was quicker."

Seth rolled his eyes. "Before we get to the lesson for baby gods, can you tell me how I did whatever I did back with Hecate?"

"I can. It's actually fairly simple," Vazi began as he lowered himself to sit on the edge of the cliff, his legs hanging over the edge. "We are the only two Lemurian gods on this plane—for now. The source of our power is the same, which meant it was easy for your power to recognize it. Using it is something that needs to be practiced and learned, of course, but there are some things that are more...intuitive than others. This was one of them."

Though the words paused, Seth said nothing, sensing that Vazi wasn't quite done. Instead, he stared out over Lemuria, just as Vazi did. Once again, he was caught by the beauty of it. And, from this vantage point, he could see that it really was a sizable chunk of land. Even with his eyesight, he couldn't make out the far edge of the land. If they lived in settlements or villages, he had no doubt thousands could call this place home.

"What was your profession before this?" Vazi asked after several minutes had passed.

The question surprised Seth, but he answered. "Depending on who you asked, either treasure hunter or archaeologist." The blank look on Vazi's face reminded Seth of just how long the god had been asleep. "Someone who investigates ruins and artifacts of the past. Finding them, deciphering their meaning, learning how people used to live."

Vazi nodded. "Have you ever been studying an artifact or ruin, then something about it just comes to you? It's not a logical leap, just a gut feeling that you *know* is right?"

Seth shrugged. "Sure. I think everyone does, now and again."

"Not everyone, but it's essentially the same thing," Vazi said, looking over his shoulder at Seth. "The power within you *knew* what to do. Knew it could help. You basically did the same thing I was doing. And it's a good thing you did."

"Oh?"

"The geas, as you called it, was strong. I'm sure it was laid on many gods other than Hecate, and I have no doubt that it was placed there by the combined effort of several powerful gods. I'm strong, but I've also been asleep for a long time, and the curse was almost indistinguishable from Hecate's power at that point. Removing it by myself was possible, but it would have taken a great deal longer, and caused her even more pain than it did with the two of us."

Seth hadn't been certain of how much he'd actually helped, so hearing that made him feel a little better. He had no idea how powerful Jalvas had been, or how powerful he now was. Yes, Jalvas had been able to open a chasm in the earth, but where exactly that rated on the scale of god powers was a mystery to him. And yes, he apparently had inherited those powers when he'd killed Jalvas, but he had no idea if he'd received all of them or just enough to make him a god.

And the idea of being a god still freaked him the fuck out.

"I'm glad I helped, then."

"As am I." He absently swirled a finger in a circle, pointed toward the ground, and had caused wind to spin gently, shifting the dirt and leaves in the area. A godly version of fidgeting, Seth assumed.

"So you're going to have to help me out before we even get to how to use my powers. Before Tempest started telling me about you guys, I'd never heard of the Lemurian gods. I have no idea what Jalvas was capable of beyond splitting the ground open."

"Well, you're aware he was the god of mountains, yes?"

"Sure."

"It's true, but not entirely accurate."

"Then what was accurate?" Seth asked, wishing Vazi would get on with it. They had too much to do for Vazi to drag this out.

"To say he was the god of stone. So while that includes mountains, it wasn't limited to them. So you can affect anything to do with stone." He smiled. "Which, if my guess is correct, will annoy your friend. She has power over stone as well, doesn't she?"

Seth's lips twitched as he realized the truth of that statement. "Oh, that's going to be fun. Let's keep that just between us for now, okay? At least until I can find a funny way to show her."

Vazi laughed. "Show, not tell?"

Feeling almost gleeful, Seth shook his head. "Oh no, this definitely calls for a demonstration."

"Fair enough. So yes, you can affect stone, such as splitting it open, but you will, I believe, always find yourself to be more powerful on mountains. Mountains on Lemuria especially. And, of course, you have god powers."

"I thought stone was my god power."

"It's part of it. It's more accurate to say that it's your god specialty, I suppose. You should be able to teleport from one location to another, but that has nothing to do with mountains, after all. And you probably have some skill with healing, sensing people, or any number of things. It's not exactly the same for every god. We weren't all created equal."

"Teleporting and healing would definitely come in handy," Seth said thoughtfully. "Hell, they would have come in handy a lot over the last few weeks."

"I imagine so." Vazi shot him a smile so full of anticipation that it made Seth nervous. "Are you ready to give it a try?"

"That's why we're here, isn't it?"

"Absolutely."

For the next hour—because Seth refused to stay away longer than that—he learned what he could do primarily through trial and error. Vazi had suggestions, of course, but since he affected the sky rather than a tangible element, he couldn't be specific.

Seth was extremely happy Vazi had moved them so far away when he accidentally caused a rockslide. Vazi found it hilarious when Seth tried frantically to halt the movement of the rocks, laughing so hard he was almost unable to help. Fortunately, between the two of them, they managed to prevent the rocks from going too far down the mountain or destroying too many trees.

Still, Seth was starting to get the hang of it. He found that he could levitate stone easily, and splitting rocks was a piece of cake—at least while they were smaller than a watermelon. He wasn't quite ready to go around destroying boulders. After the rockslide, he was also a little afraid he'd break the damn mountain.

Teleporting was a little harder, but to his relief, he was informed that it was next to impossible to do something stupid like teleporting into solid rock or wood.

By the time they decided to call it quits, Seth was surprisingly tired. He hadn't done anything physical besides stand there, but he felt like he'd been lifting weights the entire time. Despite that, Vazi suggested Seth teleport back to the others.

The first time, Seth accidentally appeared in Tempest's house, but he managed to find Kara's new house the second time, only to find Vazi waiting there, smirking.

"Don't even start," he snapped, frustration and exhaustion making his temper flare. "I've been doing this for an hour. You've been doing this for how many years?"

"I can still be entertained," Vazi corrected with a shrug. "But I'll—"

The sound of a woman screaming cut him off and their heads whipped in the direction. While Vazi turned to air to move faster, Seth didn't know exactly where he was going, so took off at a run. He dimly realized that several people were coming out of Kara's house and risked a glance back. The relief that formed when he saw Tempest dissipated when he noticed that only Aelia and Aaron were with her.

The scream had to have come from Kara.

He found her near the stream they'd been gathering water from, doing her best to climb one of the fruit trees close by. She made it to a branch about six feet in the air and looked terrified, but unharmed.

It was then he noticed the feline at the base of the tree. It was primarily white with unusual black markings, large, rounded ears, and eyes that were an extremely pale green. That was all kind of weird, but it was the size of the cat that worried Seth. It wasn't quite the same size as a panther or cougar, but it was bigger than a bobcat.

And its attention was firmly fixed on the woman clinging to the tree.

"Kara! You okay?" he yelled as he approached the feline.

Her head whipped up when she heard him and she glared at him. "Do I fucking look okay?" she snapped before manifesting a rock in her hand and tossing it at the cat. It sidestepped, sniffed the rock, then looked up at Kara once more.

It struck Seth as odd. He had no idea what kind of animal this was, but it wasn't actively trying to get to Kara, and he'd never heard of any type of cat who couldn't climb a tree. Which made him wonder exactly what it was doing.

When Aaron tried to run past Seth, he grabbed the shifter's arm and shook his head. "Wait. I don't think it's attacking her."

"It's a shade cat," Vazi said, manifesting on Seth's other side.

"They survived?" Tempest asked as she and Aelia joined them.

"What the fuck is a shade cat and why won't it go away?" Kara shouted, her gaze fixed on the cat, even when it sat and cocked its head.

"It's a type of cat native to Lemuria. We called them shades," Tempest answered.

"That's not reassuring me any," Kara pointed out. "Did you call them that because they made people shades? And why in the hell aren't any of you doing anything about it?" she demanded.

"Because it's not aggressive, and we're a little surprised," Vazi answered with a shrug. "Are you saying it attacked you?"

There was a long pause, then Kara looked up at the group. "Not exactly..." she admitted.

"Then I would say your scream probably scared it as much as it scared you," Aaron said, relaxing somewhat.

Seth glanced at him, considered, then smiled. "Why don't you see if you can lure it away from Kara? You're a cat, too."

"I'm a tiger," Aaron corrected sharply.

"That's still a type of cat," Aelia interjected. "You should try."

He looked down to her then gave in with a sigh. "Fine. Anything I should know about this shade?" he asked, looking to Vazi and Tempest.

Tempest shook her head. "It doesn't have any powers that I'm aware of. I think it's called that for the skeletal designs on its fur."

Her words made Seth look more closely at the cat and he realized that the black markings did, in fact, resemble the skeletal structure of a feline. Not exactly, but close enough. He couldn't decide if it was more cool or spooky.

"No, no powers," Vazi confirmed.

Aaron nodded and approached the cat and treed witch, keeping his steps slow and smooth. "Hey there, shade. You don't actually want the halfling in the tree, do you?" he called soothingly. When the shade cat turned its head toward Aaron, he paused his steps, then continued speaking. "Did you get curious about her and she scared you with her screaming?" he asked, lowering himself into a crouch.

The tip of the shade's tail flicked and it studied Aaron for a long moment before looking past him and to the others. When its almost white eyes landed on the Lemurians, it began to purr.

"I think it likes you guys," Aaron called.

"I don't know about that. I think it's mostly reacting to the presence of Lemurians," Vazi disagreed. "And remember, we're the first people this particular shade has ever seen."

Aaron nodded and held a hand out toward the cat. "Come on. Come away from the tree so Kara can come down, okay?" When coaxing didn't seem to work, Aaron grimaced, sighed, then...began purring. It was such an odd sound coming from the man that Tempest had to stifle a laugh. Nevermind that mundane tigers couldn't purr.

She was shocked to see the feline here. While she'd known animals were still around considering they'd heard birds, this was the first they'd seen and she was thrilled. When the shade began to approach Aaron, she held her breath. The shades were independent creatures. Back in her day, they'd normally stayed away from people, but she knew of several instances where they'd been tamed and lived with Lemurians. It was rare, but far from unheard of.

The shade cat sniffed at Aaron's outstretched hand, studied the man, then gave him a light bump with his head. Aaron ran that hand over the cat's head and looked up to Kara. "I think it's safe to come down now."

"You better be sure, or I'll find every way possible to skin a cat. And for the record, I'm meaning you," Kara warned him before she swung her leg over the branch, hung for a second, then let herself drop the short distance to the ground. The cat ignored her, so she edged around it and Aaron until she was next to Seth.

"You okay now?" Seth asked her, leaning his shoulder lightly against hers for a moment.

"Yeah. I just wasn't expecting to come down for water and run into a huge cat."

Tempest couldn't hide her smile now. The shade was less than half the size Aaron had been in his tiger form, so it was far from huge. But, if not expecting it, she supposed it would have been frightening. "If it helps, I've never heard of them attacking under normal circumstances," she offered.

"A little. Thanks."

"We should get back to work," Aaron said, giving the shade one last pet before he straightened.

"True. We've finished Kara's place, but we still need to get the others done and figure out how we're going to handle Zeus and anyone else coming after us," Aelia agreed.

Except, when they walked back into the village, the shade followed them. After some brief discussion, they decided to leave it be. If it ran off, fine, but they wouldn't chase it off.

It took some of the edge off for Tempest as they started work on Aelia's home and discussed their next move.

By the time they'd finished Aelia's chosen house, they decided they were going to kill two birds with one stone. If they were tracked by Tempest's bracelet, they'd let their enemies come to them while making trips to everyone's old homes to gather possessions. Vazi and Seth would have their powers hidden, and if they were lucky, they'd be able to trap and question anyone who came for them.

Given the way their luck had gone, Tempest doubted it. To take her mind off what could happen tomorrow, she spent half her night losing herself in Seth's arms.

CHAPTER 34

Tempest was both nervous and excited the next morning. The excitement came from not only getting to see Seth's home, but also potentially taking the target off her head. The nerves came from the possibility that their trap might fail. Or worse, backfire. If they screwed up, she might not see another nightfall.

They ate—fruit again, which made her realize they'd have to expand their menu—then Kara and Vazi shielded the energy of the gods. With everyone as ready as they could be, Vazi briefly dipped into Kara's mind to get an image of her home, then teleported the entire group to her living room.

Both Vazi and Aaron had protested Aelia coming along, but she'd stubbornly refused to be left behind. Especially since she had magic of her own. Maybe not as quick or flashy as Kara or the Lemurians, but effective.

"Remember," Seth said as he moved to one of Kara's bookshelves, "we're not in any hurry. We want them to find us."

"I'll be happier to take my time if you tell me you've got some weapons," Aaron said as he turned to Kara.

She smiled sweetly at him. "I'm a witch who can manifest stone daggers. Why would I have weapons?" His face went blank, and she sighed. "You're normally more fun to pick on," she muttered. "Yeah, come with me. Seth, want me to grab you a pistol?"

"Please. I don't know that my powers are going to be the best for today," Seth admitted as he started pulling books down and stacking them on the dining room table.

Kara found a pistol and extra magazine for Seth, and another pistol and wicked-looking knife for Aaron. The appearance of the knife had Seth rethinking and requesting one for himself. Both Vazi and Tempest refused the offer to find something for them. Tempest had Lemuria's Fire, of course, though she much preferred using her powers. Still, if they didn't end this today, it couldn't hurt to spread some of the powers of their attackers to the rest of their group. Except, she realized as she glanced at Aelia, it didn't always seem to give them to the wielder. Unless it hadn't worked for Aelia because she was human? Or maybe it was that she had apparently only wounded people with it in the past rather than killed them. If Vazi was to be believed, the transfer only happened upon death.

Once everyone was armed, they set about packing up Kara's house. Kara handled her personal possessions, though Seth and Tempest helped. Aaron, Aelia, and Vazi focused on food, blankets, and other necessities. Kara opted to leave just enough that the house could be used if necessary. Tempest thought it was a wise idea. There was no guarantee they'd all be safe after today. Besides, sometimes people needed to get away from home, no matter how much they loved it.

When they had everything sorted, Vazi flashed the piles and boxes back to Kara's new home. Then, just to make sure they gave their pursuers plenty of time, they hung around for another half hour.

Finally, Vazi took the location for Aelia's home from her mind and teleported them there. It wasn't the same place where they'd met her, but a small two-bedroom house with a surprising amount of security on it. Tempest doubted it was for Aelia, not when she caught sight of everything in the house.

The living room had basically the same furniture and electronics Kara's did, but every available wall had bookshelves that ran from floor to ceiling and were packed. But the second bedroom is what surprised everyone. The door had multiple locks on it, and even the window was wired and covered in blackout curtains. All because Aelia had a miniature museum in her spare room. Old books, scrolls, and artifacts filled the room.

"Holy shit," Seth whispered just before Aaron said, "Aelia, I think I love you."

Aelia rolled her eyes and shrugged. "I've been alive longer than most of these things have existed," she reminded them. "It's not like I went out and dug them up like you two. That said, you're welcome to pack them up if you like, since you know how to properly handle them."

Tempest thought both men looked like giddy boys on their birthday. It was charming and more than a little cute. Then Vazi picked up a statue of a man that stood about a foot tall. He examined it for a moment before turning to Aelia and arching a brow.

When Aelia spotted what he was holding, her cheeks pinkened a little and she shrugged. "I was obsessed with Lemuria. I wasn't about to let any artifacts pertaining to it get lost or destroyed. It's a good thing I was so careful, because very little remains. For all I know, only what's in this room still exists."

"What is it?" Kara asked as she stepped closer to get a look.

"Me," Vazi answered, setting the statue carefully back on the shelf he'd found it on.

Kara's lips twitched and she gave Aelia an amused look. "Do you have statues of any of the other Lemurian gods?"

"No," Aelia answered shortly before she turned to leave the room. "I'm going to go pack up my clothes."

Kara and Tempest exchanged looks before Tempest said, "I'll check the kitchen."

"I'll help you," Kara said, hurrying after.

Seth and Aaron missed the entire exchange, too absorbed in Aelia's treasures, but Vazi went with Kara and Tempest, leaving Aelia some time to herself.

They spent two hours at Aelia's, and it took almost the entire time to get everything packed up. It might have gone more quickly, except Seth and Aaron *really* liked her treasure trove and kept getting distracted.

Afterwards, they killed some time eating lunch, and everyone was thrilled to have something other than fruit to eat. She wasn't surprised when anything green was ignored by the group in favor of breads and meats. Still, nothing happened. There wasn't the slightest hint of anyone coming for them. It made Tempest wonder why, when they'd been attacked so quickly in the past.

So on to Aaron's they went. His house was shockingly different from how Seth expected. Rather than the modern apartment full of trophies, it looked...well, like a mix of Kara and Aelia's houses. It was homey like Kara's, but had the artifacts like Aelia's, though not in the same quantity or quality.

He hated to admit he liked it, but settled for keeping it to himself.

"I take it you're wanting to keep all your...keepsakes?" he asked Aaron, careful to keep his voice bland.

Aaron gave him a toothy grin. "I'll leave them here the moment you tell me—truthfully—that you don't have a single artifact or relic in your place."

Since he couldn't, Seth just shrugged. But then, he didn't know anyone in their profession who didn't have something of the past. It wasn't just their job, it was their passion.

Surprisingly, Aaron didn't gloat, just started to direct the others. He had plenty of books he wanted taken, along with supplies. Not just food and bedding, but weapons, survival gear, and magical relics. Nothing as powerful as Tempest's dagger, not by a long shot, but useful.

Seth could secretly admit he'd love to get his hands on a few of them. Aaron had some cool stuff.

The first thing he got his hands on, though, was a spare cell phone Aaron had. Since Seth's phone—all their phones—were at the bottom of the Pacific, they had some calls to catch up on.

Aelia had no family to call, and claimed she didn't want to call any friends, so Kara made the first call, assuring her parents that she was okay. Fortunately, they were used to her disappearing now and again. Usually because she had accompanied Seth somewhere, but not always.

Aaron assured his mom that he was okay as well and checked in with some of his employees to make sure nothing had imploded in his absence.

When it was Seth's turn, he stepped onto the back patio. His dad was first, but like Kara's parents, he was used to Seth not calling for a week or two at a time. Then he called Erasmus.

"Seth? I was starting to worry. You weren't answering my calls," the older man said the moment he answered.

"Yeah, kind of hard to answer a phone when it's beneath a couple miles of water. Sorry."

Erasmus sighed. "No, it's fine. I'm just happy to hear you're still alive. What's happened?"

Now Seth hesitated and glanced back toward the house. He'd talked to Tempest about the man and she'd said she would trust his judgment, but it still felt like a huge thing to drop on someone over the phone. But there wasn't a guarantee he'd be seeing Erasmus anytime soon.

"We broke the blood curse," he began.

"You did? Wonderful! How?" It took Seth too long to answer, and he heard Erasmus suck in a breath. "You found it?" he whispered in an awed tone.

"We found it," Seth confirmed.

"Unbelievable," Erasmus breathed, the soft words vibrating with excitement. "How? Where? Are you there now? What's it like? Is it—"

Seth chuckled and broke in. "I can't tell you everything, Erasmus. One day I might be able to work in a quick trip, but I will say it's even more beautiful than Hawaii. Or Greece."

"I find that last part hard to believe, but I do believe it's wonderful."

"There's a lot more to it, but, well, you understand discretion more than anyone else on the planet," Seth told him, though he felt bad he couldn't just tell the librarian everything. "Not to mention we've still got people on our tail, but I wanted to make sure you knew I was still alive."

"No, no, I understand. You definitely get yourself safe. Though I will expect to hear more details once things are settled."

"As much as I can," Seth promised.

"That's all I ask. Good luck, Seth."

"Thanks. Talk to you later."

Seth hung up and went back inside to find the others working. Aaron said he had another phone, so Seth pocketed the one in his hand and got to work.

Aaron had so much to take to Lemuria that Vazi sent it in groups rather than trying to do it all at once. The first load had just been sent when both Vazi and Seth paused and Seth's head tilted as he heard a noise that wasn't quite a sound, more like a feeling that he could somehow hear.

"Someone's coming," Vazi said, explaining what it was that Seth was sensing.

Everyone else went still but for Aaron, who double-checked to make sure his pistol was loaded and had a round in the chamber.

"How soon?" Aelia asked as she went to Aaron's stash and selected two daggers. She didn't handle them like she'd never used them before, which oddly surprised him, but neither did she hold them like they'd become an extension of her body.

Vazi's blue eyes fixed on her violet ones and he smiled thinly. "Soon."

"That's what we were wanting, though, wasn't it?" Kara asked as she manifested a short sword made of stone.

"It is," Seth said, moving to Tempest's side. Knowing she could keep herself safe—and had her dagger—didn't stop him from wanting to be there in case something happened and she couldn't. He wasn't going to lose her, not after they'd come this far. And, he hoped, this would all be over soon and she'd be safe.

If only his powers were ones he could use inside without risking them all. Since they weren't—at least not yet—he readied the weapons he'd borrowed.

When their enemy appeared, it wasn't a small group like he'd expected. No, whoever was after them brought backup, and a lot of it.

CHAPTER 35

Aaron's house was large, but in the blink of an eye it was filled with an additional twenty people. Maybe more, given they were all crammed into a space that now seemed small.

Seth had a moment to think *Holy shit,* before chaos erupted. Several of the newcomers shifted into various animals—a wolf and vulture caught his eye, but he knew there were others. A few of the intruders started throwing magic in all shades of the rainbow, while one turned to stone and sprouted wings. That wasn't good. Gargoyles were notoriously fierce fighters.

His side wasn't idle, though. Tempest flung a hand out, shoving four people back from her with a sharp blast of air. Kara faced off with the gargoyle, her sword clashing against the man's arm as he lifted it to block.

That was as much as Seth was able to take in before a tall, fierce woman bulldozed into him, knocking them both against the wall hard enough that the drywall cracked around him. Distantly, he realized it didn't hurt as much as it should have. Being a god did have some perks. She bared her teeth and went for his throat, but he twisted and threw her off. Unwilling to give up her prey, she lunged again, this time sinking her sharp canines into the forearm he brought up to block her.

Her dark eyes widened in shock as she got a taste of his blood and he knew he had to deal with her quickly, before she took too much of his blood—and his power. Vampires were dangerous enemies when they drank solely from humans. When they drank from the Arcane, they were formidable, the power in the supernatural blood lending them strength. If this one managed to make a meal out of a god? He didn't even want to think about what it could mean.

He swung the arm she clung to, slamming both it and the vampire into the wall. When it wasn't enough to dislodge her, he did it again, but she clung tightly to him, her fangs buried deep in his flesh. He dropped the knife he held and gripped her jaw with his free hand, squeezing until her hold on him loosened. The moment her canines were no longer locked around his arm, he snapped her neck. It might not actually kill her, depending on how powerful she was, so he fell to one knee, bringing her with him, and picked up the knife. The steel went straight into her heart, ensuring she wouldn't rise to attack them again.

Now able to focus on the rest of the room, he found himself surprised that he could follow the rapid pace of the pandemonium. Kara had dealt with the gargoyle and was now facing off with another witch, the two flinging magic back and forth. Aelia was battling a shapeshifter while Aaron—in half-tiger form—fought another two. Vazi was using his powers to keep the bulk of the group back and effortlessly slamming people between the floor and ceiling until they were knocked unconscious.

But where was Tempest? Had she taken her air form? Or had something worse happened? He didn't see the signs of her power use, but with Vazi using magic that was so similar to hers, he wasn't sure he would spot proof of her magic.

Seth didn't get the chance to find out, either, not when one of the group fired a shot that hit Aelia in the head. Her eyes widened as her body stilled for a second before gravity kicked in and she crumpled to the floor in a sprawled heap. Aaron roared in fury and leapt at one of the men he was fighting, shifting fully as he moved. Seth was little better. Despite being so much older than him, Aelia had taken on the role of a little sister. Hurting her was as bad as hurting Kara, and almost as bad as hurting Tempest. It didn't matter that she'd resurrect.

The ground beneath the house rumbled as he began to lose control of his powers. Fighting to keep them locked down, he dove into the fray, unwilling to let anyone else get harmed.

Magic, bullets, and knives flew through the air, occasionally redirected harmlessly into walls by Vazi. Seth learned that his punches packed a great deal more than they had when he was mortal, the first blow knocking the wolf he hit out cold. A bolt of white-hot magic hit him in the side, and he was surprised when he felt nothing more than the impact. Before, a shot like that would have, at the very least, burned him and knocked him back, but now it simply scorched his shirt. He glanced at the woman who had attacked him and fired a single bullet at her, hitting in the center of her forehead.

He was done playing around.

Aaron stood over Aelia's body in his tiger form, slashing and biting anyone who got close to her. Kara was beside him, tackling any magical attacks that were sent in their direction. But still Seth didn't see Tempest, still didn't see her magic. A cold chill went down his spine.

She wouldn't have just left them, not now. And certainly not without letting someone know. Which meant something had happened to her.

The ground shook again, more intensely than it had before. Part of the floor cracked and the few things that remained on shelves tumbled off, right before one of the bookcases fell over. One of their attackers finally realized they were dealing with more than normal members of the Arcane. "We've got gods!" she yelled.

A few of her companions took the warning to heart and disappeared, but the rest were either stupid, stubborn, or already lying on the floor dead. Still, Seth wished he had powers that were more useful in this situation. He needed every one of their enemies dead or gone. He needed to find Tempest.

"Keep one alive," he said in a low, echoing voice. He hoped that some of the people he'd knocked out were still breathing, but he didn't have time to check.

The fight was over not long after that and it was—to his shock—Aaron who left one of the attackers alive. True, the man was pinned to the floor with his throat clamped tightly in the tiger's teeth, but he was still alive.

"Hold him there for a second," Seth snapped as he quickly checked the other rooms. No Tempest. He called for her and heard only Aaron's growl in response.

He stalked to the prisoner and dropped down to one knee, moving so the man could see his face around Aaron's furred head. "Where's Tempest?" he demanded, aching to pummel the man. But unconscious men couldn't answer questions.

The man made a croaking sound and Seth looked into the tiger's furious eyes. "Ease up a little," he told Aaron, unable to soften his voice any. He knew Aaron was pissed that Aelia had been killed—again—but Tempest didn't have Aelia's ability to come back from death. He *had* to find her. She'd found Lemuria and her gods. She'd gotten back what she'd lost. Now he wanted her to be able to enjoy it.

When Aaron reluctantly complied, Seth repeated the question.

"Don't...know," the man gasped.

"Who took her?"

The man shook his head. "No...idea." Seth would have liked to think he was lying, but the terror in the man's eyes proved that he wasn't. Still, his hands flexed and the ground rumbled once more.

"We can find her," Vazi said, sounding as angry as Seth felt. "She's one of ours, remember?"

He hadn't remembered. It was going to take more than a day for him to adjust to being a Lemurian god and having a worshiper.

"We should keep him alive," Kara said from where she knelt beside Aelia's body. "If it takes us too long to find her, he might still be useful."

Seth gave a sharp nod and pushed to his feet. "We've got him, Aaron. We need something to restrain him with."

Aaron shifted back and looked to Aelia, his expression pained to find that she hadn't yet resurrected. He—all of them—had to believe she'd been right that she could survive this. It still hurt them all to see her dead, even if it was only temporary. That didn't stop him from getting rope and tying the man up. However, it might have led to the knots being tighter than was necessary.

Once he was certain their prisoner wasn't getting away, Seth glanced at the bodies, then to Vazi. The dead could wait. Tempest couldn't. "How do we find her?"

"Aren't we going to discuss how Aelia is lying there dead first?" Vazi asked coldly, the air vibrating with his rage and grief.

Kara answered before Seth could. "She'll come back. She told us—she has to—" She broke off, took a breath, then continued. "She told us she always comes back, no matter how she dies. I don't know how many times it's happened, but it sounded like a lot."

Vazi's eyes sharpened on her, and the air pulsed around them. "You swear?"

"We all saw it. She drowned on our way to Lemuria," Aaron told him, his voice still a growl. "It's the only reason I'm not flipping out."

Vazi didn't look entirely convinced and stared at Aelia's still body. Before he could turn back to Seth, Aelia sucked in a loud, ragged breath, her eyes fluttering.

"Aelia!" Aaron dropped to the floor beside her and pulled her still limp form into his lap. Vazi was only half a second behind, taking her hand in his as he knelt beside them.

"Hate getting shot," she mumbled as she struggled to open her eyes, one hand lifting to weakly rub the blood that had dripped down her forehead.

"I don't blame you," Aaron said softly as he kissed her hair. "Stop dying on me, okay? You're going to turn me gray. I wouldn't look good with gray hair."

She gave him a tired smile. "I'll do my best, but can't promise." Her eyes opened and she seemed surprised to find herself with a tiger on one side and a god on the other. "They're gone?"

"Either gone or dead, yeah. So is Tempest," Kara answered, since both men seemed too intent on making sure she was truly okay.

"Dead?" Aelia asked, shoving herself upright. "She's…"

Kara's eyes went wide as she realized what she'd implied. "Oh! No. Gods no. She's literally gone. We don't know where or why."

"What are we still doing here, then? We need to get her," Aelia told them as she tried to get to her feet. She was still recovering from her resurrection, though, and without Vazi and Aaron's help would have fallen.

"We were about to find out where she is, but you're important, too, Aelia," Seth answered. He meant it, too. For so long, his family had consisted of his dad. Then Kara had wormed her way in. In the past month, Tempest and Aelia had added their names to the list. Even Aaron and Vazi were growing on him. He couldn't explain why, but it was true.

"I'm awake now, so let's go," she insisted, and he only looked to Vazi.

It took Vazi a few seconds to focus on Seth. "Normally, I'd teach you how, but I don't think either of us want to wait even that long."

"Agreed," Seth replied without hesitation. "Find her. You can teach me later."

Vazi nodded and closed his eyes. Seth had hoped it would be an instant thing, but it took a full minute before Vazi's eyes opened. "Got her. Is everyone ready?"

Seth's fingers tightened on the butt of his pistol as he scanned the others. Aelia was bloody, but looking stronger by the second. Kara looked frazzled and battered, but determined as she manifested a new weapon. Aaron was still riding his anger from Aelia's death and only gave a single, sharp nod. "Let's go," Seth told Vazi.

For the fourth time that day, the world dissolved around them, only for them to reform in an entirely different place.

CHAPTER 36

Tempest wasn't entirely sure what had happened. One moment she'd been blasting a vulture, then she'd felt like fire was racing over her body before everything went black. There hadn't been time for her to transform to air, to call out, or do anything but stiffen in pain.

Now she was lying on a large bed with thick wooden posts and a gauzy gold canopy above her. Taking stock of herself, she discovered the pain was gone, and she felt...amazing, actually. Confused, certainly, but physically she felt good. Her clothes didn't look as though they'd been cut or ripped, so she hadn't been in a fight, which was odd since the last thing she remembered was their enemies showing up for that very thing.

Slowly, she propped herself up on her elbows and looked around the room. The rest of the furniture was heavy wood and looked like it was good quality. There was a set of French doors with curtains that matched the canopy and three interior doors.

When she went to slide off the bed, something shifted against her wrists and she glanced down, confused. Resting just above each of her hands was a band of metal, an inch wide, half an inch thick, and inscribed with symbols she didn't recognize. The one on her right wrist was almost flush against the bracelet Vazi had given her.

Frowning and not wanting more unknown jewelry on her, she studied one of them and quickly discovered that—like Vazi's bracelet—this didn't have any kind of clasp or opening. Nor was it big enough for her to slide over her hand, no matter how she twisted and pulled.

That was a problem for later, though. Putting the cuffs out of her mind, she climbed out of the bed and hurried quietly to the French doors. She wasn't surprised to find them locked. Never before had she wished she knew how to pick locks, but she did now. If none of the other doors led out of here, then she'd try breaking a pane of glass. She didn't need much to escape in her elemental form. A crack would be sufficient. Even if she break crack the glass, she could slip under the door and find another crack that led out of the house.

One of the other doors led to an empty closet, another to a large bathroom. Which meant the last door had to lead to the rest of the house—and to whoever had brought her here.

That made her hesitate, but she didn't get the chance to weigh the pros and cons of going out that door or breaking the glass.

Footsteps grew louder as someone approached her door. She stepped back and tried to transform, shocked when she stayed corporeal. Focusing, she tried again, but nothing changed. She flicked her hand and was relieved when she was able to summon a breeze. Her powers weren't gone, but something was hindering her from accessing them all. Or maybe it was just keeping her in her current form. She didn't know and didn't have time to figure it out.

Grateful she wasn't completely defenseless, she braced herself to face whoever was on the other side of the door.

It opened and she took a step back before she forced herself to stop. She wouldn't cower. Not having her elemental form made her vulnerable, but she was a powerful woman. She could handle this. She *would* handle this.

The man who stood in the doorway was about six feet tall. His lean build was covered in a charcoal gray suit that fit him perfectly. His blonde hair was long enough to style but much shorter than Seth's shaggy hair. With his tanned skin, straight nose, and bright blue eyes he was handsome enough, she supposed, but in an average sort of way.

And he was looking at her with a sick sort of glee, like she was an animal he wanted to dissect.

"Shall I skip all the small talk that I'm sure comes with situations like this, or would you rather ask inane questions?" he asked in a voice that was cultured and deep.

"Like who you are and why I'm here?" Tempest asked in a tone as neutral as she could make it, but she knew her hands weren't quite steady.

He sighed. "Yes, like those." Stepping fully into the room, he shut the door behind him, closing her in with someone who clearly didn't wish her well. "Let's cut this short, shall we? There's much to do and I don't have time to waste. My name is Joseph and you're here because I want to know why people wanted you dead."

Tempest frowned at his answer. No, she didn't like how he was looking at her, but his words almost made it sound like he was on her side. Almost. She wasn't that dumb, though.

"What makes you think anyone wants me dead?"

He tsked at her as he began to circle her, studying her from every angle. "Playing ignorant won't help you. I know people want you dead, because one of them hired me to see it done. What I want to know is why."

Fear tried to rip through her, but Tempest did her best to shove it down. Trembling in terror wouldn't save her, but maybe, if she kept her wits about her, she could get out of this. She still had her wind, and there was no way Seth and Vazi wouldn't be able to find her. The Lemurian gods had no need of worshipers like the other gods, but they could always sense those who did pray to them, and she sent up a prayer now. *Please, Seth. Find me. Vazi, find me.*

"Say that's true, that someone tried to kill me. In that case, why would I tell anything to the man who admitted to being hired to do just that? For that matter, if you were, in fact, paid to kill me, why didn't you kill me before I woke?"

Joseph narrowed his eyes at her. "Like I said, I want to know why. There's also no sense in pretending you aren't the one I was looking for. Your magical signal is impossible to mistake for anything else."

So they had been tracking her through her powers or Vazi's bracelet. Both would feel Lemurian, so it didn't really matter which it had been. She considered him for a long moment before she shook her head. "No."

"You. Will. Tell. Me!" he yelled, his voice growing in volume with each word. Worse, electricity began to crackle around him, centered in his hands, which were now clenched into fists. The glee was gone from his eyes, replaced by a desperate rage.

"Why does it matter to you?" she shot back. "Either you want to fulfill the job you were hired for, or you don't. Either way, why do you care why they want me dead? And who is *they?*"

"My father!" he snapped and a bolt of electricity shot from him to her, burning her arm and sending a painful sizzle through her veins.

She hissed and jumped back, her hand going to the injured area. "And who the hell is your father?" she asked, hoping he'd continue to give her information. It didn't seem as though he were thinking clearly, which could be an asset. When he did reply without thought, her breath caught.

"Zeus! And without me, you're never going to survive, so tell me what he wanted with you. Tell me why you had to die!" He took a menacing step toward her, more electricity—no, lightning—sparking around him. "Tell me, and I might just let you live."

They'd known Zeus was probably involved, but it didn't relieve her to have it confirmed. She had hoped he'd give her another name, but Zeus might not be working alone. She needed to find out. Maybe she could offer Joseph an exchange. Information for information. "Are you the only one he sent to kill me? Is he the only one who wants me dead? If you tell me, then maybe I'll give you the information you want."

His arm lashed out, the back of his hand slamming into her cheek and knocking her head to the side. She managed to keep on her feet, but only just. Before she could recover, his hand grabbed her throat and yanked her face toward his, so they were only a hand's width apart. "I'm not trying to deal with you, whore. You *will* tell me, or I'll snap your neck."

She pressed closer until their noses almost touched. "You plan on killing me anyway, so why should I satisfy your curiosity?" she hissed, though her heart was beating so hard it felt like it was trying to tear out of her chest.

Static electricity began to build in the hand around her throat as he made an angry sound, one that would have been less out-of-place coming from Aaron. But she knew that, Lemurian or not, she could be killed by a strong enough jolt of electricity, and as the son of Zeus, he no doubt had the power to deliver just that.

Shoving both hands at his chest, she pushed with her magic. He was thrown back, but his grip on her throat only loosened, it didn't release entirely. His hold on her threw his balance off, so with her air forcing him back, he fell and landed hard on the floor, bringing her with him.

"You fucking bitch!" he roared as his hand tightened again, cutting off her air supply. She wasn't truly concerned about suffocating—she'd never heard of an air elemental being able to suffocate—but if he squeezed hard enough, he could certainly break something she needed to survive.

Joseph tried to punch her with his other fist, but she got a hand up in time to counter it with a quick blast of air, so it did nothing more than tap her. Infuriated, he shifted his balance and rolled them so she was on bottom with him straddling her. His other hand joined the first and lightning began to build in him again, sending little pinpricks of pain anywhere he touched. Tempest hit him with her magic again, but he was either too strong or too powerful for it to dislodge him this time.

His attempt to strangle her to death gave her an idea, though. Lifting a hand, she placed it against his chest and *pulled*. Instead of trying to push him away with air, she drew it from his lungs.

She could tell he realized what she was doing when his eyes widened, a flicker of fear showing in them for only a moment before determination took over. It was a race now, to see if he would tire of the fight and break her neck before she could empty his lungs of breath. That's when fear tried to overtake her. It took only an instant to do what he intended, and minutes to die of suffocation. If she was very, very lucky, he'd lapse into unconsciousness first.

She needed to stall him, and there was only one thing she could think of that would give her the precious time she needed. The truth.

"I'm...Lemurian," she gasped as she continued to empty his lungs.

For a second, his grip loosened, and he glared at her suspiciously. "You lie," he said, his own voice weak and gasping. She was shocked her plan had worked even that well. He had to feel that he was losing more and more air by the second. Was he really that desperate to know why Zeus wanted her dead?

As best she could, she shook her head, a single movement to the right, then the left. "No. I'm Lemurian. The last."

"The last Lemurian?" He let out a choked laugh. "Won't...save you," he warned, before giving her a vicious smile.

"Yes," she disagreed, "it will." She needed just another minute. One more minute and he'd never be able to threaten her again. To give herself that extra minute she needed, she shoved her free hand down her body, grabbing him tightly between the legs and twisting sharply. His face went red, his eyes widening as pain overloaded his senses. It was enough of an opening that she was able to shove him off her.

She crawled backwards to put some distance between them while still using her magic on him.

There was a twinge of guilt at killing a man in this condition, but she knew she didn't have long before he'd try again to kill her. And he would try again. Since she couldn't transform and escape, this was her only chance to survive.

But suffocation wasn't a quick, clean death, and she couldn't quite bring herself to finish him like that, not unless she had to. There were no weapons in the room...

Her dagger. She'd had it back at Aaron's house. Did that mean Joseph had it now? It would be stupid to search him while he was alive, but she really didn't want to cause a death like this.

He was weakened, both from her magic and the blow, so she took a chance and stopped yanking the air from his body, only to pin him to the floor instead. She didn't bother standing, but quickly scrambled forward and began searching him.

Yes! He had it, wrapped in a cloth in the inside pocket of his suit. No doubt he had intended to ask her about it if she'd cooperated. She snatched it and began to unwrap it when her control slipped and one of his hands lifted. It didn't take much for him to be able to hit her with a telekinetic blast, sending her hard against the wall.

No longer pinned, Joseph shoved to his feet, swaying once. "Two can play that game," he snarled, extending an arm and curling his fingers into a fist, one that mimicked the magic tightening around her throat once more.

Desperate, Tempest wrapped her magic around the dagger and shot it toward him. She was a little dazed from hitting the wall, so when it sank into his throat at all, she was both shocked and relieved. It wasn't where she'd been aiming, but from the blood, she'd hit something vital.

It had to be enough.

The magic around her throat released, and she instinctively lifted a hand to gently cover the aching flesh.

Joseph swayed at the same instant that Seth and the others teleported in. Seth took a single step toward her when he spotted Joseph. Something beyond rage flashed on his face, only to be replaced by confusion when Joseph fell backward onto the bed and lay still.

"Tempest?" Kara said uncertainly, her gaze bouncing between Joseph and Tempest.

"I'm okay," she answered, wishing her voice didn't sound so rough. She also didn't feel quite steady either and was happy to have the wall to lean against. Except before she could blink, Seth's arms were around her and her face was pressed against his shoulder.

"I'm so sorry, darlin'. I got here as soon as I could," he said, his hold on her almost painful. There was no way she was going to ask him to ease up, though.

"I'm okay," she repeated, sliding her arms around him. "I promise, I'm okay."

He drew back and studied her from head to toe. She knew she must look horrible after the brief fight, and she tasted blood in her mouth from the backhand, but other than some aches that would fade, she really was okay. Or would be when her heart rate returned to normal. "Did he say who he was or why he took you?"

Tempest nodded and looked over at the body. "Joseph. His father is Zeus." She leaned into Seth and closed her eyes. "He wanted to know why they wanted me dead. I don't know why."

"I think I do."

Hecate's voice made Tempest's eyes open and every person in the room look to her.

"Before you answer, it looks like she's kind of banged up," Kara said, her expression concerned. "Do you think you could heal her first?"

"Of course," Hecate agreed easily. She walked over to Tempest and carefully laid her fingertips against Tempest's throat. Immediately, the ache eased and disappeared.

"Thank you," Tempest said with a faint smile. She was too tired for anything more than that.

"You're welcome." She walked to the bed and looked down at Joseph, pity in her eyes. "Zeus has literally hundreds of children. Most, I doubt he pays any attention to. A few grow...desperate...for his affection, or even just his attention." Turning back to the others, she went on. "I've seen this before, where one of his children wants any advantage they can get. To find out that one fact, obtain that one item, kill that one person. Whatever it takes to make him focus on them, even for one brief moment."

Vazi's lips curled in disgust. "He's really gotten that bad? He always was an egotistical child of a god, but to ignore his own children to that degree? It's unacceptable."

"Wait until he hears how some of those children came to be," Kara muttered to Aelia.

"I agree," Hecate agreed, ignoring Kara's comment. "But he's also more powerful than I am, and it's hard for even me to keep track of all his children. That said, I do have good news."

"He's dying of a magical STD and no one will have to worry about him for long?" Kara suggested.

Hecate wasn't the only one fighting a smile, and Aaron flat out laughed. "I'm sorry to disappoint you, but no. I was able to learn that he's convinced Tempest died in the storm he and Poseidon caused. As long as you're not blatant about what you are, and shield your powers when you leave Lemuria, you should be able to simply live your life."

"How sure are you on that?" Seth asked.

"I've been risking my own life to help save the last Lemurians. I wouldn't lie about this."

"Thank you," Tempest said again. "But if it's that risky, should you be here with us? It's not Lemuria, and we deliberately weren't warding ourselves, so it's not as safe for you."

Sighing, Hecate shook her head. "Probably not, no."

"Then why don't we all head back to Lemuria for now?" Vazi suggested.

"Yes, please," Tempest said, sure she sounded more eager than she meant to. But all she wanted right now was home. An instant later, she was there.

CHAPTER 37

V azi brought all of them—including Hecate—back to what had once been the square of the village.

Tempest swayed and Seth caught her arm before she could fall.

"I thought you said you were okay," he accused, once more looking her over.

"I am...physically," she admitted. "But I woke up in that bedroom with these on," she explained, lifting an arm to show the metal around her wrist. "I wasn't able to transform. And it felt like my air wasn't as powerful as it normally was."

Vazi and Hecate stepped closer, both studying the cuffs. "I recognize these," Hecate said grimly.

"What are they? And what are they doing to me?" Tempest asked, trying to stomp down her growing anxiety.

"It's not as bad as you fear," Hecate tried to assure her. "These were made by Hephaestus, our god of blacksmiths."

"Shit. Seriously?" Seth asked, gaze dropping to one of the cuffs and staring at it like it might bite him. "Aren't those impossible to take off except by him?"

"Or those he's granted the ability to remove them, yes," Hecate confirmed. "But these aren't his most powerful cuffs, which is good.

He's known to be able to make cuffs that can bind even the powers of gods, but he makes them rarely." Her lips twisted in a sardonic smile. "There are those who greatly fear having their powers bound like that, after all. Most commonly he provides cuffs that can cut the Arcane off from their powers." She touched a finger lightly to one of the metal bands. "That is what these are."

"Where's the good news in that?" Kara asked, also eyeing the cuffs like they were poison.

Hecate's smile warmed. "Because they were made for the Arcane that live today, not for Lemurians."

"And Lemurians have always been—on average—more powerful than other members of the Arcane," Aelia finished, smiling as well.

"Is that why I could still use my magic, just not transform?" Tempest asked, looking from Hecate to Aelia.

"It is," Hecate nodded. "It's a similar reaction that a god would have if they wore those cuffs. But I do understand that you don't want your powers limited at all."

"I really don't," Tempest agreed. "Being able to transform is my biggest defense. And while Joseph may no longer be an issue, Zeus and the others may one day realize I'm still alive."

"If I call him, will he come?" Vazi asked. "He isn't one I ever interacted with before."

Hecate thought for a moment, then slowly nodded. "He might. We can only try. If he refuses, then I'll see if I can speak with him quietly. He has no love for his father, and disagrees with most of our king's edicts. He'll keep the secret of Lemuria."

Vazi's eyes closed as he summoned the Greek god. In only a minute, a man, three or four inches taller than even Seth, appeared. He was plain looking for a god, but well-built, with short brown hair and dark brown eyes. His clothes were plain as well, a simple gray tee-shirt and jeans. And somehow he managed to look both annoyed and curious at the same time, though the annoyance faded at the sight of the Greek goddess. "Hecate?" He looked around at the others, then focused on her. "What's going on?"

"Quite a lot," she told him, voice lightly amused.

"Which I will be happy to let you explain if you can make an oath to keep it all to yourself," Vazi said, folding his arms over his chest.

Hephaestus arched a brow and cocked his head, but said nothing.

"You should swear," Hecate told him quietly. "They don't mean either of us harm. They simply want to live, and your father has already tried to kill them."

Hephaestus grimaced, then sighed. "He's always trying to kill someone," he muttered. "Well, it wouldn't be the first time I saved someone from him, or hid things from him. I swear to keep my mouth shut."

"Then let me introduce you to Vazi, god of the sky, and Seth Montgomery, god of mountains...The last two Lemurian gods still walking the Earth," she told him, motioning to each man in turn.

That got a reaction. Shock was quickly followed by confusion and a hint of doubt. "Hold on. I thought they were all dead. And since when did gods have last names?"

"No, we're not dead. We've simply been forced to sleep," Vazi told him, his frustration with the situation seeping into his voice.

"And I've only been a god for a day or so," Seth added.

Hephaestus narrowed his eyes, but nodded. "Hecate, I'll expect the full story later, but I don't imagine you called me here just to tell me Lemuria was back on the map."

"No, we didn't," Seth confirmed and motioned to Tempest, who lifted her arms. "One of your brothers put these cuffs on Tempest and tried to kill her. We were hoping you'd remove them, as apparently you're the only one who can."

"Which brother?"

"His name was Joseph," Tempest answered.

Hephaestus shook his head. "I can't say I've heard of him, but in all honesty, I doubt I've heard of half of my siblings. I've met even less. Good thing for you, I hate it when these cuffs are used for anything but subduing people who are a danger to others." He cocked his head. "You're not a danger to others, are you, girl?"

"Only if they try to hurt me or mine," she told him honestly.

He grinned broadly. "Good answer." He snapped his fingers and a seam appeared in the cuffs before they dropped off her wrists, only to disappear before hitting the ground.

Tempest sighed with relief and rubbed the skin the cuffs had been rubbing against. "Thank you," she told him.

Hephaestus shrugged. "Not a problem. I take it we're on Lemuria now?"

"We are." Vazi gave Hecate a curious look before saying anything more.

"He can be trusted, and would make a good ally, but ultimately it's your choice," Hecate said without hesitation. "The more gods who have access to Lemuria, the more likely it is that Zeus will discover you're here."

"He'll discover that eventually. I don't intend for us to hide forever. And even Zeus cannot come to this land without permission." He asked the same promise of Hephaestus that he had of Hecate and the others, giving the god permission to visit Lemuria.

"Thanks," Hephaestus said when it was done. "Now, if you don't mind, I don't like crowds, and I want to hear the rest of this story from Hecate."

"Understandable," Vazi said with a nod. "Thank you again."

Hephaestus and Hecate disappeared, and Seth gave in and wrapped Tempest in a tight hug. "Tell me you feel better now," he urged.

"I do," she promised. "But we still need to get your things from your house." Ignoring the others, who she knew were listening intently, she smiled and added, "You're planning on putting them in my house here, right?"

Seth grinned and gave her a firm but brief kiss. "That's the plan."

She arched a brow at Vazi. "Ready for one more trip?" she asked.

"If I must," he answered, feigning irritation. "But after this, Seth, you're teleporting yourself."

"I'm okay with teleporting myself. I'm just not sure I'm up for teleporting others just yet. I'm worried they'd end up in the middle of the ocean or something. I don't want to risk it until I've done it myself more than a few times."

"Probably wise." He looked to Kara, Aaron, and Aelia. "Are you three coming?"

"You kidding?" Aaron asked with a mischievous grin. "A chance to poke through Seth's personal stuff? I wouldn't miss it."

"I've seen it, and he doesn't have much, so I'll stay here unless you need me," Kara told Seth.

"No, it's fine. I know you've got your own stuff to get situated," Seth answered, though he was giving Aaron the stink eye.

"Then I'll remain behind, too," Aelia said after a few seconds. "I, too, have a lot, and today has been...trying."

"Yes, I suppose dying would do that," Vazi murmured as he considered her. "Try to be safe until we return?"

Aelia smiled slightly. "I'll do my best."

Vazi teleported them to Seth's house. True to Kara's words, there wasn't much. It really was just a place to sleep and research between expeditions, which meant everything he needed was gathered and flashed to Tempest's house in under an hour.

When Vazi returned them all to the square, they found Aelia and Kara outside, sitting in the grass with the shade cat snoozing between them. At their appearance, he cracked open an eye, let out a sleepy meow, then went back to his nap.

"You can't be done already," Seth said as he studied the cat, still not quite sure about it.

"We're not," Kara agreed as she ran a hand down the shade's back and smiled. "But we both needed a break and we had an idea."

"We?" Aelia asked, lips twitching.

Kara blew a raspberry before her grin reappeared. "Okay, fine. It was my idea, but it was a damn good idea."

Tempest hadn't known Kara long, but she'd come to understand her well, and so was instantly suspicious. "What idea?" she asked.

"A party. A housewarming party, if you like, since some of us are moving into new homes."

"You want a housewarming party for six people? Two of them who have always lived here?" Aaron asked, confused.

"Nope," she answered cheerfully. "I mean, don't get me wrong, we could absolutely have fun with just us, but I think we should get some of the people we trust—absolutely—to not go blabbing about Lemuria."

"Such as?" Vazi asked, but Tempest noticed he didn't look opposed to the idea. Truth be told, neither did Tempest. After all they'd experienced in the last few weeks, she could use a chance to simply relax and enjoy herself. And, since she knew a grand total of seven people who were still alive, it might even be an opportunity to meet more. Still, she was curious as to who Kara would choose to invite.

"Hecate and Hephaestus, of course, though I'm not sure how much of a partier Hephaestus is. He seemed like kind of a stick in the mud." Kara paused to think, clearly weighing the people she knew.

"If we do this, I'd like to invite someone," Seth said slowly. "A scholar, and someone I occasionally work for. You might actually know him, Aelia."

Curious, she asked, "What's his name?"

"Erasmus."

The slow blink she gave him in return said she recognized the name but, like him, was too discreet to say much. "Yes, he would love to see Lemuria, and he certainly knows how to keep its existence to himself."

Kara made an annoyed noise. "Should I even ask who this guy with the wizard name is?"

"No," Seth replied, "at least not yet. He might actually tell you though, all things considered. And I know a couple others who are trustworthy. A couple of them might even be fun enough for you, Kara."

"I know a few I trust, too," Aaron added.

"I like this plan," Tempest said, speaking up for the first time since the conversation began. "I do think we need to keep it on the smaller side, but I like it. I haven't had the chance to actually meet anyone besides the people here, and we're all due for a bit of fun."

Vazi was the last one to contribute to the conversation, but when he did, his gaze was on the ground and his voice was quiet and surprisingly somber for the topic. "To go from seeing the land we created full of life and laughter, then to blink and wake up to see it devoid of the people we loved and nurtured was...devastating. To know we failed our people and caused this land to slumber for six thousand years while they all died, one by one...it's unbearable."

Those eyes lifted and fixed on Seth. "To see it waking, to see a Lemurian here, is wondrous, and I will never be able to repay you for not only finding Tempest, but bringing her here safely." His gaze shifted to the two women still on the ground. "With that said, I can think of nothing better than to see life and celebration on a land that has waited six thousand years to be someone's home again."

Tempest stepped away from Seth and wrapped Vazi in a hug. "It will definitely live again. There will be more Lemurians than just the three of us. That's what we'll celebrate."

He returned the hug only to stiffen, then throw his head back and laugh. "Yes," he told her as he drew back and smiled broadly at her. "That is exactly what we'll celebrate."

But the look he gave Seth told him there was more to that statement than the god was willing to share. For now.

CHAPTER 38

They decided on the next day, a few hours before dusk, for the party. Using the phones Aaron had provided, calls were made to ensure people were free, but the details were left out. Kara thought—and everyone else agreed—that the surprise was part of the fun.

Hecate was all too happy to accept the invitation, but Hephaestus had been reluctant...at first. To Seth, it seemed that the name of one of the other intended guests had changed his mind, but Seth wasn't going to ask which one. They'd find out soon enough.

Other than the two deities, Vazi was collecting all those invited but one. Seth wanted to bring Erasmus himself, and so made sure he could do it safely.

The jump to Greece was a little jarring—it would take time to adjust to having actual powers—but it made him smile. He loved visiting the Athenaeum.

Though Erasmus knew he was coming, Seth still appeared outside and well away from the hidden entrance. The Athenaeum was all about secrecy and preserving the knowledge of the past. They were two things everyone inside took extremely seriously, and they wouldn't hesitate to kill anyone who threatened the safety of everyone and everything inside.

Seth could have likely appeared directly inside, since he'd been there before, but opted to take the 'normal' way in. Which meant he walked to the magically disguised crack in the side of the mountain that led to a small underground city. He'd been granted the ability to see it before, as he was one of the few archaeologists outside of their organization they trusted. They had even trusted him enough to give him the secrets of how to reach the actual Athenaeum, which involved passing magical locks and a labyrinth of natural-looking passages.

He wasn't surprised when Erasmus was waiting for him just inside. He would have been notified that someone was outside, and they would have recognized his face. Security made sure they knew the face of everyone permitted inside, no matter how infrequently they visited.

The head of the Athenaeum was a fit man, despite his obvious age. Almost any member of the Arcane with white hair was closing in on the thousand year mark, and Erasmus had a full head of silvery-white hair. His green eyes were warm and he smiled at Seth. "I truly wasn't expecting to see you for a while."

"Until a few days ago, I wasn't sure I would be seeing anyone again," Seth admitted as he received an affectionate hug from the older man.

"No? How curious. Can you tell me what happened?"

Seth grinned and nodded. "I can, but before I do that...you can get away for a few hours, right?"

"Of course," Erasmus agreed without hesitation. "When you asked, I ensured I would have several hours available. But what is it you need from me? Something from the archives?"

The grin widened, and Seth shook his head. "No, I thought I'd give you something instead. You might want to tell your people that you'll be gone for those hours, though."

Intrigued, Erasmus nodded and stepped away to talk to a man who stood nearby. While Seth couldn't recall his name, he did know that this was the head of security. He also didn't look happy to hear that his boss was going to be leaving the Athenaeum. "He'll be safe," he called to the man. "I swear it."

He nodded and Erasmus returned to Seth. "Lead on, my boy."

Seth laughed and shook his head. "Hold on," was the only warning he gave before he grabbed Erasmus's arm and teleported them both back to Lemuria.

They arrived back in the same square, though it had been transformed in the last twenty-four hours. Tables and chairs had been placed around the area, a few of the tables filled with food, while a cooler and some metal tubs were full of drinks. Kara had broken out a large speaker and music was playing, though at a level that didn't discourage conversation.

Mostly importantly, it was full of people. It wasn't a huge party, not when they were trying to be discreet, but for as empty as Lemuria was, it was a crowd.

Kara was busy talking to Wade and Samara, and seemed enthralled by the wings both currently had on display. They had asked that their friends come as well, and Vazi was currently cornered by one of them while Tempest stood beside him, amused. Julian, Seth had learned, was almost as much a history nerd as Aelia or Erasmus. It looked like he was having a scholargasm, while his wife, Paige, was nearby talking to Hephaestus. The two seemed close, which solved the mystery of who Hephaestus had come to see. Aaron and Aelia were sitting at one of the tables, with a few of Aaron's archaeology buddies and Hecate.

The shade cat had even made an appearance and was going from group to group, startling a few people and making others nervous, but Tempest and—to Seth's surprise—Samara offered pets whenever the cat came near.

Meanwhile, Erasmus looked at Seth in shock. "When did you gain the ability to teleport?" he asked, not yet looking around to see where they were or who was around.

"The same time I killed a Lemurian god and took his place," Seth answered with a smile.

Erasmus actually gaped at him and, for a moment, Seth worried he'd overloaded the man's brain. But then he heard someone call Erasmus's name, followed by a second voice calling for the man. Aelia didn't surprise him, but Hecate's voice did.

Once again, Erasmus looked stunned. "Hecate? Aelia? What are you two doing here? And where is here?"

Aelia laughed and gave him a hug. "Welcome to Lemuria, Erasmus. And I'm here because I was helping Seth."

"I was as well," Hecate said when Aelia stepped back. "Though I didn't know *you* were helping him, too."

"Oh. I—no—I didn't really help that much," he stammered. "There wasn't much about Lemuria, even in our archives."

"There will be now, I'm sure, though only in your private section," Hecate assured him.

"Wait, you know about the Athenaeum?" Seth asked.

"Of course."

"She's one of our divine patrons. They help protect it from discovery," Erasmus answered absently as he looked around, eyes wide. "Is this actually Lemuria?"

"It really is," Seth assured him as Aelia and Hecate nodded. But now he had a thought. He'd known that a handful of gods and goddesses had placed protections on the Athenaeum. He was a god now, too. Maybe he could add something to the mix? He truly believed in what they were doing, after all. But that was something to consider tomorrow.

"Extraordinary," he murmured. "Seth, I would like that story soon, but right now I'd like to just…"

"I get it," he promised. "Enjoy yourself."

Pleased to have shocked the man, he made his way over to Tempest, who was now fighting not to laugh as Vazi was inundated with questions from Julian.

"How long do you figure he'll give the guy before he explodes?" Seth whispered in Tempest's ear.

She smiled up at him and leaned into his side. "Two more questions, maximum."

"I'm not sure he'll get to two."

Laughing, she slid an arm around his waist and cuddled into him. "Did it go as well as you'd hoped?"

"It did. Though, apparently, he knows Hecate, too. And you should expect him to want to talk to you before I take him back to the Athenaeum."

"That's fine. I want people to know about Lemuria. I want it to grow and thrive, even if it is just in people's memories."

"Excuse me," Vazi told Julian, after only a single question, before turning his back on the man and walking over to Tempest and Seth. "Lemuria will grow, and not just in memories."

"Oh, I know," Tempest said. "It just may take some time."

Vazi shook his head and smiled. "Not that much time."

"What do you mean?" Seth asked.

In answer, Vazi laid his hand lightly on Tempest's stomach. "I mean, we have a new Lemurian already on the way."

Though none of the conversation had stopped and the music still played, Seth would have sworn he'd gone deaf for a moment, hearing only a buzzing in his ears. "I'm sorry, what?" he asked, positive he'd heard wrong.

Tempest's hand rested over Vazi's. "If you're not absolutely certain, tell me now, Vazi," she warned in a voice that should have scared even the god.

"I'm certain, though I'm sure Hecate or Hephaestus would be happy to give you a second opinion if you like," Vazi said teasingly.

"I'm pregnant?" she breathed.

"Not by much, just a week or so, but yes, you are."

Her head tilted back so she could look up at Seth. "We're going to have a baby."

It was like Seth's best dream and worst nightmare all at once. Part of him was terrified of losing the woman he loved, but the rest of him...

He turned and closed his arms around Tempest, resting his cheek against the top of her head as his emotions battled in his chest. No, he wouldn't lose her like his dad had lost his mom. She wasn't human, and they'd have people who could help. He'd find and wake up the Lemurian goddess of childbirth if he needed to. Hell, he'd get every goddess of childbirth here if necessary. He would not lose Tempest. He would love her. Her and the child currently growing in her belly.

They would be a family, and he would use every drop of power he'd gotten from Jalvas to keep that family safe.

"I love you, Tempest. You and that baby."

"I love you, too," she told him, her voice breaking with the force of emotions Vazi's words had caused.

And the god gave them several minutes to absorb the news, but that was when Kara joined them. "Everything okay?" she asked, studying them with concern.

Seth nodded and glanced at Vazi, silently asking him to answer because he wasn't sure he could talk without embarrassing himself.

Vazi, looking pleased, stepped into the middle of the square. People noticed and went quiet, one by one. "In a little over eight months, I expect each and every one of you back here to celebrate the birth of the first Lemurian baby in over six thousand years!"

Kara was the first to react, letting out an excited squeal as her arms got thrown around both Seth and Tempest. "I'm going to be an auntie!"

She wasn't the only one happy for them. Some, like Julian and Paige, didn't really know the happy couple, so just called out congratulations, but others crowded around them, equally as excited.

It changed the mood of the party. Despite what they'd accomplished, it had been more happy than celebratory, but now they all had something to celebrate. It wasn't every day a member of a formerly extinct race was conceived. Because of that, the party went on well past midnight. Vazi and Hecate offered to take the guests back home, including Erasmus, when Tempest and Seth opted to bow out early.

He wanted his own celebration.

They made love until they were exhausted, savoring each kiss, each caress. And, when they finally lie there, sated and entwined, their minds calm and drifting toward sleep, Seth rested his hand over her still flat belly and smiled.

His quest for an undiscovered temple had led him to something so much more precious. And now he had the rest of eternity to enjoy it.

EPILOGUE

Eight months later

Lemuria might not be the thriving civilization it had once been, but now it lived.

Kara and Aelia rarely left Lemuria, though it did happen when they wanted to visit friends or family, restock supplies, or work. But most of their time was spent happily restoring order to the long-dead villages that thousands of Lemurians had once called home. Kara was able to boss people around, too, when others moved to the island, as she and Aelia had essentially taken over managing things along with Tempest.

Seth's father had moved to the island. He'd been thrilled to hear that he was going to be a grandfather, and had attended the small wedding a few months prior. To Seth's delight, the man loved his new daughter-in-law as much as he did Seth himself. And, like the rest of Seth's new family, he'd thrown himself into rebuilding Lemuria.

Seth and Aaron helped, but they both continued to work as well. It was something everyone who now called themselves Lemurians approved of, since it was that work that had allowed Lemuria to be rediscovered. Neither worked nearly as much as they once had, but—to

Seth's surprise—Aaron was now working with Erasmus nearly as much as Seth was. More, actually, since Tempest was due to have the baby within days.

A fact that left Seth both terrified and overjoyed.

Fortunately, he wasn't alone in taking care of Tempest. Everyone wanted to make sure the newest Lemurian was born safely. Vazi was perhaps the worst aside from Seth, but he got it. The Lemurians had been his people for thousands of years before the bulk of the land had sunk. He wanted to see them alive and spreading across the world once more, and the baby was just the first step to seeing that happen.

They'd been discussing the possibility of allowing others, after careful vetting, to relocate to Lemuria as well. Seven people didn't even make a full village, much less a culture, but, as had been pointed out months ago, it was all too easy to see Lemurians filling the island once more. Witches, shifters, elementals, and sirens all had the possibility to have Lemurian children. They only needed to deliver on Lemurian soil. But that also led to some arguments.

Vazi wanted to allow only people from those four races to move to Lemuria, while Seth argued that they'd need more than just people to have babies to make Lemuria a viable home. If they wanted to be as self-sufficient as possible, they needed farmers and craftsmen, historians and scientists. They needed people who could contribute more than their children. Aelia had also pointed out that if race was the criteria for living on Lemuria, then she wouldn't be allowed as she was nothing more than an extremely long-lived human sorceress. That had made Vazi backtrack quickly and agree to Seth's point.

Then they had to decide how to choose which people they wanted to share the island with them. While Vazi fully intended to have

Lemuria step out of the shadows, they needed to do it carefully. They needed more than the original group to be able to stand against the might Zeus and his allies could bring if Lemuria was discovered too soon. They all agreed that trustworthiness was the first requirement people needed to have. An ability to contribute in some way was the second, right along with people who would love to see Lemuria regain its former glory.

The four of them who were from this time had ideas there, and knew others who could offer up other names, including Julian and Erasmus.

So far, they had only brought a dozen people to the island to stay, but they were working out for now, which pleased Seth. He needed a distraction so he didn't hover constantly over Tempest, but he didn't need to have something stealing all his focus.

He was with Vazi in an abandoned village to the south, ensuring it was safe and habitable, when both he and Vazi froze at the scream that tore through their minds.

"Tempest," Seth whispered before he teleported to the home he now shared with Tempest, Vazi right behind him. She was lying on the bed, her brow covered in sweat, with Hecate and Aelia standing by her feet and Kara on one side of her. An instant after he appeared in the bedroom, her back arched and she let out another scream.

"What's wrong?" he demanded, rushing to Tempest's side and sitting on the bed beside her.

"She's in labor," Aelia said dryly as she checked Tempest, who was covered by a blanket to protect her modesty as much as they were able.

"I got that," he snapped as he took Tempest's hand in his and stroked her damp hair from her brow. "Why is she in pain, though? Even humans have medicine to eliminate the pain."

"Because I only just arrived," Hecate assured him as she held a hand over Tempest's belly. It took moments only before the tension in Tempest's body eased.

"Why didn't you call me sooner?" Seth asked Tempest, kissing her forehead lightly.

"Because babies take their sweet time and you were busy," she told him, voice breathless.

"I'm never too busy to be by your side when you're delivering our baby," he told her with a shake of his head.

She smiled and gave his hand a squeeze. "I love you."

"I love you, too. Now, how are you doing? Really?"

"I've never had a baby before, but I think I'm doing good."

"You're doing better than good," Aelia said after a moment, smiling up at the expectant parents. "It's time to push."

Seth thought that once they reached that point that it would be over quickly, but it was another hour before they heard the sweet sound of a baby letting out its first cry. By that time, he was ready to tear down the walls. When his control on his powers slipped, he almost did.

"You have a beautiful little girl," Aelia said, beaming up at them as she lifted the tiny infant so both Seth and Tempest could see her. Seth was shocked to see she was a pink, wrinkled little thing, but he also instantly fell in love with her.

The ground rumbled beneath them and the wind kicked up outside, proving how overjoyed Lemuria's two remaining gods were at the birth of this new Lemurian. She wasn't a demigod, as she'd been conceived prior to Seth receiving his godhood, but she was a Lemurian in blood and magic.

Aelia dealt with the cord and offered Seth the baby once she'd been wrapped in a soft yellow blanket.

"We have a baby," he told Tempest in an awed whisper as he brushed a finger delicately over one small cheek, not caring that his own were damp.

"Let me see her," she said, holding her arms out. He placed the baby in her arms, and she smiled joyfully as she cradled the tiny demigod to her chest. "She's perfect."

"And she will be the most spoiled baby in the history of babies," Kara said, crying right along with everyone else.

"And the most overprotected," Vazi added. "But we'll give you three some time alone...For now. Don't think you're going to be hogging that baby, I don't care if you are her parents," he said, starting to usher people out of the room. He was the last out of the room, but before he closed the door, he poked his head in and grinned at them. "Just so you know, Vazi is an amazing name for a girl, too. And who better to be her godfather than an actual god?"

Tempest laughed and flicked a hand toward him, shutting the door in his face.

"We do need to decide on a name for her, though," Seth said, unable to stop touching either Tempest or the baby.

"I've been thinking about that," Tempest said, leaning her head on his shoulder. "What about Katrina?"

Seth wouldn't have thought he could get any more emotional, but his breath was unsteady as he rested his forehead against her hair. "You want to name her after my mom?"

"I do. What do you think?"

He carefully lifted both her and the baby into his lap and wrapped his arms around them both. "I think it's perfect."

Tempest smiled and closed her eyes. "Then Katrina it is."

And this Katrina would be safe. He'd spend the rest of his immortality making sure of it.

ABOUT AUTHOR

Meg M. Robinson is a fantasy author who lives in north Georgia with her husband, a teenager, and a small menagerie of animals. She's goofy and a little dorky, which greatly amuses her family.

She's obsessed with crows, sea turtles, and houseplants. And, of course, books. When she's not focused on either reading or writing a book, she enjoys playing video games, archery, and baking.

www.megmrobinson.com